Praise for Rosanna Chiofalo and *Bella Fortuna*

"Like a gondolier navigating the canals of Venice, Rosanna Chiofalo takes you on a magical ride filled with family and friends, love and loss, heartbreak and happiness. *Bella Fortuna* is a warm glimpse into Italian-American life."
—Holly Chamberlin, author of *Last Summer*

"Chiofalo, a first-generation Italian-American whose parents emigrated from Sicily in the 1960s, brings the Italian immigrant community and neighborhoods richly to life."
—*Publishers Weekly*

"Skillfully crafted . . . sure to pull the reader into the love of family and the sights and senses of romance in Venice."
—*MetroWest Daily News*

"From the streets of New York to the canals of Venice, Rosanna Chiofalo creates a warm and lively story the reader won't want to see end. Valentina DeLuca is a heroine with intelligence, heart, and courage, the kind of person every woman wants for a dear friend. Time spent with her is a sheer joy."
—Mary Carter, author of *Three Months in Florence*

"A warm tribute to her heritage, the book brings to life colorful scenes from her past as a first-generation Italian American."
—*Astoria Times/Jackson Heights Times*

Books by Rosanna Chiofalo

BELLA FORTUNA

CARISSIMA

STELLA MIA

Published by Kensington Publishing Corporation

Stella Mia

ROSANNA CHIOFALO

KENSINGTON BOOKS
www.kensingtonbooks.com

KENSINGTON BOOKS are published by

Kensington Publishing Corp.
119 West 40th Street
New York, NY 10018

All Kensington titles, imprints, and distributed lines are available at special quantity discounts for bulk purchases for sales promotion, premiums, fund-raising, and educational or institutional use.

Special book excerpts or customized printings can also be created to fit specific needs. For details, write or phone the office of the Kensington Special Sales Manager: Kensington Publishing Corp., 119 West 40th Street, New York, NY 10018. Attn. Special Sales Department. Phone: 1-800-221-2647.

Kensington and the K logo Reg. U.S. Pat. & TM Off.

eISBN-13: 978-1-61773-863-0
eISBN-10: 1-61773-863-8
First Kensington Electronic Edition: January 2015

ISBN-13: 978-0-7582-7505-9
ISBN-10: 0-7582-7505-6
First Kensington Trade Paperback Printing: January 2015

10 9 8 7 6 5 4 3 2 1

Printed in the United States of America

For Ed, my "stella mia."
This one's all for you.

Acknowledgments

My deepest gratitude to my editor, John Scognamiglio, for his careful attention to editing my books and for allaying my anxieties whenever they arise. You truly are my right-hand person, and I couldn't do it without you!

To everyone at Kensington Publishing, thank you for believing in me and my books and for your hard work in ensuring their success.

Lastly, thank you to my family for your love and unwavering support.

CONTENTS

Part Three: Astoria, New York, and Messina, Sicily
July–September 2013

PROLOGUE

A Song

Astoria, New York, June 2013

My earliest childhood memory is of a song. I remember lying in my crib and hearing the soothing sounds of a sweet voice singing to me. Many people don't believe that I can have such an early childhood memory, but I know it is real. For my father has told me that my mother sang this song to me from the first time she held me in her arms after I was born up until the day she walked out of my life.

I still remember the words to the song because after my mother left, my father sang the song to me throughout my childhood since it had always calmed me. This is the song I am singing as I tend to the grapevine in my father's small backyard of the house where I grew up. Today is Sunday and the start of the last full week in June. The grapevine is already quite lush with its vibrant green leaves. Yesterday, my father's next-door neighbor asked me which stage of the grapevine is my favorite. I can't say. In the spring when its leaves are beginning to sprout, excitement surges through me in anticipation of having the grapevine for another year. In the summer, I love seeing the grapevine in full bloom. In August, the grapes that have grown on the vines add even more beauty and are ready to be harvested. At this time, the leaves have turned the same golden hue as the spiders that dangle up and down from the clusters of grapes like yo-yos. I also love the morning glory flowers that I planted. The first thing I do when I wake up is walk to my window and look at their open blooms. By early afternoon, their petals close as they retreat once more into slumber before they awake again the following morning. The flowers' vines intertwine around the grapevine, like a child clinging fiercely to her mother.

The grapevine was planted by my mother, shortly after she and my father moved into my childhood home. I only have a handful of memories of my mother, since I was three years old when she left. And the memories aren't very clear. But I do remember the day before she left. I was here in our yard, and the weather was beautiful. I was laughing as my mother held my hand and walked with me, pointing out the names of the flowers and herbs she had planted. We spent the whole morning and afternoon outside. There's a photograph of me from that day. My mother was lifting me high up into the air as I reached for the dangling grapevine. Daddy had helped my mother create an arbor of overheard wires so that the grapevine would grow upward and create a lush canopy, which would provide shade for us during the humid summers New York City is known for. I remember giggling so hard as she held me up, and when she lowered me back down to the ground, I hopped up and down on my feet, begging, "Mama! Up! Up!" We played like that for what felt like hours. I don't even remember going back inside. But my father told me years later, I fell asleep outside in my mother's arms while she lay in a folding chair. She then carried me to bed and tucked me in. She left early the next morning before I even woke up. I don't remember that following day, but my father told me I was searching for my mother throughout the house and even in our yard. I kept screaming, "Up! Up!" as I pointed to the grapevine. My father tried lifting me so that I could touch the grapevine, but I didn't want him. I kicked and screamed, "Mama! Up!"

Daddy told me Mama had to go away, but would be back soon. And I believed him that she would be returning since I kept searching for her every day. Aunt Donna told me, years later, I finally stopped looking for my mother about a month after she'd left. And it wasn't until I started school and saw the other students' mothers that I began asking about my own.

I used to ask Daddy, "Why don't I have a Mommy?" Daddy would always look like he was going to cry when I asked him this. He never had an answer for me. He would just try to distract me by changing the subject. By the time I turned nine, I learned to stop asking and realized my mother was gone for good. But when I was fourteen, Aunt Donna told me that my mother had left us to go back to her home in Sicily. After learning this, I couldn't resist asking my father again a few times why she stayed away. He never spoke badly of her and always said my mother had been in a lot of pain. Daddy assured me that she loved us and said we needed to pray for her. I did whatever my father told me, and so I prayed for her. But it became more difficult, especially in my teens when I wished I had what my friends possessed. I wished I had a mother I could go shopping with; a mother who would cheer for me at my plays; a mother who could give me advice on boys. So I soon stopped praying for her. I'm a very religious person, and I have asked God to help me forgive my mother for leaving. But I don't know if I'll ever be able to. I came to terms with her not being in my life a long time ago. I choose to focus on the people who are in my life: a loving husband, a doting father, an aunt who would die for me if given the chance.

Shortly after we came to stay with Daddy, I was looking through a few of his photo albums. I found another photo that was taken on that day before my mother left. She was kneeling beside me as she held out a few morning glory flowers she had cut from the grapevine. She smiled, watching me inhale the flowers' sweet fragrance. I quickly shut the photo album—for it hurt too much to see my mother's tender expression.

My husband, Kyle MacLean, asked me once why I insist on still coming to my father's yard every year and tending to the grapevine since it reminds me of my mother and the pain she caused. I simply told him I love all plants, including grapevines. I could tell by the sad look in Kyle's eyes that he didn't believe me. The truth is I'm not exactly sure why. I have tried not to think about my mother a lot over the years. But when I look at the grapevine in my father's yard, I can't help but think of her. Maybe that's why I still tend to it. The grapevine is the only part of my mother I have. That and the song she sang to me as a child.

Kyle and I live in the same neighborhood where we grew up, Astoria, Queens. But we didn't know each other as children. Kyle loves to tell our family and friends how he knew he was going to marry me when he first heard my singing. He was the best man at his brother's wedding, which was held in Our Lady of Mount Carmel Church, where I volunteer and sing during Masses as well as weddings and funerals. I actually sing at a few of the churches in Astoria.

My father, Paul Parlatone, or "Paulie" as everyone calls him, is always telling me, "Julia, you're giving it away for FREE! You should be getting paid for your singing, especially since you're in such high demand."

Kyle always says when he heard me singing "Ave Maria" at his brother's wedding, he was struck by the sound of my beautiful voice. I blush whenever he tells the story even if it's just the two of us. We celebrated our five-year wedding anniversary recently. Though we've been trying, I still haven't been able to conceive. I'm forty-two years old and know that my chances of getting pregnant are growing dimmer.

A part of me craves that special bond between a mother and a child, but I was fortunate to have a father who showered me with affection as well as my Aunt Donna, Daddy's sister, who moved in with us after my mother left so she could help raise me. Love was never missing from my life. But I'd be lying if I said I never wished to have back my biological mother. When Kyle and I began dating, he asked me if I ever had a desire to find her. While I have been curious about my mother from time to time, I can say without hesitation that I have zero interest in searching for her. Why should I waste my time and energy on a mother who wanted nothing to do with her daughter?

Sometimes I think it's best that I haven't been able to get pregnant. I'm afraid I'd be a terrible mother because of how my own abandoned me. I remember my college psychology professor saying once how children learn compassion from their mothers. How can I be a compassionate, good mother when I didn't have such a role model? But Kyle and my friends have always told me I'm one of the most sensitive, tender people they've ever met. I have my father and Aunt Donna to thank for that.

My desire to be a mother has been with me since I was a girl, and I love being around children. So it's no wonder that I decided to become a teacher. I teach third grade at St. Joseph's Parochial School. It's about a mile from where I grew up on Ditmars Boulevard. Kyle and I own a one-family house on 43rd Street and 28th Avenue, just down the block from St. Joe's, but my father acts as if we live on the other side of the country. Even though he visits regularly—probably more than Kyle would like—Daddy wishes we had bought a house on his street. While my father and I are very close, and I love spending time with him, I'm also a grown woman who needs her privacy. But at the moment, I don't have a choice. Kyle got laid off from his job a month ago, and with my modest teaching salary, we weren't able to make our monthly mortgage payments. So we decided to sublet our house until he finds another job. In the meantime we're staying with my father, who's thrilled. Kyle, on the other hand, looks as if he's just been told he has a flesh-eating disease. Don't get me wrong. Kyle loves my father, and Daddy is fond of Kyle. But Daddy's also fond of teasing Kyle mercilessly about his half-Scottish heritage. Kyle is Italian on his mother's side of the family, and Scottish on his father's. What's a sore point for Daddy is that Kyle identifies more with his Scottish culture. He belongs to the American Scottish Foundation, takes bagpipe lessons, and marches every year in the New York Tartan Day Parade. I've tried asking Daddy to ease up on Kyle and all the Scottish jokes, but Daddy just can't help himself.

This is the last week of the school year, and I've decided to assign a family tree project for my third-grade students to work on over the summer. I'll be teaching fourth grade in the fall, and my principal decided to keep me with the same group of students. In addition to creating a family tree that lists their ancestors as far back as possible, the students will have to write an essay about one of their relatives. To make it more fun, I'm going to hold a contest when we return to school in the fall. The students will take a vote and decide who has the most interesting essay. The winner will receive tickets for *The Lion King* on Broadway. I thought it would be fun to participate in the project as well, but as the teacher I won't be eligible to win the contest. Even though I have the whole summer to work on my family tree, I'm excited about the project and can't wait to get started. On that note, I finish up watering my father's garden and coil the hose before going indoors.

Daddy had asked Kyle earlier to join him in a game of bocce along with his cronies at the playground on Steinway Street and Ditmars. Many of the older Italian men in the neighborhood congregate at this playground to play bocce or cards. So I have the whole house to myself this afternoon.

I head down to the basement that Daddy uses as storage unlike many of the other Italian Americans in our neighborhood who double their living space as an extension of their living quarters. I remember Daddy showing me when I was in junior high school a loose leaf binder that had our family's history recorded in it. When Daddy was in high school, his parents had asked him to record our family's ancestry so my children and grandchildren would know where they came from. Since my father is reluctant to change, especially where technology is concerned, it never occurred to him to have the history typed up or entered into a computer.

Switching on the light at the top of the basement's stairs, I begin making my way down. It smells even mustier than I remembered. As a child, I often played down here. I'm surprised Daddy never finished the basement so he could have an extra room. Though it's a two-family house, Daddy has always rented the second-story apartment, but he would've been willing to throw the tenants out and let Kyle and me take it if we had decided to move in with him after we got married. Daddy's portion of the house only has two bedrooms.

There are rows of boxes, all neatly lined up, in the basement. Their contents are written in black marker on the outside. Aunt Donna must've helped Daddy with the storage since I recognize her bold cursive on many of the cartons. My father's small, squiggly handwriting on a few of the boxes is barely legible. I walk over to a covered sofa bed, which used to be upstairs in the living room and where Aunt Donna slept when she lived with us. After she got married and moved out, Aunt Donna still kept her copy of the house keys and often let herself in as if she still lived here, much to Daddy's exasperation. But he'd never have the nerve to ask her for the keys back.

Seeing the cluttered confines of the basement, I suddenly realize my father is a bit of a pack rat. At least he's relegated his stuff to the basement and hasn't cluttered our upstairs living quarters with junk. Surrounded by all of the boxes and storage containers, I feel overwhelmed and don't know where to begin looking for Daddy's binder. I do remember when he showed it to me he had pulled it out of a large brass trunk. Scanning the basement, I don't see the trunk anywhere. I guess I'll have to wait until Daddy returns so I can ask him where it is. But then I notice a long rectangular object covered with gold and white damask drapery. Walking over to it, I pull off the drapery to reveal the trunk.

The brass trunk has tarnished greatly over the years. Unlatching its closure, I lift the trunk's lid as its hinges squeak loudly. A moth flies out, startling me. I had never wondered what my father kept in this trunk when I played down here as a kid. Two piles of *Time* magazine from the late sixties and early seventies are stacked on the left-hand side of the trunk. They're sealed in large Ziploc bags. No doubt Daddy is hoping to sell them someday. I get distracted from my original mission of searching for the binder and instead read the headlines that grace the magazines' covers. Maybe I'll bring a few upstairs and read the articles in my spare time. Taking all of the periodicals out of the trunk, I count almost seventy issues. After removing the last few magazines, I then move onto several bundles wrapped in yellow, crinkled tissue paper. I take out the first bundle, which feels soft to the touch, and open the tissue to reveal a gorgeous ruby red fabric. Unfolding the fabric, I see it's a woman's skirt. The lower half has an elaborate gold embroidered design that swirls all the way around the skirt. Its hem is cut in an asymmetrical line so that the left side of the skirt comes up just past the knee. A gold sash border encircles the hem. The style looks dated, almost like a period piece. I reach for the next bundle and unwrap it. There's another skirt, but this one is made of white cotton and has several layers of fabric. It resembles a slip that is worn beneath dresses to create extra fullness. I then remember the high-cut asymmetrical hem of the red skirt. I take the red skirt and pull it over the white slip. There is no doubt this white skirt or slip is meant to be worn underneath the red skirt.

I take out the next package, which contains a yellowing white blouse. It looks almost like a peasant blouse, but its sleeves are very unusual. There is an opening to insert one's arms, but then sewn over the sleeves is a sheer organza fabric that hangs quite loosely and dangles dramatically down to mid-thigh level. I'm reminded of a show Kyle and I went to see at Lincoln Center with Chinese dancers who wore costumes that had similar sleeves that they used, almost like fans, while they performed. The sleeves' edges are trimmed with beautiful lace. The blouse's neckline is also very striking with pleats that run from the shoulders to the bodice. In the neckline's center, the fabric is gathered to create ruffles. It reminds me of the style I've seen in recent years of wedding dresses that sport a crumb-catcher neckline.

I suddenly realize these clothes look very much like those on the Sicilian folk doll I've had since I was a little girl. I open another bundle to find a chocolate-brown velvet vest with wide gold plackets sewn down the middle and an ornate gold belt. It matches the design on the vest's plackets. A headscarf falls out. Its fabric is the same as that of the red overlay skirt. Yes! It is definitely a Sicilian folk costume. Could it have belonged to my mother?

I continue rummaging through the remaining items in the trunk. A pale blue wool coat with a faux fur–trim collar and cuffs is still wrapped in a dry cleaning bag. Several leather purses that look like they are from the seventies are covered in plastic slipcases. One is an ivory-colored clutch. I decide to take it since clutches are in style again right now. There are more women's clothes, which no doubt belonged to my mother. Upon closer inspection, I notice most of the outfits are winter clothes. I also find a few pairs of women's shoes in a black garbage bag.

Finally, I reach the bottom of the trunk and see a glossy-covered pale blue notebook. The word *"canzoni"* is written in red marker on the cover. I remember from my Italian lessons that *canzoni* means songs. Opening the notebook's cover, I'm stunned to see the name "Sarina Amato"—my mother's name—scrawled on the first page. Seeing her handwriting sends shivers down my spine. As I flip through the notebook, I see the words to songs, written in the same handwriting as my mother's name, on the first page. She must've written all of these songs. My mother loved to sing? Though I remember the one song she always sang to me, I had no idea that she had such a passion for singing as this book no doubt proves. The thought that my own talent for singing could have been passed down to me from my mother never entered my mind. I then remember a conversation I was having with Daddy and Kyle the other night over dinner. We were talking about my singing at the local churches when Daddy said my voice reminded him of Connie Francis's. But he paused for a moment before he added Connie Francis. Did he catch himself before saying my voice reminded him of my mother's? But why would he keep her love of singing a secret from me?

The trunk is now empty, and I still haven't found Daddy's binder. But as I begin placing my mother's belongings back inside the trunk, I spot something protruding from the pocket sewn beneath the lid. A leather-bound book and what looks like a pack of playing cards are tucked inside the pocket. I take out the pack of cards first. They're a deck of tarot cards. I then take out the large leather-bound book. My heart pounds against my chest, for it looks like a journal and even has a small padlock. Could this be my mother's diary?

I remember my father used to keep his toolbox in the basement on an old bookcase near the stairs. Locating the toolbox on the last shelf, I open it and take out a large pair of pliers. Running back to the trunk, I manage to cut the diary's lock off after a few attempts. I open the diary and notice the lines indicating whom the diary belongs to have been left blank, which I find odd since my mother had written her name in her songbook. Then again, maybe she intentionally left her name absent from her diary out of fear someone would find it and know her secrets.

I turn over the next page, and a tattered, yellowed newspaper clipping falls out. Though the clipping is torn, I can still make out an illustration of a crystal globe with stars floating above it. The headline is intact and reads in Italian, *"La Zingara Sa Tutto,"* or *"The Gypsy Knows All."* I silently thank God that I minored in Italian along with my music theory major. I had always wanted to learn Italian. My father used to be fluent in Italian as a child since he was born in Calabria, Italy, and lived there until he was six. But his parents encouraged him to learn and speak English once they moved to the U.S. so he lost a lot of it. He can still understand it and can get by with some basic Italian as he did when he first met my mother after going to Sicily on vacation. But other than that he rarely speaks it. Aunt Donna once told me that after my mother left, Daddy didn't like to speak Italian anymore—for it reminded him too much of the only woman he had ever loved.

The bottom of the clipping is torn, and all I can make out are the words *Villa Carlotta* and two numbers that I assume must've been part of an address. Was my mother seeing a fortune-teller? Remembering the deck of tarot cards, I pick them up and splay them before me. I'm instantly drawn to the beautiful images depicted on the cards, which look quite worn. A few of them have been taped together with Scotch tape.

I hear footsteps above, followed by Daddy's and Kyle's voices. Throwing everything quickly back into the trunk, I slide the diary into the waistband of my jeans and pull my T-shirt over it. I'll have to read the diary at night when Kyle is sleeping. Fortunately, he likes to go to bed early even on the weekends. I'm the opposite and like to stay up late reading in bed. I tiptoe upstairs and quietly shut the door to the basement, just in time before Kyle calls out to me.

Several torturous hours later, it's finally nighttime, and I'm in bed. Kyle could tell my thoughts were elsewhere, but didn't push me to reveal what was weighing so heavily on my mind. All I could think about since Kyle and Daddy came home was reading my mother's diary and finally getting to know the woman who has been such a mystery for me. My hands shake as I open the diary and begin reading. It doesn't take long for the tears to slide down my face. For the first words are lyrics of a song—the same song my mother sang to me as a child.

PART ONE

Messina and Taormina, Sicily

April–August 1969

✖ 1 ✖

Stella Mia

MY STAR

April 16, 1969

"*Stella mia, stell-ahhh mia, tu sei la piu bella stella. Steh-lah rosa, steh-lah rosa, tu sei mia steh-lahhh . . . steh-lah azurra, steh-lah azurra, tu sei anche mia . . . steh-lah viola, steh-lah vi-oh-la, tu sei la piu bella di tutte le stell-ehhh. Veramente, tu sei mia stella. Ma non posso scelgier-eehhh. Tutte le stelle sono i miei fine quando una brille piu sfogante e prende mio cuore per sempre. Stella mia, stella mia, tu sei la piu bella stell-ahhh.*"

"*My star, my star, you are the most beautiful star. Pink star, pink star, you are my star . . . blue star, blue star, you're also mine . . . violet star, violet star, you are the most beautiful of all the stars. Truly, you are my star. But I cannot choose. All of the stars are mine until one special star outshines the others and captures my heart forever. My star, my star, you are the most beautiful star.*"

With my lantern in hand, I walk along the pebbly beach near my family's home in Terme Vigliatore, Messina, singing a silly song I made up the other night as I stared at all the stars in the beautiful Sicilian sky. Every time I sing the song, I change the colors of the stars. My four-year-old sister, Carlotta, loves the song, and as soon as night falls, she takes my hand and pulls me outside so she can look at the stars and decide which colors she's going to choose.

I've been singing for as long as I can remember. Mama told me I began to sing shortly after she began taking me to Mass when I was three years old. She said I immediately fell in love with the hymns and would try to hum along. To encourage my singing, she would play the radio for me, but only when Papá, my father, was not home. For one time he caught Mama and me singing together, and he yelled at us. From that moment on, I always knew never to sing in front of Papá. Of course, my younger siblings love to hear me sing. In addition to Carlotta, there are two boys—Enzo, who is six years old, and Pietro, who is just two. I share a bedroom with my brothers and sister, and I often sing to them softly at night so that Papá cannot hear me.

Only the stars and the ocean's roaring waves are my companions tonight. It is a little past midnight, and I am the sole person crazy enough to be out alone this late. But I'm not afraid. As I make my way barefoot along the shoreline, holding my *ciabattas* in hand, I squint, trying to make out the shadow of Vulcano, one of the Aeolian Islands, on the other side of the ocean. Since it is a clear night with a full moon overhead, I am able to discern the island's ominous shadow.

This is the only time that I have to myself. From the moment I wake up to shortly before I go to bed, my days are filled, helping my mother care for my siblings.

Though I am sixteen years old, my body often aches like that of a sixty-year-old woman. I started doing heavy chores when I was seven years old. Working hard and rearing my sister and brothers is the only life I know. The sole comfort I have is in my singing and attending church on Sundays.

My mother and I share few moments of laughter. For like me, she is burdened with the crushing load of running a household and tending to her children, not to mention keeping at bay my father's fury. My poor mother started receiving beatings at my father's hands not long after she married him at the tender age of fourteen. She had me when she was fifteen. Though she is now thirty-two, she looks closer to fifty. My father is a decade older than my mother. I've witnessed his hitting my mother for as long as I can remember.

Though I've become accustomed to my father's abuse, I still wonder why he is so cruel toward my mother and me. I received my fair share of lashings when I was a child, but the older I got the more intense his abuse became. I remember the first time he hit me. I was only eight. He came home from work and found me outside playing in our garden. I loved the flowers, plants, and herbs my mother had planted. She had begun teaching me how to garden and pick the herbs for both our cooking and to make healing ointments. I took it upon myself that day to help my mother by picking a few herbs. But when my father found me, he yelled at me for cutting too many herbs. I tried explaining to him, but that only angered him more, and he smacked me so hard that I fell to the ground. I was shocked, but I believed I deserved his punishment because I had done something wrong by picking too many herbs. Mama had come out in time to witness Papá hit me, and she yelled at him, but then he slapped her across the face, too. My mother soon learned not to intervene when he hit me because she would always get hit and often much worse than just a slap. Mama does whatever she can to ensure my father remains calm so he will leave me alone. But her efforts are rarely successful.

Even as young as three and four years old, I felt intimidated. Perhaps because Papá rarely said a kind word to my mother or me. Sometimes, he would surprise me by talking to me about how many sardines he had caught in a day. My father is a fisherman, primarily of sardines, which are abundant in the waters surrounding Sicily. I would take advantage of these few instances and engage him in the conversation, acting excited about the large catch of fish he'd caught and asking questions. He seemed pleased that I was interested. But there were few moments like these.

I was ten years old when my brother Enzo was born. My father was the happiest I'd ever seen him, and he remained in good spirits for several months afterward. My mother had had several miscarriages and two children who died shortly after birth before she had Enzo, Carlotta, and Pietro; hence, the large age difference between me and my siblings. Each of the miscarriages and the two babies who died had been boys. When I saw how elated Papá was after Enzo's birth, I began to suspect he hated me because up until that point I had been the only baby who had survived and grown. But I wasn't the boy he wanted. Yet just when I thought I understood my father's actions, he resumed hitting me when Enzo was six months old. And as I approached adolescence, his abuse got worse. After one grueling beating, I asked my mother why Papá hit us so much. She merely shrugged her shoulders and said, "It's his nature. It's simply who he is."

On my fourteenth birthday, Mama gave me a beautiful sundress she'd sewn. It was a rich emerald-green hue that complemented my auburn hair perfectly. I never loved anything I owned as much I loved that dress. A week later, I came home from buying a few groceries Mama needed for dinner that night. When my father saw me, he demanded I take off the dress. As I walked by him to head to my room to do as he ordered, he pulled me toward him by my braid.

"If I ever catch you again wearing something so suggestive, I'll cut off all of your hair."

And then he grabbed the hem of my dress and tore it with his hands.

"No!" I screamed. But it was too late. My beautiful dress was ruined. I glanced at Mama who was standing behind us in the kitchen. Her face looked pained. No doubt she was thinking of all the hours she had put into making my dress. And I'm certain my father's cruel act of destroying my dress was not just meant to hurt me, but also my mother. From that day forward, my dislike of him grew to an intense hatred.

Taking these late night walks to the beach could be the death of me if my father ever found out, but I don't care. I used to be terrified of him, but I am growing numb to his beatings and to the fear that he might kill me one day. Tears fill my eyes as I think about how I actually welcome death sometimes. At least then, I would finally be free of him.

I reach my favorite spot on the beach, where several immense boulders sit close to the water's edge. Climbing on top of one, I let my legs dangle off the edge. Staring out across the ocean, I fix my gaze once more on Vulcano. Maybe someday I will be daring enough to try and swim all the way there, and my father would never find me—that is if I don't die first from exhaustion. Sighing, I lie down on my back and stare at the stars once more, getting lost in all their twinkling lights. I close my eyes and listen to the soothing sound of the waves crashing against the shore.

Rain is falling down on me, but the pellets feel unusually heavy and sharp. Maybe it's hailing. Suddenly a sharp pain throbs throughout my head. I wake up and see pebbles and small rocks bouncing off my chest. As I sit up, my heart drops when I see my father is the one hurling the rocks at me.

"*Brutta puttana! Ti ucciderò! Ti ucciderò!*" Papá screams. His eyes look more deranged than usual as he calls me a whore and promises to kill me.

"Papá! *Prega di fermarsi!*" I plead with him to stop, but that only angers him more. He now resorts to hurling mounds of wet sand at me. Shielding my face with my hands, I sob uncontrollably. But I am not crying because of the rocks and sand hitting me. All I can think of is that I will no longer have this haven I can escape to, for he will now keep an even closer watch on me.

"Aiii!" I scream as my father yanks my hair, slapping my face with his free hand. He then releases my hair and begins undoing his belt.

I decide to make a run for it and jump off the boulder. Though I can smell liquor on his breath and suspect he's very drunk, he still manages to catch up to me. I run into the water, oblivious to the fact that I'll surely drown. But when my feet no longer feel the sharp rocks that line the ocean's floor, my father reaches me and grabs the nape of my neck. With little warning, he thrusts my face down into the water and then lifts my head up just enough so that I have a quick gasp of air before he plunges me back underwater. At first, I fight back, trying to overcome my father's massive strength. But on the third plunge, I give up. Isn't this what I wanted after all—to die and be rid of him forever?

As I discovered a long time ago, my wishes and prayers never come true. I'm amazed that I even love attending church and still pray to God. For it's become quite clear, He's forgotten about me.

So why should now be any different? Instead of killing me as my father had vowed to do, he carries me out of the water, dropping me on the sand. He sits down next to me, holding his head in his hands. I turn over onto my stomach, coughing and spitting up water. My chest heaves as I gulp in whatever air I can. When my father sees I'm struggling, he merely comes over and gives my back a hard thump with his fist, which only elicits more coughing. And the stench of fish, which is always on my father because of his trade as a fisherman, makes me want to gag.

"Why do you disobey me? Why?" Papá's expression is full of hatred.

"You never told me I was not allowed to come here." I cringe in anticipation of my words provoking another attack.

"You know you are not to go anywhere without a chaperone and at this time of the night? You do not need me to tell you that you are forbidden from leaving the house so late. I rarely allow you to go outdoors alone during the day. Do you really think I would allow it in the dead of night? There could only be one reason why you would do such a foolish thing. Who were you meeting?"

"No one. I swear, Papá. It is the only time I have to myself and don't need to worry about the children."

"Ah? So now you need time to yourself? What is his name? I will make sure he never walks again. Tell me his name. Now!" My father towers over me with his hand raised in the air.

"Please, Papá! Just think. Where could I have met anyone? I am always with you and Mama and the children."

"Here! You could have met him here. How do I know he isn't hiding behind one of these boulders right now, quivering like a coward?" He squints, trying to see in the darkness, and screams, "Come out! You hear me? Come out! Be a man!" Then he begins searching for my imaginary lover, looking behind each of the boulders that sit along the shoreline.

My father's search momentarily rescues me from another thrashing. But I know it has just bought me a few minutes. For when he doesn't find anyone hiding behind the rocks, he'll beat me until I tell him who I was meeting. Tears stream down my face. I don't know how much longer I can go on living like this.

"I'll find you! You hear me? Maybe not tonight, but I will find you!" Papá continues yelling into the night, his voice only muffled by the waves crashing against the shore. "Come on, Sarina. That boy's blood will be on your hands. You have disgraced me and your mother. She will be so disappointed in you." He pulls me up by my arm, dragging me back home. I try shrugging his grip off me, but he sinks his fingernails into my flesh until I wince from the pain. My body is always covered in scratches and bruises.

When we reach my house, I see the light on in my parents' bedroom. I can make out my mother's form behind the window. But as soon as she sees us approaching, her shadow disappears, and the light goes out. No doubt she is afraid of angering my father. Sometimes I wish she were stronger and would stand up more to him. I feel so alone. The only consolation I have is that she was worried and waited until she saw I was all right.

"I have lost sleep because of you," my father says once we're indoors.

I begin making my way to the bedroom I share with my younger siblings, but Papá comes over and blocks the entrance.

"You wanted to sleep outside like an animal, so you will have your wish." He turns to the cabinet in our kitchen and takes out from one of its drawers a long rope. Wrapping the rope around one of my wrists, he creates a tight noose. Then as if I were a dog on a leash he pulls the rope, leading me outside and to the fig tree in the yard behind our house. He kicks me hard in the shins, causing my legs to buckle as I fall to the ground. Undoing the noose around my wrist, he places the rope instead around my body and ties me tightly to the tree. The rope's fibers dig into my skin. I begin shivering from my wet clothes.

"You are lucky I decided not to give you another beating once we got home. But you do not appreciate anything I ever do for you." He walks away, slamming the door of our house.

This is not the first time he has tied me to this tree and left me out all night. He has been doing it since I was ten years old. I used to beg him not to leave me all alone in the dark, which I was afraid of until last year, and I also pleaded with him to let my cat Tina stay outdoors with me. But of course my pleas always fell on deaf ears.

Eventually, I stopped being frightened. For I realized it wasn't the dark I needed to be terrified of, but rather my father.

I suddenly hear a twig snap behind the tree. Sitting up, I see two glowing yellow eyes beaming right at me.

"Tina! How did you get out?"

I didn't hear the door open after my father went inside, and I know he would never feel any compassion toward me to give in to my request of having my cat stay with me so that I wouldn't be terrified. She must've been out earlier, and no one had noticed she wasn't inside when they went to bed. My father always keeps her indoors at night to ensure she catches any mice we have. That is his sole purpose for having the cat. He's always frowned whenever one of us showers any affection on Tina and treats her like a beloved pet.

"Meow!" Tina rubs up against me. I tilt my head toward her and let her lick my cheek.

I start sobbing, feeling so wretched tied to this tree with only my cat to console me. My distress only elicits further meows from Tina. She's always hated it when one of us cries. She senses our anxiety and in turn becomes agitated. Tina is now licking me more frantically until finally I stop sobbing. Content that I have calmed down, she curls up against my side, keeping me warm. Even her purring soothes me as it reverberates throughout my body. Comforting myself as I always have by singing, I whisper the words to the song I sang earlier, *"Stell-ahhh mia, stell-ahhh mia,"* imagining I am one of the stars up in the universe and far, far away from my cruel father.

∼✷ 2 ✷∼

Una Tazza di Porcellana

A PORCELAIN TEACUP

April 30, 1969

Though all of the days are grueling for me in my household, today is particularly difficult. All of my younger siblings have come down with the flu. My mother and I have hardly slept, caring for them as well as staying on top of our chores. And now Mama and I are starting to get sick as well.

"Sickness does not stop a house from running," Papá likes to say, for when my mother and I are ill, we must carry on as always. We do not get to lie down in bed and have someone take care of us as when my younger siblings or my father fall ill. Naturally, Papá never lifts a finger to help my mother and me with our added burden of tending to sick children. The daily routine must run as smoothly as usual. All three meals must be cooked fresh every day, the beds must be turned out and made, the floors scrubbed, and the children must be kept comfortable enough so that they are not crying their heads off when he comes home in the evening and does not wish to have his dinner disturbed. Even through crippling body aches and high fevers, I have my hands deep in ice-cold water as I wash the laundry. If my father so much as hears me complain of a physical ailment or sees me take a moment to catch my breath, he is quick to raise his voice or even slap me like a mule to force me to resume. If I didn't love God as much as I do and respect His commandments, I swear I could murder Papá in his sleep.

"Sarina, bevi questo," my mother whispers as she hands me a cup of tea with fresh-squeezed lemon juice and honey.

"Grazie, Mama." I quickly gulp the tea, ignoring its scalding temperature out of fear that Papá will catch us taking a momentary break from our chores. I leave some tea for my mother and implore her to drink the rest.

"No, ho già bevuto. I already drank mine. This is all for you. Hurry, before he comes back." Mama glances nervously over her shoulder, toward the front door.

Nodding my head, I drink the last of my tea. My mother takes the cup and hides it in her apron pocket in the nick of time since my father comes in a moment later. I resume my ironing. The steam along with the tea I had is making me extremely hot. I press the back of my hand to my forehead and notice it's burning up. Quickly I glance in my father's direction. He is at the kitchen sink, washing the sardines he has caught in the ocean. My mother stands beside him, shelling beans. Taking my handkerchief out of my bra, I dip it in the glass of cold water I use for filling up my iron and dab my face. Suddenly my mother's anguished cries reach my ears, followed by something crashing to the floor. I'm afraid of the sight that will greet me as I turn around.

"Ai! Ai!" Mama repeatedly screams as she presses her hands to her right eye. Blood rivulets gush down. The cup I had drunk tea out of now lies shattered by her feet. Papá must have seen it bulging from her apron pocket.

"While I am out toiling hard, you decide to take a coffee break?"

"It was just tea. I am sick. You know that."

I am surprised that my mother has dared to speak back to him.

"Sick! What is this nonsense? Are you one of the children now?"

I want to rush to my mother's side, but I know that will make matters worse for both of us. He will not only lash out at me, but he might hit Mama again.

With great effort, I turn around and resume my ironing, pretending I have not witnessed Papá beating Mama.

My shoulders shake as I hear more china being shattered. My father has taken from the cupboard another one of my mother's prized china teacups and throws it on the floor. He then stomps on the broken teacups, ensuring they cannot be glued back together—the ultimate insult to my mother. For he knows how much she loves her china, the only wedding gift she received. Her china set has grown smaller over the years, each piece destroyed after yet another of my father's volatile fits. All that exists now are three dinner plates, one pasta bowl, and a creamer. I feel guilty that because of me my mother has lost more of her treasured china. I don't know why she didn't use one of the cheaper glasses we drink out of every day. Perhaps because it is rare that she has an occasion to use her beloved china, and she is tired of just seeing it sit in her cupboard. We rarely have guests out of fear of my father's unpredictable behavior.

"Some nights I don't know why I come home at all when this is what welcomes me. Utter disrespect for my wishes. I should have never taken you off your father's hands. You aren't worth the paltry dowry he paid me." And if his words don't sting enough, he spits on the floor beside my mother's defeated, crumpled form. Her arms are wrapped over her head, and her body shudders visibly. Papá passes me as he makes his way to his bedroom. I keep my eyes lowered; my heart races and doesn't slow down until I hear his bedroom door close. I wait a few seconds to be certain he's not coming back out before I rush over to Mama. Untying my apron, I press it to the cut above her eye to stop the bleeding.

"Go away, Sarina, before he comes back and hits you, too. I will be fine."

"He's probably deep in sleep already. Here, let me help you up." I hoist my hands beneath Mama's arms and pull her up. Her lips are shaking, and tears threaten to spill from her eyes, but she's attempting to be brave for me. I smooth back the strands of her hair that have escaped from her bun. Taking a glass from the cupboard, I fill it with cold water and hold it to her lips. She takes a few sips.

"*Grazie,* Sarina. Don't worry. It's just a little cut."

"I'll get you a bandage." I walk over to one of our kitchen drawers and search until I find one. Bandages don't last long in this house.

"Let me see if the bleeding has stopped." I take the compress from Mama's hand. The cut is still bleeding, but only lightly now. I run my apron under the kitchen sink faucet and clean up some of the blood that has dried on her skin. I then pat her skin dry with a dish towel before applying the bandage.

"There. You will be as good as new." I smile at Mama, who momentarily returns my smile before her smile disappears as her eyes fill with sadness once again. Her gaze wanders to the broken fragments of her teacups that are strewn all over the kitchen floor.

"*Quelle erano le mie ultime tazze di porcellana.*" She shakes her head as she repeats again, "Those were my last porcelain teacups."

The teacups were her favorite part of the china set, and now none remain.

"Don't worry, Mama. Someday I'm going to buy you the best china set in the world."

Mama laughs. "How will you do that? By marrying a rich man?"

"Ha! I refuse to ever get married and be another man's slave again. I will earn my own money. Once I do that, I will get you and the children away from Papá."

"You dream too much, Sarina." Mama gives me a sad smile.

We jump as we hear footsteps coming from my parents' bedroom. We nod quickly to each other before I resume my post at the ironing table. Mama begins sweeping up the shattered china. Papá comes out of the bedroom. He stops in front of me. I dare not meet his gaze. After what seems like forever, he walks toward the door and steps out. Soon, the scent from his pipe reaches my nostrils.

Silently, I pray to God to make Papá fall sick with an incurable disease. And I vow that somehow I will find a way to keep my promise to Mama. She will have the most beautiful china set in the world.

❦ 3 ❦

La Lumaca

THE SNAIL

May 7, 1969

My cousin Agata and I are skipping through the fields of the land my father and uncle inherited after their parents passed away. We are deep in the countryside, about five miles from our home by the beach. Agata and her family live a few houses down from ours. We love to come here because we are left alone for hours without our fathers' ever-watchful glares. Though we are hard at work, harvesting the crops, mainly grapes, that our parents grow, Agata and I don't mind since we have each other's company and can talk freely. Every so often, we chase each other like little girls or hold hands as we're doing now, singing and skipping through the lush vegetation.

I have a small plot of land, on which my father allows me to grow whatever I want—one of the very few kindnesses he has shown me. He seems to take pleasure in the idea that I've inherited his love of gardening. I especially love to cultivate herbs and have become quite an expert in those with medicinal properties. The other night my mother suffered from terrible stomach indigestion. I added a couple of bay leaves to a pot of water and let it come to a boil. I poured the water into a cup and stirred in a teaspoon of honey so that Mama could easily drink the bay leaf water. Within minutes, her stomach cramps subsided. I've also used the bay leaf water for whenever one of us feels nauseated.

Once Agata and I are done picking the ripe grapes from their vines, we head over to my garden. I'm busy snipping oregano, rosemary, and thyme with my garden shears. I inhale deeply the herbs' fragrances. Agata snips bouquets of basil—no doubt to make her famous pesto sauce.

"You are planning on charming our fathers with some pesto tonight?" I smile as I glance up momentarily from the rows of neatly planted herbs.

"Whatever works for their bestial temperaments, Sarina." Agata glances over her shoulder, making certain our fathers are not within earshot.

"They always seem to be in a better mood once we visit the farm. Maybe we should move here?" My thoughts wander as I fantasize about living in the countryside with a father who rarely gets cross with his wife and children. Sighing deeply, I shake myself out of my reverie, knowing that will never happen.

"Nothing will change our fathers. Mama tells me that old age softens people. But I have also heard it can make them worse. My hunch is that my Papá will be just as mean when he is old." Agata takes a break and plops down on the ground. She pulls her hair out from the bun it's in and quickly braids it. We both have very long hair, reaching down to our waists, and as such often wear it braided or coiled in a bun.

"I love it when you wear your hair in braids. It looks like two perfect husks of wheat. I wish my hair were your golden hue instead of this coppery shade—or as Papá likes to call it 'the hair of the devil.'" I stare longingly at Agata's hair.

"Zio Salvatore forgets that his own mother had your same auburn hair. I doubt he called her a devil."

Salvatore is my father's first name.

"Poor Nonna. I can't believe she is no longer with us." My eyes well up at the thought of my grandmother who died the previous year of a stroke. True, I never witnessed Papá utter a harsh word toward her, but I often wondered if Nonno hit her and that's where Papá learned to beat his own wife and children. I asked my mother once if she knew if Nonno had beaten his wife and my father, but she told me she didn't believe he did. Zio Mario, Agata's father, is also known for his bad temper, but his punishments are less severe than those my father doles out. He slaps Agata when he is mad at her, but he never beats her viciously or ties her to a tree for an entire night like my father has done to me. And I don't believe Zio Mario has ever laid a hand on Zia Carmella, Agata's mother. I think about how sweet Enzo and Carlotta are, and I know without a doubt that they will continue to be kind, gentle people when they grow up. Pietro is still too young for me to know what his temperament will be like, but the more I ponder my father's violent behavior, the more I become convinced he is just evil and there is no explanation for his outbursts.

"Enough sad talk. Have you noticed the son of your new next-door neighbor? He is quite handsome. He said hello to me the other day when I was coming to your house." Agata smiles mischievously.

"Did you talk to him? I cannot believe this is the first I am hearing of this."

"I could not risk your father's eavesdropping on us."

"Ah! True. Don't keep me in suspense any longer. Did you say anything to him?"

"I just nodded my head and gave him a hint of a smile. Again, I was too terrified of Zio Salvatore's hearing me and then telling my father, who would no doubt accuse me of acting like a whore merely by returning a greeting."

I laughed. Though it seems absurd, our fathers consider any attention a woman gives to a man to be inappropriate until they are married. Before then, one must never glance in a man's direction, talk to him, or do anything else that might encourage him.

"Do you have any idea what his name is?"

"I heard his mother calling him the other day. His name is Giuseppe." Agata is smiling to herself as she inhales the scent of the herbs I've placed in my basket on the ground.

"I wouldn't get carried away with any fantasies, Agata. Sometimes I think our Papás intend for us to become old maids so we can take care of them forever." I now add to my basket of herbs a bunch of sage leaves I've picked. I like using them in my soups. Lately, I have been cooking dinner more to give Mama a break. She's been looking more tired than usual. Wiping my brow with my apron, I close my eyes and enjoy the warmth of the sun on my face.

"When our fathers are ready, they'll arrange our marriages to the sons of some well-off merchants or landowners. That is after all the only value they see in having daughters. I heard Papá say so to Mama once." The joy that was evident in Agata's face moments ago is now replaced by the usual somberness I'm accustomed to seeing.

"We'll run away before that can happen. Don't worry."

Agata laughs. "You and your plans of running away. How do you expect to get far when we live with two bloodhounds who sense everything?"

"I'll kill myself rather than let my father barter me like some chattel." My face is drawn into a scowl.

"Sarina! Don't ever say such a thing! I would never forgive you—nor would God! You'll burn in hell. Then Zio Salvatore will surely think he was right in saying you possessed the devil's hair."

Our glances meet, and we break out into laughter.

Agata becomes serious once again. "Please, Sarina, don't ever joke like that."

I shrug my shoulders. "I am too much of a good Catholic to ever commit suicide. But that does not mean I cannot fantasize about it now and then."

"Agata! *Dove sei?*"

Agata quickly jumps to her feet at the sound of her father's voice.

"*Hai trovato la tua figlia?*" My father asks his brother if he's found his daughter. My heart fills with sadness at the thought that our afternoon to ourselves has come to a close.

Reluctantly, I also stand up. Our fathers wheel their bicycles toward us. Zio Mario and my father had ridden their bicycles up the mountains in search of *le lumache,* or snails. It rained all of last night, and whenever we've had a good soaking, my father treks out on his bicycle in search of snails. A few Mason jars sit in the baskets that hang on the front of their bicycles.

"Did you catch a lot?" I ask my father.

"*Si,* Sarina. We filled every one of our jars except for one." My father proudly holds up two of the jars. I can see the snails clinging to the glass.

"I will cook them tonight, Papá, just the way you like them."

"*Si,* Sarina. Be careful you don't burn any like you did the last time. Maybe you should just let your mother cook them."

Though his words are offensive, he does not say them in his usual hostile tone, perhaps because Zio Mario and Agata are still with us.

"I pulled lots of basil, Zio Salvatore. I'm going to make my pesto sauce that you and Papá love so much." Agata holds up a bunch of basil.

"I cannot wait, Agata!" My father smiles at her. My heart sinks. Why can't he ever utter a kind word to me?

We make our way to Zio Mario's car and begin the drive down the mountain. I wish Zia Carmella and my mother had come with us. But they claimed they had too much work to do. Suddenly, the realization comes to me that Agata's mother and mine might have bowed out of this excursion to the countryside so that they, too, could have some time to themselves and away from their husbands.

Our fathers are chatting animatedly all the way back home. Their good humor lasts throughout dinner. We say good-bye to Agata, Zia Carmella, and Zio Mario shortly after dinner. Agata is an only child, and that is another reason why she is so close to me and even my younger siblings.

The long day has tired my father out, and he retires to bed shortly after dinner. I pretend to go to bed, but a few hours later, once I'm assured that my family is sound asleep, I get up and tiptoe to the kitchen. Leaning against the sink, I cross my arms and stare longingly at the stars outside, wishing I were on one of my late-night strolls to the beach. But after my father almost drowned me and accused me of having a lover, I know I cannot risk venturing out again. For I am certain he would kill me the next time. Turning away from the window, I walk over to a crudely made wooden shelf Papá carved for Mama's plants. He always likes to keep a couple of snails alive for a few days. As soon as he gets tired of seeing them, he throws them outside. This time, he's only kept one *lumaca*. I watch the snail crawling on the underside of a turned-over drinking glass. My heart fills with sadness as I watch the trapped creature confined to its narrow space.

✺ 4 ✺

Gattina

LITTLE CAT

May 14, 1969

"*Bestia! Bestia!*" Papá screams before he throws our cat Tina against the wall of our kitchen.

"*No, Papá! Per favore, lasciala stare.*" I plead with him to leave Tina alone. But once more he charges toward her. Tina's back hunches, and her fur stands on end as she repeatedly hisses at Papá. Though her eyes are filled with terror, she's also prepared to defend herself.

I run toward my father and grab his arm, but he shoves me so hard that I lose my balance and fall. That's when Tina decides to strike, lunging for my father and clinging to his arm with her teeth and claws. He tries shaking her off, but to no avail. She then scratches his cheek.

"*Maledette disgraziata! Ti ammazzo!*" Papá curses Tina and grabs her by the scruff of her neck, but she manages to swipe him one last time with her claws, scratching his eye.

"Aiii!" He drops her.

Tina runs out the door just in time as Enzo comes home from school. Even though he is just six years old, he walks to and from school by himself. Fortunately, the schoolhouse is only around the corner from our street, so he doesn't have to cross any roads. Papá forbade my mother or me from accompanying Enzo, saying we couldn't afford to take any time away from our chores. "Besides, Enzo needs to become a man, and that's not going to happen if he has the two of you holding his hand," he'd said.

"What happened?" Enzo looks from me to my father, no doubt thinking Papá has beat me once again and I have finally rebelled. If only I had the courage to do so.

I shake my head at my brother, imploring him not to ask any more questions. He stares at the floor and walks quickly to the bedroom, but my father begins screaming anew, causing poor Enzo to freeze in his tracks.

"You had better hope that wretched cat has run off for good! If she comes back here, I will take her to the beach and drown her! I should have done so months ago when I discovered she wasn't catching any mice. What good is she? That is the only reason why I've kept her and fed her. I've wasted my money on that despicable creature." My father walks over to the kitchen sink and spits into it, as if his words aren't enough to convey his disgust.

"But, Papá, she's been a good cat. She is kind and always looks worried when Carlotta, Pietro, or I are crying. She even licks us to make us feel better."

"And you let her? Who knows what germs that filthy beast is carrying?" Papá glares at Enzo, who quickly averts his gaze. His eyes are welling up with tears.

"Go wash up, Enzo." I walk over and prod him gently toward the bathroom.

My father shakes his head, running his hand through his hair as he walks over to the cupboard and takes out a small bottle of grappa. He takes a long swig from the bottle and returns it to the cupboard. He then walks into his bedroom and slams the door shut.

I know I must act quickly and find Tina. This isn't the first time he's hit her, but he's never come close to killing her as he did today. Maybe she's too afraid to return home, but I know how loyal she is toward us. We're the only family she knows.

I remember the day Agata and Zio Mario brought Tina to our

house two years ago. They had found her outside their home. She was only a couple of weeks old. They said she looked as if she were searching for her mother. Agata and Zio Mario already had a cat that helped catch their mice. Zio Mario knew we'd been having problems with mice and thought we might want her.

"She won't be ready to catch mice for months," my father said, shaking his head.

"Cats grow quickly. Give her a few months, and she'll be killing mice left and right. Our cat was only a few months old when we got her, and she wasted no time," Zio Mario said with apparent pride in his voice.

You would have thought he was talking about some great feat Agata had performed instead of a cat whose sole purpose was to kill pests. They hadn't even named her. Agata was aloof when it came to their cat and didn't pay much attention to her.

My father finally agreed to take Tina.

"You'll have to feed her with a doll's bottle. We tried giving her a bowl of milk, but she almost fell into it! I got the idea to use one of my doll's bottles." Now Agata was the one beaming with pride.

"You still have your dolls?" I asked incredulously. My mother had wasted no time in giving my one doll to Carlotta even though part of me wanted to keep her. Although I knew I was too old to play with her, I wanted my doll for myself. Perhaps because she was a reminder of the childhood I once had, if only briefly.

Agata's face flushed at my question. Instead of answering, she took out of her dress's pocket the doll's bottle. "I brought mine just in case you didn't have one."

Zio Mario handed the kitten to me. I gingerly took the kitten in both of my hands. It was the first time I looked into her face, and I couldn't help exclaiming, "Ahhhh! *Cosi bella!*" Without a doubt, she was the most beautiful little creature I'd ever seen. And the thought of having to bottle-feed her only made her more adorable. Even when we showed the kitten to my mother, her beautiful smile, which she rarely displayed, showed her admiration.

Tina grew quickly, and my siblings and I were all disappointed to throw out the bottle when the time came. Enzo still tried to feed her with it, but even Tina knew she was too old and staunchly refused the bottle. We still hadn't chosen a name for her. Enzo kept calling her "Gattina," or little cat. Though "Gattina" seemed like a simple name, it was also cute and charming. But Carlotta, at two years old, could only manage to say "Tina." So we decided to go with this name since it would be easier for Carlotta to pronounce.

With a sleek, shiny silver coat, a little splash of what looked like milk on her chest, and stunning yellow eyes that resembled a tiger's eye jewel, Tina possessed a regal feline splendor. I became curious about what breed she was since we'd never seen any of the stray cats in our village look like her. So one day, I went to the library and found a large reference book on cats. About fifty pages into the book, I saw a photo that was a dead ringer for Tina. Her breed was Russian Blue. I knew we had a special cat, not just due to her unique breed, but also by her sweet personality and her complete devotion to me and my family . . . well, except for my father.

Sometimes, when my parents weren't home, I would take out of my mother's jewelry box her thick eighteen-karat-gold rope chain. An oval filigreed pendant hung from the chain and in its center lay a stunning aquamarine gem. My father had given my mother this necklace when they became engaged. It had belonged to a wealthy great-grandmother of his. I called the necklace Mama's Cleopatra necklace since it looked like jewelry the famous African queen would have worn. My mother promised me that she would leave the necklace for me after she passed away. I loved to drape the Cleopatra necklace around Tina's neck. "Gorgeous! You are so beautiful!" I whispered to her and imagined Tina's ancestors belonging to the Russian aristocracy, who would have adorned their cats in the same fashion every day.

Tina is like a baby to me. And now I must give her up. I'm too terrified that my father will make good on his threat and drown her if she comes back home. With tears in my eyes, I go searching for her, but shortly after I step outside, Enzo follows.

"We have to find her." His eyes are red-rimmed. My heart breaks for him. I wish that at six years old he didn't have to witness my father's cruelty.

"I know. I'm going to look for Tina. Go back inside."

Enzo shakes his head. "I want to help you."

"Okay. Let's go."

It doesn't take us long to find Tina. She's curled up in a small opening that has eroded from the bottom of one of the large boulders that sit on the beach. It's one of her favorite spots. When Tina sees us, she comes running out, meowing and rubbing against our legs. I pick her up lest she run off from us again. Pain pierces through me at what we must do. I shut my eyes tightly, forcing back tears. I can't lose it in front of Enzo. But now comes the difficult part. I wish I could shield him from the truth, but he deserves to know.

"Enzo, you know we can't bring Tina back into the house? Something might happen to her."

Enzo nods his head. "Papá might hurt her again and maybe worse the next time."

I nod my head. "*Sì.* I need to take her away from here. Somewhere far where Papá can't find her. I'll make sure she is in a safe place. I promise."

"I want to come with you, Sarina. I want to be able to say good-bye to Tina."

"You can say good-bye now."

Enzo shakes his head vehemently. "No, no, no!" He begins pummeling my chest with his little fists, startling Tina, who almost jumps out of my arms.

"All right. All right. Calm down. You can come."

With one last glance over my shoulder to ensure Papá isn't following us, I urge Enzo to hurry as we quickly make our way behind our house where I keep my bicycle. Placing Tina in the basket that hangs in the front of my bicycle, I motion for Enzo to take the seat. I then straddle the bicycle and ride it standing up since there isn't enough room for both of us to sit. I am accustomed to giving Enzo and Carlotta rides on the bike, so pedaling standing up isn't difficult for me.

I ride all the way into Barcellona Pozzo di Gotto, or Barcellona as the locals call it. I'm headed to the veterinarian's office. Someone had once told me that occasionally he took a few strays in and gave them up for adoption. It's almost two p.m., and the high sun along with the extremely muggy air we're having today is unbearable. My sundress is sticking to me. Pulling my dress's hem up, I bend over at my waist and quickly wipe the perspiration from my face. My ponytail is coming loose. I take out my hair and retie it into another ponytail, tightening my ratty rubber band. Enzo only looks marginally better than me. I lick my palms and smooth down the cowlicks in his hair.

"Tuck your shirt in. We don't want to look like some miserable beggar children."

Enzo nods and does as he's told. He then takes Tina out of my bicycle's basket. Fortunately for us, she's always loved riding in the bicycle's basket and is used to it. A cat jumping out of my basket on Barcellona's busy streets is all I would've needed. That's what I've also always loved about her. She's never been a typical skittish cat.

Before we walk through the vet's door, Tina twists her ears, and her eyes open wide. She seems nervous, almost as if she can sense there are other animals behind the door. When we walk in, a large sheep dog tries to lunge for Tina, but its owner quickly restrains him with his leash. Tina nearly jumps out of Enzo's grip.

"May I help you?" The receptionist is a pretty blond woman who looks to be in her early to mid-twenties. She smiles kindly at us.

"We heard that Dr. Lombardi sometimes takes in strays and finds homes for them. Our mother is allergic to our cat, and we were hoping he could find her a good home." I smile back at the woman, but her pleasant demeanor from a moment ago has vanished, and she's now frowning.

"I'll ask Dr. Lombardi, but our boarding room is getting full. Unfortunately, not too many people have been adopting the animals lately. Have a seat, and I'll ask him when he's done with the patient he's now seeing."

"Thank you. Please, whatever you can say to him would be greatly appreciated." I plead with my eyes to show her how important this is to me. The receptionist glances down as if my begging is embarrassing her. Or is it that she's embarrassed *for* me?

We wait for about half an hour, but it seems like an eternity. I'm sure Papá must be awake from his siesta and looking for us. No doubt, Enzo and I will both have a beating waiting for us. He doesn't go beyond a few slaps or spanks for the younger children. He saves the more severe beatings for my mother, and especially for me.

Finally, the receptionist motions to us with a wave of her hand. We follow her to the back of the vet's office. She leads us into an examination room. The veterinarian has his back turned to us. I see him placing vials of blood onto a tray.

"Here are the children I was telling you about, Dr. Lombardi." The receptionist holds her hands out in our direction as if she is presenting prize horses. I can't help but bristle at her use of "children" since I'm almost seventeen.

"Thank you, Bianca." Dr. Lombardi still keeps his back averted. Bianca returns to the reception area.

Enzo and I wait another minute before Dr. Lombardi turns around and gives us his attention.

"I'm sorry. I need to focus on what I'm doing so that I don't make a mistake mixing up the blood vials. I had told Bianca to give me another five minutes, but she doesn't seem to be able to tell time." Dr. Lombardi rolls his eyes.

"We're sorry for bothering you, Dr. Lombardi, but we can no longer keep our cat. Our mother is allergic. We were hoping you could take her and possibly find her a new family?" I hope that my voice doesn't sound too desperate.

"She's a good cat, doctor. Very kind. She's never scratched anyone," Enzo says without diverting his gaze from the doctor.

I'm amazed at how well he can lie, since he and I know what a good job Tina did of scratching my father today. But that's the only time she ever attacked anyone.

"Let's see what we have here." Dr. Lombardi walks over to Enzo and takes Tina from him. He pets her and begins cooing softly in her ear. Tina looks up at him and then licks his chin.

"A Russian Blue! I've never seen one here in Italy. She's beautiful." Dr. Lombardi's eyes glow. Maybe he wants her for himself? I can't help wondering.

He places Tina on the exam table and begins pushing her fur back, inspecting it. At first, I don't know what he's doing, but then I realize he's checking for fleas and ticks. I hear him every so often utter, "Hmmm . . . hmmm." My heart starts to race. For I know she must have fleas or ticks since she spends so much time outdoors. But surely, Dr. Lombardi is a veterinarian. He can treat her, and she'll be as good as new.

"What are you doing?" Enzo asks as Dr. Lombardi turns up Tina's ears and inspects them as well.

"I'm looking for ear mites. Earlier, I was checking for fleas or ticks. I'm sorry to say your cat has ear mites and fleas. The ear mites aren't so bad, but she's quite infested with fleas. I'm sorry, but we can't take animals with fleas, ticks, or ear mites." Dr. Lombardi looks pained as he says this.

"Please, Dr. Lombardi. You can treat her for the fleas and mites. You do that for the other animals that are brought here." I try to keep my voice calm, but my anger is beginning to swell.

"*Sì.* But you want me to keep the cat boarded here with the other animals I have. I cannot afford to have the other animals come down with fleas. I cannot have people adopt them if they have fleas. *Mi dispiace.* I am very sorry. I wish I could help." Dr. Lombardi shrugs his shoulders.

He then looks us over from head to toe. He slightly shakes his head as he takes in our clothes and appearance. And in that moment, I realize he has seen through my lie about my mother's being allergic to Tina. My cheeks flush hot as shame fills me. It is as if Enzo and I also have fleas. Dr. Lombardi must think we're too poor to care for our cat or possibly he suspects it is one of our parents who has forced us to give the cat away.

I hear Enzo utter an almost inaudible "thank you" as Dr. Lombardi hands Tina back to him. I don't bother expressing my gratitude since he wasn't able to help us. Clenching my hands into fists, I say to Enzo, "Let's go." We walk quickly out of the exam room. We pass by Bianca's desk, and she doesn't even look up to say good-bye. No doubt she must have been eavesdropping and heard everything.

We step outside. The sun feels even more brutal. My spirits sink as I realize where we must go now. There is no other choice.

I try telling myself that this is life. Sacrifices must be made. At sixteen, I had learned this lesson young in my family. My father's wishes were the only ones that counted in my household, and while we lived under his roof, we did not and could not make the decisions—even where a beloved family pet was concerned, a pet who had lived with us for two years and who had known no other owners besides us. True, our father did not tell us we had to give her away, but neither Enzo nor I trusted him. If it weren't this time, there would surely be another instance when he would hurt Tina and possibly even kill her. He'd almost drowned me that night at the beach. If he could do that to his own child, why would he spare the life of a cat that he saw as nothing more than an animal without a soul and not worth saving?

Enzo continued to hold Tina as I got my bicycle. He was about to put Tina in the basket, but I stopped him.

"We're going to the piazza. We can walk from here. Just hold her unless you're getting too tired."

"No, she's light."

"Good." I pat his head.

"We can't go back home with her, Sarina."

"I know, Enzo. That's why we're going to the piazza."

"We're going to leave her there all alone?" Enzo looks at Tina. He's stroking her head. This was a mistake. I should have insisted he not come. What had I been thinking?

"She won't be alone. Look at all these people. Someone will see her and how different she is from most other cats, and he or she will take Tina home. People often feed the stray cats and dogs. I've seen them do it when we've come here with Mama and Papá."

"You have?" Enzo asks a little too quickly.

"She will be all right. I know it." I reassure Enzo, but can't help feeling as if I'm the one who needs to be reassured.

We walk over to the piazza and sit down on one of the benches. It is around four in the afternoon now. The piazza is still quite empty except for a few vagrants. Most people are still taking their siestas or just awakening from them. I see a few of the shop owners returning to their businesses. We could leave Tina now under a bench, and no one would notice. But I'm not ready to leave her just yet. Enzo doesn't question me as to what we're waiting for. I know he is savoring what little time we have left with her.

Tina is examining her surroundings, curiosity getting the better of her as she squirms to wrest herself free from Enzo's grip. Finally, he lets her jump onto the bench. She sniffs the vines that are reaching toward us from the garden that's situated behind the piazza's benches. Her eyes then fix on a red-breasted robin that's just flown over to the branch of a palm tree. Her pupils dilate as she continues staring at the bird. Now would be a good time for us to slowly walk away before she notices. I try to will my feet to move, but they remain cemented to the ground.

Taking a deep breath, I look once more toward the shops across the piazza's way. I see a plump woman sweeping the sidewalk in front of a butcher shop. She wears a white apron. Her face looks kind. She turns around and goes inside. I can make out her form behind the meat counter. I glance to the side of the butcher shop and see a door that must lead to their kitchen.

"Let's go!" I all but shout to Enzo as I quickly pick up Tina and scramble across the street, making my way to the butcher shop.

We walk by the entrance door, which is open. Going to the side of the butcher shop, I pray that the door is unlocked. The metal latch is scorching hot from the sun's rays, and I almost burn my hand. Ignoring the sensation, I pull down on the latch. It opens!

Pulling the door slightly ajar lest anyone see me, I peek inside. Slabs of meat hang from the ceiling. I see the back of a rather portly man who is sharpening his cleavers. Crouching down, I drop Tina into the kitchen. She looks at me with a surprised expression, but then notices a piece of raw meat on the ground near her and picks it up with her mouth, chewing ravenously. The butcher is still sharpening his cleavers. I take one last look at Tina. Enzo is peeking over my shoulder. Our eyes meet. I nod my head, signaling that it's time we leave. He returns my nod. Quietly, I close the door. Enzo and I hurry away, keeping our gazes down. I look over my shoulder once we're close to the corner, and I see the woman who was sweeping in front of the meat shop earlier making her way over to the side entrance. She has to be the butcher's wife. I wish she hadn't come out just yet. I wanted to wait for a little while to see if the butcher would toss Tina back out once he noticed her. At least the butcher's wife didn't see us. I pray they keep her. At least we weren't leaving her out in the piazza.

We make our way back to where I left my bicycle. I wasn't even afraid that it would be stolen. My thoughts were focused on getting Tina inside that butcher shop. I struggle to keep away the pain that is trying to inch itself into my heart by repeating to myself that it was something we had to do. No choice. We had no other choice whatsoever. But it's no use. The pain fills every pore in my body, and the tears I've been fighting back are now swimming fiercely down my face. I can't glance at Enzo. I can't bear to see the hurt that must surely be on his face.

When we reach the spot where I left my bicycle, I'm relieved to see it's still there. The weight of all that we had to do is too much for me. I all but collapse on a nearby bench and place my face in my hands and sob uncontrollably.

"Sarina, she'll be fine. That man and lady in the butcher shop will feed her and take care of her. Did you see how she went for that piece of meat on the floor? She's in cat heaven now." Enzo puts his arm around my shoulders. Once again, I'm amazed at the maturity he has displayed today. Someday, he will make a fine man and husband. I pray my father's evil nature never touches his pure heart.

I hug Enzo. "You are so funny! But yes, you are right. Tina is in cat heaven, or should we say meat paradise?!" I pull away from Enzo, and his cheeks are also stained with tears now. But he manages to laugh. I hug him once more, placing a kiss on his forehead.

"We'd better get going. Mama will be worried."

"Papá is going to be really mad."

"Don't worry about him."

We get on the bicycle. Enzo's grip around my waist feels tighter on the way back home. I pedal much slower than I did when we set out for Barcellona. My energy has been spent.

When we finally get home, it is dinnertime. My pulse quickens at the thought of what will await us when we step inside. Holding hands, we walk through the threshold. The front door was left open. My parents and Carlotta are eating dinner. Pietro is in the bassinet near my mother, who's rocking it with one hand while eating with her other. No one looks over at us. I know it is only moments before my father lashes out.

I take Enzo to the bathroom and wash his face for him even though he is capable of doing it for himself. I then quickly splash water on my face. Enzo waits for me, too fearful to go to the dinner table alone.

We take our places at the table. Still, no one says a word. Our minestrone has gotten cold, but Enzo and I eat it hungrily, oblivious to its temperature.

"Where is Tina? I can't find her." Carlotta tugs at my dress. Coldness washes over me. I had forgotten about Carlotta and what we would say to her about Tina.

I struggle to think of a plausible excuse that will satisfy Carlotta's curiosity, but then my father says, "She's gone."

I look at him, horrified. Carlotta is too young to hear the truth. Then again, Enzo was also too young to be my accomplice in abandoning Tina.

"Gone? At the beach?" Carlotta looks at me for an explanation.

"Your sister and brother had to abandon her. She attacked me. We could not trust her anymore. She could have hurt you or the baby." My father gestures with his head toward Pietro, who is still sleeping soundly. My mother's face appears grim, and her eyes look sadder than usual.

"Tina would never hurt Pietro or me. She loves us!" Carlotta says. Her voice is starting to crack. "Where did you take her, Sarina?"

"She's with an old man and woman. Don't worry. They will take good care of her." I try to stroke Carlotta's head, but she pushes my arm away.

"No! She's my cat! How could you have done that? How could you? She was my baby." Carlotta is now bawling.

"We had to, Carlotta. She hurt Papá, and he's right; we don't know if she would have done that again, or to you or the baby or even Enzo. Please, Carlotta. Don't be upset."

"No! Tina loved me. She would have never hurt me." Carlotta then turns to my father. "She hated you! You were mean to her.

That's why she hurt you." Carlotta is pointing her chubby, little index finger at Papá, whose face looks ashen. He places his hands on his belt and begins unfastening it.

I rise out of my chair and pick up Carlotta, heading quickly to our bedroom before Papá can get to her. He is now following us.

"Let me go, Sarina! I don't want you anymore. You took Tina away from me." Carlotta is kicking me and hitting me with her tiny fists.

Entering our bedroom, I throw Carlotta onto the bed and quickly run out, slamming the door shut behind me. I then block the door with my body.

"Move, Sarina. Carlotta must learn not to disrespect her father."

"She is only four years old, Papá. Beat me. Not her."

"She is learning from you." My father strikes me across the face with his belt. My body slumps down, yet I still refuse to get out of his way. But it doesn't matter. For now he has settled on taking his anger out on me instead of Carlotta.

A couple of hours later, everyone has gone to bed. I have not gotten up from the floor. My father pushed me into the corner of our kitchen so that Enzo could go to sleep. I'm in too much pain to get up. I'm surprised Papá didn't force me to stand and go to bed.

I hear my mother come out of her bedroom and go into the bathroom. The sound of rushing water reaches my ears. I don't even notice when she's kneeling beside me. Mama unties the strings of my sundress and lowers it. She places a wet washcloth to the welts on my back that have sprung from the repeated lashings Papá gave me. I cringe every time she dabs them with the washcloth. She then applies a natural healing salve I made from a combination of chamomile, calendula, comfrey, plantain leaves, olive oil, lavender oil, honey, and beeswax. I keep it stored in a jar for whenever we need it, which tends to be often in this household. After Mama is done, she helps me sit up and gives me a glass of water.

"I hate him, Mama. I hate him." I'm crying as I say this.

"Shhh. You have to stop standing up to him."

"And let him beat Carlotta? Never!"

My mother helps me to my feet and walks me to the bed. She

taps Enzo on the shoulder and whispers to him. He gets up, taking his pillow with him, and sleeps on the floor.

"Enzo, you don't need to do that."

"You need more room or your body will stiffen and you'll be in even more pain tomorrow," Mama whispers.

I decide not to argue with my mother. I'm exhausted. She pushes Carlotta to the side of the bed, making even more room for me. Carlotta does not stir. My heart still aches at how upset she was about Tina.

Mama pulls the sheet over me and kisses me on my cheek before walking out. I close my eyes but, although I'm so fatigued, I can't fall asleep. Will Carlotta ever forgive me for abandoning Tina? Will I ever forgive myself? I had to do it. The alternative would have been worse. At least now, Tina is alive and has a chance with the butcher and his wife. But in my sister's eyes, I was every bit as abominable as my father, since I was the one who committed the crime of abandoning our beloved cat. I was the one who took Tina away from Carlotta.

Soon, I fall asleep and dream of Tina. She has found her way home to me. I hug Tina, asking her to kiss me with her nose as I had trained her to do. I am ecstatic that she's back in my arms until I open my eyes and realize it was all just a dream and Tina is never coming back home again.

❧ 5 ❧

Vita da Sogno

DREAM LIFE

June 13, 1969

It is the morning of my seventeenth birthday. As soon as I wake up, I kneel in front of my bed. Making the sign of the cross, I pray to God to give me strength, for today, I will be running away from home.

The day after I abandoned Tina, I realized the time had come for me to finally leave home for good. Over the course of the weeks that followed, I began plotting the details of my escape. Every night, I sat at our kitchen table and carefully planned my *vita da sogno*—the dream life I had always fantasized about, but thought was not within reach.

I cannot wait any longer. I will never have the courage to run away unless I act now. Tears fall down my face. I haven't forgotten my promise to my mother that I would buy her another china set and take her and my siblings away from my father. But I am also not a fool. I know how difficult it will be, helping that many people to escape. I also know of the very real possibility that I will never see my mother alive again. And my siblings are so young that they will probably forget me even if we are reunited years from now when they're adults. Insecurity takes hold of me, but then I look once more at the snail we still have in the jar, and in that moment all doubt vanishes.

I chose to run away on my birthday, for I wanted my *vita da sogno* to start on a date that I would never forget. June 13 is also the feast day of St. Anthony of Padua—the patron saint of recovered items. People pray to him when they have lost a treasured possession, imploring the saint to help them find the missing object. St. Anthony is also the patron saint of travelers and for those who suddenly find their lives taking a new direction. I could not help but see the irony that I had chosen this particular saint's day to make my escape and turn over a new leaf. But this is not the only reason I decided to run away from home on this day. My family and I will be going this evening to Barcellona, where festivities are held in honor of St. Anthony of Padua. The celebrations kick off tonight and last for a week. It will be easier for me to slip away during the feast with its large crowds and many distractions. The fact that it is the feast day of St. Anthony of Padua makes me feel all the more assured that the saint will be protecting me.

Every week since I decided I would leave home, I have been stealing a few liras from my father's secret box, which holds his savings. As my mother once told me, he has never even imparted to her where he keeps his money. But when I was a little girl, I used to love crawling under my parents' bed whenever they weren't looking. I discovered a loose floorboard that had not been pushed back completely into place. Beneath the loose floorboard, I found a large boot box and my father's money. I had never before taken any of the liras in the box, for I was too afraid of my father's finding out. Now it was a risk I was willing to take in order to make my dreams of escaping become a reality. I only took a few liras every week, but last night I took much more. It was enough money for me to take a bus to the resort town of Taormina, where I planned on going door to door of the many hotels there and asking if they could use another maid. I placed a note in my father's money box telling him I would repay him someday. Though he does not deserve any kindness on my part after the way he has mistreated my mother and me, my belief in God compels me to do what is right.

I stayed up late at night, sewing by hand a large, voluminous skirt with plenty of ruffles to conceal the extra layers of clothes I'll be wearing when I run away. It's the only way to be able to take a few clothes with me without raising my father's suspicions, since it would look strange for me to bring a bag larger than a pocketbook to the feast. I also sewed a few pockets in the lining of my underwear to hide my money. Except for my clothes and money, the only other possessions I am taking are my ruby red rosary, which my mother gave to me for my first Holy Communion, a small Bible, my diary, and a photograph of my family that was taken a few years back. Fortunately, my father was the one to take the photograph, so he's missing from the portrait. My Bible is small enough to fit in my pocketbook, but I will have to place my diary in the waistband of the slip I'll be wearing. I sewed additional elastic around my slip's waistband to give it added reinforcement so that I won't lose my diary.

I woke up much earlier today so that I could complete all of my chores about an hour before we leave for the feast. But it's as if my father suspects I have ulterior motives. Just when I think I'm done, he throws more work my way. I forgot that I not only need to iron his suit, but also my siblings' dress clothes. Working at a frantic pace, I try to hurry so that I have enough time to get ready. The heat of the iron coupled with my anxiety makes me sweat profusely. Finally, with just twenty minutes to spare, I'm done ironing. I grab the bundle with my extra clothes and the few possessions I'm taking with me and am about to walk out of the room I share with the children when Carlotta calls me.

"Sarina, I need help with my stockings."

I halt in my tracks. Without turning around, I say, "Carlotta, I have shown you more than once how to put on your stockings. You will never learn if I am always dressing you."

"Please, Sarina! I promise this will be the last time."

Shutting my eyes tightly, I force back the tears, for I know with certainty that Carlotta will be able to keep her promise after tonight.

I walk over to my younger sister and do my best to keep a stern face lest my true emotions betray me and I break down.

"*Grazie,* Sarina! Now I'm all ready for the feast! Do you think

Papá will buy me *zeppole?*" Carlotta looks into my face expectantly. The fried doughnuts are one of her favorite sweets sold at the feast.

"Most certainly and, if he's in one of his grumpy moods, then I'll buy you *zeppole*. That is, if you're a good girl. But that's our secret, Carlotta. You must not tell Papá or Mama that I have some money. Okay?" I place my hands on either side of Carlotta's face, forcing her to look me in the eye. She nods her head.

"I always want you to remember that I will carry you in my heart forever. *Ti voglio bene*." I hug Carlotta tightly.

"I love you, too, Sarina."

"Now run out. I need to get ready."

I watch Carlotta run to the front of the house and join my other siblings. How can I leave her? How can I leave my mother and the rest of them? But my sanity depends on it. Walking to the bathroom, I'm relieved no one is in there. I step in and quickly wash my face. I then put on the layers of clothes I'm taking with me. Why did I even bother taking a bath today since I will no doubt be sweating in all these clothes, not to mention it is a warm June day? As I finish getting dressed, I hear my father yell, "Sarina, where are you? It's time to leave."

My heart races. I take one last look at myself in the mirror above the tiny sink in our bathroom. The face that greets me in the mirror is full of fear. Shrugging the feeling off, I walk out of the bathroom purposefully.

I notice my mother is staring at my skirt, and I pray she does not ask me in front of Papá if it's a new skirt. No doubt Mama is wondering when I could have had the time to sew myself a skirt with all my chores. I glance nervously at her. She lightly nods her head and walks away. Breathing a sigh of relief, I wait until all of my family has stepped out before I join them. Looking over my shoulder, I take a mental snapshot of our small house before shutting the door.

The sounds of trombones, trumpets, and a thumping bass drum fill the air as a long parade winds its way through the narrow streets of Barcellona. A few men, both young and old, carry the towering statue of St. Anthony of Padua. I stare at the benevolent saint's face and then transfer my gaze to that of the infant Jesus that he carries in his arms. St. Anthony's devotion to the baby Jesus is evident in his tender expression.

Cries of delight from Enzo and Carlotta reach my ears. They are standing at a *zeppole* stand, waiting for my father to buy them the powdered sugar sweets they love so much. Carlotta and Enzo reach their hands high, bouncing on their little feet in anticipation of the *zeppole*. My father is in a good mood tonight, for he is buying the children almost any treat they desire. I silently thank God. This way, I will not have to hold my promise to Carlotta to buy her *zeppole*. I need all of the money I have.

Savory aromas vie with sweet ones. The smoke from sizzling sausages and bracciole stings my eyes. Men shout out their goods as if the sight and smells aren't enough to lure customers to their stands. Normally, I cannot wait to have many of the delicacies found at the feast. But tonight my thoughts are racing. All I can think about is my escape. Agata bought a bag of *zeppole,* which she is sharing with me. I nibble on one as we stroll through the crowded streets. Our parents walk behind us. While our fathers are engaged in conversation and are enjoying the feast, they still keep their eyes on Agata and me to ensure no boys approach us.

"Sarina, are you not feeling well?" Agata asks me as she pops what must be her fourth *zeppola* into her mouth.

"I'm fine."

"You are hardly eating. I've never known you not to sample most of the food at the feast. And I can't believe you turned down the fried zucchini blossoms—your favorite! You seem preoccupied. What's the matter?" Agata looks at me with concern written all over her features. Whenever she is worried, she unconsciously tightens the muscles in her forehead, creating a deep crease between her brows.

"I'm fine, Agata. The last feast we went to, I actually had a bad upset stomach when I got home. I don't want that to happen again." Guilt washes over me that I've lied.

"I know what's worrying you, Sarina. You're afraid that my plan of secretly meeting Giuseppe tonight will not work, and you will get in trouble for covering for me."

"Yes, I am a little nervous about it, Agata." I muster a small smile, which my sweet cousin returns.

Agata had managed to talk to Giuseppe when she last visited me, and they agreed to meet briefly tonight during the fireworks display, which we would be watching from the roof of the house that belongs to my father's friend Luigi Milazzo. Luigi's house is one of the best from which to view the fireworks. It will be too dark for our families to notice Agata slip away, and they will be distracted by the fireworks. I am to cover for her in case anyone takes notice and just say she went to the bathroom. Agata is supposed to meet Giuseppe in the alleyway behind Luigi's house. She has promised me she will be back before the fireworks are over.

"Don't worry. If I'm caught I'll tell our fathers that you tried to talk me out of meeting Giuseppe. I'll make you look like a saint!" Agata pats my shoulder.

"You would do that for me? Take all the blame?" I cannot look Agata in the eyes. She is noble, a trait I am lacking in as I envision what I must do later.

"Of course. You're the closest thing I'll ever have to a sister since my parents detest each other and can't bear to couple again to give me any siblings. I would do anything for you, Sarina."

A feeble laugh escapes my lips. Agata's words touch me, and I must resort to humor before I lose all control and break down crying. "Have you ever thought that perhaps your mother could not get pregnant again after she had you rather than assume your parents have no interest in being intimate?"

"No one knows this, Sarina, and please do not breathe a word of it to your mother or father, but my parents have not slept in the same bed for years. Papá sleeps on a cot in a storage closet he cleared out so he could turn it into a makeshift bedroom."

"I'm sorry, Agata. I had no idea."

"If there was ever any love between those two, it's long vanished." Agata's eyes look sad as she says this.

I, on the other hand, know there was never any love between my parents. My mother was just doing her duty as an obedient daughter by agreeing to her father's request that she marry Papá. Of course, I have no doubt that Papá found Mama beautiful and was attracted to her. But in terms of loving her, he is incapable of it. I don't believe he even loves his children. My mother, siblings, and I are merely present to help him with his work and keep his house in order.

"It's time!" Agata startles me out of my thoughts. I glance at my watch. It's 9:50. The fireworks are scheduled to go off at ten p.m. We wait for our families to catch up to us before we head over to Luigi's house. My heart races. The evening has dragged on insufferably. And I still have a very long night ahead of me.

Luigi, his wife, and three sons are standing in front of their house. They greet us warmly. We follow them inside and make our way to their roof. It is pitch-black, and we are all moving slowly, trying to see in the darkness, until Luigi turns on a few flashlights.

"We will keep them on until the fireworks start." Luigi is smiling as much as his sons. I guess this is the highlight of the year for him. I can tell he takes pride in the fact that he can give his friends the best view of the fireworks. There is something depressing about the fact that all this man has to look forward to is the annual feast in the village where he was born and that he will most likely never leave. Yet I get the sense that Luigi is content with his simple life and has no regrets. Many of the people in our villages are this way. I cannot understand them and how they would not want to leave the confines of their small towns and explore what is waiting outside of these peripheries.

Suddenly, bursts of color erupt through the night sky, showering prisms of light so close I almost believe I can actually touch them.

"*Veloce! Spegnere le torce elettriche.*" Luigi tells us to hurry and turn off our flashlights.

We all stand in silence, staring up at the dazzling display before us. I allow myself a few seconds to take in the beauty. But it is hard for me to relax. Usually, this is my favorite part of any saint's feast. I love watching the fireworks from Luigi's roof since from this height the fireworks appear so near. It feels very magical, and when you've had a life that is filled with as much hardship as mine, you stop believing that there is any magic or wonder left in the world.

A sharp elbow nudges my arm.

"*Ora!*" Agata whispers "now" loudly to me.

Glancing nervously at our families, I'm relieved they haven't heard her. But they'd have to be standing close to us to hear with the din of the fireworks.

"Be careful."

Agata nods her head and is about to walk off when I grab her arm. She gives me a frustrated look. I stare into her eyes, knowing this will probably be the last time I ever see her. I then let go. She disappears at the perfect time since there is a short pause before more fireworks erupt, allowing the darkness to completely cloak her before anyone notices her exit. I know from all the years that my family and I have watched the fireworks from Luigi's roof that there are at least three pauses throughout the show. It seems to be taking longer than I remember for the second interval to come.

"*Guardate questo! È bellissimo!*" My father is holding Enzo up, imploring him to look at an exceptionally beautiful shower of fireworks. Papá's face is lit up momentarily in the fireworks' glow. He is smiling, and if you didn't know him, you'd never suspect there was so much evil inside him. I cannot help but think back to when I was Enzo's age and the few times Papá was kind to me, like when he talked to me about all the fish he'd caught, and I wonder how long it will be until he begins hitting Enzo. Sometimes, I think he takes pleasure out of beating Mama and me. Does he ever realize how horrible he is toward us? Something tells me he has no idea, and even if he did, I am almost certain he would have no remorse.

"Ooh! Mama! *Guarda!*" Carlotta is standing on the ledge of the roof, but my mother's arm is wrapped tightly around her tiny form. They are completely transfixed by the fireworks. My gaze then falls on Pietro, who is in his carriage and is somehow able to sleep even with all the noise from the fireworks.

I turn away. I cannot wait any longer lest I lose my nerve. Edging slowly to the stairs that lead back down to Luigi's house, I continue to watch my family. Taking one last look at their huddled forms, I quickly turn around and run down the stairs. Tears are racing down my face. As I walk through Luigi's living room, I freeze in my tracks at the sound of voices. I see an open window and realize the voices are coming from outside. It then dawns on me that the shadows I can barely make out are Agata and Giuseppe. Afraid someone will come down and hear them, I rush over to the window and close it quietly. I can't resist peeking out, but I make sure to stay out of their sight. Giuseppe has his hands around Agata's waist, and he is kissing her. Her eyes are closed, yet I can still detect a glow of happiness in her face.

I smile and whisper, "Good-bye, my dear cousin." I then tiptoe to the front door, closing it gently behind me. Once outside, I begin running. The crowds are too preoccupied with the fireworks spectacle to pay me any heed. I keep running until I know I am a good twenty blocks away from Luigi's.

I head over to the Duomo of Saint Sebastian, which is the largest church in Barcellona. I pray that her doors are kept open this late at night. As I approach the cathedral, I see light streaming through the stained-glass windows. I climb the steps and breathe a sigh of relief after pulling open the heavy wooden door. Thankfully, no one is inside. I step into the last pew and pull up the knee rest. Then I crouch down and sit on the floor. This will be where I will sleep for the night. Once morning comes, I will make my way to the bus station. I will not fully let down my guard until I am on the bus and out of Barcellona. I am nearly drenched in sweat. Taking off the top layer of my clothes, I roll them into a makeshift pillow. Sighing deeply, I stretch out underneath the pew and close my eyes. But sleep eludes me. The faces of my little brothers, sister, and mother haunt me. Will I ever see them again? Forcing these thoughts out of my mind, I focus instead on what lies ahead of me and the new life that I am about to embark upon.

❦ 6 ❧

Gioiello del Mediterraneo

JEWEL OF THE MEDITERRANEAN

June 14, 1969

I am on my way to Taormina. I woke up at dawn and was able to sneak out of the Duomo of Saint Sebastian without being noticed. Fortunately, the streets were nearly deserted that early in the morning, since most of the residents were sleeping in after staying up late to watch the fireworks. Once I left the cathedral, I quickly headed over to the bus station. There, a bus would take me from Barcellona to the city of Messina, where I would transfer for Taormina.

As soon as my bus gets on the highway, cutting through the mountain tunnels, I breathe a sigh of relief. Finally, I can relax. My heart races in excitement. My escape worked! I'm finally free and far away from my father's clutches. I will never suffer another of his beatings. But as soon as I feel joy, guilt immediately washes over me for leaving Mama and the children behind. They are on their own now. They will not have me to protect them from Papá's wrath.

Though I have been surrounded by Sicily's vibrant landscape my whole life, I feel like I am only now truly seeing her. Suddenly, something my teacher once said comes to mind. She described Sicily as *"il gioiello del Mediterraneo"*—the jewel of the Mediterranean. Looking out my bus's window, I can see why. The verdant mountains . . . the azure waters of the Mediterranean Sea . . . abundant sunshine that graces the island for most of the year . . . towering palm trees lining the streets . . . farms that thrive because of the island's rich soil that allows almost any crop to be grown . . . orchards full of fig, olive, and citrus trees . . . prickly cactus pear plants. This is my beautiful home.

The bus slows down as it comes to a road that has been made narrower because of construction. We pass under a rain cloud, and rivulets of water quickly pellet the driver's windshield. The driver does not even bother turning his windshield wipers on, for within seconds we've cleared the clouds and are cloaked in sunshine again. I see a rainbow and smile, feeling like it is a good omen. For me, rainbows have always been proof of God's existence. Every time I see one, I feel God's presence even more.

Though I am elated to be heading toward a new adventure and home in Taormina, I'm also terrified. I try not to think about the possibility that it could take some time to secure work. If I am very meager with my meals and skip breakfast and just allow myself a little bread and cheese or a piece of fruit, I can make my money last a couple of extra weeks. I am not ashamed to beg, but I will offer people something for their money. I am prepared to sing on the streets and the beaches of Taormina. But surely, with all of the hotels and resorts that line the beach, I will be able to secure work as a maid in one of them. Squeezing my eyes shut tightly, I pray to St. Anthony, asking him to help me find my way.

I open my eyes in time to see the highway sign pointing to Taormina. Her beauty has been written about for centuries. I wonder if she will live up to her fame. My stomach growls, reminding me I have not had anything to eat since the *zeppola* I nibbled on last night. I saved two of the *zeppole* for my trip. I take them out and pop one in my mouth, chewing ravenously. Something catches my peripheral view. I see a dirty boy with disheveled clothes leaning forward, staring at the *zeppola* I'm holding that I haven't eaten yet. His mother is asleep beside him, and she has the same ragged appearance. I try to ignore the boy watching me, but my conscience won't allow it. Suddenly, it's not this strange boy's face before me, but the face of one of my younger brothers. I hold out my hand, offering my last *zeppola* to him.

"Take it."

The boy casts one nervous glance at his mother, who still remains sound asleep, and turns back around, quickly snatching the *zeppola*. He nods his head in thanks to me. I smile and turn my attention back out the window. My eyes feel heavy, and I want to sleep, especially since I only slept in spurts the night before. The hard floor and cramped space beneath the church's bench made it hard to sleep through the night. My anxiety also kept awakening me. My dreams mingled with both happy images of what my new life promised me and images of my father chasing me, dragging me back home. Sometimes it was a monster chasing me, but then the image transformed into my father. While I would like nothing more than to take a quick nap on the bus, I must be on my guard. Pickpockets are notorious for riding buses, and I have already seen a few of the men watching me. Traveling alone as a female is one of the risks I am prepared to take. I forgot to steal my father's knife that he uses to skin the rabbits he kills and prepares for dinner. I just pray that no one bothers me until I reach Taormina and can steal a knife from a merchant's shop or even from a table at one of the many restaurants in the coastal town.

I take out my rosary beads and begin praying, fingering each bead as I go through the Our Fathers and Hail Marys. Hopefully, this will help me pass the time as well as keep my nerves at bay.

An hour later, the bus driver announces that we are entering Taormina. His voice startles me out of sleep, much to my dismay. I quickly feel my pelvis, making sure the lumps are still there. Of course, it would be next to impossible for anyone to steal my money without waking me up since I've hidden it in the pockets I sewed in my underwear. A thief would have to rip my clothes off to find out. I shudder at that thought, once again becoming aware of the fact that I am a woman traveling alone who could be subject to attacks.

We make our way along hairpin turns, taking us higher into the hills of Taormina. Soon, her coastline comes into view. I gasp. I've never seen such a vivid shade of blue water. I always thought the beach where I lived was beautiful, but it pales in comparison. The turquoise shade of the Ionian Sea truly looks celestial. Though this is all that I've seen so far of Taormina, I can already tell her famed beauty that has been written about is well-deserved.

The bus finally comes to a stop. I cannot wait to descend and explore the town. Putting my rosary beads around my neck, I stand up. My body is still sore from sleeping on the church floor as well as from sitting for so long on the bus. The bus driver's eyes meet mine as I am about to descend the stairs exiting the bus. He winks at me. I quickly turn my head and climb down the stairs as fast as I can, thankful that there are more people behind me.

Many of the bus's passengers have heavy luggage and are lining up to take taxis up the hill to their hotels. Since I cannot afford to spend any additional money, I begin walking up the hill. I'm glad I was not able to take more than my meager belongings and can easily make the ascent. Throngs of tourists, mostly young ones who don't mind the hike, are walking up as well. The women mostly wear sundresses over their bathing suits. A few wear only skirts over their bathing suits, letting their cleavages remain exposed in their swimsuits. Many of the men do not wear shirts and a few are just in their swimming trunks. I blush when a teenage boy catches me staring and smiles at me. I look away. Suddenly, I feel self-conscious in my long ruffled skirt and my blouse, which is now sticking to my back from all my sweat. I realize that my clothes are too heavy for being by the beach. I thought since they were linen, I would be fine, but aside from standing out from the rest of the people here, I will be sweltering every day. Perhaps I can get my hands on a pair of scissors and cut the sleeves off my shirt. Of course, the only way I will be able to do that is if I pilfer the scissors. Shame fills my heart that I will have to sin by stealing until I have the means to purchase what I need. I say a silent prayer to God, asking him ahead of time to forgive me and to understand I must steal out of necessity.

By the time I reach the top of the hill, I sense a headache coming on, no doubt from being dehydrated. My stomach is grumbling once more. Walking to the shade of an immense palm tree, I use my skirt's hem to wipe the perspiration from my forehead. I then no-

tice a drinking fountain that's built into the wall of one of the hotels. A lion's head is carved into the stone wall, and the lion's mouth
is open, revealing the bubbling fountain. A man stops in front of it
to let his dog drink. Once they leave, I head over. When I reach the
fountain, I bend over and cup some water with my hands, wetting
my face. Then, I take a long drink from the fountain. Immediately,
I feel much better.

"That's my fountain!"

I look up, startled to see a girl about ten years old giving me the
meanest scowl. She is dressed in a Sicilian folk costume and even
wears a scarf over her head. And I thought I was overdressed in this
heat. Black curls peek out from either side of her kerchief. Her
hands are clenched into fists and rest on her hips. She is beyond
adorable, and I cannot help but laugh out loud.

"What's so funny? And didn't you hear me? That's my fountain.
Go!" The girl stomps over to me, pointing her index finger into the
distance.

"*Va bene!* All right." I hold my hands up in resignation. "No
need to get so upset. I thought this was a public fountain and anyone could drink from it. I'm new to town."

"Well, no one is supposed to drink from it. It belongs to this
hotel. I would get in trouble too if they caught me drinking from it
or filling my pitcher." She pulls out from a deep pocket in her skirt
a terra-cotta pitcher, much like the ones that are sold as typical Sicilian souvenirs. She then looks around her, making sure no one has
seen her, before she puts the pitcher back into her pocket. I can't
help but think that those extra deep pockets were sewn that way
for a reason and wonder what else she is concealing in them.

I don't believe her claims that the hotel does not want anyone
drinking from the fountain, but for her sake, I play along.

"It's our secret." I press my lips tightly together and with my
right hand gesture as if I'm locking them. I then put my imaginary
key into my cleavage, which causes the girl to erupt in giggles.

"You're funny—and pretty." She stares up at me.

"*Grazie.* You're pretty too. Do you live near here?"

"*Si.* On the beach."

She doesn't look like she comes from a wealthy family. I cannot imagine how they would be able to afford to live in one of the houses that overlook the beach, which is what she must be alluding to.

"You must have a nice big house." I smile.

"No. We live *on* the beach in a tent."

I suddenly feel bad for having made the nice house comment, but she doesn't seem to be bothered by the fact that her home is in a tent.

"Is that where your family is now? Why aren't you with them?"

"They're out working. I'm supposed to be working, too, but it's so hot today that I needed a break and wanted to fill my pitcher with water. That's when I saw you drinking from my fountain."

"Wow! Your family must be very proud of you for working and helping them with money."

She nods her head.

"So what work do you do?"

Her face grows serious, and she looks down at her feet. "Different things."

Even though I'm dying to know exactly what kind of work this little girl is doing, her sudden sad expression along with the deep pockets in her skirt confirm my suspicions that she must be a pickpocket. Not wishing to make her feel any more uncomfortable, I change the subject.

"My name is Sarina. What's yours?"

"Isabella. I'm named after one of the Spanish queens. My family says our ancestors came from Spain, and there's a good chance we are even royalty. Someday, I'm going to be a queen." She is kicking up the pebbles on the ground, and her face glows now, no doubt from her dream of becoming queen someday.

"You will make a good queen. I can tell by how you stood your ground and had no problem telling me this fountain was yours."

Isabella nods her head.

"I should get going. You wouldn't happen to know of any hotels that are hiring maids, would you, Isabella?"

She ponders my question for a moment, then shakes her head no. I'm tempted to ask her what her parents do, but if they are also professional pickpockets I don't want her to feel ashamed again.

"Come to the beach some time. You can help me make the castle I will live in when I'm queen."

It takes a moment for me to realize she means a sand castle.

"Sounds like fun."

"Our tent is red. It's the only red one of the tents on the beach."

"There are more?"

"Yes."

I'm surprised that the town police or even some of the hotel proprietors with hotels on the beach don't kick them out. Even though the beach isn't private property, I could still see the hotel owners being concerned that the squatters could turn off their guests. It's obvious Isabella and her family are vagrants.

"Red. I'll remember that. You have a nice day, Isabella, and be careful." I pat her head.

"Of what?"

"It's always good to be careful."

"Okay. Bye, Sarina."

I wave and begin walking away.

"Sarina, wait!" Isabella runs after me.

"If you can't find any other fountains, it's okay if you drink from mine. Just don't tell anyone else."

I touch the side of her face. "That's sweet of you, Isabella. *Grazie mille!*"

Isabella returns my smile, then skips away. I can hear her singing a popular nursery rhyme. I can't help thinking that while she is still a child, she has been forced to be an adult by stealing for her family. I had thought I wouldn't encounter poverty in a place as wealthy and beautiful as Taormina, but I see now how foolish I was for entertaining such an idea.

Sighing deeply, I smooth out the wrinkles that formed in my clothes from sitting so long on the bus, and make my way into the entrance of the first hotel where I will inquire for work. I wish I could just relax my first day in Taormina and stroll through the town. Maybe even take the aerial tramway that leads to the beaches. But I know it's more important for me to find a job before my money runs out. There will be time to explore Taormina. After all, this is my home now.

҉ 7 ҉

Gli Zingari

THE GYPSIES

June 21, 1969

A week has passed since I arrived in Taormina, and I still have not been able to find work. I've gone to a dozen hotels, but have been told they don't need any other workers. I even offered to wash dishes or do any job that might be needed. But nothing. I have only been using my money when I feel faint from the little food that I have been able to steal from the many restaurants that have outdoor seating. Often, I take the leftovers before the waiters have cleared the tables.

Today I have my sights set on the man who sells blood oranges and figs out of his cart. I can almost taste the juicy fruit as I stare longingly at them. My opportunity comes when a customer walks over to the cart and asks the vendor questions about the fruit. Walking quickly over to the cart, I drop a few coins on the ground. As I stoop over to pick them up, I am able to grab two blood oranges. I would have liked a fig too, but didn't dare waste any more time. Picking up my coins, I quickly walk away.

"*Signorina! Signorina!*" I ignore the shouts. Surely, no one is calling to me here. Besides, I have never been referred to as *signorina*. I am too young. But then I realize I am no longer a child but a young woman. *"Signorina! Signorina, per favore, vieni qui."* I dare to glance over my shoulder, making eye contact with a woman standing in the doorway of a bread shop. She nods her head to me and motions with her hand for me to go over. Swallowing hard, I walk over to her.

"Aspetta un attimo, signorina." She smiles kindly as she asks me to wait before stepping into the bread shop. I return the smile, wondering what this woman wants from me.

A few moments later, she comes back and is holding a white paper bag.

"Per voi." She hands the bag to me. I look questioningly at her, but she waves her hands in a hurried gesture toward me, indicating I should open the bag now. I peer inside, and the most heavenly aroma of bread reaches my nose. A few brioche rolls are inside the bag. My cheeks grow warm as I realize she must've witnessed my stealing the blood oranges from the street vendor.

"Anytime you are hungry, please feel free to come by. I always have extra rolls."

"Grazie, signora. But I cannot take these." I try handing the rolls to her, but she pushes them back toward me.

"I know you are hungry. I saw you steal the fruit from the vendor a few minutes ago. And I've seen you before, walking by the restaurants and taking whatever food the patrons have left behind on their plates."

I'm too embarrassed now to say anything, but for some reason I don't want this stranger thinking the worst of me. Mustering the courage, I say, "I never have stolen before in my life. But since coming to Taormina, I have not been able to find work. Once I do, I will leave money at all of the places from which I have stolen. I promise. And I will pay you back for your kindness today."

"That won't be necessary, but thank you for the offer. I wish I could give you work in my bread shop, but my husband and I cannot afford to hire anyone at the moment. We do all the baking and selling ourselves. But I want to help you, so please do not feel ashamed to come by anytime you are hungry. How old are you anyway? You should be with your family, not on the streets begging for work and stealing. You must have family?"

"I cannot go home. And I am not that young. I am seventeen," I tell her.

"I see." The bread shop owner's eyes convey sympathy. "I did not mean to offend you. I was merely expressing concern. My name is Angela."

We talk for a few more minutes, and then I take my leave, promising Angela I will return to visit her. I summon whatever energy I have left and head over to the aerial tramway that takes passengers to the beaches of Taormina. I know there are hotels and restaurants on the beaches. If I am not successful there, I might have to leave Taormina and find some other village where I can possibly find work. The thought saddens me since in the few days I've been here I have fallen in love with this beautiful village.

I'm reluctant to pay the fare to buy a ticket for the tram, but I also do not want to risk getting caught sneaking on. How embarrassing would that be in front of all the wealthy tourists? So I shell out the necessary liras for the tram, cringing as I think about my ever-depleting funds.

The view from the tram takes my breath away. Mount Etna looks so close. A ring of clouds crown the volcano's mouth. The sun is glistening off the azure waters of the Ionian Sea. I overhear one of the tourists reading aloud to his wife from his guidebook that Taormina is about 820 feet above the sea. I'm amazed by the fact. At this height, I truly feel like I am in paradise. Tears fill my eyes. Although the past few days have been difficult, I am happy to be here. Somehow, I must find a way to make my new life work.

Once the tram reaches the station, I descend and begin making my inquiries at the hotels that line the beach. Before stepping through the doors of the first hotel, I pray to God, asking him to let this be my lucky day.

After several hours of going from hotel to hotel and receiving the same response that no workers are needed, I'm exhausted. It is now almost half past eight in the evening. There arc more beachfront hotels, but I don't think I can handle any more disappointment today. My stomach grumbles. I saved a few of the rolls Angela gave me. I take one out and eat it as I make my way down to the beach. Taking off my sandals, I traipse along the shoreline, staring at the ocean. Closing my eyes, I free my mind from all thoughts and worry and just let the balmy breeze blow through my hair. The water is quite warm, but still feels refreshing beneath the soles of my feet. Hundreds of pebbles are strewn on the sand.

A fiery orange streaks through the horizon as the sun begins to set. I stop to stare at the vibrant colors. That is when music reaches my ears. I look off to the right and see a group of people dancing in a circle. Drawn to the music, I slowly walk toward the small crowd. As I get closer, I can make out the sounds of *il friscaletto,* which is an ancient folk flute from Sicily, and even the clashes of several *tamburelli,* or tambourines. Both are famous instruments in Sicilian folk music. Ever since I was a little girl, I always dreamed of owning a tambourine someday.

I stand about twenty feet away, not wishing to disturb the group. They are all so busy dancing, singing, and laughing that at first they don't notice me. I tap my foot in time to the song that is being sung by a woman, who looks to be in her mid to late thirties. She is quite pretty, and her long, thick, wavy hair hangs down to her waist. The song's lyrics make me smile:

"Non abbiamo molti soldi. Ma tutti abbiamo bisogno di essere felici sono cibo, riparo, e di amore. Finché abbiamo questi, soprattutto l'amore, siamo davvero i ricchi e saremo felici per sempre."

"We don't have much money. But all we need to be happy are food, shelter, and love. As long as we have these, especially love, we are truly the rich ones and will be happy forever."

"Sarina!" A child's voice startles me. It's Isabella, the girl I met by the fountain my first day in Taormina.

"Ciao, Isabella." I return the hug she gives me. You would think we had known each other for years and are the best of friends.

Glancing up, I see that the pretty dark-haired woman has stopped singing and is staring at me. In fact, everyone in the group is now looking at me. That is when I notice for the first time the red tents hoisted in the sand. This is Isabella's family. A few of them are dressed in Sicilian folk clothes like the ones Isabella wore the first time I met her. Tonight, she is only wearing a long sundress. I notice Isabella and the woman who was singing share the same jet-black hair color and thick, wavy hair. The singer must be Isabella's mother.

"Mama, this is the girl I told you about the other day. The one who drank from my fountain." Isabella leads me to her mother by the hand.

"How many times do I need to tell you that fountain is not yours?" her mother says sternly. But then she meets my gaze and smiles warmly. "*Ciao.* You are prettier than Isabella said you were. My name is Maria."

"I am Sarina. I'm sorry. I did not wish to disturb you. I merely wanted to hear more of your beautiful singing."

"*È niente.* Please, don't apologize. Thank you for the compliment. You love music, too?" Maria is now plaiting Isabella's hair. Suddenly, a memory of when my own mother braided my hair flashes through my mind. My face must register the pain I'm feeling since I see Maria looking at me with concern.

Trying to keep my tone light, I answer, "Yes, I love music very much. I like to sing, too, but I am not as good as you."

"As artists, we are always toughest on ourselves. Let someone else be the judge of your talent. Why don't you sing for us now?"

I'm surprised to hear her refer to singers as artists. I never thought of myself, or any singer, that way before. But I guess she is right. There is a certain artistry in singing and when one writes his or her own lyrics. My thoughts keep me from responding to her question.

"Are you all right, Sarina? Or are you just too embarrassed to tell me you don't want to sing in front of a group of strangers?"

"I'm sorry. I did not hear you. *Si, si. Sto bene.* I am fine. *Grazie.* I am too tired to sing tonight, but perhaps another time?"

"*Va bene.* But you must come back. I am now curious to hear if your voice is as lovely as your features." Maria pushes my hair back off my shoulders before she kisses me on either cheek. "Isabella told me you were looking for work at the hotels. Were you able to find any?"

I can't believe Isabella told her mother so much about me. Then again, she is just a child and was probably excited about meeting someone new.

"No, I have not been able to. I've been to almost twenty hotels now between the ones near the piazza and a few on the beach. But I have not finished inquiring at all of the beachfront hotels yet."

"Forgive me for saying so, Sarina, but you look very pale. Have you eaten tonight?" Maria places her hands on my arms and forces me to meet her gaze.

"I ate at lunch, but I'm afraid to say I lost track of time and did not have a proper meal this evening. I ate a roll a little while ago, so I'm fine." I feel my face flush slightly. I know Maria knows I'm pretending not to be hungry.

"Please, eat with us. There is plenty." Maria takes my hand and leads me to a bonfire.

A man who looks to be around Maria's age and three teenage boys sit around the fire, holding skewers of fish over the flames. They are talking animatedly and laughing. The smell of the roasting fish makes my stomach grumble. They fall silent when they see Maria approaching with me. The teenage boys scan me from head to foot, making me feel more ashamed and uncomfortable. I can only imagine what I must look like. I have not paid much attention to my hair and clothes in the past week. I've been too preoccupied with finding work.

Maria addresses the older man. "Gianni, this is Sarina. She befriended Isabella in the piazza the other day. She is our guest tonight. Please give her one of those skewers of fish as soon as they are ready. Sarina, I will be right back. Please make yourself comfortable." Maria walks away before I can protest and say I'll follow her wherever she is going.

I cannot believe she's left me here alone with this man and the teenage boys. I look for Isabella, but I see her off in the distance kicking a soccer ball to a boy about her age. Well, we're not completely alone. The other women in the group are just a few feet away. I know I am overreacting, but I have never been alone in the presence of one man, let alone several. As if sensing my unease, Gianni begins talking to me.

"How long have you been in Taormina?" Gianni looks at the teens and, with a slight nod of his head, they all return their gazes back to the fish they're roasting.

Feeling less self-conscious now that I'm not being gawked at, I begin to relax a bit.

"I've only been here for a week."

"Sit down, Sarina. There's a rock behind me so you don't have to get sand all over your clothes."

I walk behind Gianni and sit down on the rock. It feels good to be sitting after the long day I've had. He hands me one of the skewers of fish he's roasted.

"Grazie molto."

"Prego." Gianni smiles.

One of the teenage boys looks at me and says, "My name is Tonio. I am Isabella's brother, and these are my cousins, Marco and Felice." Tonio points to his cousins, who each give me a shy smile. I'm glad to know I am not the only one who feels awkward.

"I'm sorry, Sarina. I forgot to tell you who I am in relation to these thieves." Gianni laughs and winks at the others. "I am Maria's husband and Isabella's father."

"And my father as well unless you and Mama have been keeping secrets from me all these years." Tonio nudges his father's arm playfully with his elbow.

"No, no. You are definitely my son. Your brash demeanor attests to that." Gianni shakes his head, but the grin on his face shows he is just teasing Tonio.

"Do you read cards, too?" Felice asks me.

"Cards?" I ask, confused.

"The tarot," Felice clarifies.

Of course, they are *zingari*—gypsies. When I met Isabella, the thought that perhaps she and her family were gypsies had not crossed my mind. I just assumed they were pickpockets. But their clothes are not shabby at all, and in addition to the fish that the men no doubt caught themselves, there are several loaves of bread and platters of fruit and vegetables on a blanket that is spread on the sand. Surely, they must have paid for some of this and not stolen it all. Now that I know they are gypsies, I am not surprised by all that they have. They must do fairly well reading people's fortunes.

"No, I don't read tarot cards. I have been trying to get work as a maid at one of the hotels, but have had no luck so far." I attempt to eat my fish slowly so that my hunger isn't apparent. The fish tastes like mackerel and is coated in a breaded batter.

"Jobs at the hotels do not open often. People know how valuable those jobs are. This is Sicily, not the north where there are more opportunities," Marco says in a grim tone.

I suddenly feel foolish for not having thought of this. Of course, growing up in Sicily, I have always known of the bleak prospect for jobs. I cannot believe this hadn't crossed my mind when I made my plan to run away from home and find work. *Stupida!* I mentally chide myself.

"Papá, maybe we can teach her?" Tonio looks at his father.

"See, you are my son. I was just having the same thought." Gianni pats Tonio on the back.

"Teach me what?" My hunger from the past few days has made my brain foggy. I am also beginning to feel sleepy. Gianni pours wine from a small jug into a wooden cup and hands it to me.

"How would you like to learn how to read the tarot, and you could travel and work with us?" Gianni asks me. "My mother is slowly going blind. She had to stop reading cards six months ago. We have lost money. She was one of our best fortune-tellers." Gianni looks over to where a group of women is sitting. He points to an old lady with a gold shawl over her head. She is smiling, but even in the twilight, I can tell she cannot see well. She talks to the other women, but her eyes hold an empty gaze. She seems content, and I see her laugh every now and then, revealing a top row of missing teeth.

"Oh, that's kind of you, but I don't know." Though I'm tempted to take Gianni up on his offer, I'm also not sure how I'd feel about conning people into thinking I can predict their future. I don't believe for a moment that Gianni and his family have special abilities and are psychic. I often heard my mother talk about gypsies who had swindled people out of all their savings. But then again, this might be the only way I can make some money—at least until I can find some other work. Besides, since being on my own, I have had to put my morals aside to steal food.

"Let me talk to Maria first. I don't make important decisions without consulting her. You can think about it in the meantime. You know where to find us. Even if you decide not to work with us, you are still welcome to come by and eat with us anytime you wish." Gianni stands up. "I must take a walk. I ate too much, and it is not sitting well with me." He pats his belly and laughs. *"Buonanotte!"*

"Buonanotte, Gianni. Thank you for the fish. It was very good."

Gianni merely holds his hand up as if to say, "It was nothing," and makes his way to the shore. He walks slowly, and every few steps bends over to pick up pebbles and toss them into the sea.

"I should go, too. It is getting late." I stand up to leave.

"Where have you been sleeping?" Tonio asks me.

I shrug my shoulders, not wanting to say. I shouldn't feel ashamed in front of *gli zingari.* They are accustomed to living on the road and doing whatever is necessary to survive. But while they live in tents on the beach, it is still more of a home than where I have been sleeping.

Thankfully, Tonio does not pressure me to answer him and instead says, "It is always safe to sleep on the beach. We have plenty of sheets if you want one to sleep on."

"Thank you. I will keep that in mind. It was nice meeting all of you. Thank you for your hospitality." I wave to Tonio, Marco, and Felice. They nod their heads. I can feel their gazes on my back as I walk away.

While I don't want to see Maria for fear that she will try to convince me to stay with them for the night, I know it would be rude of me to leave without thanking her for dinner. I head over in the direction of where the women are still seated, but I don't see Maria.

"Excuse me, I was looking for Maria," I ask a plump woman with graying hair. She is rubbing olive oil into the thick folds of her hands, which are quite large. Again, a memory of Mama comes rushing back to me as I remember she used to massage olive oil into her hands, which were severely chapped from all the washing and cleaning she did.

"She went to put Isabella to bed. I don't know if she will return. She mentioned not feeling well tonight and that she might retire early."

Secretly, I'm relieved, since it looks like I will be able to leave without Maria's asking me to stay. I don't know if I can bear to see her look at me with worry yet again.

"*Grazie, signora.* Please tell her that Sarina was looking for her and that I'll visit again soon."

"Be safe, my child." The woman holds her hand up in front of me and makes the sign of the cross as if she is a priest giving me his benediction.

"*Grazie. Buonanotte.*"

"*Buonanotte!*" all the women chant back to me.

It is quite dark now, and I still do not know my way around the beach area. When I was by the piazza in Taormina, I had been sleeping inside St. Augustine's Church, crouched down beneath the pews as I did at the Duomo of Saint Sebastian in Barcellona the night of my escape. Fortunately, St. Augustine keeps their doors unlocked all hours of the day and night. And I feel safe there. I will have to sleep on the beach tonight, but I don't want the gypsies to know. I still have some pride in me. Though I enjoyed the gypsies' company, I also felt overwhelmed. I need to be alone tonight.

I am about a hundred feet away from the gypsies' tents when I hear their music start up again. Stopping, I look over my shoulder, but all I can see are shadows of their forms as they bounce back and forth in rhythm to their instruments and singing. Pulling my gaze away, I keep walking until I find a shed. Praying that it's un-locked, I am relieved to see its door is slightly ajar. I open the door and step in. Something falls on me, causing me to yelp. I feel cold metal and fabric. I open the shed door wider, letting the light of the moon illuminate the object. A beach umbrella. I am then able to make out several beach umbrellas and folding chairs stacked up in the little shed. It is quite stuffy inside. There's no way I can sleep in there. Taking one of the chairs out, I unfold it. I sit down, releasing a deep sigh. My bones have felt achy from sleeping on the floor of St. Augustine's Church for a week now. Though the chair does not allow me to stretch out much, it still feels more comfortable than the cold floor of a church.

Sinking lower into the chair so that my head rests on top of its back, I lay my hands on my belly and watch the moon, listening to the waves softly crash against the shore until I am lulled to sleep. My dreams are filled with the singing and dancing *zingari,* but soon they are replaced by images of flashing tarot cards as I struggle to decipher their meaning and see what the future holds for me.

❧ 8 ❧

La Ruota della Fortuna

WHEEL OF FORTUNE

July 22, 1969

"*La Morte.*" I am giving a tarot reading and am seated under a beach umbrella by the shoreline to feel the ocean's breeze. Every time I draw the Death card, my clients' faces become ashen, and they look like they might actually die.

"Do not be afraid. It does not mean you or a loved one will die. This is a very good card in the tarot deck. It signifies great change—a time of renewal and transformation."

The young man sitting before me looks to be in his mid-twenties. A scar runs from the left side of his forehead down across his brow bone, giving him an angry expression. His jet-black curly hair and close-set eyes detract even more from his appearance. We are nearing the end of his reading. He didn't notice when I laid out his cards that the Death card was among them. He was too busy ogling me. I'm even surprised he's actually heard me mention the Death card.

"Do not lie to me," he says in a very hostile tone.

"I am not lying to you. One cannot merely look at the illustration depicted on the tarot card and assume it has a literal interpretation. The cards and their meanings are quite complex. If you will just let me finish my reading, you'll see you have nothing to fear."

"Go on." He gestures with his head for me to continue.

My words seem to comfort him. Now, instead of staring at my cleavage or trying in vain to get me to stare into his eyes as he's been attempting since he sat down across from me, he is closely examining not only the Death card but the other cards in the spread. Worry lines slash through his forehead. What could a man so young have to worry about? Then again, I am younger than him, and I have had my share of worries.

"You will come to a crossroads in your life, one that will force you to embrace the inevitable change that will occur. Think carefully before you make your choice."

"I thought you said this was a good card? Change in my life has almost always been bad. It also sounds like you are warning me. That can only mean you see some misfortune ahead." He crosses his arms in front of his chest as he leans back in his folding chair, rocking it forward and back. He seems to be oblivious that he is sinking the chair deeper into the sand. I want to laugh, but dare not.

"The card is positive in the sense that it is alerting you to be ready for whatever change is coming your way. Even if it is a wonderful stroke of good luck, the card is still asking you to be cautious. Also, you cannot just look at this one card. You must take every card into account and see the overall message they are giving you. At the beginning of the reading, *la Ruota della Fortuna,* the Wheel of Fortune, card appeared. Again, this card indicates change in your life. We cannot control what God and fate have in store for us. We can only control how we will react to the change and learn from the lesson that is being imparted."

"You are being vague. What will happen to me? What is this great change you keep referring to? Am I destined to repeat my father's miserable existence of running a filthy pig farm for the rest of my life? Will I become successful and live the life I know I was born for? Perhaps this is the change that the cards are alluding to? I will come into my wealth someday?" The man's face looks desperate.

For a moment, I feel sorry for him, but I also know in my heart he will make the wrong choice, and, even if he does become rich, he will place too much importance on it and ultimately destroy himself. The gypsies, who have now become my second family, constantly told me to trust my instincts when they instructed me in how to read the tarot. I was overwhelmed by all the cards in the major and minor arcana. Maria kept reassuring me that, in time, I would master each card and its divination. That is why I need to listen closely to my heart and feel what the cards are trying to communicate to my clients. While I am fascinated by the tarot, especially when my clients feel like I have given them an accurate reading where their past and present are concerned, I cannot help but still feel insecure when I predict my clients' futures. It has only been about three weeks since I started giving readings.

After just one week of lessons in tarot card reading, Maria and her family insisted I was ready, even though I still couldn't remember well what each card signified. I sensed that their patience would run out soon if I did not start bringing in my share of the money. Though I would have preferred more time to learn the tarot better, I also felt uncomfortable continuing to eat the gypsies' food without compensating them for it. I still searched for other work since Maria and her family do not stay in one location for long. They told me they would be in Taormina until the end of the summer before they headed to their next destination. If I can secure a more stable job in Taormina, I will not be forced to leave with the gypsies. As I have said before, I've fallen in love with Taormina. Also, I do not want to go much farther away from Mama and my siblings. Though I no longer live with them, creating more physical distance between us would only widen the hole in my heart. Knowing they are not too far offers a small consolation to me.

I am snapped out of my reverie by my client's fist slamming down on my small folding table, sending several of the cards flying.

"Answer me? What is the matter with you? Your silence is proof that some calamity awaits me."

I continue to ignore him as I rush toward my cards, which are flapping in the breeze, inching closer to the water's edge. A wave is about to crash along the shore. I scramble, picking up whatever cards do not escape my reach. Too late. The wave hits, sweeping a few of my cards out to sea. These cards were a gift from Gianni, Maria's husband. Well, I insisted I would repay him once I could. I had tried to give him the money for the cards when I began earning money. But he insisted the cards were a gift. Now I will be forced to spend the little money I have earned to buy another deck so that I can continue my work.

I walk back toward my table. The bottom half of my skirt is completely wet. The man is still waiting for me, but he's standing now.

"I demand my money back," he says. His black eyes shine even darker as they stare at me with obvious contempt.

"I gave you your reading. I do not give refunds merely because a customer is unhappy with his reading." I return his stare defiantly.

"You didn't finish the reading. I want my money back."

"We can finish the reading now. You are choosing to end it." I turn my back toward him as I walk toward my chair. He pulls me toward him.

"A few of the cards from my reading blew away. You can't finish it. Therefore, I want my money back. Now!" His hands dig painfully into my arm.

"Let go of me! I will report you to the *carabinieri!*"

"Ha! Do you think the police will believe a swindling gypsy and *puttana?*" He lowers his face, bringing his lips closer to mine before he begins kissing me. I knee him in the groin. He yelps in pain, pulling away from me.

"*Puttana!* You are nothing more than a whore, tempting men with your cleavage that is all but spilling out of your dress and your devil's red hair." He slaps me across the face, causing me to lose my balance as I fall onto the scorching sand. He pounces on top of me and begins fondling my breasts, which he's yanked out of the bodice of my dress. I struggle, but he is too heavy.

"Please! Stop it! I beg you!" But my cries go unheeded. Tears blind my eyes.

It is the middle of the afternoon. Most people are taking their siestas, and the beach is all but deserted. The gypsies never give readings at this time and are also taking their siestas. But I need whatever money I can earn, so I still set up my table in hopes that someone who cannot sleep and who wants a reading will come by. I have found that a few people who do not want their families or friends to know they are getting a reading like to come at this time since there is a much lower likelihood they'll be discovered. Now I wish I was taking a siesta on the makeshift cot that Maria prepared for me in her family's large tent.

"Get off her before I kill you with my bare hands!" a man's voice booms loudly. He doesn't give my attacker time to follow his order. He grabs him by the nape of his neck and flings him face-down into the sand. I quickly cover my breasts with my arms. But the stranger is too busy thrashing my client to notice I am half naked. I try to retie the bodice of my dress, but it's torn. My hands are shaking so hard, but I'm relieved someone helped me.

"Rinaldo! I should have known it was you!" The stranger is still screaming. He kicks Rinaldo repeatedly in his ribs. "Get up, you coward!"

Rinaldo comes to his knees. "What do you care? She's nothing more than a cheating gypsy and *puttana!* Why do you think most of her customers are men?"

My face flushes. He's right. Most of my customers have been the young men in town. Even a few older men have come for readings. But none of them ever made an advance toward me or even suggested anything improper. True, I had noticed many of them staring, but I know that is men's nature—to stare at women. Though I felt uncomfortable at first, Maria told me to become accustomed to it since I was a very pretty girl. "Besides, you will get more customers because of your beauty. Use it to your advantage," she had said. She even bought two dresses with lower-cut bodices for me— another gift. When I tried to tell her the dresses felt tight and were too revealing, she told me they were supposed to fit that way. I knew I couldn't refuse her gift because of the generosity she and her family had shown me. Besides, the clothes I had come to Taormina with were too warm for the beach, where I conducted most of my readings. The new dresses were lightweight and sleeveless. Now I cannot help but wonder if Maria's intent in buying me the dresses with low-cut bodices was to lure more men, thereby increasing the profits that I split fifty-fifty with the gypsies. Anger rages through me. Maria and her husband used me. Here I am thinking they're helping me and that they are my newly adopted family when all they were thinking about was how to increase their pot.

The stranger who has rescued me is now punching Rinaldo's face. I cannot look.

"Please! That's enough!" I scream.

The stranger stops and looks at me. I lower my eyes, still ashamed by Rinaldo's accusations. I'm sure this man believes them.

"This swine deserves it and more. My father used to employ him. We caught him stealing a large sum of money." The man gives Rinaldo another kick in the ribs.

"Enough! Enough! I will repay you. The reading she gave me showed I will come into a great fortune someday. You and your father will see I am true to my word." Rinaldo begins sobbing.

"You'll have to make your riches elsewhere. Get out of Taormina. If I ever see you again, you will wish I had just ended it for you now. For this is nothing compared to the beating and torture you'll suffer if I catch you in this town again. Get up."

Rinaldo struggles to stand. Once he's risen, he begins to walk away, but the stranger stops him.

"Apologize to the woman first."

Rinaldo opens his mouth as if to protest, but the stranger takes a menacing step toward him.

"Mi dispiace." Rinaldo bows his head and then scampers off.

"Are you all right?" The stranger hands me his beach towel. "Wrap this around yourself."

"Grazie." I take the towel. The stranger turns his back to give me privacy. I drape the towel around my shoulders, using one of the pins that were holding my hair in place to keep it securely closed.

I notice the stranger is wearing swimming trunks. He must have just come out of the water when he spotted Rinaldo attacking me. Droplets of water still cling to his bronzed skin and a few fall from the wavy strands of his dark blond hair. His eyes are a deep emerald green like the waters of the Costa Smeralda off the island of Sardinia. My teacher once showed us a postcard she had purchased when she went to Sardinia for vacation. I had been envious of her and had dreamed that maybe someday I, too, would be able to secure work that would allow me to make some extra money to travel someplace as beautiful as Sardinia.

"I must repay you for helping me. Would you like a reading?" I ask him. My voice is hushed. I cannot stop thinking about what he must think of me after hearing Rinaldo's ugly words about my reputation.

"Are you covered?" he asks.

"*Sì.*" I keep my eyes averted from his as he turns around.

"*Grazie.* But please, don't feel that you must repay me. It was my pleasure to help you." He is now staring at me just as intently as Rinaldo had been during his reading. I feel my face burning up and look off into the distance, toward the beach.

"You have the most beautiful hair I have ever seen. It is the color of a Scottish woman's hair or even a German's, and with your olive complexion, the contrast is very striking. Your ancestors must've been from one of the Germanic tribes that invaded Sicily many centuries ago."

"Thank you. Yes, my mother says we have German in us. She has flecks of red in her hair, too, but it's not as fiery as mine. My father has always hated it and called it the devil's hair. It's funny. Rinaldo called it that today, too." I smile shyly at him. His face grows somber, and for a moment, I feel as if he's caught a glimpse into my soul—all the pain I've endured at my father's hands, my heartbreak over leaving my mother and siblings behind, the shame I am now feeling over Rinaldo's attacking me and hurling the most foul insults at me.

"May I ask what your name is?"

"Sarina. And yours?"

"Carlo. Where are you from, Sarina?"

"I'd rather not say."

Carlo nods his head and looks off to the surf. He then asks me, "How long have you been in Taormina?"

"A month and a half."

"You are here all alone."

"Yes. The gypsies who live in that large red tent by the Vulcano

Cabana have taken me in. They taught me how to read cards so that I could make a living."

"I see." Carlo's face looks pensive, but he remains silent.

"Thank you again for helping me. I should probably make my way back toward the tent."

"Are you here every day?"

"Yes. I also go into the village once a week and do readings in the piazza. But some weeks I don't make it up there. It depends on how much money I've made the previous week and if I can afford the fare for the aerial tram."

"I will most certainly see you, if not here on the beach then in the village. Maybe I will come for a reading, but I will pay. I insist."

"Va bene." I begin packing up my things.

"Let me help you." Carlo closes my beach umbrella and folds my table. "Surely, you don't lug all of this stuff back to the gypsies' tent? That's quite far off."

I gesture with my head toward the beach umbrella shed that I had found that first night after I met the gypsies. "I store them in there. The man who rents the beach umbrellas and chairs doesn't mind. I actually bought this umbrella from him."

"Well, let me carry them back for you."

"Mille grazie."

Carlo places the folded beach umbrella under his arm before grabbing the table and chair. He walks quickly through the sand as if he is carrying only one object.

When he returns, he asks, "Can I walk you back to the tent?"

He sees the hesitation in my eyes.

"I just would feel better knowing you were safe even though I'm sure that coward Rinaldo is long gone by now."

I look around on the beach. It's still quite vacant. "All right."

We walk slowly. I love staring at the ocean as I stroll along the beach. Listening to the sounds of the waves and the seagulls has always soothed me. If I lived on the beach all the days of my life, I would be content. Unlike Rinaldo's, my goals in life are simpler. I just pray to God to keep me and my family safe so that I can see them again someday. I also ask God to give me enough money to sustain me. Well, I do ask for a little extra money so that I can bring it to my mother when I am able to. Closing my eyes, I fight back the tears that threaten to overtake me as I wonder when I will see Mama and the little ones again. When I open my eyes, I see Carlo staring at me. His eyes look sad, but thankfully he does not ask me if anything is wrong.

We are about thirty feet away from the tent when I stop and say, "Thank you, Carlo, but you don't need to walk me any farther. I'll be fine from here."

"*Ciao.* I will look for you again so that I can get my reading."

I laugh. "*Ciao.*"

Carlo smiles and waves to me before walking off. I watch him. The sea breeze blows his wavy hair lightly to and fro. His physique is lean but solid. He looks about 5'9" tall. He felt taller standing next to me, but at my stature of 5'2", almost anyone feels a lot taller. I make the sign of the cross and say a quick prayer, thanking God for letting Carlo walk by on the beach when Rinaldo attacked me. A shiver runs through me as I contemplate what almost happened.

"Sarina! I was about to come looking for you. Why is that towel wrapped around you? Did you go into the water?" Maria comes over to me, concern written all over her features. She tries to put her arm around me, but I step back, remembering how I was almost raped and how she insisted on my wearing those low-cut dresses.

"Leave me alone!" I walk around Maria and head toward the tent. But she follows me.

"Sarina! Please! Why are you so upset? What is wrong?" She catches up to me and reaches for my arm, trying to stop me. Instead, she pulls at my towel by mistake, and it falls off my shoulders, revealing my torn dress.

"*Dio mio!* Who did this to you?" Maria grabs me by the shoulders, looking into my eyes.

"You did this to me! You insisted I wear these dresses. Now I know why most of my customers have been men. I was almost raped this afternoon, and he accused me of prostituting myself to all the men who have been coming for readings. You encouraged me to use my beauty to my advantage."

"Sarina, I had no idea this would happen. Do you really think I would do anything to harm you? We've only known each other for a short time, but I already think of you as one of my own. I would never let any harm come to you, just as I wouldn't let any harm come to my own children. Taormina is very safe. Nothing like this has ever happened here. Please, believe me." Maria's eyes fill with tears. I can see she is being sincere, though I still feel like the need to make as much money as possible was foremost in her mind when she bought those dresses for me.

"I don't know if I can keep doing this, especially after what happened today."

"Sarina, you have a gift. I know it hasn't been long, but I have watched you when you give your readings, and you not only read the cards but use your intuition to feel the situation. Please, don't let what happened today influence you. I will ask Gianni or any of the other men to always be nearby when you do a reading, and I forbid you from doing any more readings during siesta. The beach is too quiet then. No wonder this happened. Have you seen this man who attacked you before? Gianni and the other men will find him and give him a good beating. He'll never bother you again. Trust me."

"No, I never saw him before, and don't worry. He already got a good beating."

"You hit him?" Maria asks as she looks at my petite frame, incredulous that I could have done much damage.

"No. A young man saw what was happening and came over to help me. His name was Carlo. After he was done beating my attacker, Carlo told him to leave Taormina and never come back. Apparently the man who attacked me had worked for Carlo's father and stolen from him. So Carlo knew him."

"What did this young man who helped you look like?"

"He had wavy dark blond hair and green eyes." My face flushes slightly as I remember how handsome Carlo was.

"I don't believe I know him. Did he say what his father does?"

"No. He was very kind. He even helped me carry my umbrella and table to the shed, and then he insisted on walking me back here."

"I thank God the Fates were looking out for you by sending this Carlo along. Come inside and rest. Don't worry about helping me with supper." Maria takes my hand and leads me toward the tent.

After taking a sponge bath, I change into the slip that I use as a nightgown. Lying down on my cot, I feel all the aches in my body from when Rinaldo attacked me. Bruises dot my arms and chest. Though I feel worn out from the rough day I've had, I know I will not be able to sleep. I just want to rest for a bit before joining everyone else for dinner. My mind drifts to Carlo, and I wonder where he is right now. He didn't say much about himself. Then again, I didn't either, especially when I refused to tell him where I'm originally from. He mentioned that he would probably see me either in the piazza or on the beach, so he must spend his time equally divided among the two. I feel foolish in my thoughts as I suddenly realize most people in Taormina spend as much time on the beach as they do in town. The crazy day I've had is making me lose my ability to think clearly.

I rest for another half hour. The smell of calamari reaches my nose and is too tantalizing for me to resist. Standing up, I put on a dress that Maria has left for me. It is a bit large, but I take the belt tie from my other dress and wrap it around the waist of this one, making it tighter. Instead of a low-cut bodice, this dress has a square neckline that covers my cleavage adequately.

Holding up Maria's brass handheld mirror with one hand, I brush my wavy, waist-length hair with the other. I remember how Carlo stared at it and how he told me it was beautiful. I had never really thought of my auburn hair as beautiful since it wasn't commonly seen and since my father had always made me feel like I was cursed to have such red hair. He tolerated the little bit of red in my mother's hair because hers also had hues of soft brown and didn't draw as much attention as mine. I coil my hair into a bun and reach for a few pins to fasten it, but on second thought, I decide to leave my hair down, draping it on either side of my shoulders before I step out of the tent.

Only a few people are still eating by the campfire. Several of the men are getting their instruments ready for the night's music. This has been my favorite part of staying with Maria and her tribe of gypsies. They sing and dance every night. Even on the days when they haven't made much money, they still appear happy.

"Sarina! Sarina!" Isabella comes running in my direction and throws herself into my arms once she reaches me. She then leads me by the hand toward the campfire and sits on a small stool Gianni carved for her. She pats the empty folding chair beside her. "Sit next to me."

Doing as she asks, I cannot help but laugh after seeing Isabella take a handful of calamari that are sitting in a large pot and pop them all into her mouth.

"You really love those, don't you?" I stroke her hair. Isabella's playful personality reminds me so much of Carlotta's that sometimes it is hard for me to be around her, but I never let her see my anguish.

"They're my favorite! Yum!"

I eat my share of calamari and a tomato and green bean salad one of the women has made.

Maria and Gianni have just finished singing a duet about a husband and a wife who are miserable together yet can't live without each other. Laughter and whistles go around the group.

"*Grazie! Grazie mille!* Can I have everyone's attention? *Silenzio, per favore!*" Maria implores the gypsies to be quiet.

"You have all helped me welcome Sarina into our fold." Maria gestures toward me with a nod of her head and smiles. I return the smile, but begin feeling anxious, not sure where she is going with this. And I hate being the center of attention. Now everyone is looking at me, but I only see kindness in their faces.

"Though she has only been reading for a few weeks now, she is a fast learner, and I can see she will be one of our best tarot readers. She truly has a calling for it."

"*Si, si.*" Many of the gypsies voice their approval. Even Gianni's mother, Concetta, manages to make me out in her half-blind state and waves a feeble hand in my direction.

"But what you do not know is that Sarina is also a gifted singer."

"Ahh!" Gasps of surprise reverberate among the gypsies. Even I'm stunned. For I have not sung in front of the gypsies yet. The only time I allow myself to sing is when I'm alone. Maria must've heard me sing when I was washing my clothes the other day by the water.

"Sarina has been shy about her talents as a singer. But I think it is time she share with us her beautiful voice. Sarina, we would be honored if you would take the stage."

My heart freezes. I'm terrified, but I also know I cannot disappoint them, not after all that they've done for me. I know this is also Maria's way of still trying to make amends with me over what happened with the dresses. I remember how I spoke to her earlier, and regret fills me.

"Sing, Sarina! Sing!" Isabella is now standing and hopping up and down, holding her hands together as she begs me to sing.

I stand up and make my way toward Maria. Everyone applauds and cheers.

Maria hugs me and whispers into my ear, "You are a very brave young woman. I love you."

I am moved and hug her back. Maria kisses me on both cheeks and then walks over to Gianni, who wraps his arm around his wife's waist.

Clearing my throat, I begin to sing.

"*Mama . . . Ma-mahhh. Come ho potuto lasciarti? Non c'è nessuno al mondo come te. Il tuo amore é eterno. Il tuo amore non giudica mai. Il tuo amore sempre conforta. Mama . . . Ma-mahhh. Come ho potuto lasciarti? Ho battuto il mio cuore ogni volta che penso a te e il dolore mia partenza deve aver sicuramente causato. Non potrò mai perdonare me stesso. Ohhh, Mama . . . Ma-mahhh. Come ho potuto lasciarti?*"

"*Mama . . . Mama. How could I have left you? There is no one in the world like you. Your love is eternal. Your love never judges. Your love always comforts. Mama . . . Mama. How could I have left you? I beat my heart every time I think of you and the pain my departure must surely have caused. I will never forgive myself. Oh, Mama . . . Mama. How could I have left you?*"

There is complete silence once I am done singing. My first thought is that I sounded horrible. But then I see many of the gypsies crying, even a few of the men. I then realize my hand is clenched into a fist and is over my heart. When I sing, I often close my eyes, completely immersing myself in my song and the place it takes me to. I did not realize when I was singing that I was actually beating my own heart every time I thought about my mother and the pain I must have caused her after I left.

The silence only lasts for a moment more, then everyone starts applauding. Many of the older women, mothers themselves, run up and embrace me.

"Povera ragazza," or "poor girl" several of them say before kissing me on the cheeks. A few others say, *"Bravissima! Che bella voce!"*

Maria is back at my side. *"Si, che bella voce!* I told you Sarina has a beautiful voice. Let us applaud her and her moving song once more."

More rounds of applause and cheers ring out through the crowd. Maria hugs me. Then she pulls me away and says softly so no one else can hear, "I had a feeling that first night I met you that you were a gifted singer. My gypsy intuition was correct once again. I could see in your eyes how much you loved music and even from the way you talked about it. I'm sorry that I didn't give you any warning, but I knew, if I had asked you to sing tonight, you would have turned me down again as you did the night we met. I know how shy you can be. But when I heard you singing by the beach while you were washing your clothes the other day, I knew you needed to stop hiding that voice. You must grace us with your singing every night. You hear me?" Maria pushes my hair back off my shoulders and holds my chin up—an action I have often seen her do with her own daughter, Isabella.

"I'm sorry, Maria. I'm sorry I talked to you the way I did before."

"You have nothing to be sorry for. You were right. I should not have encouraged you to use your beauty to get more customers. I am terribly sorry. Please forgive me."

I embrace Maria and say, "All is forgiven."

Maria turns her attention back to the crowd and yells, "Who is next?"

Tonio comes up with a stool and his mandolin. He plays it expertly, but does not sing. He told me the other night that he leaves the singing to his parents.

I am listening to Tonio and tapping my foot to the playful sounds of the mandolin when someone taps me on the shoulder. Looking up, I'm surprised to see Carlo.

"I'm sorry. I didn't mean to startle you. I've been trying to get your attention, but you're quite the star tonight." Carlo looks at me with what appears to be an expression of admiration and respect.

"You heard me sing?" My cheeks burn. I feel exposed since my song was very personal.

"Yes. It was incredible. I don't think I've ever heard anyone sing like that."

"You don't need to flatter me. But thank you."

"I'm not flattering you. I'm serious." Carlo's voice sounds hurt, as if I implied he was lying.

"I'm sorry. I just hate being the center of attention. I guess you can say I don't receive compliments well."

"How are you feeling? I know you had quite a bit of a fright earlier today with that scum Rinaldo."

"I'm fine. Just a little tired. Thank you for asking."

"Do you think we can take a walk? We don't have to go far from the gypsies, just enough so that I can talk to you without shouting above the music."

"I'd like that. Let me tell Maria, in case she comes looking for me."

I walk over to Maria, who is drinking wine out of a wooden cup. Her arm is slung around her husband's neck, and she is sitting on his lap. I can tell they are still madly in love with each other even after all these years of being married. It is strange for me to see that since I never saw such love in my own parents' marriage.

"Maria, I am taking a walk with my friend. We aren't going far."

Carlo is standing behind me. He extends his hand toward Maria. "Carlo. It's a pleasure to meet you, *signora*."

"Maria, please. This is my husband, Gianni."

Carlo shakes Gianni's hand.

"So you are the one we have to thank for rescuing our Sarina earlier today."

Carlo shuffles his feet as he glances down at them and then back up at Maria and Gianni. "You don't need to thank me. I'm grateful I was there when I was."

"It was nice to meet you, Carlo. Enjoy your *passeggiata*. Please join us later. We have plenty of wine." Gianni holds up his wine bottle and laughs. He is already a bit drunk.

"Thank you. We will." Carlo places his hand on the small of my back as we walk away. Maria catches my eye and winks.

Carlo and I walk farther away from the tent and the din of the gypsies. It is a cloudy night, and the stars are hidden, much to my disappointment. Looking at the stars is one way I feel close to my younger siblings, especially Carlotta. I imagine that when I am staring up into the night sky, Carlotta is singing "Stella Mia," the song I taught her, and looking at the stars as well.

"I know you didn't want to tell me earlier where you are from. Is it because you ran away from home?" Carlo asks.

"I guess I cannot deny that after the song you heard me sing tonight."

"You don't have to be afraid of me, Sarina. I would never betray your secrets."

"I'm sorry, Carlo. I have learned to be wary ever since I left home and have been on my own. Besides, I had just met you. I don't give my trust easily."

"Even though I saved you?" The hurt that was evident in Carlo's tone earlier is back.

"That is true. Forgive me?" I cannot help but give him a sly smile.

"That will be easy, especially when you flash me that pretty smile." Carlo's eyes light up.

"I'm sorry about your mother," he continues. "Why did you leave home if you miss and love her so much?"

"I had to if I hoped to stay alive."

Carlo's brows knit together. He stops in his tracks and takes my hands. "Who tried to hurt you?"

"My father. He beat me and my mother many times. It kept getting worse. Even if he never did kill me, I could not take my miserable life there anymore. Only my mother and siblings kept me going. Though I am happier now, I cannot stop feeling guilty over having left them."

"You did what you needed to. I'm sure your mother understands."

"I hope so."

We continue walking. The red tent now looks quite far off in the distance, but I'm not worried. I feel safe with Carlo.

"How long will you be here?"

"What do you mean?"

"I know gypsies often roam. I've lived in Taormina my whole life, and we've seen our share of different nomadic gypsies. I doubt it is any different with this group."

"Yes, Maria told me they plan on staying here only through the end of the summer."

"And you will be leaving with them too?"

"I'm not sure yet. I would like to stay in Taormina. The town has captured my heart."

"Yes, although I was born and still live here, I have no desire to leave."

"You live in town?"

"Yes, near the piazza."

I'm about to ask him what his father does since he had mentioned Rinaldo had worked for his father, but I'm distracted when suddenly Carlo takes my hand. I'm too stunned to say anything else. We continue walking hand in hand. My pulse is racing, and my head feels slightly woozy. His hand feels so big wrapped around my small one.

"We should start making our way back. I don't want Maria to worry."

"Of course."

We walk the rest of the way back in silence. I'm grateful, for I don't know if my mind can form right now any coherent responses to questions Carlo might ask me.

As we get closer to the crowd, I let go of Carlo's hand, too embarrassed to let the gypsies see.

Gianni gives Carlo and me two cups of wine. Maria is singing once more, and the other women are dancing around her.

"Sarina, I know it's late, but is there any way you can give me a reading now?"

"I don't see why not. We can sit by the bonfire so I can see the cards. Let me get them."

I walk inside the tent and look for my cards. I then remember my deck is not a complete set after a few of the cards were blown into the sea. They will have to do.

I step outside and see Carlo is already by the bonfire. He's looking into the flames. Suddenly, I realize I feel nervous. But I also feel good. There is a happy feeling inside of me that I have never experienced. Slowly, I walk over to him, hoping my nerves will calm by the time I reach Carlo.

Forcing my voice to sound light, I say, "Carlo, I must warn you that your reading might be off. When Rinaldo got upset, he pounded my table with his fist, sending a few of my cards flying and into the water. I wasn't able to retrieve all of them. So you'll be getting a reading with several cards missing from the deck. If that makes you uncomfortable, we can wait to do the reading until I replace my deck of cards with a new one."

"Perhaps those cards disappeared so that they would *not* appear in my reading for one reason or the other." Carlo laughs.

"Perhaps." I also laugh and shake my head.

Unfolding a sheet that I brought to lay the cards on, I spread it on the sand. Carlo helps me smooth out its edges and then takes off his sandals, placing them on two corners of the sheet to keep the sea breeze from folding it. I take off my own *ciabattas* and place them on the other two corners of the sheet. We sit down cross-legged on opposite sides of the sheet, leaving the center free for the cards. Flipping through my deck, I pull out the court cards—King, Queen, Knight, Page—of each suit. I shuffle only these cards and ask Carlo to take the one from the top with his left hand and place it face up in the center of the sheet.

"Knight of Swords. This is your Significator, the card that represents the person who is receiving the reading. It also identifies the person by their sex, age, and astrological sign and may also reveal other traits such as personality, work, and other characteristics. Usually, the person who pulls this card has an astrological sign of either Aquarius, Gemini, or Libra. Do you know which sign you are?"

"Yes, I am Aquarius." Carlo swallows hard, then licks his lips. He is no doubt impressed that the card accurately depicted his zodiac sign. For a moment, my gaze is fixed on the rosy hue of his mouth and the extra fullness his upper lip has.

"Aquarius. So that means your birthday is either at the end of January or beginning of February."

"I see you know your astrology. I was born on January 21, 1947."

I mentally note that he is twenty-two, and five years older than me. I thought he was no more than nineteen.

"We both share the suit of swords as our Significator cards. Mine is Page of Swords."

In order to learn the cards and their meanings, I had done readings for myself, and naturally I had wanted to know which of the cards was my Significator.

"What is your astrological sign?" Carlo asks. "Don't tell me we also have Aquarius in common?" He gives me a mischievous grin.

"No, we don't. I am a Gemini. My birthday is June thirteenth."

"Ahh! Nonna Lucia, my grandmother, is also a Gemini, and she is an avid follower of the zodiac. She's told me that Geminis and Aquarians are compatible. So I guess we do have a lot in common." Carlo crosses his arms, and his grin widens. He looks quite satisfied with himself.

"It takes more than having compatible astrological signs and common Significator cards for two people to get along." I say this in a very matter-of-fact tone and don't dare look up as I do my best to keep a serious expression.

"Of course. But it does help to have the universe aligned. Don't you agree?"

I glance up. Carlo is staring at me intensely. I quickly avert my gaze and shrug my shoulders as I say, "Perhaps. Getting back to your Knight of Swords Significator." Forcing my attention back to the card, I close my eyes and try to listen to what my intuition is telling me about Carlo.

"You are a generous person, sometimes too generous. Be careful. While this is an admirable trait to have, it can also be used to the advantage of your enemies if you trust the wrong person." I glance up at Carlo. He nods his head knowingly.

I continue. "When you commit yourself to a project, idea, or even to someone, you do not hold back. You give it everything you have."

"That is true." Once again Carlo nods his head.

I exhale a sigh of relief. So far, my reading seems to be accurate. I am afraid of being so off that he will surely believe Rinaldo's accusations of my being a swindling gypsy.

"I also see, Carlo, that you are not afraid to take risks. But again, you must exercise caution. Think well before making any weighty decision. Your ability to charge forward and not be intimidated will aid you when you are faced with obstacles. But your fearlessness could also blind you and lead you to believe that you are invincible, thus causing you to take risky measures that could backfire. If you learn to harness this gift, especially when helping others who are in need, you can greatly benefit from it."

Carlo's face looks pensive.

I keep the Significator card lying where it is, but put back the other court cards into the remaining deck of cards. I shuffle the cards and then hand them to Carlo.

"Think of the question you want to ask me while cutting the deck of cards into three piles. Use your left hand to cut the deck. Then lay the cards out in three separate piles from left to right. Do not tell me your question until *after* I am done with the reading."

"Why must I use my left hand to cut the cards?"

"Because it is the hand of the heart—the life force that determines your path."

"Do I have to tell you my question? Can you just tell me what the cards say?"

"I will not betray your confidence to anyone if that is what you are worried about." I look Carlo directly in the eyes so he knows I am sincere in giving him my word.

"That is not what I'm worried about. I can tell you are a person of integrity. I'm embarrassed to say the question is of a personal nature." Carlo seems slightly nervous.

"Why don't you rephrase the question so that it's vague yet is along the lines of what you want to know?"

"That should do." Carlo takes a deep breath as he begins cutting the cards. After placing them in three separate piles as I had instructed him to do, he clasps his hands and places them in his lap. He watches me as I begin turning over the cards. Though I've become accustomed to my male clients staring at me while I give my readings, none of them have managed to unnerve me like Carlo has. I feel my pulse race and know I must be blushing. At least it is nighttime, so I'm hoping he won't be able to see my face burning up.

I line up nine cards in the Celtic Cross Spread because it gives a very detailed reading. I learned two other more complex spreads from Maria and Gianni, but they encouraged me to go with the Celtic Cross Spread since I was still new to the tarot. The Celtic Cross is one of the simpler tarot spreads to learn. I personally like this layout the best of the three I learned because I have discovered that my clients usually want to know about a certain aspect of their lives, whether it relates to love, fortune, or any other area in which they need more in-depth clarification. Since this spread gives a very descriptive reading, I can give my clients additional clues that will help them find the guidance they're seeking.

I take a quick glance at all of the cards and notice the majority of them are split among the suit of cups and the major arcana. The seventy-eight cards of the tarot deck are split into the major and minor arcanas. The major arcana is the core of the deck, as Gianni explained to me. These cards represent universal facets of human experience and the influences that are intrinsic to human nature. A few of the major arcana cards instantly convey their meaning, such as the Temperance, Strength, and Justice cards. Others represent people who embody a certain life aspect, such as the High Priestess, the Fool, and the Emperor. And then there are the cards with astronomical images, such as the Moon, the Star, and the Sun.

These symbolize the powerful, mysterious forces related to the universe. Gianni explained to me that the major arcana cards are very important in that they show the different transitions, or stages, on an individual's life journey, especially in relation to his or her spiritual or inner growth.

The minor arcana are the cards comprising the four suits—wands, pentacles, swords, and cups. Each suit is made up of fourteen minor arcana cards, including ten numbered cards (Ace through the number ten) and four court cards (King, Queen, Knight, and Page). The numbered cards signify life situations one encounters, while the court cards are people and/or personality characteristics.

In addition to several cups and major arcana cards, Carlo's spread also contains a suit of swords card and a suit of wands card.

Clearing my throat, I begin. "The first card. Page of Cups. There will be a new beginning in your life, most likely a romantic one. You welcome this new chapter in your life and have been waiting for it."

"So far, that's true." Carlo smiles.

"You don't need to give me confirmation after each card. Hear the entire reading before you decide if I have been accurate or not."

"I'm sorry, Sarina. Please go on."

"That's all right. I just want to remind you that I am still fairly new to reading the tarot. I don't want to disappoint you or raise your expectations."

"Don't worry. You could never disappoint me." Carlo's eyes lock with mine. I swallow hard before returning my gaze to the cards.

"The second card represents your hopes and goals. We have the Nine of Cups. You seek the ultimate happiness and fulfillment. Most of your cards are pointing to a romantic partnership; however, you could also be seeking fulfillment in a creative aspiration you have. If it is a romantic union you desire, the woman you meet will be your soul mate. You both will have the perfect harmony—understanding each other like no other person has before. If you are seeking the fruition of a creative or artistic idea, again you will reach your goal. But you must be careful. For life is a balance between good and bad. Wonderful events happen as well as bad events. You must enjoy the moment when life is good and not take it for granted. Do not take the people who treat you well and love you for granted. If you realize the fulfillment of a creative dream, appreciate the rewards of it. For you can never know when the tide will turn, and you will have a tough journey ahead. Do you understand?" I glance up at Carlo, who is staring at the Nine of Cups card. He nods his head without looking up.

"The next card represents your future. Wheel of Fortune. This card complements the first card in that it shows there will be change in your life. And it also reinforces the second card in that it is reminding you that since change is inevitable, you must enjoy your blessings when you receive them."

"Will it be a good or a bad change that will occur?" Carlo asks.

"I cannot be certain. But my intuition, as well as what the cards are telling me so far, is that the change will be a happy one. Still, there will be a turn of events. It is unavoidable. Again, the card is advising you to be cautious when that change occurs. How you react to the situation is important. Just because there will be a time of trial does not mean it will last forever. Remain optimistic and try to learn the lesson that is being given to you when events change for the worse."

Carlo's face looks worried. Taking a deep breath, he says, "Go on."

"Ace of Cups. This card represents the possibilities of what can happen. I don't know if you've noticed that the majority of your cards are the suit of cups?"

"I have noticed. What does that mean?"

"The suit of cups generally relates to emotions and love. It can also relate to creativity, desires, or wishes. Since most of your cards are cups, I am almost certain that the answers you seek are related to your emotional state and matters of the heart. It does not have to represent a romantic love. It can also point to emotional conflict and even quite possibly to your being blinded in a sense because you are thinking with your heart rather than with your head. If this is the case, the suit of cups cards also serve as a warning to have caution and take a moment before acting too rashly or making an important decision. Be certain that you are also giving thought to your choices."

"So far your reading is quite accurate. I'm sorry. I know you asked me to wait until you were done." Carlo grins sheepishly at me.

"Well, I am happy you are satisfied so far. Let us see if the feeling lasts through the end of the reading." I laugh.

"We will see." Carlo laughs with me.

"Going back to your fourth card, the Ace of Cups. This love that will enter your life, or the emotional conflict you will have, will be a consuming one. You will never have felt like this before. You will be at your best, wanting to give and show your feelings as much as possible. Do not hold back. Be generous with your love even when you become insecure, and accept fully the love that is being offered to you. Don't let any feelings of doubt cloud what you feel. Be willing to take the risk and jump completely into the water.

"Fifth card. Ten of Swords. This card represents the obstacles you will face in reaching your goals. You must be prepared for a setback. Again, this card indicates there will be change, and from reading the previous cards, I am more convinced now that you will have both positive and negative changes in your life. But the change that this card alludes to is one that you will have a difficult time accepting."

"Is there anything I can do to stop this negative event from happening?" Carlo asks.

I shake my head. "No. This card is not only a warning that a negative transition will occur but it also indicates that a force greater than you will bring about this change. Perhaps someone will betray you, and there is nothing you can do about it. As I said earlier, both good and bad happens in life. We can't always avoid difficulty or choose the outcome we'd like. Though you will suffer from this sudden, painful transition, this card is also positive in that it is reminding you that you can overcome this difficulty and learn from it. How you react to this trying time is in your hands."

"I'll try to remember that when I'm at my lowest," Carlo says, sighing deeply.

"Yes, you must. Remember, the tarot is not just for getting an answer you seek to your question and determining your future. It also serves as a guide for deep introspection as well as for learning from all of your experiences."

"That does make sense."

"Nine of Wands. The sixth card. This will give us an idea of what will happen in the near future."

"I will grow a beard and get fat!" Carlo blurts out, and looks at me with a twinkle in his eye. "Sorry! I couldn't help myself. I thought we could use some humor since this reading got so heavy in the last few minutes."

I shake my finger playfully at him, "Behave!" He's right. We needed that moment of levity. I was feeling myself tense up as well with the reading from his last card. I haven't been completely forthcoming with Carlo's reading, for I didn't have the heart to tell him that I also sensed he would suffer great loss.

"Please, continue, Sarina. I see there are just a few more cards left until I know my ultimate fate."

"The Nine of Wands card indicates that while you will suffer greatly, you have the strength and resilience to surpass any misfortune that befalls you. You must not give up even if obstacles are still being thrown your way. The obstacles could be in the form of enemies, and you might not even realize you have these opponents. Remain strong, and do not give your trust easily."

"That will be easy. My grandmother used to always tell me I question everything and everyone."

"There is nothing wrong with that, Carlo. It is better than rushing into a situation without weighing the consequences. But I feel that this card might be implying you need to also be careful with people you already know and who have your confidence already. Sometimes it is the people closest to us who let us down and don't want the best for us." My voice sounds sad as I think about my father and how he's treated me more like a foe than a daughter. Sometimes I think perhaps he is jealous of me, although I'm not exactly sure why. But suddenly a memory comes to me. I caught him staring intently at Mama once as she and I worked together on our garden. We were laughing and joking with one another. Instead of looking angry as I would have expected from him, his expression was somber, almost sad. Was there a time, perhaps before I was born, that Mama joked with him and laughed with him more as she was doing now with me? I don't ever remember Mama sharing much joy with Papá. They barely even seemed to share a conversation other than to discuss practical day-to-day matters. Is that possibly the reason why Papá detests me so much? Is he jealous of the special bond Mama and I share? And does he feel I've stolen her affections away from him?

"I will be extra cautious. This reading is going to make me paranoid." Carlo laughs, startling me out of my thoughts.

I smile and look at the seventh card. "The Emperor. This figure often represents either a father or authoritative male figure in your life, which is perfect for where we are at in the reading since this card represents your family and/or friends who will either help or hinder you in reaching your desires. Unfortunately, in your case there is a very powerful male figure who wants to exert his influence over you and does not care about your own wishes or dreams. You must remain firm in what you want and not let outside forces sway you in what you feel is the path you should take in your life. Be very careful. This person will do his best to make you fail."

Carlo's lips are pressed into a tight grimace, and his brows are furrowed together.

"Are you all right?" I ask.

"*Si, si. Grazie.* Please, go on."

"We're almost done. I know it's getting late, and you must be tired."

"I'm fine. In fact, I could sit here all night with you."

My heart stops at his words. I do my best to act as if they've had no effect on me.

"The eighth card. Ten of Cups. This card is reversed. That's the only card in your spread that is reversed." I tap my index finger along my chin, weighing the meaning of this card and taking my time before I interpret it.

"Is that bad?" Carlo's voice sounds worried for the first time throughout his reading.

Without thinking, I place my hand over his and reassure him, "Remember, we cannot avoid when bad things will happen. The tarot can help us to be prepared and to be careful when we face a difficult path."

"I'll remember your wise words when I cross that bridge."

Carlo turns his hand so that his palm is facing upward, allowing him to curl his fingers around my hand. I want to pull my arm back, but I can tell by his firm grip that won't be so easy. Although I only met him today, I also don't want to offend him. He's been so kind to me. But his touch is making me nervous and sending tingles throughout my body.

I wait a moment to see if he will let go of my hand, but he doesn't. Not wanting to draw any further attention to myself, I focus on finishing the reading.

"When a card is reversed in the tarot, its meaning is the opposite of the card's meaning when it is in its upright position. We have the Ten of Cups. In its upright position, it is a very positive card, representing the perfect harmony and union between two people. Oftentimes, this card alludes to a possible marriage. But in the reverse, it signifies a broken marriage or values that are at odds with the values of someone close to you. The eighth card in this spread is supposed to relate to your work and how it will influence your primary relationship. Since your reading overall seems to be indicating a romantic involvement, there is a chance your work could affect this partnership.

"And at last we are up to the ninth and final card. The Lovers. A very good card, and it is also very good when the last card in a reading is a positive one, because even if most of the previous cards are predictions of a tough journey ahead, the last card is offering hope."

"Grazie, Dio!" Carlo shouts as he makes the sign of the cross and then holds his hands up in prayer as if he is thanking God.

"Don't make fun of your reading or tempt the Fates." I try to say this in a stern voice, but am having a hard time since Carlo looks so funny. But I want to be certain he's taking this reading seriously.

"Again, I'm just trying to lighten the mood. But I must admit, I have ulterior motives as well for making jokes. I love seeing you smile and hearing your laugh."

I ignore his compliments and change the subject quickly before he can make me blush even more than he already has.

"The Lovers card represents the ultimate union and can again point to marriage or a perfect joining of two people. The bond you will have with this woman will be on a very high level. She will be your soul mate and will know you like no one else ever has. There is a strong attraction between the two of you that only deepens your spiritual connection to this person. This card can also symbolize your beliefs and values. At this point, you may feel more secure than you did earlier in your journey to make your own decisions and not let others influence you. Again, this card reflects back to the Emperor card. I saw a powerful male figure who will try to sway you and convince you to go against what you believe is just. This person does not have your best interests at heart. Though you might fall prey to this person, the Lovers card shows that in time you can become strong enough to ignore external forces and listen to yourself. Let your own intuition guide you. This card is also a warning, in that it shows you will be faced with a moral dilemma and must take time before deciding what action you will take.

"My overall sense of your reading is that there will be a new beginning or transformation in your life, most likely a new romantic relationship. While you will receive the satisfaction you have always desired in a partner, you will inevitably be faced with obstacles that will force you to reevaluate what is most important in your life. You must be careful with the people in your life and whom you place your trust in. You can succeed but only after much introspection. Do you have any questions?"

"I guess you cannot predict if this woman whom I will meet is the one I am meant to spend the rest of my life with?"

Glancing down at the cards, I try to get a feeling to see if I can answer Carlo's question. But nothing appears in my mind. I feel blocked. In the short time I have been reading the tarot, this has never happened before. For some reason, the cards do not want to reveal the possible outcome.

"I'm sorry, Carlo, but the cards are not giving me any clues indicating if this woman will remain in your life for a short or a long time. It could be that the moment is not right for the cards to reveal this fate. If you'd like, I can give you another reading in a month or so and see if I can give you more clarification. I won't charge you since I wasn't able to answer this question for you."

"That won't be necessary. I'll pay you for your time and work. I am satisfied with the reading you gave me tonight. I did feel a lot of what you said made sense, and I must admit the question I had in mind was of a romantic nature."

I remember how normally a client tells me his or her question at the end of a reading, but I get the feeling Carlo does not want to share his question with me even though I told him earlier that he could phrase it more vaguely.

"I will walk you back to the tent. It seems that most of the gypsies have gone to bed. I was so engrossed in the reading that I didn't even notice the music had stopped." Carlo stands up and waits for me while I collect my cards.

"I hadn't noticed either. Gianni and his son Tonio are still up."

We walk back toward the tent. I stop a few feet away, not wanting to get too close to Gianni and Tonio, who are talking animatedly to one another, probably debating some political issue as they often do. I'm tired and don't feel like getting into a prolonged conversation with them.

"Thank you for walking me back, Carlo. I hope the reading proves useful for you, and I hope you will remember some of the warnings and advice the cards were giving you."

"Thank you for the reading. Oh, I almost forgot." Carlo pulls out of his pants a thick wad of liras. I'm surprised at how much money he is carrying. Without asking me how much I charge, he pulls out several liras and hands them to me.

"This is too—"

"I insist, Sarina. You earned it. You gave me a very thorough, detailed reading. Please, accept the money."

I hesitate. There is no doubt I can use all this money, but I also feel that I am already indebted to Carlo for rescuing me from Rinaldo. But I sense Carlo is a true gentleman, and my refusal of his generosity would offend him.

"*Grazie molto.*"

"*Buonanotte,* Sarina. I enjoyed very much spending time with you this evening. Perhaps I will come by again another night so I can hear your beautiful singing." Carlo takes my hand and places a light kiss on the back of it.

Merely nodding my head, I whisper back, "*Buonanotte,*" and

walk toward the back of the tent so that I can enter through the second entrance. It is late, and I don't want to enter the tent from the front since I would have to walk among the other gypsies' cots and would possibly wake them. My cot is located toward the back of the tent.

Suddenly I notice out of my peripheral vision that Gianni and Tonio have ceased talking and are looking toward Carlo and me. I'm mortified as I realize they must've witnessed Carlo's kissing my hand.

"*Buonanotte,* Gianni. Thank you for the wine," I hear Carlo say just as I am stepping inside the tent. I'm surprised he has not left yet. My instincts tell me in that moment he must've been staring at me the entire time I was walking away. A ripple of small waves courses through my belly.

Thankfully, Isabella is sound asleep. I'm sure she would have had a bunch of questions for me about the stranger with whom I spent so much time. She's taken to sleeping beside my cot instead of her parents'. I don't mind, for her presence comforts me. Kneeling beside her cot, I stroke back a few strands of hair that are clinging to her cheek. I lift her sheet and cover her shoulders.

Yawning, I take off my dress and step into the slip I go to bed in. I close my eyes, but sleep escapes me, for all I can think about is the way Carlo kissed my hand.

❧ 9 ❧

La Cantante

THE SINGER

July 29, 1969

A week has passed since I gave Carlo his reading. He hasn't come by again even though he'd told me he would love to hear me sing. I try convincing myself that I'm not disappointed, but I know I am. He's been in my thoughts since that fateful day we met. I call it fateful because it was sheer luck he was on the beach and was able to prevent Rinaldo from attacking me.

"*Sciocca.*" I am nothing more than a silly girl I whisper to myself as I take in the view of the Mediterranean Sea from the aerial tramway that is taking me back into town.

I'm silly for thinking that perhaps Carlo and I shared an attraction. He was probably just being polite by acting as if he were interested in hearing me sing a second time. But then why did he insist on holding my hand during the reading and later kissing it before we parted? Does he do this with all the young women he meets?

With some of the extra money Carlo gave me for his reading, I decided to buy my tram ticket. While I love the beach and spending most of my time there, I need a break—not just from the scenery but also from the gypsies. Though I love them, it's difficult to have a few moments to myself. Maria refuses to let me give readings alone any longer because of what happened with Rinaldo. And even when I'm walking along the shoreline while the gypsies are engaged in another activity, someone eventually calls out to me to join them. They've also asked me to sing every night. I don't mind that as much. Tonio has even been giving me lessons on his mandolin and lets me practice when he's not using it.

I was afraid when I told Maria this morning that I would be heading into town that she would say she was coming with me, but thankfully she didn't. She just asked me to be careful. I think she feels less worried about my giving readings alone in the piazza because it is so crowded. But I've decided not to work today. Part of me feels guilty that I will not be making any money, but I want some time to myself to relax and not have to predict my clients' destinies. But there is another reason for my going to the piazza. I want to see if by any chance one of the hotels or even the restaurants finally needs more maids or any other workers.

Although I have at least another month before Maria and her family leave Taormina and travel to the next town where they will set up camp, I want to begin looking for other work now. I'm beginning to prepare myself that the likelihood of staying in Taormina is quite low. But still, I must do my best to at least try and find other employment that would allow me to stay here.

As I walk along the Corso Umberto, I pass several fancy clothing shops. But I dare not loiter in front of them, for staring at merchandise I might not ever be able to afford will only make me too sad. The scent of fresh brioche reaches my nose, and I see I am approaching Angela's bread shop. I was planning on visiting her after I made my inquiries at the hotels and restaurants. Deciding to see my friend and buy a brioche, I step into the shop.

Angela is behind the counter, placing brioche that have just come out of the oven onto an ornate platter.

"Buongiorno, Angela."

"Sarina! *Che bella sorpresa!* What a nice surprise!" She comes around to the front of the counter and hugs me. "Why have you stayed away so long? I was beginning to think you had left Taormina and you had not even wished me good-bye."

"I know how much you like surprises so I thought if I waited this long to visit you, you would definitely be surprised!" I laugh.

"Tsk . . . tsk." Angela shakes her head. "*Basta!* Enough with the jokes! Is everything all right? I was worried about you."

"I'm fine, Angela. I've actually been busy working. That's why you haven't seen me, although I must admit this isn't my first time in town since you last saw me over a month ago. I'm sorry I didn't stop by the other times, but I was quite busy and needed to be able to catch the last tram to the beach before they suspended service for the night."

"You are staying by the beach? No wonder you are so tanned. You secured work at one of the hotels overlooking the beach?"

"No. I had no luck there either." I hesitate before continuing. I know what so many people think about gypsies, but I don't want to lie to Angela, either. She fed me when I was starving those first few days after I had arrived in Taormina.

"*Dio, mio!*" Angela makes the sign of the cross. "You didn't become one of those women, did you?" Angela's eyes open wide. I have no idea what she means at first, but then I realize what she's suggesting.

"No! Of course I did not become a *puttana!*"

"*Ah! Grazie, Dio!*" Angela clasps her hands and holds them up over her head, thanking God that I haven't resorted to becoming a prostitute. "I'm sorry, Sarina. But it seems like you are reluctant to tell me what you are doing for work, so naturally my mind rushed to that awful conclusion."

"It's all right. I met a family of gypsies, and they've been very kind to me. When they heard I had no success in finding work, they offered to teach me how to read tarot cards and work with them. I mostly do my readings on the beach. We make good money with all the tourists staying there and even the residents from town who go to the beach for the day. But sometimes I come up to the piazza and offer readings on the street."

"Sarina, listen to me. You must not trust *gli zingari!* Of course they were kind to you. They wanted to ensnare you and use you to help them make more money. When you least expect it, they will steal all of your savings. My mother used to say, '*Gli zingari non hanno le anime,'* and as such cannot feel guilt for conning and hurt-ing others."

"That is absurd, Angela! Where does it say that gypsies don't have souls? They are just trying to make a living like the rest of us. I know the horrible reputation that gypsies have. Yes, it is true that a few swindle people and have no remorse for doing so, but Maria and her family are different. Besides, gypsies aren't the only ones known for conning people."

"I hope for your sake, Sarina, you are right. Well, I am not going to spend our entire visit lecturing you. All I ask is that you be care-ful. Please promise me that." Angela places her hands on my arms, forcing me to look into her eyes.

"I will. Thank you for your concern, Angela. I will probably just be reading the tarot cards until the end of the summer. The gypsies plan on leaving Taormina then."

"That makes me feel better. But I would relax more if you left them before their last day in Taormina. I fear they will find a way to get the upper hand with you. Have they told you the exact date they plan on leaving?"

"No."

"Ah! They are clever. I might be wrong about them as you say, but I always believe it is better to err on the side of caution. See if you can get them to pinpoint the exact day they plan on leaving. That way you can disappear conveniently and be certain your money is safe with you."

Silently, I laugh to myself over Angela's paranoia. But I am also touched that she is looking out for me, much the way she would if she had a child. Angela and her husband were not able to conceive. By the tenderness she's shown me, I can tell she would have been an excellent mother.

"You are a very wise woman, Angela. You are right. It never hurts to be careful. I am always telling my clients that when I give them a reading."

"Maybe you can come back later and give me a reading? That is if you have the time and won't risk missing your tram back to the beach. Who knows? Maybe you'll see that I will come into an in-heritance from an unknown wealthy relative, and I can finally be the one relaxing by the beach and shopping at all the exclusive boutiques in Taormina!" Angela winks.

"You never know!" I laugh.

"I will pay you, of course."

"No, please. After all the food you've given me, I could not take money from you. Please think of it as my way of repaying your generosity. I didn't come in here just to visit you, Angela. The smell of your heavenly brioche made its way to my nose out on the street. I must buy one." I take some money out of my small leather satchel that I purchased from a street vendor shortly after I began reading fortunes.

"Put your money back into your purse!" Angela hurries away and steps behind the counter before I can protest. Picking up a brioche with a pair of tongs, she places it in a napkin before handing it to me.

"*Grazie.* But that really isn't necessary, Angela." I take a bite of the still-warm brioche and savor its subtle sweetness.

"You will be paying me with the reading. That's enough."

"So how is business?" I can't help noticing that the bread shop has not had one customer since I walked in. Usually, the mornings are the busiest time.

"It's been a bit slower lately. But it happens. I'm not worried. That is how it goes—up and down, much like life, right? At least the few hotels that buy from us are still being loyal and not going to a couple of the new bakeries that have surfaced in the piazza."

"I will tell my clients whom I give readings to in the piazza to come here if they are hungry or are looking for good bread."

"*Grazie,* Sarina. Is that what brings you to town today? You will be working?"

"No. I decided to take a break today. I want to try and see if any of the hotels have openings for work now or even at the end of summer. As I mentioned earlier, the gypsies will be leaving Taormina, most likely in August, so I'd like to find other work that would allow me to stay here."

"I thought you said you made pretty good money giving readings?"

"I do, but I'm afraid that once summer ends and most of the

tourists leave, I won't be making enough money to continue supporting myself."

"That is true. But I must warn you. It will be even harder for you to find work at the hotels or restaurants this late in the season or even for the fall. Many of them hire temporary workers for the busy summer season and then let them go once autumn approaches."

I hadn't even thought of that, but Angela is right. My spirits sink.

"If only you could sing! Ha! Villa Carlotta is looking for a singer to entertain their guests in the evenings. But that is the only available job I have heard of." Angela begins wiping her display counter with a wet towel.

"What did you say? A singer?" My heart stops beating for a moment.

"*Sì.* They used to have an opera singer. She was quite good. A man from the famous opera house in Milan, Teatro alla Scala, was vacationing at the Villa Carlotta and heard her sing. He offered her a job. Talk about luck! She moved to Milan two weeks ago, but Silvano still has not been able to find someone to replace her."

"Is Silvano the owner of the Villa Carlotta?"

"Yes. Silvano Conti. He's quite wealthy and is in the process of building another hotel, but this one will be in Enna. He's been away a lot, overseeing the construction of the new hotel. But he was here yesterday and told me he'd be staying put in Taormina for at least another week or two because of work that needs his attention at the Villa Carlotta. It's an exquisite hotel. I'm sure you must've noticed it when you were trying to find work. Did you ever inquire there?"

I shake my head no. "The name doesn't sound familiar. Perhaps I did go in it, but did not take notice of its name. I would've remembered it." I do not tell Angela that my little sister's name is Carlotta, and that's why I would've remembered the hotel. I also don't reveal to her that I sing for I'll feel like a fool if I don't get this job at the Villa Carlotta. I know it is a long shot. Surely, Signore Conti will want a seasoned singer. But I must try. It might be my only way of staying in Taormina.

"Where exactly is the Villa Carlotta?"

"It's on Via Pirandello, just a few minutes from the Corso Umberto. You can't miss it."

"Maybe I didn't inquire there for work when I first arrived in Taormina. I don't remember going onto Via Pirandello."

"You probably didn't. Like I said, it is an exquisite hotel. You would have most certainly remembered it."

Glancing at the clock that hangs on the wall by the shop's entrance, I say to Angela, "I should get going if I want to make my inquiries and have enough time to return and give you your reading before the last scheduled tram departure. Thank you for the brioche, Angela."

"*È niente.* It's nothing. I look forward to your reading." Angela smiles and waves to me as I leave the shop.

I walk as quickly as I can to Via Pirandello, but then I realize I'm just making myself sweaty, and I don't want to show up at the Villa Carlotta looking disheveled. Forcing myself to slow down, I pray fervently to God, asking him by some miracle to let me get the singing job. Perhaps the hotel's being called "Carlotta" like my sister is a good omen.

After what feels like an eternity to me, I finally reach the Via Pirandello. I walk down the street, but do not notice an elaborate hotel as Angela described the Villa Carlotta. Then again, many of the hotels in Taormina are gorgeous. I begin to make out a large brick building that has arched windows, giving it a Middle Eastern feel. Many of the buildings and even the churches in Sicily have Middle Eastern traits from when the Arabs occupied the island. I remember learning in school that many of the churches used to be mosques. That's why so many of the churches feature large rounded domes. Once I get closer, I can make out the words **Hotel Villa Carlotta** etched in black cursive at the center and top of the building. I remember a few of the other hotels in Taormina choose to use the English word for hotel instead of the Italian word *"albergo."*

My pulse is racing. For a moment, I contemplate walking away. Closing my eyes, I will my nerves to calm down. Taking a deep breath, I enter the hotel, and at last my breath is taken away. The interior of the hotel is beyond grand and much more impressive than its exterior. The walls are painted in warm shades of coral and orange. Beautiful, enormous vases stand in various corners and niches around the lobby. Windows surround the interior, giving majestic views of Taormina's natural beauty.

"*Buongiorno, signorina.*" A middle-aged man with a thick mustache, a deep olive complexion, and the most intense black eyes I've ever seen greets me.

"*Buongiorno, signore.*"

He looks at my hands, no doubt noting I don't have any luggage.

"May I help you?"

Swallowing hard, I'm tempted to say I walked into the wrong hotel and leave, but I know I must take my chance or else I will always be wondering. "Someone in town mentioned to me that the hotel is looking for a singer. Do you know if the owner is here today, and if so may I speak to him?"

The man sizes me up from head to toe before saying, "I am the owner of the Villa Carlotta. My name is Silvano Conti."

"*Mi dispiace.* I'm sorry. I did not know. My name is Sarina Amato."

"*Non preoccuparti.* Do not worry. You said someone in town told you I was looking for a singer?"

My spirits lift. So it is true. "*Si.* Angela, who owns the bread shop." I suddenly realize I don't know Angela's surname. "I'm sorry. I do not know her surname." My face blushes slightly.

"Everyone knows Angela and her famous bread! We carry her bread in our restaurant." Silvano laughs. Something about the way he laughs bothers me slightly.

"I am sorry to disturb you. But I would like to apply for the position. That is unless you have hired someone else already?"

"No, no. I have only had a handful of people come to me, and I wanted to run when each of them sang. I was about to give up the idea of even having a singer. So you sing? Where have you worked before? You look quite young if you do not mind my saying so."

"Yes, I sing. I have not sung for money before, but I have been told my voice is strong by those who have heard it." I silently pray he at least gives me a chance and lets me audition.

"*Sì, sì.* I suppose it would not hurt to hear you sing." He says this with what sounds like resignation in his voice.

He has probably heard the same from the other people who applied and believes I will be as atrocious as them. Anger begins to fill my veins, as my mother always liked to say—usually in reference to my father, of course. Signore Conti seems to have already made up his mind without knowing a thing about me. I will prove him wrong. My hesitation and fears from a moment ago vanish as I focus instead on singing the best I ever have.

"*Grazie, signore,*" I say, forcing my voice to sound sweet.

"Follow me. We'll go into the bar. Our previous singer usually sang on the dining patio outside while our guests had their dinners. But when it was raining or in the cooler months, she sang indoors."

"So you do not hire singers just for the summer months?"

"No. Our hotel has quite a reputation. While our rooms are not completely booked in the cooler months, we still get enough guests for me to be able to keep the nightly entertainment."

I'm pleased to hear this since if I am hired I won't be forced to look for other employment in the fall and winter.

"The singer who left us was quite talented. She was an opera singer. Though I was upset to lose her, I am also quite proud that one of my singers is now at the famous La Scala, the opera house in—"

"Milan. Yes, I have heard of it." I cannot hide the irritation in my voice this time. Again, Signore Conti is making judgments.

"Ah! Of course you have heard of it."

"Did she usually sing opera here?"

"Sometimes, but I asked her not to sing it often. I wanted a more relaxed environment. After all, the tourists are coming to Taormina for rest. While I am an opera enthusiast myself, there is a time and a place for it. However, I must say the few occasions she did sing opera the guests did not seem to mind and were also pleasantly surprised. Perhaps I should have let her sing it more often." Signore Conti shrugs his shoulders. "You don't sing opera, do you?" He has an amused expression.

"No, I do not."

"That is what I thought. Well, enough talk. You came here to sing after all. You can stand over here." Signore Conti gestures toward the open windows to the back of the bar. Now that we are no longer talking, I can take in the room that houses the bar, which is exquisite. What looks to be limestone rocks make up the wall behind the actual bar. A few arches are carved out of the limestone rocks, and elaborate silver sculptures sit in the open spaces. The windows are not as large in this room, creating a dimmer interior. I can imagine how it must look at night.

I walk over to where Signore Conti has gestured for me to stand. He goes behind the bar and takes a glass and a decanter of liquor. Pouring himself a drink, he comes back around the bar and takes a seat on one of the stools. A worker, no doubt the bartender, arrives and nods his head at Signore Conti as he begins lining up clean glasses on the counter behind the bar. He isn't wearing a bartender's uniform, but just as I think this, I notice he heads for a door to the back. He doesn't even glance my way. I look around the room and notice there is just a maid cleaning the small tables that surround the bar area. Relieved there aren't more people to witness my audition, I clear my throat a few times.

"Would you like some water before you begin, Sarina? Or perhaps something stronger to calm your nerves?" Signore Conti smiles derisively. My anger returns.

"No, I am fine. But thank you."

"*Va bene.* Whenever you are ready." He gestures toward me with his glass of liquor and then takes a huge gulp.

Instead of singing the folk-style songs that I normally love to sing, I decide to sing a popular song from the 1950s that was sung by Teddy Reno called "Piccolissima Serenata"—small serenade.

Closing my eyes, I begin to belt out the lyrics of the song. When I open my eyes, I try to avoid looking at Signore Conti, but I can tell from my peripheral vision he is giving me his full attention. The bartender has come out from the back and is now in his uniform. He leans his elbows on the bar, resting his chin in his hands as he watches me sing. Even the maid has stopped her cleaning and is tapping her foot along to the tempo of my singing. Seeing I have a rapt audience makes me bolder as I begin to swing my hips and snap my fingers. I am completely losing myself in the singing and don't care anymore what Signore Conti thinks of me. And for the moment, I don't even care if he gives me the job. All that matters right now is my love of singing and the joy I am feeling. I am truly happiest when I sing.

I finish the song, and everyone applauds—even Signore Conti! He stands up and says, *"Bravissima! Bravissima!"*

I merely nod my head and say, *"Grazie."*

"That was amazing. How long have you been singing?" the bartender asks me.

"Since I was a young girl."

"Forgive me. My name is Gaetano." He walks over, extending his hand.

"I think I liked your version of 'Piccolissima Serenata' better than Teddy Reno's!" the maid gushes like a teenage groupie. She walks over and also introduces herself. *"Mi chiamo Grazia."*

"Sarina." I point to myself. "It's nice to meet you, Grazia. What a beautiful name. I can see a song being made with your name." I smile warmly at her.

"Do you also write your own songs? Maybe you can write a song just for me!" Grazia giggles. Though she has to be in her late twenties, she still exhibits a schoolgirl's demeanor.

"Maybe!" I laugh.

"So you do write your own songs?" Signore Conti asks. He is looking at me differently than he was at the beginning of our meeting. I now see respect in his eyes.

"Yes. I usually like to sing my own songs, but of course I have favorites from popular musicians, too."

"I forgot to mention that I also have a piano player who accompanies the singer." Signore Conti gestures toward Gaetano.

"I thought you were the bartender?" I ask in surprise.

Gaetano laughs. "I am. But I need the extra money, so Signore Conti agreed to hire me as a pianist as well. It's helped greatly since we lost Anna, the singer we had."

"I take it you don't sing?"

"No. My voice is okay, but just that. Besides, I'm happier just playing the piano."

"Can you start tonight?" Signore Conti asks me.

"Sì. Grazie molto. I will not disappoint you or your guests."

"I'm sure you won't." Signore Conti laughs and pats my shoulder. He then turns to Gaetano and Grazia. "Can you please excuse us? I want to discuss some details in private with her."

Gaetano and Grazia walk out of the bar.

Signore Conti tells me how much he will be paying me. I try to hide my elation since it is much more than I had hoped for.

"That is generous. *Grazie, signore.*"

"Where do you live?"

My face immediately turns crimson as I cringe at the thought of having to tell him I live on the beach. I cannot think of a lie and decide to be honest.

"I am living on one of the beaches. I had a difficult time securing work when I arrived in Taormina last month. There is a group of gypsies on the beach. They were kind enough to let me stay with them in their tent." I do not meet Signore Conti's gaze.

"Gypsies do not act kindly toward others without getting something in return." Signore Conti lowers his face until his eyes meet mine.

"They offered to teach me how to read tarot cards. I split what I make with them. They pay for my food as well."

Signore Conti begins pacing back and forth, looking pensive as he smoothes down his mustache with the fingers of his right hand.

"How would you feel about reading fortunes here in addition to singing? I've never had a fortune-teller, and whenever I'm at the beaches, I see all the fools who flock for a reading. I will pay you an additional five liras a week. Also, you will need to be much closer since you will be working at night and the tram suspends service in the evenings. I can offer you room and board. Of course, it will be a room in the staff's quarters, but I'm sure it will be more comfortable than the gypsies' tents on the beach."

"Thank you. I was worried about where I would live since it would be hard for me to take the tram every day, not to mention the expense."

"*Va bene!* It is all decided then." He looks quite pleased with himself.

"Signore Conti, I'm sorry. I know I told you I could start right away, but I just realized that the gypsies I have been staying with will be worried if I don't return tonight. They have treated me well, and I don't want to give them cause for concern. Would it be possible for me to start work tomorrow instead? This would also give me a chance to get my belongings."

"You give these gypsies too much thought. If it were the other way around, trust me you would be far from their minds. But that is fine. I've been without a singer for weeks now. One more day won't break me. Actually, I almost forgot. I take it you do not have a larger wardrobe?" Signore Conti takes in my dress disapprovingly.

"It is quite hot on the beach so I have had to resort to wearing sundresses. I can buy more appropriate dresses for work after I make my first earnings."

Signore Conti reaches in his back trousers' pocket and takes out his wallet. He pulls out several liras and says, "I'll pay you for this week now so you can go buy a couple of dresses that would be suitable. Since you don't have to be at work until tomorrow evening, you have the rest of today and tomorrow to shop. Go to Gisella's. She is across the street from Angela's bread shop. Tell her you will be my new singer, and she will know what you should purchase."

"Grazie molto, signore!" I am absolutely beaming now. I cannot believe my good fortune.

"If you do not have any other questions, I must leave for a meeting now."

"No. I do not have any questions. Thank you again, Signore Conti. I will see you tomorrow evening."

"Yes. Please don't be late. Ah! I don't believe I told you when to arrive. Come by four p.m. You can rehearse for a bit in here before the bar opens."

I nod my head. *"Arrivederci, Signore Conti."*

"Arrivederci." Signore Conti looks at his watch and then hurries away.

I take my time leaving the Villa Carlotta. Reveling in its grandeur, I feel giddy at the thought that soon I will be spending most of my time in such a magnificent place.

Once outside, I walk quickly to Angela's. I cannot wait to tell her my good news. On my way to Angela's, I decide to visit the Church of San Nicola in the Piazza Duomo to say a quick prayer in thanks for getting the job at the Villa Carlotta. The medieval church is also known as the Duomo of Taormina. A gorgeous Baroque fountain with a centaur is situated in the center of the piazza. I remember learning in school that the centaur is the symbol of Taormina.

Once inside, I step into one of the pews and sit on the bench. After I thank God for all the blessings He has given me since I arrived in Taormina, my thoughts drift to my father. If only he could see me now.

❧ 10 ❧

Una Grande Sorpresa

A BIG SURPRISE

July 31, 1969

I am getting dressed in the small, but very pleasant, hotel room that Signore Conti has given me. Tonight will be my second working at the Villa Carlotta. While I was nervous performing in front of so many people last night, it went well. Everyone seemed to enjoy my performance, and I even had quite a few guests who were interested in having their cards read.

Signore Conti wasted no time in having posters printed announcing that I would be singing at the hotel. He also had flyers advertising my services as a fortune-teller. The posters were placed all around the piazza in Taormina and of course on the hotel's property. Earlier when I was rehearsing, Signore Conti came over and showed me the local newspaper, which also contained an advertisement he had placed about my fortune-telling. The ad included an illustration of a crystal globe with stars floating above it. The headline read, *La Zingara Sa Tutto. The Gypsy Knows All.* This bothered me since I've only been reading tarot for a short time, and I'm not God. I don't "know all." But of course I cannot say anything to Signore Conti. He is my boss now and is paying me generously.

It was tiring having to read fortunes while taking my singing breaks, but I'm not complaining. I know how fortunate I am to have found work and to be living out my dream as a singer—a dream I thought impossible only a couple of months ago when I was still living under my father's roof. I was sad to tell Maria and the other gypsies that I would no longer be working with them. Though she and Gianni seemed disappointed, they understood that I want to stay in Taormina. They made me promise to visit them a few times before they leave at the end of the summer.

Signore Conti asked Grazia to do my hair. In addition to working as a maid at the Villa Carlotta, she is also attending school to receive her beautician's license. A knock on my door brings me out of my thoughts.

"Come in!" I shout.

"Are you ready to have me do your hair?" Grazia walks over and kisses me on both cheeks. She is a very warm and kind person.

"*Sì.* Please do not style it elaborately. Simpler is better."

"Bah! I am the hairdresser, and as such, you need to trust my judgment. Besides, how can you know if you won't like an elaborate do if you've never had one? I assume you have never had a beautician style your hair?"

"No. I haven't. My family could never afford such a luxury. Not even my poor mama got her hair done. She would give me trims, and since I wear my hair long, that was enough. Of course, she braided my hair and put it up in buns, but that was about it. I know it's not so fashionable to have long hair still." I look longingly at Grazia's stylish short bob. She has lustrous light brown hair that is thick and straight. A beautiful white sash headband stands in perfect contrast to her dark locks.

"I can cut your hair short some time if you like, but I think you should keep your hair long. It works on you, especially when you sing. There is something very alluring about long hair and even more about gorgeous red hair like yours."

"Perhaps. I will give it more thought before I let you shear it all off!" I laugh.

Grazia takes the chair at my dresser and turns it away from the mirror.

"I won't be able to see," I protest.

"Exactly. I want to surprise you. So let me do my work."

I sit down and remain silent as Grazia tugs at my hair for what feels like forever, but only amounts to maybe twenty minutes.

"Finito!" Grazia announces. "Are you ready to see my masterpiece?" Grazia smiles. I can tell she's pleased with my hairstyle.

I stand up and turn around. "Ahh!" I gasp, placing my hand over my mouth. "Is this really me?"

Grazia laughs, *"Sì, bella!"*

"I look like that French actress. What is her name? Brigitte—"

"Bardot. Yes. That is who I was thinking of. But you are a redheaded version."

My hair is pulled up into a high bun or beehive. Grazia has inserted two yellow roses, which she took from the vase on my dresser, in the side of the bun. Though my hair is swept up, she has managed to loosen it so that it is not pulled back severely. She also coaxed waves and soft curls out of my hair.

"I am just missing the bangs that Brigitte Bardot has." I tilt my head from side to side, admiring Grazia's work. "You truly are talented, Grazia! Thank you!"

"My pleasure. If you want, I can cut some bangs the next time I do your hair. I am off tomorrow so I won't be able to style your hair. I'm sorry."

"That's okay. I don't need my hair styled every night. Yes, I think I would like the bangs."

"That way you will have a new look without dramatically changing your hair by cutting the length so much." Grazia looks at her watch. "It's almost time for you to go on." She kisses me again on both cheeks. "Good luck! I'm sure you will be as fantastic as you were last night!"

"If I don't see you later, have a good night."

"Ciao, Sarina!"

"Ciao!"

I stare at myself one last time. I truly am almost unrecognizable. The two dresses I bought are gowns. One is an emerald green that complements my auburn hair well, and the other an ivory hue. They are both fitted and long. I almost look like a film star. I felt a little uncomfortable at first when I wore the ivory dress last night. But as always when I sing, I am able to completely lose myself in the singing, and I even felt glamorous in the gown as I performed. I could not bring myself to wear the bolder emerald one last night. But Gisella from the boutique had insisted I buy it. I see how right she was now, especially with my hair styled and swept up. Taking a deep breath, I leave my room and make my way to the outdoor dining patio.

Tonight is more thrilling for me than last night. And the audience is larger. I sing a few popular songs and even a few of my own folk songs. Everyone seems to be enjoying my original songs as much as the songs by other musicians that I am covering. I decide to end the night with a song I wrote about my cousin Agata and her growing love for Giuseppe. My mind goes back to the night I witnessed them kissing behind Luigi Milazzo's house as the fireworks were erupting and I was making my escape. Tears fill my eyes as I think about my dear cousin and how I have abandoned her, too. Is she angry with me for leaving her? Fighting back tears, I finish singing the last lyrics of my song. The audience applauds thunderously.

"*Grazie mille! Mi chiamo Sarina. Spero che tutti voi avete goduto voi stessi.*" Thanking the audience, I express my hope that they enjoyed the performance.

"*Brava! Brava!*" they shout, continuing to applaud. I bow my head.

"Sarina, I think they love you more than they did Anna," Gaetano says as he stands up from the piano and takes his sheet music.

"Oh, I don't know about that, Gaetano. This is a new round of tourists, not the ones who heard Anna. It's not a fair comparison. But thank you for your kind words and your beautiful piano accompaniment." I smile.

"*Buonanotte.* I see you have a fan waiting to talk to you." Gaetano nods toward the bar.

I glance over and freeze. Carlo! I had all but given up hope I would see him again. He continues staring straight into my eyes. Slowly, a grin spreads on his face. He steps off the bar stool and makes his way toward me. I do my best to appear calm as if his presence has not completely rattled me.

"Ciao, Sarina. Che grande sorpresa!"

I cannot help thinking that I am the one who has had a big surprise. But I dare not say so.

"Sarina, I had no idea *you* were the amazing singer my father had hired."

"Your father? Signore Conti is your father?"

"Yes. I thought I had mentioned to you when we met on the beach that Rinaldo worked for my father."

"You did, but you never said what you or your father did. Actually, I don't know much about you, I'm afraid to say." I offer a shy smile.

"Well, we will be seeing much more of each other now that you are working here. So you will get to know me very well. And I hope I will get to know you better, too." Carlo looks at me intensely.

"Were you away? I haven't seen you."

"Yes. Perhaps you've heard. My father is building another hotel in Enna. We take turns going there to oversee the construction."

"I had heard. And what are your responsibilities at the Villa Carlotta? Do you manage the hotel?"

"Mostly. I also help out if one of our staff falls ill. Today, I was forced to deal with some plumbing problems."

"You even do that kind of work?" I ask incredulously.

"Yes, Sarina. Just because I am the owner's son, I do not place myself above the other workers, although my father wishes I would. But he and I are quite different."

"I'm sorry. I did not mean to offend you."

"You didn't. If you aren't too tired, would you like to stay and talk to me for a bit? We could even take a walk to the piazza."

"All right. But let me change my clothes. I feel too dressed up."

"No. You are perfect as you are. Truly stunning. Please don't change."

I don't know what to say to Carlo's request. Although I am pleased that he has noticed how beautiful I look tonight, I feel a bit silly going to the piazza like this. Although many of the tourists get dressed up in the evening, my gown still feels too formal. But I don't want to displease him. "*Va bene.* We can go for the walk now."

We make our way to the piazza.

"May I ask about your mother? I haven't heard your father mention her to me, and I would think I would have met her in these past two days."

Carlo purses his lips. His eyes look sad, and I immediately regret asking him about his mother.

"Her name was Carlotta. She died giving birth to me. I was named after her. My father changed the name of the hotel from Albergo Conti to Villa Carlotta after she died, in honor of her."

"I'm so sorry." I place my hand on Carlo's arm.

"Thank you. My father's mother raised me. Nonna Lucia and I are quite close. Remember I told you during my reading that she knows the zodiac well?"

"Yes, I do remember. Does she stay at the hotel? I haven't met her yet."

"She does, but she is getting quite up there in years. Lately, she's been spending most of her days in bed. Nonna has very bad arthritis, as well as a few heart problems."

"My little sister's name is Carlotta."

"It must be destiny then." Carlo's eyes twinkle.

"How so?"

"The irony of it all. The energy from my mother's and your sister's name brought us together." His eyes lock onto mine. I quickly glance away.

"You believe in the forces of fate? Most men do not believe in such nonsense."

"Surely, that's not true. Rinaldo said you had many male customers."

I blanch.

"I'm sorry. I did not mean what Rinaldo was implying. I know you are not a swindler or . . ." His voice trails off. Now he looks embarrassed.

"It's all right, Carlo. I am a fool. I did find it odd when I began giving readings that so many of my customers were men. But I was just so happy to be making money I didn't give it much thought. I know it is usually women who frequent fortune-tellers. I let myself believe the men in Taormina must just be superstitious."

"I've been guilty of seeing what I want to as well. We all make that mistake."

Carlo and I pass a bench beneath a large palm tree.

"Do you mind if we sit for a little while? My feet are beginning to hurt in my shoes."

"Ah!" Carlo hits his forehead. "I should have let you at least change your shoes so you would be more comfortable. Forgive me. Please, sit down." Carlo gestures for me to sit down and waits until I am seated before he sits next to me. He drapes his arm around the back of the bench. I can see out of my peripheral vision that he is staring at me.

"Sarina, I have never believed in wasting time so I am going to take my chance and be quite candid. I would like to spend more time with you. I like you a lot."

His honesty surprises me. Again, he's managed to leave me speechless.

"I'm sorry if I've embarrassed you. But I have been thinking about you since the day we met on the beach. I wanted to come see you the next day, but then my father dropped on me that there was an emergency at the new hotel's construction site and he needed me to go take care of the problem. He had another urgent matter to tend to here so he couldn't leave. You cannot imagine my shock and pleasure when I saw you tonight at the Villa Carlotta. Even though your hair is so much different from how you normally wear it, I instantly recognized you. I can't even describe the sense of happiness I felt when I saw you again and then to realize that you were the singer my father had hired. I had never even thought to ask him what her name was."

Carlo removes his arm from the back of the bench and takes hold of my hand before saying, "If you don't feel the same, Sarina, just tell me, and I swear I will never bother you again. We can be good friends and nothing more. But if you feel something, too, please tell me. I know I can give you whatever you desire and make you happy."

I swallow hard and remain silent as my shyness takes over. Carlo looks nervous. I've never been romantically involved with anyone. Though I have fantasized like many other young girls about some-day meeting someone who would treat me kindly, I didn't give it much serious thought, especially when I was living under my father's roof. As I'd told Agata that day we were in the country, I couldn't envision my father's ever granting anyone permission to marry me since then he would lose another slave in his household.

"Sarina?" Carlo lowers his head so that I'm forced to look into his eyes. And in that moment, my shyness disappears.

"I like you, too." My heart is pounding so hard against my chest.

"I knew there was something between us!" Carlo's face lights up.

"But Carlo, will your father approve? I am after all from a poor family, and now I'm practically a gypsy. It's one thing for him to hire me to work in his hotel, but to accept me as his son's girlfriend is an entirely different story."

Carlo's face grows somber, and I know I have touched upon the truth.

"I won't lie to you. My father does care about social status. He always has. That is how we're different. But he also has a good heart. I think in time he could accept the idea of our seeing each other. That is if everything works out. My intuition tells me it will." Carlo smiles mischievously.

"I don't know. I wouldn't feel right going behind your father's back. If he found out, he would fire me. I need this job, Carlo. Remember I am on my own."

Carlo takes my face in his hands. I think he is going to kiss me, but then he says, "You are *not* on your own. You have me now. I will never let any harm come to you. Do you understand?"

I still have my doubts, but with Carlo holding my face so near his, I feel I have no choice but to nod my head.

He takes one hand away from my face and begins stroking my cheek with the backs of his fingers. I feel weak. Carlo's eyes fill with longing. He leans over and kisses me softly on the lips. Then waits, making sure he has permission to continue. I lean into him, show-ing him I want to kiss him as much as he wants to kiss me.

The kiss is wonderful, leaving me feeling satisfied and immensely happy all at once. We continue kissing. I have no idea how much time has passed. I just know I am a little disappointed when Carlo finally pulls away.

"You've made me very happy, Sarina."

Carlo hugs me. I want to tell him he's probably made me happier than I've made him, but I decide to remain silent and just enjoy his embrace. Resting my head on his shoulder, I can't help but notice there's one star in the sky that seems brighter than all the others. Maybe Carlo is right about fate bringing us together. Maybe this is another sign that the universe is sending us, and we are meant to be together.

❦ 11 ❦

Isola Bella

August 5, 1969

The sweet scent of flowers fills the airs. I'm surrounded by bougainvilleas that stand out in splendid contrast to the indigo blue sea that stretches before me like a velvet carpet.

"*Siamo in paradiso,*" Carlo whispers to me, before planting little kisses down the side of my neck.

"*Si.* I can't believe how gorgeous Isola Bella is. Beautiful island—her name is truly fitting. I thought no place could compare to Taormina, but this is even more splendid."

"Well, Isola Bella is part of Taormina."

"I know, but you know what I mean." I playfully elbow Carlo in his ribs.

"I'm glad you like it."

"You have yet to disappoint me, Carlo!" I giggle.

And it's true. The past week has gone beyond any fantasy I could have imagined. Almost every day Carlo has taken me out. We've mainly gone to the different beaches of Taormina or strolled through the piazza, where he has taken me to fine restaurants and even insisted on buying me clothes, shoes, and purses from the boutiques along the Corso Umberto. I didn't want to accept such expensive gifts, but my protests fell on deaf ears.

We've been able to see so much of each other because Signore Conti has been tied up in Enna at the new hotel's construction site. Whenever I think about Signore Conti returning to Taormina, I feel both despair and dread. Despair, for I will not be able to see Carlo as freely, and dread that his father will discover our affair. But for now, I push all thoughts of Signore Conti out of my mind and focus on the wonderful man before me.

"Sarina, I will be right back." Carlo stands up and slips into his sandals. I can't help but admire his well-toned physique. Both of us are still in our swimsuits. It's too hot to wear anything over them since we are by the beach. When I ran away from home, I didn't bring my swimsuit, so Carlo insisted on buying one for me. I felt too shy to buy the bikinis that so many young women are now wearing, so instead I bought a one-piece suit in a beautiful coral shade.

"Where are you going?"

"Trust me." He smiles and blows a kiss to me with his hand as he hurries off.

I sit up and watch him, shielding my eyes from the sun with my hand. He is now walking along the sand and heading east. Soon, he is just a speck in the distance. Where could he be going that is so far? But he told me to trust him, and I will.

Standing up, I pull a few bougainvillea from their stems and inhale their sweet fragrance. Shielding my eyes from the sun with my hand, I look out toward the waves. There is something exhilarating about watching waves break against the shoreline. My mind soon drifts to thoughts of Carlo's kisses and his gentle caresses. I want to show him fully my love, but I am torn. I always imagined that if by some miracle my father did grant permission to anyone who asked to marry me, I would be a virgin until my wedding day. Yet I cannot see any wrong in being intimate with Carlo. How can expressing your love in every way possible be a sin? But my Catholic upbringing has taught me so.

A breeze whips up from the sea, blowing through my hair. Though it's hot, I decided not to pin my hair up since Carlo loves it down. I lie back on the sheet Carlo brought for us. Before I know it, I've fallen asleep. I don't know how much time has elapsed when I wake up.

Opening my eyes, I almost scream when I see a huge beast towering over me. It takes me a few moments to realize it's a horse. Thinking I'm dreaming, I stare at it incredulously a moment longer until I hear Carlo laughing. He comes up from behind the horse whose reins he's holding.

"Surprise!"

For a moment, I'm speechless. Then I say, "What are you doing? Whose horse is this?"

"I have a friend who owns a few horses on his secluded property. I asked him if we could borrow one of them today."

"And he let you?"

"Of course! We're friends. And when I told him I wanted to take a gorgeous woman horseback riding along the beach, there was no way he could refuse me."

"Why would you want to go horseback riding on the beach?"

Carlo laughs. "Because it is beautiful, especially when you are with someone as lovely as you."

I blush and suddenly realize that this must be something the rich do. No wonder I have never heard about it. In my world, horses are for utilitarian purposes—to carry a farmer's harvest, do work in the fields. I had read about the English riding their horses for pleasure, but I had never known of people to do it along the beach.

"Do people ride horses on the beaches a lot here in Taormina?"

"Mainly the tourists and a few of the rich people. Enough questions. It's time to ride."

Carlo folds up our sheet and places it in his satchel. He then hides his bag under one of the bougainvillea bushes.

I begin putting my sundress over my swimsuit, but he places his hand over my shoulder.

"Leave it. Just roll it up and place it with my bag under the bush."

I do as he says as a strange sensation slowly washes over me. For I will be sitting very close to him on the horse, and this is the closest we will have come to embracing with hardly any clothes on.

Carlo strokes the horse's mane and whispers to it. It is a beautiful black horse. I don't believe I've ever seen a horse with such a lustrous coat. Carlo can see the admiration in my eyes.

"He's magnificent, isn't he?"

"*Sì.*"

"He is a stallion and used to race. But he is retired now."

I laugh, covering my mouth with my hand.

"It's true. You think I am joking? My friend used to race him, but after an injury that put an end to his equestrian career, he retired and so did Notte."

"Notte? He has a name?"

"Yes. All race horses do. I'm sure you can see from his glossy black coat why my friend named him after the night. Anyway, race horses must have names or else how would people know which one to place their bets on?"

"*Vero.*" Nodding my head in agreement, I cannot help but feel stupid. Carlo must sense my embarrassment for he comes over and tucks my hair behind my ears before holding my face up toward his. He gives me a quick kiss.

"I love introducing you to experiences you've never had. Your pleasure upon discovering something new makes me happy. You know that is all I want? To make you happy?"

I smile. Carlo hugs me.

"Are you ready to mount Notte?"

"*Sì.* I must warn you. I am a bit frightened. He is so big, and I'm afraid he'll throw us off his saddle. So I will be holding on to you like my life depends on it."

"Even better! I don't mind." Carlo's eyes suddenly look sultry as his gaze wanders lazily down my body.

Bending over at the waist, he clasps his hands and turns his palms upward, instructing me to place my left foot in them. I do as he asks and with a quick thrust, he lifts me up. I grab the handles of the saddle and hoist myself higher before I drape my right leg around Notte's back. Notte stirs a little, causing my stomach to flutter as I take in how high off the ground I am. Once Carlo mounts the stallion, I feel more secure.

"Don't worry. We'll take it slowly. I want you to enjoy yourself.

You can go ahead and wrap your arms around my waist now. You might want to sit closer to me so you'll feel more secure and won't have to lean as far forward to hold onto me."

I take Carlo's suggestion although my heart starts racing at the very close, intimate contact. Carlo leads Notte toward the shoreline. I cringe for a moment when the stallion's hooves sink lower into the sand.

"Is it all right for him to traipse through sand?"

"*Si. Non preoccuparti.* No need to worry. It is actually very good exercise for a horse to traverse through sand. It works out their muscles more."

"You seem to know a lot about horses."

"We had a couple of horses when I was a child. But my father eventually sold them."

"Why?"

"Money. It is always about money where my father is concerned. He wanted the money he could get from the sale of the horses, not that we needed it. But he used the money to reinvest it into the hotel. He expanded Villa Carlotta, made renovations."

I cannot help but detect a hint of bitterness in Carlo's tone.

"You were upset that he got rid of the horses. Weren't you?"

"Yes. I grew up with those horses, and I loved them. But that's life, right? We don't always get what we want—even us rich boys."

Notte reaches the wet, firm sand along the shoreline. The ride feels smoother now. I finally feel myself relaxing. The sun is beginning to make its descent. Carlo points it out to me.

"We'll be able to catch the sunset while on horseback."

"You planned it that way, didn't you?"

"Of course. I think of everything, Sarina."

Every time Carlo says my name, pleasure washes over me. I don't know why. It's just something about the way he says it. He is not only kind and tender, but also very romantic. This can't be real. I cannot be here living this life—sitting on this horse, taking in this magnificent panorama, singing to adoring crowds every night. When I longed for a new life while under my father's thumb, I only hoped to be able to find work to support me and to be free of his abuse. Tears fill my eyes. God has truly looked out for me. But as always, the moment I feel joy, guilt begins to seep in. Guilt that my days are no longer filled with backbreaking household chores and the fear of my Papá's beatings. My family still endures their miserable existence, while here I am living the life of a wealthy tourist. I promise, though. I will make it up to my mother and siblings one day.

Carlo switches the reins into his right hand, leaving his left hand free. He places it on my thigh. His touch causes my pulse to beat wildly.

"Are you enjoying the ride, Sarina?"

"*Si, molto. Grazie, Carlo.* This past week has been wonderful." And to further show him my appreciation. I rest my head on his shoulder and tighten my grip around his waist. He squeezes my thigh in return.

From that moment on, we ride in silence, absorbed in the sunset and the beautiful colors that are being cast over the shimmering waters.

"Let's rest here for a bit." Carlo pulls back on the reins, signaling to Notte to stop. Carlo helps me dismount.

"You're a sweet horse. Thank you for not bolting off while I was on your back." I stroke Notte's mane as I talk softly to him. He tilts his head to the side and perks up his ears to my words.

Carlo laughs. "Maybe we'll take him out again another day, and I will let him gallop. It's quite a whole other experience." Carlo's eyes twinkle.

"You would not dare do that to me!" I say crossly.

"I really think you would enjoy it, Sarina. Have I led you astray so far?"

I shake my head.

"And I won't ever. Come. Let's sit on the sand and watch the sun sink behind the horizon." He sits cross-legged on the sand and reaches for my hand, pulling me down onto his lap. Placing his arms around my waist, he rests his chin on my shoulder. I wrap my arms around his. I can feel his heart beating against my back. The sun finally disappears into the water, leaving behind a coppery, orange hue similar to that of the golden peaches on the trees behind the Villa Carlotta. I turn my head and look at Carlo. He knows I want him to kiss me. I still cannot bring myself to be the initiator and kiss him first. It feels unladylike, but lately I have entertained the idea and know I will catch him off guard someday and kiss him first. But I haven't worked up the courage yet.

Carlo kisses me softly. I drape my arms over his shoulders and stroke the back of his neck. He goes crazy as a soft moan escapes his lips. Pulling me closer to him, he kisses me with abandon. His thumbs swirl around my back. A small shiver tingles throughout my body. Suddenly, Carlo pulls away and lifts me off his lap, placing me gently on the sand.

"Is something wrong?" I ask.

Carlo shakes his head. He is out of breath. "We need to slow down. That is all."

"But why? I was enjoying myself."

Carlo looks at me, and the lust I saw a moment earlier while he was kissing me is back, but he looks away. "We have to be careful, Sarina. And I don't want to take advantage of you. This isn't merely a fling for me. I care about you. The time needs to be right. Do you understand what I am saying?"

"I do. But weren't you the one who told me that you don't believe in wasting time? If we both feel the same way, what is the harm in being more intimate? I want to show you how much you mean to me."

Carlo looks pensive for a moment before saying, "You really care about me, Sarina. I am not just imagining it, then?"

I edge closer to his side and get up on my knees. "I can assure you, Carlo, you are not imagining it." I lean in and kiss him. We kiss for a while, but this time Carlo contains himself. His hands do not wander down my body even though I wish they would. But I know he is treating me like a lady. I must be patient for when the time is right.

Carlo stops kissing me. Sighing deeply, he says, "We should get Notte back before my friend thinks I've made off with him. I could remain here with you the whole night."

"*Dio mio!* My God! What time is it? I'm supposed to be singing tonight. I cannot believe I forgot." I stand up in a panic.

"Relax! I asked Gaetano if he could cover for you tonight."

"But he does not sing. He just plays the piano."

"People like listening to the piano by itself, too, Sarina." Carlo laughs. "What do you think we did when we lost our last singer?"

I nod my head, feeling foolish. "I just do not want anyone to think I am abandoning my duties. I take my work very seriously."

"Yes, and you have been working hard between your singing and all those tarot readings. You deserve a break."

"I have Sundays and Mondays off. That is generous. What did you tell Gaetano? He doesn't know—"

"It is all right. He does not suspect about us. I told him you had an urgent matter to tend to. That's not a lie. I urgently needed to spend all this time with you today." Carlo flashes a devilish grin.

I cannot resist hugging him. "You're too much. But what if Gaetano or one of the other hotel staff sees us coming back?"

"I will let you enter the hotel first. I'll wait a few minutes. Even if any of them suspect, they wouldn't tell my father. If you haven't noticed, he doesn't treat them as kindly as I do. Respect goes a long way."

I nod my head. Carlo seems to be a bit too trusting. Perhaps because he has never had to fend for himself the way I have.

"Let's go, my Circe." Carlo holds my hand as he leads me to Notte.

"Circe? Is that your new name for me?"

"Absolutely. For like the famous sorceress from Greek mythology, you have enchanted me with your singing, your beauty, and that kiss you gave me earlier." Carlo touches his lips to the back of my hand before helping me up onto the horse.

We ride all the way to Carlo's friend's house. I am no longer anxious riding so close to him. I plant little kisses on his neck from time to time. A full moon lights our path tonight. Every so often a haze of clouds floats over the moon. I will never forget this magical day and night we shared on Isola Bella.

∞ 12 ∞

Un Amore Magico

A MAGICAL LOVE

August 14, 1969

Carlo leads me deeper into the sea at Giardini-Naxos. The lucid waters allow me to see straight down to my feet. Giardini-Naxos is a popular seaside resort, but it is also famous for being near what was the first Greek colony in Sicily. We stop wading just before the water gets deep. Carlo draws me to him and holds me.

"Each day I'm with you, Sarina, you only grow more beautiful." Carlo strokes my back. Then pulls away and looks into my eyes. He pushes my wet strands of hair behind my shoulders before lowering his head and kissing me.

I close my eyes and let myself be enveloped by his kiss as I feel my body melt into the sun's warmth. Carlo seems to know just when my breaking point is. For he always manages to stop kissing me right before I lose all control—or is he the one who's afraid of surrendering completely?

Sighing deeply, I swim away from Carlo, deciding to play a little game with him.

"Where are you going?"

"What does it look like? I'm taking a swim!" I shout back.

"Wait for me!" Carlo swims after me. Having lived by the beach my whole life, I'm quite a strong swimmer, as is Carlo. I slow down, letting him catch up to me. But then without warning, I dive underwater, swimming a few feet before I come back up. Carlo is treading water, looking at me with an amused smile.

"You're going to tire yourself, Sarina."

"No, I'm not." I flip over onto my back and continue swimming away from him. Of course, I've just proven to Carlo that I am getting tired since it takes less energy to swim on one's back. But I don't care as long as I manage to elude him a bit longer.

Carlo swims after me once again. It is hard for me to see how close he is since I am on my back. I decide to stop for a moment and tread water so I can see how far he is. But as soon as I do so, I feel my foot being tugged. Suddenly, I'm underwater. Carlo has his hands around my waist. He then swims upward, taking me back to the surface.

He's laughing. But I am absolutely fuming. Giving him a hard shove, I make my way back toward the shore.

"Sarina, wait! I was just having a little fun with you as you were having with me. Don't be mad!"

All the swimming I've done is catching up to me, and I finally feel short of breath. I keep pushing on until I'm back where our feet were touching the bottom of the sea. I stop, but remain turned away from Carlo. He reaches my side.

"You scared me, Carlo!" I give him my most angry stare.

"Do you really think I would have let any harm come to you? I brought you back up in an instant. But you're right. I shouldn't have startled you that way. Please, let's not waste any time being angry with each other." Carlo takes my hands and kisses each one of them. This is the first time I've been angry with him, and I'm having a difficult time staying mad.

"Don't ever do that to me again!"

"I won't. I promise. Let's float on our backs and relax. I don't know about you, but I'm exhausted after all that swimming." Carlo leans back, splashing me with water as he kicks up his feet and floats.

I stare at him. He is perfect. From his bronzed physique to the way his hair waves softly, he could have been one of the gods whom the early Greek settlers on Sicily worshipped. But it's not just his looks that are perfection. His tender, kind personality belies his privileged upbringing. Every day at the hotel, I see how kindly he treats the staff.

Keeping his eyes closed, Carlo says, "How long are you going to ogle me? Or are you contemplating drowning me after I gave you such a scare?"

I float onto my back and take hold of his hand. We both remain silent as we enjoy the cool water against our skin.

A few hours later as the sun begins to set, we're driving along the winding road that leads to the medieval town of Castelmola. This is my day off from work, so we don't have to worry about rushing back to the hotel in time. Carlo and I have been waking up early so that we can spend most of the morning and afternoon hours together before I work in the evenings. Every day for the past couple of weeks he's taken me to a different attraction in and around Taormina. Signore Conti has been gone longer than we expected. Fortunately, he hasn't sent for Carlo. I know we won't be able to spend as much time together once Signore Conti returns. But I decide to forget about Signore Conti and let myself fully enjoy these days while I have Carlo all to myself.

"Wait until you see the panorama from Castelmola. It will take your breath away." Carlo steals a quick sideways glance toward me before he returns his attention to the twisting turns in the road.

"Carlo, you don't have to impress me with a new site every time we see each other. I would be content just enjoying your company."

"I know. But it makes me happy to show you these places. Your eyes sparkle when you've discovered something new. I love seeing you this way."

"You're too good to me. I still wonder sometimes if this is all real."

"It is. And it will only get better. I promise you."

Carlo parks the car, and we get out. I can make out the ruins of the medieval castle that once stood in this idyllic mountain village. Fragments of ancient ruins are strewn about the grounds. And Carlo was right about the views. The sea surrounds us from atop this hill, and as the sky gets darker, the lights begin to flicker on all around Castelmola.

"Let's go to one of the cafés. We can still enjoy the view from there."

We sit down at one of the small tables outside a café that has a few other patrons. Many of the tourists are snapping away at the panorama with their cameras.

"Grappa, per favore." Carlo orders his favorite liquor.

"E per voi, signorina?" The waitress asks me what I would like to order.

"Un bicchiere di vino della casa." I ask for the house wine.

"We should get something to eat, too. We haven't eaten since before we went swimming."

We both order panini with prosciutto and *Provoletta* cheese. Then for dessert we have *Tetu,* which are clove-scented chocolate cookies. I love them so much that Carlo insists on buying more for me to take back home.

By the time we're done eating, night has fully taken over. Castelmola is aglow. Carlo has moved his chair next to mine. He wraps his arm around my shoulders as we continue taking in the serenity of the landscape.

"Stay with me tonight," Carlo whispers in my ear.

My heart races.

"Nothing has to happen. I just want to hold you in my arms for the night and watch the sun rise with you on the beach in the morning."

I cannot stop the smile that is slowly spreading across my face. I want to tell Carlo that I am ready to fully show my love to him. But how can I when neither of us has uttered the words "I love you" yet? Maybe tonight will be the night that I tell Carlo I am falling in love with him.

"I can think of nowhere else I would rather be than in your arms tonight, Carlo." I hold his gaze. Without saying a word, Carlo stands and takes me by the hand. We make our way back to Carlo's car, descending through the sleepy hilltop town of Castelmola. The darkness that blankets us feels comforting.

After a short drive, we get out of the car and head over to the beach. Hand in hand, we stumble in the dark through the sand.

The moon is hidden behind a thick covering of clouds tonight. I'm not even sure which beach we are at, but it doesn't matter. All that matters is that I am with Carlo. As usual, he's come prepared for our outing and pulls a sheet out of his car trunk. I help him spread the sheet out onto the sand, close to where the waves break against the shore.

We lie down, and for a few minutes we just listen to the soothing sounds of the surf. Carlo turns his head toward me and kisses me, but nothing more. I feel myself drifting off to sleep, but I try to fight it off. It's no use. In Carlo's arms, my body completely melts. Just as I am falling asleep, Carlo whispers, *"Ti amo, Sarina. Ti amo molto."*

My eyes flash open. I am fully awake now.

"Amo anche te." I tell Carlo I also love him. Moving closer, I rest my head against his chest. *"Mi hai dato un amore magico."*

He holds me tightly. "No. It's you, Sarina, who has given me a magical love."

13

La Marionetta

THE PUPPET

August 15, 1969

After we spent the night on the beach, Carlo woke me up in time to watch the sun rise. We have now arrived at Villa Carlotta. It is about seven in the morning. We do our best to walk quietly among the pebbles strewn along the ground in the back of the Villa Carlotta.

"Get some rest. I have some work I need to take care of, but we can go to the piazza around noon if you'd like." Carlo kisses me on the forehead.

"You should try to get some rest too. I will see you later." I turn around to leave, but freeze in my tracks. Signore Conti is standing a few feet away, smoking a cigarette as he makes his way toward us. I'm too frightened to say anything.

"Papà, you're back." Carlo's voice sounds faint.

"Where have you been, Carlo? I returned yesterday morning. No one knew where you were."

"I took the day off."

"How convenient, and on the day Sarina is off." Signore Conti looks at me. Fury is in his red-rimmed eyes. What must he think of me now, seeing me return with Carlo so early in the morning?

"If you will both excuse me." I nod my head in Signore Conti's direction and walk as quickly as possible to the back entrance of the hotel that leads to my room. Thankfully, Signore Conti doesn't demand I stay. I can hear heated whispers between him and Carlo.

Once in my room, I climb into bed, not bothering to take my sundress off. There is no way I can rest now. I'm afraid for Carlo. Because of me, he is now in trouble with his father. Though Signore Conti spared me, I know it was just a brief reprieve. I have no doubt he will confront me when he is ready to do so. He was more concerned with his son at the moment. Will he fire me? Where will I go? The gypsies left a few days ago. I went down to the beach looking for them, but all of their tents were gone. The man who rents umbrellas told me they had left the previous day. I was surprised since I thought they would stay until the end of August, especially since today is the national holiday of Ferragosto, and Taormina will be swarming with even more visitors and tourists. All the umbrella man could tell me was that they left in a hurry. He was convinced they had conned someone who didn't take lightly to being swindled and that they were forced to leave town as quickly as possible. I don't believe that they conned anyone. I never witnessed any of the gypsies intentionally swindle their clients. Still, it was odd that they left in such haste. When I discovered that Maria and her family had left, I felt alone. Although I have Carlo, I had come to think of the gypsies as my second family. Maria and Gianni had become surrogate parents to me. And of course, Isabella was like a little sister. Even her brother Tonio had struck up a friendship with me, and I felt like he was watching out for me as well. And whenever I was feeling sad and missing home, the gypsies' contagious happy nature had always managed to lift my spirits. It had felt nice belonging to their tight-knit clan. If only I could have said good-bye to them.

I sigh deeply. It's no use. I can't rest. Getting out of bed, I pace my room until I hear a knock at my door. My stomach twists in knots. It has to be Signore Conti. I open the door.

"Carlo! What are you doing here? If your father catches you," I whisper to him, glancing nervously down the hall.

"Don't worry about him. I told him I couldn't sleep and went out for a walk along the beach and just happened to run into you on the way back."

"And you think he believed you? Come on, Carlo!"

"He did tell me he wasn't stupid, but I refused to cower before him. Let him believe what he wants."

"This isn't good, Carlo. He will probably fire me now."

"There is no way you are going anywhere. He is making so much money with all the people who are coming to the restaurant to hear you sing. Before it was mostly the guests at the hotel dining at our restaurant, but word has gotten around Taormina of your beautiful voice, not to mention your gifted tarot card readings, so we have more locals visiting us too. We've never had the crowds we now have at the restaurant. My father loves money above all. He would be a fool to fire you."

"Carlo, I think we need to consider that our seeing each other won't work. It's obvious your father doesn't approve by how angry he appeared earlier."

"Shhh!" Carlo places his index finger on my lips. "Trust me. I told you he will come around. We just need to be patient."

"But—"

"Stop worrying, Sarina. Now get some rest or else you'll be exhausted for work tonight."

I nod my head. "You should go before he sees you."

I begin to close my door, but Carlo stops me. He gives me a quick kiss on the lips and then leaves.

After shutting my door, I lean my back against it and take a deep breath. I want to trust that Carlo will be able to sway his father and convince him to accept us as a couple. But I cannot see how Signore Conti would ever accept me. I can tell that in his eyes I am nothing more than the hired help and a gypsy. Signore Conti has never even asked me about my background or my family. He doesn't care. While he has yet to utter a cross word to me, a few of the other employees have told me how he berates them on a regular basis. I keep wondering when it will be my turn to receive his scorn. And now that he suspects Carlo is romantically involved with me, it will just be a matter of time. I am certain of it.

After siesta, Gaetano and I are rehearsing for the night's performance when Signore Conti comes into the bar. I try to act absorbed in my singing and not let my voice betray my nervousness.

"Excuse me, Gaetano, Sarina."

"Buonasera, Signore Conti." Gaetano greets Carlo's father. I merely nod my head, forcing a small smile to my lips. But I dare not meet his gaze.

"I am sorry to interrupt, but Sarina, I would like you to begin wearing this costume for your performances." Signore Conti holds a bundle wrapped in tissue paper out to me.

A gift? He all but knows his son and I were coming back from a secret rendezvous, and he has a gift for me?

"Grazie, signore." I pull apart the folds of tissue paper and take out a traditional Sicilian folk costume in stunning hues of red, brown, and gold. The costume is gorgeous. I remember seeing photographs of my grandmother when she was younger. She wore a costume that looked very similar to this one.

"A few of the guests have been filling me in and have told me of your love of folk songs. I thought the costume would be perfect, not to mention the tourists love anything in relation to Sicilian culture."

"You want her to dress up like a puppet!" Carlo's voice booms behind Signore Conti. His eyes are roiling with venom. *"Lei non è una marionetta!"*

"Don't be silly, Carlo. I know she is not a marionette. Do you see strings attached to the back of this costume? Look at what an elaborate costume this is. Such intricate stitching and embroidery! She will look like one of the gypsies in town who wear Sicilian costumes. It's perfect since she reads tarot cards. People appreciate the authentic experience."

"I know what you are doing, Papá. I will not have it." Carlo storms over to me and tries to take the costume out of my hands, but I won't let it go.

"Carlo, it's all right. I do not mind wearing the costume. Your father is right. It is quite beautiful." I try pleading with Carlo through my eyes, but to no avail.

"We don't need to parade Sarina to attract the tourists. She is already bringing in a large audience. People come to hear her sing and *not* because she is wearing a costume that heralds to the peasant days of Sicily. I know you don't want to disobey my father, Sarina, but you do not need to wear this costume."

"Carlo, you are forgetting your place. I am the owner of Villa Carlotta, and, until I am dead, you and my staff will take orders from me. And people are not just coming to hear Sarina sing. They are also coming to hear their fortunes told. While the gowns I asked her to purchase are lovely, she does not look quite right in such glamorous dresses when she is reading the tarot cards. I did not think of it when I asked you to buy those gowns, Sarina. And like I said, this costume is especially perfect for when she sings her folk songs."

"I will wear the costume, Signore Conti. Thank you. I will go try it on now." I walk to my room before Carlo can try taking the costume from me once again. I hear something smash. Looking over my shoulder, I see a decanter of liquor in pieces by Signore Conti's feet.

"This is not over, Papá!" Carlo screams at his father before storming out.

"He's been under added stress with his responsibilities here as well as overseeing the construction of the new hotel in Enna. His mood will pass in no time." Signore Conti gives a slight snicker as he says this to Gaetano, who is cleaning up the mess Carlo made.

I turn around and continue to my room. Once inside, I sob uncontrollably. Signore Conti was making a point by buying me this costume and insisting I wear it. He was showing Carlo and me that he rules here, and he was reminding us that I am not on their level.

Wiping my tears away, I put on the costume. I did mean it when I said it was beautiful. But I cannot help feeling ridiculous wearing it now that I know Carlo thinks I will look like *una marionetta*. Well, he did not exactly say that. He felt more that his father was using me as his instrument, as his puppet to lure tourists and guests to the hotel. But I cannot help feeling that Carlo was also trying to pull my strings in insisting that I not wear the costume rather than letting me handle the situation with his father on my own.

These past few weeks have been a fairy tale. But fairy tales are not real. Carlo and I have been living in a dream. I don't know what I was thinking allowing myself to fall in love with a rich man's son.

✎ 14 ✎

Furia dell' Etna

ETNA'S FURY

August 20, 1969

Mount Etna has been erupting for the past five days. The tourists cannot believe their good fortune at being in Taormina right when the volcano is erupting and can talk of little else. I, on the other hand, feel it is a bad omen of sorts. Ever since I have begun reading the tarot, I am becoming more superstitious and relying increasingly on my intuition. I also cannot help but notice the irony, for it isn't just Mount Etna who has been exhibiting her fury. Ever since the night Signore Conti asked me to wear the Sicilian folk costume and I agreed, Carlo has been furious. He and his father barely speak to each other when they are in the same room. And even when Signore Conti isn't looking, Carlo has not given me his encouraging smiles. He must be upset with me for wearing the costume. But he knows I need this job.

Signore Conti stated this morning that he would not need to go to Enna until the end of September. The construction plans on the new hotel finally seem to be going smoothly. He made this announcement to the hotel staff in the morning when he called an impromptu meeting. He also said he was calling the meeting to remind staff of his rules, one of which was that there could not be any fraternizing among the hotel workers. When he said this, he looked directly at me, and then he let his eyes travel over to Carlo before returning his gaze to me. I swallowed hard and lowered my head.

After I eat my midday meal, I notice Signore Conti drive off in his car. Ever since he's returned from Enna, he rarely leaves the hotel. And when Carlo and I are in the same room, Signore Conti makes certain not to leave us alone.

I need some fresh air and decide to go out into the hotel's courtyard. Walking around, I admire the beautiful flowers and plants that have been planted with such care. My thoughts wander to my father's land in the country. I miss picking my herbs and preparing my homemade remedies. If Signore Conti were to discover that I also have a passion for herbal remedies, he'd think I was a witch in addition to being a gypsy.

"Sarina, I was looking for you." Carlo walks over to me.

"Your father left a little while ago, but he might be back any minute."

"I know. He is driving to Messina to pick up a few hotel supplies he can't find here in Taormina. He won't be back anytime soon. Don't worry."

"Carlo, I'm sorry that you're upset with me for going along with your father's plan of wearing the costume, but you have to understand I cannot lose this job."

"You think I am upset with you?"

"You've barely looked at me, Carlo, since that night."

"That's because *he* is constantly around. I can't take this anymore. At night, I can't sleep. I miss holding you in my arms and spending our mornings and afternoons together."

"We need to be patient. And now is not the right time for you to talk to your father about me."

"I don't know, Sarina. I'm beginning to think you might be right. I was foolish to think that I could reason with that stubborn mule. After what happened with the costume and his making a point to remind me that he is in charge here, I've been thinking it's time I forge my own way. All my life, I was brought up to believe that the hotel would be my future. I never questioned it. While I do love working here, I cannot continue doing so when my father allows me little input as to the management operations. I am a grown man now. But he forgets that fact."

"What would you do?"

"Someday, I would like to start my own hotel. I'm still waiting for all of the money that my father promised I would receive when I turned eighteen. It's been four years now, but he keeps making excuses as to why I can't have my inheritance yet. Even though I'm twenty-two years old, my father treats me at times like I'm twelve. I've been thinking maybe I can get a job managing one of the hotels on the Aeolian Islands."

"I see." My voice is barely audible. This is what he has come to tell me. He is leaving. Reason has finally sunken in, and he knows we can't be together.

"In fact, I placed a few calls yesterday. I'm friends with a hotel owner on the island of Lipari, and he needs a manager. If I take the job, I can start as soon as I want."

I muster up the courage to say, "That's wonderful. I'm happy for you, Carlo. Has your father given you his blessing?"

"He doesn't know yet, and I don't think I will tell him until I'm in Lipari. It will come to blows between us if I get into another argument with him. And surely the news of my abandoning him to help another hotel owner get rich will just infuriate him even more."

I glance at my watch. "I'm sorry, Carlo, but I need to go rehearse with Gaetano. I'm sure I will see you before you leave." I walk by him, but he grabs my arm.

"Sarina, you haven't let me finish. I want you to come with me."

Tears fill my eyes. He still wants me. He wasn't planning on abandoning me.

"You do?"

"Of course. Has all good sense left your head? First you think I was upset with you over that stupid costume, and now you think I was going to start my new life without you?" Carlo's eyes are wide-open, and a hint of a smile dances along his lips.

"Carlo, I don't know. What would I do there? It was so hard for me finding this job at your father's hotel, and I'm so blessed to be singing. Never in my wildest fantasies did I think I would be making money to sing. I'm not sure if I can give this all up."

"But you can give me up?" Carlo's voice sounds pained.

"I don't want to give you up, but I don't see how this will work out."

"Sarina, you forget that you have me. I will provide for you. You do not need to work."

"I know it is common for husbands to provide for their wives, but we're not married. Besides, I have come to love being able to provide for myself and not depend on anyone. In my father's home, I was dependent on him. Now I finally have my freedom."

"And you would still have your freedom with me, Sarina. And who's to say you couldn't find work as a singer at a hotel in Lipari? You are talented. And you also have your tarot cards. But again, you could live like a queen and never work if you wanted to. You could be *my* queen." Carlo takes my hand and holds it to his heart.

I'm torn. I want nothing more than to be with Carlo. It is impossible for me to imagine living without him. And in that instant, I know what my decision will be.

"Are you sure about all of this?"

"*Cento per cento!*" Carlo laughs and picks me up, spinning me around.

"You haven't even heard my answer yet!" I giggle.

"I can see it in your face. It's yes!"

Carlo kisses me, then says, "We'll leave in the middle of the night. I will come get you around four in the morning. We'll have to wait at the dock until the ferries begin operating in the morning, but we have to leave that early if we hope to elude my father. You've made me so happy, Sarina. And wait until you see Lipari! I will also take you to the other Aeolian Islands in our spare time. You will not regret this. I promise!"

Carlo hugs me. Though I am happy we will be together, free of his father's watchful glare, I'm also scared. But right now my heart is fully in control, and I can't leave the man I love.

It's five o'clock in the evening. In eleven hours, Carlo and I will be leaving Villa Carlotta for our new life in Lipari. I cannot believe in just the span of two months, I will be running away once again. While I can see Carlo's rationale for waiting to tell his father that he's moving to Lipari, I can't help also feeling it's a mistake.

I'm seated at one of the tables in the restaurant, looking over my song list for tonight's performance—my final one at the Villa Carlotta. Though I am happy that I will be with Carlo, I'm also sad that I will no longer be singing at the hotel. Contrary to what Carlo thinks, I hold little hope that I'll be able to secure work as a singer in Lipari.

Men's voices reach my ears. I look over to the French doors that lead out into the courtyard. I see the back of Signore Conti. He's waving his hands in an animated fashion as he talks to someone else. I can't see who he's speaking to, but soon I hear another man's voice. There is something familiar about the voice.

I begin warming up my voice. Gaetano had a doctor's appointment today, so I'm rehearsing alone. I'm so absorbed in my singing that I don't notice the French doors open until I hear a man shout my name.

"Sarina!"

Shivers run throughout my body as I suddenly realize where I've heard that man's voice before. I look up and am face-to-face with my father. It can't be. How did he find me?

"You worthless, thankless child! You have made your mother so ill with worry, leaving the way you did. And your younger brothers and sisters have not stopped crying since you left! This is how you repay me for the kindness I showed you over the years? We thought you were dead. I was just about ready to give up searching any longer for you."

I'm too dumbstruck to say anything. At the mention of my mother and siblings, tears stream down my face.

"Sarina, I'm sorry, but you must go with your father. I had no idea you had run away from home." Signore Conti looks at me grimly. I want to say, *"How can you have known I ran away if you never asked me anything about myself?"*

"I am sorry for any trouble she has caused you, Signore Conti. I am not a man of much means or else I would pay you for your trouble and for feeding my daughter."

Signore Conti holds up his hand. "There is no need for that. Sarina was working while here. I do not give handouts."

"Working?" Papá looks at me, thinking the worst.

"She was singing for our restaurant's patrons."

Thankfully, Signore Conti omits that I was reading tarot cards. But I'm sure learning of my singing is just as bad for my father.

Papá walks over. When he reaches me, he lifts my arm, forcing me to stand. I try shrugging my arm free, but his grip is too strong.

"I have a life here, Papá. People treat me with kindness. Mama did not tell you that I sent her money a couple of weeks ago? I could help you and the family with the money I make here."

"Money? What money? Either you are lying or your mother is keeping secrets from me."

I suddenly realize my error, for now my father will beat my mother for hiding money from him.

"Sarina, please do not make this situation any more difficult than it already is. You belong to your father. I cannot continue to employ you against his wishes," Signore Conti says.

So that is it. I am nothing more than my father's property even though I have been living independently for weeks now and making my own living. Even though I've earned the respect of all those who come hear me sing.

"Let me just get my belongings, Papá."

"I am coming with you in case you get any ideas. You made a fool of me once before. I will never let you out of my sight again." Papá keeps his painful hold on my arm.

"That won't be necessary, *signore*. I will have one of our maids accompany her." Signore Conti motions to Grazia, who was mopping the floor behind the bar but has been fixed in place staring at the scene before her. My cheeks burn with shame. She hurries over. Papá seems reluctant, but finally releases my arm. I head to my room as Grazia follows me. Neither of us says a word.

Once in my room, I take out the large embroidered bag I bought from a street vendor not long after coming to Taormina. I pack the few dresses I own but decide to leave behind the fancy gowns Signore Conti had me buy when I first got the job at the Villa Carlotta. I almost leave behind the Sicilian folk costume, but for some reason I decide to throw it in my bag. I also take my tarot cards even though I know that if my father finds them he will think I've surrendered to Satan's ways. He's always said fortune-telling is evil. Tears flow freely down my face as I pack.

Grazia whispers, *"Mi dispiace, Sarina. Mi dispiace."*

But her apologies do little to console me as my mind begins to flash through all the wonderful places I've visited since arriving in Taormina. And Carlo! I will never see him again.

It is around midnight. When Papá and I arrived at our house a few hours earlier, all the lights were off. No one came to welcome me back. Not my mother or my siblings. I didn't blame them, however. For my father gave me the worst beating he's ever given me. I wanted to scream, but my pride refused. He took away my freedom. I wouldn't allow him to also take my dignity. But my silence seemed to enrage him more. Once he was done beating me, he tied me to the tree outside. Although he had sworn earlier he would never let me out of his sight, he knew I wouldn't be able to free myself from the ropes tied around my body.

Just when I think I can no longer take the pain from my battered body, I hear my mother's soft whispers. *"Mama è qui. Mama è qui.* Mother is here. Mother is here."

At first, I think I'm imagining hearing her voice. I'm too exhausted to even open my eyes to see if it's really her. But then I feel a wet towel pressed against my wounds. She rubs something on my cuts and bruises. The smell of herbs and oils reaches my nose, and I realize she is using my homemade healing salve.

"Mama, perdonami. Please forgive me for leaving you, Mama." I cry.

"Mia figlia. Non c'è nulla da perdonare. There is nothing for me to forgive, my daughter. I knew you could not stay here any longer after what happened to poor Tina." My mother strokes my hair back and tucks it behind my ears. She picks up the washcloth and presses it to my forehead once again. *"Dormi.* Sleep now. Get some rest."

But at the mention of my beloved cat Tina, I sob even harder. Suddenly, the weight of all that I have had to endure over the past few months comes bearing down on me—my father's beatings growing more severe, abandoning Tina, running away from home, struggling to find work to support myself, worrying about Mama, Carlotta, Enzo, and Pietro.

"Mama, please believe me when I tell you that I have thought about you and the children every day since I ran away. I have felt so guilty for leaving and for finally being free of Papá."

"My dear child, I was so worried about you, too. I wondered if you were eating and where you were sleeping. I was afraid you would be attacked since you are a pretty young woman. Every night, I prayed to God and all the saints to protect you. I am happy to see you are safe. When you sent money to me, I saw the return address was Messina. But I did not believe you would have mailed a package from where you were actually staying and risked your father's seeing it. Where were you staying?"

"I went to Taormina, Mama, but I had one of the workers at the hotel where I worked send the money to you when he went to visit his parents in Messina. I wish you could see Taormina, Mama. It's beautiful beyond words. A paradise on Earth. I had always dreamed about seeing Taormina. That added to my burden. I felt guilty that I was having a life I had fantasized about, while you and the children were suffering so much."

"Please, Sarina, stop feeling guilty. I have always wanted nothing but the best for my children, especially you. If all my children could escape and have wonderful lives, I would be so blessed. My life is over, but there is still hope for my children."

"Oh, Mama." I begin crying again as I press my head against my mother's chest. I wish I could hug her, but I know she cannot untie me.

Mama strokes my hair and, as if reading my thoughts, says, "I should cut these ropes so that you can run away again, but I'm too afraid of what he will do to the children."

Her voice sounds strained. I look up into her face and see how tormented she is over wanting to help her daughter but fearing her action will only make circumstances worse for her and my siblings.

"So he still beats you? And from what you have just said, he is now beating the children, too? I feared this would happen after I left. Sometimes I thought about returning for this reason alone."

"He began beating me more, and he started hitting Carlotta and Enzo on a more regular basis. When you were around, he only spanked them from time to time. Enzo has been rebellious, which has only incensed your father more. But he controls himself more with them. Carlotta's and Enzo's punishments have not been as severe as yours were. It's as if there is a small, rational part of him that realizes they are still too young. He doesn't hit Pietro since he is only a toddler."

"I guess the devil hasn't completely possessed Papá," I say with much sarcasm in my voice.

"He has tried to find you every day since you left. He's gone to Barcellona and Messina, showing your photograph to people and making inquiries."

"I'm surprised he wasted so much time on me."

"Your father has never liked to lose. Your managing to run away and stay hidden for all these weeks has made him feel like you got the upper hand over him." Mama shakes her head. "He is not a man but rather a child who must always get his way."

"It's my fault that he now hits Carlotta and Enzo and that his beatings of you have become more frequent. It is probably for the best that Papá found me and brought me home. At least now we are all reunited again, and I can protect the children from him."

"He will still beat us, Sarina. You were not always able to protect me when you were here. Remember when he broke my teacup? You know, as well as I do, that sometimes it's better not to intervene because his fury just gets worse. I know you often threw yourself in his path when you thought he was about to hit the children. But he will not allow you to stand in his way anymore. Remember, he is stronger than you. Look at how brutally he beat you tonight. And his future beatings of you will be even more merciless, especially after the way you disobeyed him and embarrassed him by running away."

"Embarrassed him by escaping this hell? He should be embarrassed over the way he treats his family. *That's* what he should feel humiliated about," I all but scream.

"Shhh, Sarina. He will wake up. I should go back inside. He

gets up regularly in the night to use the bathroom. His drinking has only become worse since you left."

"All right. *Grazie, Mama.*" My mother hugs me and kisses me on both cheeks. Before leaving, she tries to loosen the ropes binding me so that they're not cutting into my skin too deeply. But Papá has tied them with iron strength.

"Don't worry, Mama. Go before he discovers you're gone."

Mama nods her head. Picking up the washcloth and the healing salve jar, she hurries back into the house.

Tears run down my face. Although I suspected that Papá would transfer his beatings of me onto Carlotta and Enzo, hearing proof of it from my mother is almost too much for me to bear. And Mama is right. He will absolutely show no mercy on me from here on out. I might as well try and find a way to end my life before he does it.

Staring up at the stars, I try to let the serenity of the night sky soothe me.

"Sarina!"

My heart races. I see a dark form rush toward me.

"Who's there?" I cry out.

"It's me." The moonlight shines on Carlo's face as he comes closer.

"Carlo! How did you find me? Please, you must leave before my father discovers you!"

"I'm not leaving you. Oh my God! What has he done to you?" Carlo kneels beside me, which allows him a better view of my battered face. And when he sees I am tied to the tree, his face twists in anger. I have never seen him look so mad.

"He's a savage brute! I will kill him!" Carlo's voice rises.

"Shhh! Please, Carlo, calm down. You will only make things worse for my mother and my siblings. Please, just go back home. Forget about me. I should never have run away. My family needs me. As I suspected all along, my father has now transferred his beatings of me onto my sister and one of my brothers. And he beats my mother even more than before. I was a foolish girl thinking I could have the life I've lived these past couple of months. I was not born to that world. I need to be a dutiful daughter and help my mother and siblings."

"Sarina, you have told me that it did not take much for your father to unleash his anger on you and your mother. He sounds completely insane! There is no reasoning with someone like that. There is no way you can continue to live here. He will beat you even worse. Look at you!"

I begin crying again. Carlo and Mama are right. There is no doubt that my father's abuse toward me will be much more severe.

"I don't think I can leave my family again, Carlo. The guilt over abandoning them before has stayed with me every day that I've been away. I don't think I can take leaving them a second time, and now that my mother has confirmed for me that he also hits my younger siblings . . ." My voice trails off as I shake my head.

"It won't be your choice, then, Sarina. I am kidnapping you. The guilt lies with me." In an instant, he takes out from his trousers' waistband a pocket knife and cuts my ropes.

"No, Carlo!" I try to protest, but Carlo places his hand over my mouth.

"Sarina, please don't cry out. As you said earlier, if your father discovers me it'll only make matters worse for your mother and siblings. I will report your father to the local *carabinieri* for domestic abuse. That should put the fear of God in him, and he will stop hitting your mother and siblings."

"Ha! That is what you think? The police do not get involved in domestic matters. You know that."

"They do when they're paid enough. Everyone in Sicily knows how corrupt the *carabinieri* are. I will pay them generously to warn your father, and I will also ask them to make regular visits to ensure there is not so much as a bruise or a scratch on your mama and little brothers and sister. I promise you, Sarina. No harm will befall them again. I will also secretly come by from time to time to check in on them."

"But if my father catches you—"

"Don't worry, Sarina. He won't even know I'm here."

"You would do all of this for me, Carlo?"

"Of course I would. I love you."

"I love you, too. I thought I would never see you again after my father took me away from the Villa Carlotta."

"You'll never lose me, Sarina. Now we must go. We cannot waste any more time."

"Wait. I want to see my little brothers and sister. I have not seen them since I came back. I just want to see their faces one last time."

"Sarina, it is too risky."

"Are you saying that if my father wakes up and discovers we are fleeing, you will not put up a fight for me?" A hint of a smile escapes, for I know what his answer will be.

"No one is taking you away from me again, Sarina."

"That is what I thought. I will only be two minutes. Wait here."

I stand up carefully since my legs are cramped from being tied and walk quietly to my house. Opening the door very gingerly, I step inside. My father's snoring reaches my ears, and my anxiety lessens since I know he is in a deep sleep. I enter the bedroom that Carlotta, Enzo, and Pietro share. Even in the dark, I can tell they have grown quite a bit in the two months since I've been gone. Part of me wishes I could wake them up and talk to them just for a moment. However, though I trust Carlo would not leave me here, I don't want him getting into a fight with my father. And I don't want Carlotta and Enzo witnessing that. I notice on the floor beside their bed my bag with the few belongings I took before leaving the Villa Carlotta. Papá must have thrown it there. Taking out my deck of tarot cards, I place them beneath Carlotta's pillow. She will know they are from me once she and Enzo hear I was here. For of course, Papá will throw a fit when he learns I have run away again. I feel slightly comforted in knowing that at least I can leave this small gift for Carlotta and Enzo. In Sicily, tarot cards are also often used as playing cards. A vision of Carlotta and Enzo sneaking off to one of their beloved outdoor hideaways on the beach and playing with the cards comes to my mind. Smiling, I lightly kiss my sister and brothers on their cheeks before stepping out of their lives once more.

PART TWO

Aeolian Islands

August–November 1969

❦ 15 ❧

Vulcano

August 21, 1969

Carlo and I are en route to Lipari. The first port of call for the ferry that takes passengers to the Aeolian Islands is Vulcano. Carlo decided to start his job a few days later so that we could have some time to ourselves and explore Vulcano. I think he did this to help ease the pain of leaving my family.

After we left my house, we spent the night in Milazzo, near the ferry station. We slept in Carlo's car—or rather he slept. I was awake most of the night, sobbing and thinking about Mama, Carlotta, Enzo, and Pietro. Every so often Carlo would wake up and hold me in his arms as he whispered to me that everything would be all right.

Carlo had made arrangements to meet Gaetano at the ferry station before we departed so that he could give him his car keys. Carlo trusted Gaetano and knew he would not betray our whereabouts to Signore Conti. Gaetano was going to keep Carlo's car at his parents' house in Taormina. Carlo had explained to me that on a few of the islands, cars were not allowed. Besides, the islands were so small that one didn't really need them.

Gaetano agreed to mail a letter to my mother once he arrived in

Taormina. While I was up last night, unable to sleep, I found a note pad in Carlo's glove compartment. I let Mama know that a friend had helped me escape, and that I was safe. I apologized to her for leaving once again and acknowledged that she was right when she told me life would be even harder for me in my father's home. I also let her know things would be different from here on out for her and the children. Of course, I didn't tell her what Carlo had said about how he was going to bribe the police so that they would warn Papá and check in on Mama and the children from time to time. Mama would realize what I meant once the police visited Papá.

Carlo had thought to ask Gaetano if he could get some makeup from Grazia to cover up the bruises on my face. When Gaetano handed me the makeup, I was barely able to look at him. I felt so ashamed of the beating my father had given me, even though I knew it wasn't my fault. I quickly put the makeup on, still trying to keep it looking as natural as possible since I rarely wore any, and then handed the makeup to Gaetano to bring back to Grazia. But he told me Grazia wanted me to keep it. Secretly, I was relieved since I knew it would take a few weeks for my bruises to fade.

"Porto di Levante!" The ferry's captain announces we've arrived at Vulcano's port.

I was so absorbed in my thoughts that I didn't even notice we were approaching land. My thoughts drift back to the nights I snuck out of my family's house and stared at Vulcano on the other side of the beach, wishing I could escape to the island. Now here I am. As the ferry gets closer to the dock, the smell of hard-boiled eggs reaches my nose.

Carlo sees me scrunch up my nose and says, "That's the odor of the sulfur coming from the mud baths, the Laghetti dei Fanghi. They're not far from here. We'll take a dip in them later."

"Ewww! I don't want to sink myself into mud even though I have heard the minerals are good for your skin."

"Everyone who travels to Vulcano must indulge in the Laghetti dei Fanghi. It'll be fun!"

I shrug my shoulders. "If you insist."

"And wait 'til you see the beaches, Sarina. I won't say anything more so that you'll truly be surprised." Carlo puts his arm around me as we disembark from the ferry. I merely nod my head. Though I am trying to remain upbeat and joke with Carlo, it is difficult for me. My spirits are still so low.

"I know you are terribly sad over leaving your mother and siblings, Sarina. But you will see them again someday. Now is not the right time. You understand that, don't you?" Carlo's eyes look concerned. I touch his cheek.

"I do. Don't worry. I'll be fine. I just need some time. Please be patient with me, Carlo."

"Always."

"You still haven't told me how you found out that my father had taken me away from the Villa Carlotta and how you find my home."

Carlo sighs.

"When I came home last night and discovered you weren't singing, I asked Gaetano where you were. He told me how your father had found you and insisted you go back home with him. I became enraged when I found out that my father didn't even try to intervene to prevent you from leaving. I went to find him. I asked him how he could've let you go. I told him how your father beat you, and that that was why you had run away. My father told me he could no longer employ you, knowing you'd run away from home, and that as a minor, you still belonged to your father. I grabbed him by the lapel of his shirt and threw him against the wall. I told him he was a coward and that the real reason he didn't attempt to intervene is that he wanted you gone so that I could no longer see you. My father then said he had known we were involved, and it was for the better that things didn't work out. He asked me to listen to reason and told me we came from different worlds. He said you would prove to be nothing but trouble for me. Besides, I was still young and had no idea what I truly wanted and neither did you. My hands curled into fists. I know he is my father, Sarina, but I almost hit him in that moment. Instead, I told him he didn't know me and would never know what I truly desire in life. I then walked away.

"I went to your room and searched among your things to see if there was some clue as to where your family lived. To my extreme relief, I found your Bible with an address written on the first page.

I prayed it was the right address. I knew once I found you, I would take you with me and never return to the Villa Carlotta. Besides, we were planning on leaving for Lipari that night anyway. So I packed a bag and set off to find you. And thank God, I did."

"I can't believe I left my Bible behind, but I guess I'm not surprised since I was so upset and in shock that my father had found me. I'll never forget what you are doing for me, Carlo."

"It's not entirely unselfish of me, Sarina. When I thought I might've lost you forever, I felt so desperate. I couldn't imagine you absent from my life."

I hug Carlo. We then walk hand in hand away from the dock.

"I suppose we'll find a hotel first? Will we be able to find a vacancy? I noticed all of the tourists on the ferry."

"I also have a friend who owns a hotel here in Vulcano. When I went to get us espresso this morning, I called him. Fortunately, he had a few rooms left. So we'll be fine, Sarina."

"You have a lot of friends, thankfully for us. Can we trust them not to say anything to your father?"

"Yes. I've already told both Tomaso, my friend here in Vulcano, and Michele, my friend for whom I'll be working in Lipari, not to let my father know of our whereabouts if he calls. However, I don't think he'll be looking for me. He has more important business to attend to with his hotels and becoming even richer than he already is." Carlo's voice sounds very bitter.

"After we drop our bags at the hotel, I thought we would take advantage of being up so early and go hiking to the top of Vulcano della Fossa. We can go to the beach after lunch."

"They let people climb to the top of the volcano?" I ask incredulously. My heart starts to pound a bit, realizing how high that must be. While I don't have a fear of heights, I also have never been that high up before.

"Of course. That's one of the main attractions that tourists flock to here in Vulcano. We'll need to stop by a few stores and get ourselves proper shoes. You'd never make it up there in your flimsy sandals. We'll also need water."

"As always, you think of everything, Carlo." I smile at him.

"Well, one of these days I'll forget something." Carlo winks.

Tomaso, Carlo's friend, is at the hotel's front desk when we arrive. The hotel is simply called L'Albergo Vulcano. It is nowhere near as grand as the Villa Carlotta, but seems more practical, probably catering to tourists who are not wealthy.

"Carlo! It's been a long time!" Tomaso shakes Carlo's hand, then kisses me on both cheeks as he introduces himself. *"Piacere, Sarina. Sei molta bellissima!"*

I blush at Tomaso's compliment. *"Grazie.* It is nice to meet you, too."

"I'm sure you will be comfortable here. Are you certain you cannot stay longer than two nights, Carlo?"

"Yes, I will be starting work in Lipari the day after tomorrow."

"Work? And at another hotel? Did your father disown you?" Tomaso laughs.

"Not yet, but I'm sure he will when he learns I have struck out on my own."

"I see. That is commendable of you to want to forge your own path, Carlo. Nothing wrong with that. Well, here are the keys to your room. I will let you get settled. Of course, let me know if you need anything. Enjoy your stay in Vulcano. *Arrivederci!"*

I am too focused on the fact that Tomaso gave us keys to just one room to return his farewell. But what did I expect? I wouldn't want Carlo to spend money on two hotel rooms. Perhaps there are two beds in the room, but I'm too embarrassed to ask Carlo.

We arrive at our room, and I breathe a sigh of relief when I see there are two twin-size beds in the room. Though I want to show my love fully to Carlo, I'm still frightened of what my first time will be like. I guess I'm not as ready as I thought I was recently.

We drop off our belongings and use the restroom before heading back out. I take my bag, but empty it of some of its contents.

"Should I pack my swimsuit so that we can go to the beach directly after eating lunch?" I ask Carlo.

"Yes. This way we don't waste any time. I'll take the towels in the bathroom. We can get more later." Carlo looks at his watch. "I want to go to the volcano early before it gets too hot. We can rest on the beach after lunch. *Va bene?"*

"That's fine."

Carlo gives me a light kiss on the lips. *"Sei perfetta, mio angelo."*

"I'm not perfect nor an angel!" But I'm delighted by his endearments.

We make our way back to the shops in town. After buying hiking shoes, we head over to a grocery store to buy water.

"Ah! *Cioccolato!*" Carlo picks up a small box of chocolates. "We'll need these to give us some strength after climbing to the top of Vulcano della Fossa. You've had Baci chocolates, right?"

A memory flashes through my mind of my father's bringing home a box of chocolates for my mother one year when it was her birthday. I was no more than four or five years old. That is the only memory I have of him doing something nice for her. I remember the box was a dark blue like the one Carlo is holding. My mother had secretly shared her chocolates with me out of fear that Papá would be insulted she was giving them away—even to her young daughter. The chocolates were heavenly.

"*Sí.* They are quite good. But it has been a long time since I had them."

"Let's buy two boxes then!"

"How will we carry all those chocolates and our water to the top of the volcano? It's too much, Carlo!" I laugh.

"I'll take the chocolates out of the boxes and keep them in this paper bag. Don't worry. I'll carry them, and besides, we'll be eating them as we hike. The load will be light in no time!"

"*Signore*, would you also like to purchase tickets to the tour of Vulcano della Fossa? I can give you a discount," the store's clerk asks Carlo.

"What time does the tour depart?"

"In five minutes."

Carlo shrugs his shoulders. "Why not? It'll give you a chance, Sarina, to learn more about Vulcano." Carlo pulls out his wallet and pays for the tickets.

A few minutes later, we're with a small group of tourists and a man who is our tour guide. He's short and probably in his sixties. He wears navy blue shorts and a white button-down shirt tucked into his pants. A white canvas hat and sturdy-looking black hiking boots complete his ensemble. His arms and legs are deeply bronzed. I also notice his calf muscles are well-defined. No doubt from all the hikes he's taken up the volcano.

"Gather around, please. *Mi chiamo Fulvio.* I will begin giving the tour while we hike. This way, once we are at the crater, you can relax and enjoy the scenery as well as take photographs. If anyone has questions for me, I am happy to answer them, but please wait until after we reach the volcano's summit."

"Fulvio must love to hear himself talk," Carlo whispers to me. I give him a scolding look and silently mouth "Shhh," but I can't resist laughing softly.

As we make our ascent, I'm grateful Carlo thought to buy the hiking boots. The ground is quite pebbly, and the higher we get, the steeper the incline becomes.

"Ah!" Carlo slaps his forehead. "I knew I was forgetting something. Sometimes it can get quite cool at the top, especially in the morning. We should've bought sweaters at the shops, too. I guess we will have to keep each other warm." Carlo leans in close to me as he says the last sentence. My stomach flutters. And then I remember how we will be spending the entire night alone together in the same room. True, we already spent a night together when we slept on the beach in Castelmola. But this feels different, more intimate, perhaps because of the hotel room's small quarters.

"Attenzione, per favore!" Fulvio shouts for attention as he directs his gaze toward us.

Carlo and I giggle, but remain quiet for the duration of the guide's history on Vulcano, which I'm actually enjoying and finding quite fascinating.

"Vulcano was known to the Greeks as Hiera or Holy Island and can often be found in mythology whenever there is a reference to the Aeolian Islands. In *The Odyssey*, Ulysses came to Vulcano, which was supposed to be the gateway to Hades, or the underworld. The Romans named the island in honor of Vulcan, the god of fire.

"The island was formed from the fusion of several volcanoes. Vulcano della Fossa is the largest of these volcanoes. It is still active, but it hasn't erupted since 1890. Its crater, which we will be seeing once we reach the top, is known as Gran Cratere, or Big Crater for you tourists who speak English."

Fulvio then goes from speaking Italian to speaking English as he diverts his attention to an older British couple.

"Do the other volcanoes have names?" one of the Italian tourists asks Fulvio, who looks miffed not only because his discussion with the British tourists has been interrupted, but also since a question is being asked now rather than at the summit as he had instructed us to do.

"*Sì.* We have Vulcanello to the north. Monte Aria, which is inactive, and is especially popular with geologists, and Monte Saraceno."

Fulvio goes on to talk more about the island of Vulcano in general. Carlo has been handing me Baci chocolates along the way. Since the last time I ate them I was so young and did not know how to read yet, I hadn't realized that each chocolate was wrapped in a little love note. Every time Carlo hands me a Baci, I stop listening to our guide so that I can read the love note. Deciding to save the notes as a memento of this trip, I put them in my bag.

While the Baci chocolates are even more delicious than I remember, they're making me quite thirsty. But we only have so much water, and I'd rather wait to drink since we also have to make our way back down from the crater. Fulvio told us at the onset of the hike that it would take about an hour and a half to reach the top. He mentioned hikers who are in very good shape can make it in an hour, which I can't imagine right now, for I'm feeling quite winded.

It's also getting dusty from all the sand that we're kicking up. Carlo insists I drink more and tells me we are nearing the summit. I stop to take just a couple of sips of water. Carlo waits with me. We let Fulvio and the rest of the tour group go on ahead without us, but no one seems to notice. Soon, I hear several elated cries of joy. No doubt, they've reached the top of Vulcano della Fossa and are amazed by Gran Cratere.

"*Dio mio!* That man sure can talk."

I laugh. "Let's go see what all the excitement is about." I elbow Carlo's side playfully. He jerks away.

"You know how ticklish I am yet you delight in torturing me." Carlo gives me a quick hug. We join the rest of the tourists, walking with our arms around each other's backs.

My breath is taken away when I see the landscape before me. It looks like the photos I saw last month in a Taormina newspaper of the American astronauts who had landed on the moon. The volcano's crater has the same craggy, gray surfaces as the images of the moon. As we approach the crater's edge, we see clouds of white smoke billowing from its opening.

"I forgot to talk a little about the fumaroles. The smoke that you are seeing is coming from what's known as fumaroles, openings in the planet's crust often found near volcanoes. The smoke is from gases and steam that are being emitted from the fumaroles. The steam is created when water is heated to extreme temperatures, and the pressure suddenly drops when it is released from the ground. As you can see, the smoking fumaroles add to the crater's dramatic appearance." Fulvio smiles as he looks at the scene before him with obvious admiration.

I would think that after all the times he's been up here with his tour groups, he wouldn't be astounded anymore. Then again, this is an incredible sight that probably never ceases to amaze.

"This is magnificent, Carlo. Thank you for taking me here. I love it!"

"I'll never forget how amazed I was the first time I came here. Let's get closer and look into its depths."

Carlo keeps his arm protectively around me as we lean slightly to look over the crater's edge.

I shiver a bit staring into the abyss. Carlo notices and pulls me back slightly.

"Afraid?"

"It's just a lot to take in, but no, I'm not afraid. I'm more in awe. I can't believe how much it looks like the moon from the pictures that the American astronauts sent back."

"Yes. Just think of it this way, Sarina. I've taken you to the moon—well, the closest you can get to the moon on our continent."

"I like that. It's kind of romantic. Let's pretend we are on the moon and this is our new home."

"Okay," Carlo laughs.

A few hours later, we're relaxing on the Spiagge Nere. Just when I think that Carlo can't shock me anymore with the sights he's introduced me to, he does it again. The Spiagge Nere features black sandy beaches! I had never even heard of beaches with black sand. Carlo told me there are several in the world.

"Is it my imagination, Carlo, or has it gotten extremely hot in the half hour that we've been here?" I fan myself with my floppy straw hat.

"It's the black sand. I should have thought of that. We're approaching the middle of the afternoon, the worst time you can be on any beach, but especially here because of the black sand."

"This might be a good time to go to those mud baths, Carlo."

"Let's go."

I pack up our belongings as Carlo folds up the lounge chairs and umbrella we rented.

It's easy to find the Laghetti dei Fanghi, for all one needs to do is follow the stench of the sulfur.

While Carlo pays for our admission, I walk closer to the mud baths and watch the tourists bathing. Most of the tourists have covered their faces with the mud. It is a bizarre sight, and listening to the different languages being spoken only adds to my feeling that I am on another planet.

Carlo joins me after paying for our admission. "Ready?"

I take off my long skirt and halter top. Carefully, I step into one of the little lakes of mud. It's quite hot, but immediately the sensation relaxes my body, especially once I fully submerge myself. If it weren't for the odor of the sulfur, I could probably fall asleep.

"Ah! This is the life. Are you feeling better, Sarina?"

"I am. Visiting the attractions on Vulcano has helped to take my mind off of everything else." I can't even say "my family." My heart tugs whenever I think about them.

"Good. Hey! Look over there! What's that!" Carlo's voice sounds alarmed as he points off in the distance. I follow his finger. Then I feel something mushy and hot hit me in the face.

"Got you!" Carlo laughs as he gets ready to throw more mud at me.

Before he can do so, I quickly sling up some mud and hit him in the mouth. He spits it back up, coughing.

"Oh, Carlo! I'm sorry. I didn't mean to get you in the mouth!"

But just when I lower my guard, he throws more mud at me. We continue throwing mud at each other, laughing the entire time, until we're out of breath. When we finally stop hurling mud at each other, we notice many of the tourists are looking at us with disdain. But we don't care.

"You know what's after this, right?" Carlo asks.

"Siesta? I'm getting quite sleepy."

"Shopping!"

"I brought enough clothes with me, and I'm sure you did, too."

"Did you bring a second swimsuit?"

"No. I don't own a second swimsuit."

"So we are going shopping then. You'll understand why when we shower the mud off ourselves."

"Must you always be so mysterious, Signore Conti?"

"Don't call me that. It makes me think of my father."

But Carlo is smiling. We head over to the outdoor showers and rinse the mud off. I now see why we must buy new swimsuits. The mud has discolored our suits.

"If I'd known that my swimsuit would get ruined, I wouldn't have gone into the mud. We bought this suit only a month ago in Taormina."

"The new swimsuit will be my gift. Besides, every woman should own more than one."

"Thank you, Carlo, but I can't let you keep paying for me. I have money."

"And I am rich."

"But you don't know if you will ever see the rest of your inheritance."

"I have plenty of money in the bank. And now I'll be making more at my new job in Lipari. We'll be fine."

Since Carlo has continually asked me to place my trust in him, I will. I only wish I could be as confident as him where our future is concerned. Perhaps it's my upbringing that has made me more cautious—or perhaps it's my intuition that the gypsies taught me to rely on.

It's midnight. Carlo and I are getting ready for bed. While Carlo washes up, I climb into my bed and release a deep sigh as my body sinks into the downy mattress. The bed I shared at home with my siblings was so flat from the weight of all our bodies in it. My back often hurt when I woke up in the morning. Within minutes, I'm drifting off to sleep, but just as I begin to dream, Carlo nudges my arm lightly.

"Sarina, are you asleep yet?"

"I was. Is something wrong?" I look up into Carlo's face. He looks slightly nervous.

"I'm sorry. I thought you hadn't fallen asleep yet. I've only been in the bathroom for five minutes."

"I guess I'm exhausted."

Carlo nods his head. He then kneels down on the floor beside my bed. He strokes my hair.

"You know I love you very much?"

"*Sì.* And I love you very much." I sit up in bed and lean forward to kiss him.

"I have thought about this probably since the first day I met you, if you can believe it. But I wanted to make it more special. However, circumstances are forcing me not to waste any more time."

Carlo takes my hand and slips a braided gold ring onto my finger.

"Sarina, I want to make you my wife. But I want to give you a proper wedding first. I was thinking maybe in a month, we can do that. Of course, it would just be a small wedding, but I still want you to get married the proper way in church and all. We can go back to Taormina or even Messina and get married there. As I'm sure you realize, we cannot sleep in the same room without people gossiping that we are sinning. I told Michele, my friend in Lipari, who gave me the job at his hotel, that we had eloped here in Vulcano. Besides people talking, I was also afraid that Michele would not have felt comfortable having us share a room. His hotel, the Villa Athena, is one of the most popular hotels in Lipari and is almost always fully booked, sometimes even in the less popular winter months. I wouldn't feel right taking an additional room away from him when a guest could be paying for it. So we will have to pretend that we are already married. While we must play this charade, please know that I absolutely do intend to and will make you my wife as soon as we have become more settled in Lipari. That is, if you'll agree to be my wife."

I can feel Carlo's hand shaking while he holds mine. I close my own over his. Tears fill my eyes.

"I can't believe you want to marry me. I would be honored to become your wife. But . . ."

Carlo's face registers surprise as he frowns. "But what?"

"I feel I'm still too young to marry. And so much is still unsettled in our lives. Can we have a long engagement?"

Carlo kisses my hand. "Well, yes, I suppose we could. But I must admit, I can't wait to make you mine. I understand, however, and I don't want to make you uncomfortable if you feel you need more time."

"I am yours already, Carlo. Getting married won't make me any more yours than I am now. You have my heart." I reach over and place my hand on his cheek.

"You've made me so happy, Sarina. I just feel that marriage would bring a certain legitimacy to our love."

"I know what you are saying. But my heart also knows it must be right. I don't want us to rush to get married because we're afraid of what people will say if they find out we're not."

"I realize that, too. That is why I said we can wait until next month. As for what you said about being too young, Sarina, you aren't."

"Yes, I know. My mother was only fourteen when she wed my father. But again, she had no say in the matter. She was just a child. I am only a few years older than her. I have always vowed I would never make the same mistake she made."

"So that's what this is about." Carlo pulls away from me and looks off to the side.

"Don't be mad, Carlo."

He sighs. "It's just . . ." His voice trails off as he lets out a deep sigh.

"What? You can tell me."

"I sometimes feel that you cannot let go of your past and just focus on us and the blessings you now have in your life."

My heart races as anger quickly fills it.

"You want me to forget my family?"

"No, Sarina, of course not! I want you to be happy, but I know you are still haunted by your father's beatings, that you still feel guilty that you are not with your mother and siblings. I don't blame you. It's natural for you to feel that way. I just want you to give yourself a break, too. I can tell you feel as if you don't deserve happiness because their lives are still so hard. But don't you see? By your leaving, you can someday help your mother and siblings. And you *have* helped them. You've sent them money. And once we're settled in Lipari, I will go back to Messina and ask the *carabinieri* to keep an eye on your family."

"That's no guarantee, Carlo. The *carabinieri* are not always there in my family's house. And when my father gets drunk or goes into one of his rages, he has little control over his actions. I'm grateful to you for wanting to talk to the *carabinieri*, but I am also realistic."

Tears fill my eyes, and now it's my turn to look off.

Carlo takes my chin in his hand and forces me to look at him.

"I'm sorry, Sarina. I didn't mean to upset you. Whatever you want, we'll do. You do want to marry me though, right?"

I wrap my arms around Carlo's neck and place my head on his shoulders. "Yes. I can't imagine being with anyone else but you. Can we just wait more than a month? At least a few months—until we are more settled in Lipari. I haven't even found work yet."

Carlo strokes the back of my head. "I told you, Sarina, you don't have to worry about finding work. I can provide for both of us."

I pull back and look at Carlo. "I know. But I really enjoyed working for your father in the hotel and making my way. Even when I was reading the tarot, it felt good to be able to take care of myself. I miss singing at the Villa Carlotta. For the first time in my life, I felt respected—people admired my singing and complimented me. It gave me a sense of purpose. I cannot be your wife and just tend to our home. I know that idea might seem unusual for many women today, but I don't care."

"*Va bene.* I must admit you were radiant when you were singing. I think you are at your most beautiful when you sing. Your passion comes through. And as I have always said, I want you to be happy."

"*Grazie*, Carlo. I still don't know what I did to have God send you to me."

"Let's just be grateful we did find each other. Now, will you wear this ring? Unless you can't even bear the thought of pretending we're married." Carlo smiles.

"Yes, I'll wear it. The ring looks brand-new. Where did you get it?"

"I bought it at one of the shops today. Remember when you were trying on swimming suits I told you I was going to buy a newspaper? Well, I ran into a jewelry store. I knew it would take you some time to try on all of those suits I gave you." Carlo gives me a mischievous grin.

"So you had a plan all along. You can be quite deceptive." I giggle and touch my nose to Carlo's. He playfully rubs mine with his.

"Actually, I want you to think of this as an engagement ring, but of course we won't tell anyone that. We'll let them think it's your wedding ring. When we are ready to get married in church, I want to give you my mother's wedding ring. I would have given you her ring now, but I forgot to take it when I left the Villa Carlotta."

"You're too much, Carlo. But that's why I love you."

Carlo kisses me longer this time.

"So you won't have a problem going along with my lie and letting everyone in Lipari think we are married?"

"No. While I do not like lying, I know we must."

"Sarina, I hope you don't think this is presumptuous of me, but would you mind if I slept with you in your bed tonight? I just want to hold you. Naturally, I want to wait for us to make love until it is our wedding night. Again, I plan on doing right by you, Sarina. You deserve only the best."

I move over so Carlo can get into my bed. The narrow twin-size mattress forces us to lie very close together. Our arms will be wrapped around each other throughout the night. I look at the ring Carlo gave me. It is beautiful in its simplicity. The ring's braided shape makes me think of my cousin Agata's braids. The ring feels odd around my finger. I'm sure I will become accustomed to it.

Though I try to fall asleep, all I can think about is what my future with Carlo will be like. While everything I told him about wanting to wait to get married was the truth, I did not tell him everything. How could I tell him that when he brought up marriage, I felt anxious and as if I might suffocate? I do want to marry him. Then why do I feel such dread when I think about it? I know why. It's because of my father. Deep down, I'm afraid that Carlo will change and become the monster my father is, though I know that's highly unlikely. Still, the fear remains. I'm afraid the freedom I have had these past few months since I ran away from home will be taken from me once I become another man's wife. Carlo has been wonderful. I know he is different from most men. Still, what will happen when we have children? I doubt he will be as tolerant of my wanting to work, let alone sing. But who am I fooling? How could I continue to work with children?

I hear Carlo's deep breathing, alerting me that he's asleep. I gently lift his arm off me. My heart is pounding and, with his arm resting on my chest, it feels harder to breathe. Closing my eyes, I will myself to calm down. Soon, my breathing returns to normal. At least I have bought myself some time. Hopefully, my nerves will disappear in a few months when Carlo brings up the subject of our getting married again. I do love him so much. I cannot bear to hurt him and I won't—even if it means sacrificing my own needs and happiness.

❧ 16 ❧

Lipari

August 28, 1969

Carlo and I have been in Lipari for a week. Of the Aeolian Islands, Lipari is the largest and most populated. As such, it offers the largest number of ferry and hydrofoil rides to the other islands, as well as the mainland, all year round. The marinas are almost always bustling with throngs of visitors.

I haven't seen much of Carlo these past few days, for he's been busy training and working at his new job. Of course, he's promised to make it up to me even though I told him that wasn't necessary. While I miss him, I've also enjoyed being alone with my thoughts. I've mostly spent my time on the beach, but yesterday I visited a few hotels and restaurants to ask if they were interested in hiring me as an entertainer. I was told since summer was pretty much over no new employees would be hired until next season—just as Angela had warned me.

Today, I am venturing to Lipari's old town, which is built within ancient walls. During the mid-sixteenth century, the Spanish erected these walls in order to put an end to the many pirate raids. And they built the castle rock, or "the old castle," as it's also known.

In order to enter the walls of the old town, visitors must go up a ramp in the Piazza Mazzini.

Once I reach the top of the ramp, I see a ticket office for admission to the Museo Archeologico Eoliano, or the Archeological Museum of the Aeolian. Carlo encouraged me to visit the museum and told me it's one of the most popular tourist destinations in Lipari.

Once I'm inside the museum, I am immediately transported back to prehistoric times as I learn about the Aeolian Islands' early inhabitants. I stop to admire ancient archeological finds such as theater masks, water jugs, and various other relics. I'm especially fascinated to see a few of the artifacts were found underwater. I move on to the volcano exhibits, which are even more interesting for me now that I have hiked to the top of Vulcano della Fossa and stared into its crater's depths.

My museum ticket also includes admission to the Parco Archeologico, which is an open-air archeological park. While the park features many impressive artifacts, the most striking are the ancient Greek sarcophagi, or stone coffins, which date back to the fifth through third century BC.

The Cathedral of St. Bartholomew is next door to the Museo Archeologico Eoliano. My breath is taken away once I step inside and see the magnificent Norman-Baroque architecture. I overhear a group of tourists talking and learn that St. Bartholomew is actually the patron saint of Lipari.

I enter a pew and kneel. Making the sign of the cross, I pray to St. Bartholomew and ask him to protect Carlo and me in our new home here in Lipari. I also ask him to watch over Mama, Carlotta, Enzo, and Pietro and to reunite us someday. After my prayer, I sit on the bench and just let my eyes wander around the remarkable cathedral. I decide to leave once I feel my stomach grumbling.

Carlo told me if I got hungry I could head over to the Marina Corta after taking in the sights of the old town. I descend the broad steps of the Via del Concordato, which are right in front of the Cathedral of St. Bartholomew, and cut through the ancient fortifications. The steps lead me to the Via Garibaldi, which wraps around the bottom of the castle rock between Piazza Mazzini and the Marina Corta.

True to its name, the Marina Corta is a short, or small, harbor, unlike the Marina Lunga, or long harbor, which is the main port in Lipari. Fishing boats bob gently on the water along with a few other boats carrying tourists who are either lounging in the sun or taking in Lipari's idyllic serenity. Cafés and *trattorie* surround the piazza. I can smell focaccia, which must have just been pulled from the oven. I let my nose follow the aroma, and soon I see a small establishment with the sign FOCACCE E PIZZETTE.

Since I'll be eating with Carlo later, I decide to just have a small snack to hold me over. I order a pizzetta with sausage at the counter and take it with me as I head over to the Marina Corta. Eating my pizzetta standing up, I notice a few street vendors along the port. They are selling the popular Sicilian souvenirs of terra-cotta vases, jugs, carafes, and various other trinkets. Maybe I'll buy a few terra-cotta pieces to decorate our hotel room. While our lodgings at the hotel where Carlo works are temporary, it would be nice to add a personal touch.

Before deciding which souvenirs I'll purchase, I peruse all of the vendors' tables to make sure I'm not missing any merchandise that is for sale. I wouldn't want to immediately buy a souvenir only to see another that I like better. I examine a terra-cotta vase that is the size of my palm and is painted garishly with the colors of the Italian flag. Opting for an unadorned vase that is simpler in its terra-cotta form and looks more like an authentic ancient artifact, I ask the vendor to wrap it for me when I hear a woman call out, "Sarina?"

Turning around, I'm shocked to see Maria standing behind a vendor's table.

"It is you!" Maria rushes over and embraces me.

"What are you doing here, Maria? Is Lipari where you and your family are now staying?" I look around to see if any of the other gypsies are nearby, but none of them are in sight.

"Sì. But I'm sorry to say, Sarina, things have not been so good for us since we last saw each other." Maria's eyes fill with tears.

"Is everyone all right? I came by the beach in Taormina, looking for you, but I was told you all left rather abruptly. I thought you were planning on staying in Taormina until the end of August?"

"We were, but one of our clients contacted the *carabinieri* and told them that Gianni had swindled him out of all his money. Gianni was arrested, but the police had to let him go since they didn't have any real proof. I think they arrested him more to scare him. So we decided to leave earlier. We were afraid that man would become angry if he saw the police had released Gianni and try to create some other trouble for us."

"But why are you selling souvenirs?"

"The police have been trying to clear the gypsies out of Lipari. If we had known, we would never have come here. But we cannot afford to leave Lipari just yet. I used some of our savings to purchase a vendor's permit and these souvenirs to sell. Gianni and the others are trying to be discreet by feeling people out on the beach and in town to see if they would be interested in private readings. But we have not been able to bring in as much money as when we are openly set up to do readings like we were on the beach in Taormina."

"I'm so sorry, Maria. I wish I could help you after all you and your family did for me."

"Thank you for the sentiment, Sarina, but it is all right. Seeing you again is enough." Maria smiles.

"How is Isabella?"

"She's fine. She loves going to the old town and exploring, pretending the castle is hers and that she's a queen."

I laugh. "Yes, I remember when we first met she told me she was going to be a queen someday."

"Sarina, why don't you come by where we're staying tonight? I know Isabella would be thrilled to see you."

"Of course. Where are you staying?"

"We have our tents set up on Spiaggia Bianca. Have you been there yet?"

"*Si.* I know where it is."

"You still haven't told me why you are here in Lipari. Did you come just for a day visit?"

I shake my head. "I'm here with Carlo."

"Ahhh! I knew there was something between the two of you. I could see just by looking in your eyes how taken you were with him. That's wonderful. When do you go back to Taormina?"

"We moved here. My father learned I was at the Villa Carlotta. He brought me back home and beat me the worst he ever has. Carlo rescued me. We were planning on moving to Lipari even before my father found me. Carlo's father, whom I worked for when I sang at the Villa Carlotta, suspected that we were seeing each other, and he didn't approve. Carlo wanted to be free of his father, so he secured work at his friend's hotel. He hopes to open his own someday."

"How wonderful! And what does his father think about Carlo's abandoning him?"

"He has no idea. Well, he must now since we've been gone for a week. But Carlo hasn't contacted him yet to let him know we're in Lipari. I'm beginning to think he won't bother, Maria. I can't help but feel terrible, like this rift between Carlo and his father is my fault."

Maria reaches out and touches my cheek. "It is *not* your fault. Carlo is a grown man and must forge his own way. If it's anyone's fault, it is his father's. He cannot treat his son like a boy and interfere with his life and forbid him from seeing you. You both made the right decision. Forget about his father. Focus on Carlo and your new life together."

I nod my head. "I'll try. *Grazie*, Maria. It is so good to see you, too. I've missed you."

A few tourists come by Maria's table.

"I should get going. Bring Carlo tonight. There will be singing and dancing. Everyone will be happy to see you and hear you sing again."

"Ciao, Maria."

Maria nods her head good-bye before turning her attention to her customers. I suddenly realize I haven't paid for my souvenirs. The vendor has been staring at me and looks frustrated. I should buy the souvenirs from Maria since she needs the money and is like family to me. I put back the souvenirs I was going to buy from the first vendor and walk over to Maria's table. The first vendor scowls when he sees me walk away. I wait until the tourists Maria is taking care of have made their purchases.

"Did you forget to tell me something, Sarina?"

"I was going to buy a few terra-cotta vases and pottery to decorate our hotel room. Since you are selling souvenirs now, I might as well help out a friend and buy them from you."

"You are too kind, my child."

I buy five different terra-cotta pieces, more than I was planning on, but it is my small way of helping Maria out.

"I'll see you tonight, Maria."

"*Arrivederci,* Sarina. I cannot wait. We'll have fun just as we did in Taormina!"

I wave. At least the gypsies and I will be reunited. If I can't have my own family, they are the closest thing to family for me now—and of course Carlo. With that thought, I hurry back home. I cannot wait to tell Carlo that Maria is here.

Villa Athena, where Carlo works and where we are now staying, rivals the Villa Carlotta in its grandeur. On our first day here, Michele, Carlo's friend and owner of the Villa Athena, gave us a tour. The hotel is named after Athena, the Greek goddess of war and wisdom and Zeus's favorite daughter. The building is surrounded by Corinthian columns, which give it the appearance of an ancient Greek temple. Olive trees surround the property. Michele told me that Athena is often associated with olive trees, and so he thought it was fitting to plant them since she is his hotel's namesake.

I'm waiting in our hotel room for Carlo to finish his morning shift so we can have our midday meal together. In addition to Michele's giving us a room as part of Carlo's pay, he also invites us to eat with him and his family every day. Carlo and I have taken him up on the offer since we are trying to save money.

Unlike our room at the hotel in Vulcano, our room in Lipari has a queen-size bed. But Carlo has remained true to his word and only holds me at night. Well, he kisses me too. I have heard him sigh deeply after he kisses me, and sometimes he moves to the far side of the bed. I think it's becoming more difficult for him to keep his promise and not make love to me until our wedding night. I know I've been tempted.

"*Bellissima!*" Carlo storms into the room, startling me.

"You scared me!"

"Mi dispiace, mia principessa!" Carlo lifts me in his arms and spins me around.

"You have a lot of compliments for me today! Why are you in such a good mood?"

"I have been in a good mood every day since you told me you will become my wife. And when does a day go by that I don't tell you how beautiful you are or that you're my princess? Eh?"

"Oh, I'm sure there has been a day here and there when you've forgotten to call me beautiful or your princess." I frown.

"Stop teasing me!" Carlo lowers me to the ground. "Are you ready to eat?"

"Yes, but I wanted to tell you first, you'll never guess who I ran into today!"

"My father?"

"Of course not! Speaking of him, when are you going to call him? He must be worried about you."

"Trust me, Sarina. He is not wasting his time worrying about me. I'm sure he's figured out that I've run away with you."

"Still. I would feel better if you would at least let him know you're fine. You don't have to tell him you're here or of your decision to stop working for his hotel."

"That would make me a complete coward." Carlo runs his hand through his hair and turns away from me. When he turns back around, he nods his head. "You're right. I haven't been acting like a man. I'm sure my grandmother must be worried, too. Then again, he's probably lied and told Nonna Lucia I'm in Enna, taking care of business there. I will tell him the truth—even where we are. Let him try to make me return. I'm sure I'll get a response to my letter, informing me that he's disinherited me."

"You're going to write instead of call him?"

"Why not? If I call, we'll just get into an argument, and I'm through with that. He doesn't deserve more from me. He's lucky I'm even letting him know I'm still alive. I know the day will come when I'll have to confront him face-to-face, especially since I plan on visiting my grandmother once we're more settled here. But for now, it's best that we don't see each other. Who knows? Maybe the distance will somehow get him to see reason, but I'm not holding my breath."

"Well, I am glad you are going to let him know you're okay."

"You're so kind. After my father did nothing to prevent your father from taking you back home and after I told you that he didn't approve of our seeing each other, you can still find it in your heart to feel compassion for him." Carlo walks over and hugs me. "Now, don't keep me in suspense any longer. Who did you run into?"

"Maria!"

"The gypsies came to Lipari?"

I fill Carlo in on what Maria told me and let him know she invited us to see them tonight.

"I should warn them," Carlo says when I'm done.

"Warn them of what?"

"I've heard that the police want to crack down on any vagrants, including gypsies. They're even saying they're going to try and rid the island of the beggars who are seen by Marina Lunga. Apparently, many of the business owners have been complaining that they are losing customers, especially the wealthier tourists, to the other islands that are more 'cleaned up' as they put it. They feel that the homeless, gypsies, and beggars detract from Lipari."

"She already knows about the police crackdown. That's why she's selling souvenirs. They hope in time they can do private readings, but how many could they possibly get since they have to do it secretively? It's ridiculous that the police think the gypsies are detracting from Lipari and turning off visitors. I see plenty of tourists who disembark from the ferries at Marina Lunga make their way over to the hotels. And as you mentioned, the Villa Athena is fully booked, as are a few of the other hotels."

"Well, the police are worried about the tourists cutting their stays short once they see the gypsies and the beggars, and they're afraid Lipari will get a reputation as being an island for vagrants. I do think they're acting paranoid. Wherever you go in Italy, there are homeless people and beggars as well as gypsies. I'm sure it must also be because of the business owners and their discomfort when they see the vagrants. They must've put pressure on the police to do something about them. I hate to say this, but the best thing for

Maria and her family to do is leave Lipari. They will only run into more trouble and risk getting arrested."

"But they haven't been reading tarot in public anymore."

"What if one of the people they approach about private readings rats them out? Also, they're still camped out on the beach. Remember, it's all vagrants the police are targeting, not just fortune-tellers. I don't know how much longer they can continue living there before the police force them to leave."

"Maria will be heartbroken. She already looked sad when she told me of their recent misfortune."

A few hours later, Carlo and I are riding the scooter he purchased to make getting around Lipari easier. We're on our way to the Spiaggia Bianca where the gypsies are camping. I haven't been able to stop thinking about what will become of Maria and her family since Carlo told me about the police forcing all vagrants from Lipari.

For the remainder of our ride, I try to focus on the beautiful colors of orange, purple, and pink that streak across the sky as the sun sinks deeper beyond the horizon and twilight begins to take over. I close my eyes, letting the soft breeze coming from the sea soothe my spirits. I wish there was a way I could help Maria and her family after all they've done for me.

Music reaches my ears as we arrive at the Spiaggia Bianca. We make our way over to the large band of gypsies who are dancing the *tarantella*.

"Come on! Let's join in!" Carlo grabs me by the hand and runs over to the gypsies. We quickly jump into line and begin hopping to the rhythms of the *tarantella*.

"Sarina! Catch!"

Gianni throws his tambourine to me. I catch it in the nick of time. Several gypsies have tambourines, holding them high up in the air as they shake them in a wild, frenzied motion while they dance. A few of the men are standing in the background, playing the *friscaletto*, or flute, and mandolin. One man is even blowing on a *ciaramedda*, a popular Sicilian instrument.

We continue dancing, switching partners as we link our arms together and break away every few seconds to tap our feet as we hop from one foot to the other. Seeing the gypsies like this, one would think they do not have a care in the world. Again, their love of life always comes through, even when they are facing difficult times as they are now.

I glance at Maria and tiny Isabella. Their faces glow in the light of the bonfire that has been built by their tent. I look at all of the gypsies and try to freeze this image in my mind. For I know that soon they will be forced to move on once more. And this time, I doubt I will be lucky enough to cross paths with them again.

✂ 17 ✂

Panarea and Filicudi

September 13, 1969

Carlo has not had a day off from work since we arrived in Lipari, so his boss has let him take this weekend off to recuperate. We're taking a day trip to Panarea, the smallest of the Aeolian Islands. Later this afternoon, we will set off for the island of Filicudi, where we will spend the night and all of the day tomorrow.

Panarea, like Taormina, is popular with the rich. But for some reason, the wealth seems even more ostentatious here. Though I saw plenty of wealthy people in Taormina, it was still hard for me to get accustomed to seeing how they were able to splurge with their money, when in my family every lira spent was carefully weighed before the purchase was made. Luxuries like eating at fine restaurants and having our hair done at a salon were not realities for us. While I have grown a bit more accustomed to Carlo's beautiful gifts and his treating me to nice restaurants and taking me to other wonderful places, once again I cannot rid myself of the guilt, especially when I think of my family's struggles. All I can pray for is that someday I can share with them a bit of the lifestyle Carlo has introduced me to.

"Dove sei?" Carlo intrudes on my thoughts, looking at me with

worry etched in his face as he picks up my hand and kisses the back of it.

"Nowhere. You should be used to my drifting off all the time." I offer a small smile, knowing Carlo sees through my feeble excuse.

"*Sì.* I am used to your daydreaming a lot. You look so sad when I catch you. Are you happy with me, Sarina?"

"Of course I am, Carlo. I've never been this happy. You know where my thoughts often are." I purse my lips tightly and avert my gaze as I feel tears threatening to spill.

"Your family. I know. They are always with you. I promise they will be a part of your life again someday. But for now, please try not to feel bad that you aren't with them. We've discussed this before. There's no way you can return. Your father cannot be trusted."

"I'm sorry. I didn't mean to cast a cloud on our weekend together. I promise no more daydreaming or sadness. Let's have a good time."

Carlo pulls me to him and hugs me tightly. I return his embrace.

"I love you so much, Sarina."

"I love you, too."

Our ferry has left us off at the pier in San Pietro, the largest of the three hamlets on the east coast of the island. Sky-blue waters with gleaming white yachts and sailboats, both at dock and at sea, adorn the landscape. The image before me looks too perfect and surreal. I feel like I am seeing it in a dream or in a book. So far, of the three Aeolian Islands I've been to, Panarea is the most beautiful and reminiscent of paradise. Cars are not allowed on Panarea, and the best way to explore the island is by *gozzo,* a small wooden motor-boat with a sun shade. We head over to rent one.

"I'll let you navigate the boat."

I look at Carlo horrified. "Me? I have no idea what to do!"

"*Gozzi* are easy to navigate. Even someone with no experience manning a boat can easily steer one. Trust me, many of the tourists here have no experience navigating, and that doesn't stop them from renting a *gozzo.* It'll be fun, and I'll be by your side." Carlo places his arm around my shoulders and gives me a reassuring hug.

"The line to rent is quite long."

"Yes, unfortunately, there's no avoiding that. *Gozzos* are the best way to explore a few of the inlets that are along the coastline and inaccessible by land. Also, we'll be able to stop at any one of the numerous coves we come across and take a swim. Best part of all is that we'll be alone, away from all these tourists."

"Sounds nice."

"And romantic," Carlo adds, giving me a lazy smile.

After waiting in line for twenty minutes to rent our *gozzo,* we're finally out on the water. Once we're farther away from the other *gozzi,* Carlo lets me navigate. He's right. It's quite easy, and I'm actually enjoying it.

We pull into a cove and drop anchor.

"Ready?" Carlo asks me as he pulls off his shirt and shorts to reveal his swimming trunks, and then dives into the water.

I take off my sundress and follow him. Once I reach the surface, I tread the water, enjoying the sun's rays on my face. Carlo treads alongside me.

"It's so beautiful here."

"Not as beautiful as you, *stella mia.*"

"What did you call me?"

"*Stella mia.* You are my star."

Though I promised Carlo there would be no more sadness today, I cannot help my expression.

"Sarina, what is it?" Carlo treads closer to me.

"I just can't believe you called me that. I made up a song called 'Stella Mia' that I used to sing to my little sister Carlotta as we looked up at the stars. I miss her so much. I didn't even get to talk to her when my father brought me back home."

"I'm sorry, Sarina."

"No, don't be. You had no idea, and I'm moved that you think I am your star." I touch Carlo's cheek. He takes my hand and brings it to his lips.

"I don't know what I would do if I ever lost you, Sarina. Don't ever forget that."

We swim around the cove for another half hour before heading back to the *gozzo.* Carlo takes over the steering so that I can relax and enjoy the panorama.

"Where to now, captain?"

"I thought we'd go over to two *isolotti*—Lisca Bianca and Basiluzzo."

"I overheard tourists in Taormina talking about these *isolotti*. They were quite taken with them."

"It's hard not to become enchanted. If I were a millionaire, I would live here in Panarea, although I don't know if I could tolerate the snootier rich people." Carlo laughs. "Anyway, there will most likely be hordes of tourists at Lisca Bianca. Let's go first to Basiluzzo, and on the way back, we'll stop at Lisca Bianca. There's a special place I want to take you to."

As we approach the *isolotto* of Basiluzzo, a wall of rock greets us. Carlo drops anchor near a limestone wall.

"The color of the water!" I exclaim upon seeing the emerald green waters.

"I know. It's amazing, isn't it? There are even a few Roman ruins here in Basiluzzo. I have a friend who scuba dives, and he told me there are also Roman artifacts on the seafloor."

Wasting no time waiting to enjoy the crystalline waters, we jump in. I follow Carlo's lead as he swims closer to the limestone wall.

"Let's just float here and rest a bit from swimming."

Carlo leans back and lets his body float along the surface of the water. I wait a few minutes before floating alongside him, not wanting to take my eyes off the scenery.

When we're ready to leave Basiluzzo, we get back into our *gozzo* and head over to Lisca Bianca.

"Notice the color of the rocks here is much lighter than that of the rocks on Basiluzzo? That's why it's called Lisca Bianca."

I note how perfectly the colors complement the landscape.

Soon we see many couples swimming toward an arched grotto. Once they are beneath the grotto's arch, they stop swimming and instead tread water. And then the couples kiss. I raise my brow questioningly in Carlo's direction.

He smiles. "This is the special place where I wanted to take you. It's called Arco degli Innamorati. Lovers' Arch."

"*Sì.* I can see that." I cannot hide the annoyance in my voice. Does he really think I will feel comfortable kissing him here in front of all these other *pazzi?*

"You think they're crazy, don't you?" Carlo bends over, laughing uncontrollably.

"It's not funny! Why did you bring me here? I don't want to be romantic with you here in front of all these crazy people!"

Carlo wipes tears from his eyes. "Sarina, they're not crazy, and neither am I for bringing you here. There is a legend that says any couple who kisses beneath the arch will be together forever."

"Ah!" I blush when I realize how I must've sounded.

Carlo takes my hands in his.

"Sarina, call me a superstitious fool, but I want to take any measures necessary to ensure that we will be together forever. That's why I brought you here."

I look up into Carlo's eyes. He leans forward and kisses me.

"Let's go," I say.

Carlo drops anchor and once again we dive into the water. We wait for a few of the couples to clear the arch before swimming over. When we're beneath the Arco degli Innamorati, Carlo holds me so tightly to him that I don't need to tread the water as much. His strength amazes me sometimes. He kisses me softly at first, then passionately. As I return his kiss, I send out a prayer to God, asking him to never separate us.

Later, after we've made our way back to the port and returned our *gozzo* rental, Carlo suggests going north to Ditella, where there are whitewashed houses and the sweet fragrances of jasmine, hibiscus, and bougainvillea compete with one another. It doesn't take long for the footpath to become steep and narrow.

"Didn't we get enough exercise today with all the swimming we did?" I ask Carlo as I trudge up the path.

"Trust me. You won't regret the exertion once we get to Timpone del Corvo."

I don't protest any further since I've learned to place faith in Carlo. His excursions have yet to disappoint me. I cannot help but wonder why we didn't do this earlier in the day since the sun is beating down on us this late in the afternoon. Taking my time, I finally catch up to Carlo, who has already reached the top and is shielding his eyes from the sun as he takes in the view.

"I was beginning to think you'd never make it." Carlo snickers.

"Funny." I'm about to make another sarcastic comment, but get distracted by the incredible view. From up here, one can see all across Panarea. And in the north lies the Aeolian Island of Stromboli.

"Absolutely gorgeous!" I wrap my arms around Carlo's waist. He places a kiss on my head as he wraps his own arms around my shoulders.

"So the hike was worth it?"

"*Si, si!* I'm sorry I ever questioned you, my lord." I pull away from Carlo and bow dramatically.

"The more I get to know you, Sarina, the more you surprise me with your humor. Did you ever realize how funny you are?"

I shrug my shoulders. "No. There was hardly any time for laughter in my house, although I did share some funny moments with my cousin Agata."

"I don't doubt it."

As the sun sets, Carlo and I are on the ferry taking us to Filicudi where we'll spend tonight and all day tomorrow. The sky and waters are cast in a translucent gold as the sun sinks farther beneath the horizon. I lean into Carlo who stands behind me as he holds me.

Our ferry pulls into the Filicudi Porto, and immediately I sense the difference in atmosphere. Unlike Panarea with its glitz, noise, and crowds, especially around the San Pietro port, where most of the hotels, restaurants, and nightclubs are housed, Filicudi is very quiet. And from the little I can make out of the surrounding area along the port, it's quite rustic. While Panarea was gorgeous, I feel more comfortable here.

"We must hurry before the scooter rental closes."

Carlo takes me by the hand and begins running toward the scooter rental booth. Sure enough, the old man behind the booth looks like he is getting ready to leave for the day. When he sees Carlo running and waving at him, he immediately comes out and greets us, much different from the person we rented our *gozzo* from in Panarea, who barely thanked us for our business. Of course with the numerous rich tourists in Panarea, he could afford to be rude.

As our scooter zips along the pebbly roads in Filicudi, night soon shrouds the tiny island. I cannot believe how eerily dark it is. I don't even see lights behind the windows of homes.

"Is it always this dark here?"

"Ah! I forgot to tell you, and I guess you have never heard. There is no electricity in Filicudi. And this road that we are on is the only one. By day, you will see farmers, and even people who just want to travel to the port, on mules. And you'll hardly see any tourists. This is considered too remote and off the beaten path for them. Plus, many of the wealthy cannot do without the luxury of electricity."

I hug Carlo tighter as our scooter curves along the jagged coastline. Part of me wants to close my eyes so that I can't see how close we are to the edge of the road. But it doesn't matter since it's so dark and I can't see much anyway. I decide to try and relax and trust Carlo.

Before I know it, Carlo slows the scooter as we approach a small stone structure. A lantern hangs outside, to the side of the door. I then see another similar structure about fifty feet away, also with just a lantern hanging outside. Carlo gets off the scooter, and then helps me off.

"Are these rentals?"

"No, they're people's homes. Since not many tourists come here, there are few rentals. I asked Michele if he knew anyone on the island who would be willing to give us even a room for the weekend. We lucked out. The owners of this house are quite elderly. Their children are all grown and live in Messina and Palermo. They have a few rooms, and said we could have the entire second level to ourselves if we wanted. Of course, I offered to pay them more."

"There's a second level? The house looks so small from the outside."

"It's too dark for you to see, but it extends quite a bit to the back."

"You didn't have to spend all that money to rent the entire second floor, Carlo. One room would've been enough. We'll only be here for one night."

"I know. But I wanted you to be comfortable."

"I don't need much, Carlo. I know you're accustomed to . . . to . . . a more spacious lifestyle."

Carlo laughs. "You can say it, Sarina. I am a spoiled rich brat."

"No, that's not what I meant. Though you did grow up with money, you are so different from the other wealthy people I've seen in Taormina and even in Lipari and when we were in Panarea. I know you would be happy even if you found yourself poor someday."

Carlo walks over to me and takes my face in his hands and then kisses me lightly on the cheeks.

"Grazie, Sarina."

"For what?"

"Thank you for seeing who I truly am. Thank you for not judging me based on who my father is and where I came from."

"I would never judge someone without knowing him or her first."

"I believe that. Now, let's head inside. I'm sure our landlords must be wondering where we are. They tend to go to bed quite early on this island."

Carlo takes my hand and leads me to the house. Before we make it to the front door, an elderly man and woman come out. The man is holding a very large lantern. The woman wraps a shawl around her shoulders. There has been a constant breeze since we got off the ferry.

"Buonasera." The man walks over to Carlo and shakes his hand. *"Mi chiamo Gregorio. Questa è la mia moglie, Ivana."*

"Piacere. I am Carlo. My wife, Sarina." Carlo gestures toward me.

"Piacere, signore, signora." I nod my head in their direction. It still feels odd for me whenever I hear Carlo refer to me as his wife.

As if reading my thoughts, the old lady, I notice, immediately looks at my left hand. No doubt she wants to ensure that we really are married. I cannot help but wonder if they ever had a couple who wasn't married try to stay with them.

"Thank you for letting us rent your rooms. I know it was short notice," Carlo says.

"Eh! We rarely have boarders so it was no trouble. Come. You must be tired."

Once Gregorio and Ivana turn their backs to us, leading us indoors, Carlo looks at me and smiles. I know he is thinking what I am. Gregorio and Ivana are the ones who are tired and can't wait to go to sleep.

The house has a rustic charm. It almost reminds me of my family's home, but ours did not have a second level. Gregorio leads us up a narrow, very steep staircase. We then walk down a long corridor. He explains that his bedroom is to the front of the house while ours is to the back. He then looks over his shoulder and winks at Carlo. My face reddens immediately.

We will have three rooms to ourselves—our bedroom, bathroom, and a small room with a sitting area. Again, I mentally chide Carlo for paying extra money since I doubt we'll use the last room. We'll be exploring Filicudi all day tomorrow and then returning to Lipari.

"I've placed fresh towels in your bathroom. I will change your sheets in the morning after you leave."

I didn't even hear Ivana coming up from behind me.

"Grazie, signora."

"You can join us for breakfast if you like. We eat at seven a.m., but we understand if you wish to wake up later. I can leave some food out for you if you decide to sleep in," Ivana adds.

"Thank you. We want to see as much of Filicudi as we can since tomorrow will be our last day here, so we'll be up early, too. We would love to have breakfast with you." Carlo smiles.

"Good. Good. *Buonanotte!*" Gregorio waves before he heads back down the stairs with Ivana.

The next morning, after we have breakfast, we are back on our scooter and on our way to Capo Graziano, the site where excavations of two Bronze Age settlements lie. Now that it is day, I can see Filicudi's gorgeous landscape with its dramatic cliffs and rocky terrains that hug the coastline. I can even make out paths that seem to run straight down to the beach.

"Do you see all these paths leading to the beach?" Carlo shouts to me above the scooter's din.

"Yes, I see them."

"The locals call them *'sciare.'* The paths were carved into the rock by eruptions from the island's volcanoes before they became dormant."

Once again, another Aeolian Island manages to captivate me with its beauty and long history. As we approach the Capo Graziano, I realize we saw maybe three people on the road, and all of them were on foot. Filicudi's tranquility is very soothing. There is almost a spiritual aura here. I remember once a monk, who was visiting from northern Italy, spoke to the congregation at the church where my family and I attended Sunday Mass. He told us that God is not just found in church or in the Bible, but everywhere, especially in nature and when there is nothing but silence surrounding us. I was only eleven when I heard the monk speak, and I didn't quite know what he meant by being able to find God when silence surrounds us. But now, as the monk's words come back to me, I fully understand what he meant.

After visiting the Bronze Age excavations, we walk along the two beaches that are on either side of Capo Graziano—Spiaggia del Porto and Spiaggia di Pecorini. Both are pebbly beaches. No sandy beaches exist on Filicudi. Since it is still quite early in the morning, the sun isn't beating down on us yet, and there is a light breeze as we walk hand in hand along the shoreline. As we approach the northern end of the island, we come across a huge basalt rock called Giafante, which means elephant in the Sicilian dialect.

About two hours later, as the sun and humidity get higher, we can't take the heat, so Carlo asks a fisherman who is getting ready to set out if we can catch a ride with him. The fisherman seems to be glad to have the company and begins chatting away.

"Have you heard of the Grotta del Bue Marino?" Carlo asks me.

"Yes. My cousin Agata used to say she wanted to go someday with her prince. She had learned of it in school and seen photographs. She told me it looked very romantic."

Carlo laughs. "It is. But the one time I went there, I was just a boy and had no princess. Now I do." Carlo puts his arm around me. I blush when I see the fisherman has overheard Carlo and is looking at me and smiling.

There are countless caves along Filicudi's coastline, but the Grotta del Bue Marino is the most famous as Carlo explains.

"Wait until we swim into it!"

Carlo's face beams much like a schoolboy's. I'm touched by his apparent happiness over introducing new things to me.

After we dive into the water, the fisherman tells us he will come back for us in about half an hour. We wave to him as his boat jets away.

Carlo and I swim slowly toward the cave's opening. We are the only ones here, and again I'm amazed by the intense serene atmosphere this unique island affords us. Carlo enters the cave first, waiting for me to catch up. When I do, he senses my hesitation and beckons me toward him by waving his hand.

"You don't like small spaces, do you?"

"It's just so dark in here."

"You'll be fine."

I follow Carlo deeper into the cave. A low moaning sound reaches my ears. I almost jump out of my skin. I ask Carlo nervously, "What is that?"

Carlo laughs. "It's just the sound of the waves echoing in here. Actually, the sound of the waves is how the cave got its name Grotto del Bue Marino, or the Cave of the Sea Ox—because the echoes sound like oxen."

Relieved that there isn't some unknown creature with us in the cave, I relax. Once I get accustomed to the echoes, I realize the sounds can be soothing.

Suddenly, the color of the water inside the cave becomes an extraordinary shade of turquoise. Carlo turns around and smiles once he notices the look of awe on my face.

"No wonder you wanted to take me here, Carlo. It's absolutely breathtaking."

"It is."

We tread water, basking in the glow of the cave's light. Carlo comes closer to me.

"Wrap your legs around my waist. I want to hold you."

I do as Carlo instructs. We kiss for a long time. Our kisses become more heated; Carlo holds me tightly to him. I kiss the side of his neck. Without warning, he drops me into the water. I come up for air, choking a bit. He's laughing. I splash water his way and try to jump on top of him so I can push him down beneath the surface. But I don't have the strength. He catches me, and I squirm against him, trying to break free. He stills me by kissing me again.

We let our bodies float so we can relax and hold hands, staring up into the cave's darkness.

"I wish I had thought to bring you here last month. That's when the Festa del Mare happens. It's a beautiful feast. A candlelit procession of boats come to this cave. And then a statue of Eolus is dropped onto the seafloor."

"We'll just have to come back next year." I turn my head toward Carlo. He turns toward me and smiles.

"*Si.* You will be my wife then. We can make it our *luna di miele*— our honeymoon—although we'd have to delay it if we still plan on getting married in a few months."

My stomach flutters at the mention of our wedding. I don't say anything and close my eyes, pretending that I am resting.

The time flies by, and we make our way out of the cave and wait for the fisherman to pick us up. He drops us off at the Filicudi Porto, but not before giving us a small bundle of sardines from his morning's catch. We thank him.

"I guess we'll have to take these back to our lodgings since we have no way of cooking them ourselves. It'll be a gift for our hosts. I'm sure they'll invite us to eat our midday meal with them anyway."

As we make our way back to Gregorio and Ivana's house, the clouds are moving in, so that by the time we reach our destination, the skies are no longer sunny. The air is now stifling with an unbearable humidity, and the wind has picked up.

"Let's hope we're just in for a passing shower. We'll have to wait until it's over to take our ferry back to Lipari this evening."

But a few hours later, a series of raging thunderstorms are battering the island.

"Even if the storm lets up soon, the ferry service will most likely be suspended. The waters will still be too rough to traverse. You might as well plan on staying here for the night," Gregorio warns us.

"That's all right. It gives us an excuse to spend another night in paradise."

Carlo looks at me. I notice Ivana is smiling, but she acts like she hasn't heard Carlo as she busies herself washing the dishes from our meal. She made Pasta alla Norma, a pasta dish with eggplant and a salty ricotta cheese. She also prepared the sardines the fisherman gave us by stuffing them with breadcrumbs. My mother used to make sardines this way as well.

Carlo and I spend the rest of the afternoon and early evening in the room with the sitting area. I guess it came in handy after all. We dip hazelnut biscotti, which Ivana baked, into small flutes of Vin Santo, a sweet dessert wine. Gregorio and Ivana are taking their siesta. Carlo and I have become accustomed to foregoing our siestas so we can spend more time together, whether it's back home in Lipari or when we've explored other islands.

We watch the rain and lightning storm that is playing outside our window. It looks quite striking.

A few hours later, I am awakened by Carlo's shaking my shoulder. I'm still sitting in the settee where Carlo and I were watching the rain.

"What time is it?"

"It's a little past eight o'clock. I didn't want to disturb you, so I had a little snack with Gregorio and Ivana. She gave me this panino for you and a few figs and cactus pears."

"You should have woken me up, Carlo. Gregorio and Ivana must think I'm lazy."

"Nonsense. They know we didn't take a siesta and assume that's why you fell asleep later. They've already gone to bed for the night."

"I wonder how early they wake up," I say as I bite into my panino that has mortadella and *Provoletta*. "Hmmm. This is so good."

"Gregorio told me he wakes up shortly before four a.m. to begin fishing. Ivana wakes up with him so she can prepare his breakfast."

After I'm done eating, we decide to go to bed early so we can catch the first ferry back to Lipari in the morning. But since I took a nap, sleep eludes me.

"Are you awake?" I ask Carlo.

"Yes. I'm not used to going to bed at nine o'clock. Besides, this heavy rain is also keeping me up. I can't believe it's still pouring."

I sit up in bed. "Well, there's no use pretending to sleep if we can't."

"Let's go out."

"In this deluge?" My eyes open wide in disbelief at Carlo's suggestion.

"It'll be fun. Come on. We can tell our children and grandchildren someday how we walked in a wild thunderstorm on the abysmally dark island of Filicudi."

Carlo always has a way of making me feel like we're on an adventure even when we're going about our mundane daily routines. It's one of the things I love so much about him. I asked him the other day if he had any gypsy blood in him since his carefree, live-in-the-moment demeanor reminds me of Maria and her family's approach to life.

"I can never say no to you." I lightly kiss Carlo on the lips.

"That's what I like to hear."

We grab the lantern from our sitting room and quietly tiptoe down the stairs so we don't wake up Gregorio and Ivana. We don't even have light jackets or umbrellas. But we don't care.

Once outside, we make our way toward the water. Carlo leads of course since he has a better sense of direction in the dark than I do. By the time we reach the beach, we're absolutely soaked.

"I think we can turn around now," I say.

Suddenly, I realize just how insane our idea to come out here was, and I can't stop laughing. Carlo joins me. He holds the lantern with one hand and keeps the other arm wrapped around my shoulders. His face glows in the light of the lantern. He kisses me, and in this moment, I feel everything—the heavy rain pelting us, our wet clothes clinging to our skin, the warmth of Carlo's lips pressed against mine, the rapid beating of our hearts, the smell of the sea, the pebbles from the beach that have slipped into my sandals.

"*Ti voglio bene, Sarina, per sempre.*"

"I love you forever, too, Carlo."

"Look, the rain is letting up! The gods must've looked down on us and felt bad that we were being drenched and decided to show us some mercy."

"Maybe. But I would wait until we know for certain the rain will completely stop," I laugh.

"Let's walk along the shoreline. There's something about being cloaked in this eerie darkness that I love."

"That's funny. I feel the same way. It's as if no one can see us. It's very comforting."

"Well, no one can see us on Filicudi. This island is practically a ghost town."

"That's part of its charm."

We walk along the shoreline with our arms wrapped around each other's waists. It's now stopped raining. The only light to guide our way is Carlo's lantern. But soon, we catch a glimpse of light coming from the other side of the sea, peeking beneath the clouds, which are slowly beginning to lift.

"It's the moon rising." Carlo points to it. "I don't believe I've ever seen the moon rise before. Let's wait and watch."

Like a sheer white curtain, the veil of filmy clouds slowly lifts, revealing more of the moon. And soon the beach is lit from the moon's glow.

"The moon looks enormous tonight." I rub my hands over my arms. A light breeze is coming off the water. The humidity from earlier has completely faded now that the storm is over.

"I wish we had a blanket so we could spend the night here," Carlo says.

Once the moon has fully risen, we decide to return to our room. Our path on the beach is lit much more now thanks to the moon. But the farther away from the beach we get, the darker it becomes again.

When we reach our bedroom, I light the two candles on our night table.

"I can keep the lantern on if you want more light, Sarina."

"No, turn it off. I like the candlelight better."

Carlo turns off the lantern. While he has his back turned to me,

I begin taking my clothes off, but instead of slipping into my night-gown I remain naked. I wait for Carlo to turn around.

"I'm definitely ready for sleep now. But first . . ." Carlo's voice trails off when he sees me naked.

Though we've shared a bed, I've never changed in front of him. His eyes wander slowly down my body. As his eyes make contact with each part of my body, it's as if he is touching me in that partic-ular spot.

"I'm sorry, Sarina. I thought you had changed already." Carlo turns back around, but I step over to him, placing my hands on his shoulders.

"I want you to see me," I softly whisper into his ear.

Carlo looks at me over his shoulder as if he is still afraid he is overstepping a boundary. But the look in my eyes is all he needs to know I am serious. Slowly, he turns around. I lean over and begin kissing him with a passion I have never displayed. It is too much for him. He wraps his arms around my body and kisses me back just as hungrily. He lifts me and carries me to the bed. Pulling away from our kiss, he strokes my face tenderly with his fingers. Then his hand slowly travels down, stroking my neck, my décolletage, the soft concave curves of my abdomen, the tops of my thighs, behind my knees and down my calves, and then my feet. Tears slowly slide down my face as I realize what he is doing. He is showing me he loves all of me and can wait to take me.

I place my hand over his as he guides it over my body. We look into each other's eyes.

"I can wait until we are married, Sarina. I don't want you to re-gret your first time."

"I know you can wait. But I can't."

Carlo swallows visibly at my admission.

"It feels right, Carlo. How can we waste this perfect night in this perfect place?"

To show him I am ready, I begin stroking him the way he stroked me, beginning with his face and ending with his feet. But I take it a step further and begin undressing him. He doesn't fight me. When he is naked, I lie on top of him, pressing my body closely against his. Closing my eyes, I feel the warmth exuding from his body, and then I listen for his heartbeat. Carlo begins stroking my hair. He then places his hands on either side of my face and pulls me toward him as we kiss again.

The rain starts up again outside, gathering in intensity as another storm gets under way. Carlo takes his time with me, as he leaves a trail of kisses from my lips all the way down to my legs. He repeatedly whispers, *"Ti amo, Sarina."* I whisper back, *"Ti amo, Carlo."* My love for him feels so overwhelming that I begin crying softly. When Carlo notices, he kisses my cheeks and looks into my eyes. His own eyes fill with tears, and I know he is feeling exactly as I am. We kiss for a long time before Carlo begins caressing me. I wrap my arms around him. The rain muffles my soft moans and cries. After we make love, Carlo holds me tightly to him. His heart is still beating as rapidly as it was while we made love. I have never felt so loved as I do in this moment. Soon, Carlo falls asleep in my arms. I am wide awake, not wanting to let go of the memory of our lovemaking as I recount over and over in my mind every detail. These past few weeks, I have felt that Carlo is my soul mate, but tonight I am even more certain of it.

I don't remember when I finally drifted off to sleep, but a few hours later, I wake up in the middle of the night and feel Carlo stirring beside me. Even in the darkness, I can make out that he is awake and staring at me.

"I have something for you."

I laugh. "I guess you can't wait to give it to me since you're up."

"Tonight has been so special. Why not make it even more special?" Carlo smiles and turns his back to me as he lights the candle that is on the night table. He then picks up an envelope and empties something from it. Turning around, he holds it out for me to see. It's a white gold bracelet with a charm dangling from it. I take a closer look and see the charm is of a fish. The fish gleams in what looks like blue sapphire, and its eye is a tiny diamond stone.

"Così bello! Carlo, it's stunning."

"I thought you would like it. I bought it when we were in Panarea. Let me put it on you."

"And you waited until now to give it to me?" I ask incredulously as I hold up my wrist.

"I just wanted to give it to you at the right time. And now I'm glad I waited. Every time you look at this bracelet, you'll remember the night we first made love."

"Ti amo molto, Carlo."

I wrap my arms around his neck. He whispers, *"Ti amo, Sarina."*

Once more we join our bodies. In this moment, I know without a doubt that my heart will always belong to Carlo.

❧ 18 ❧

Stromboli

September 21, 1969

We trek ever higher up the rocky, dark slope. The smell of ash is burning our nostrils. Our eyes are fixated on the fiery glow coming from the peak known as the Sciara del Fuoco, or Stream of Fire.

Carlo has the night off, and he wanted to take me to see the evening eruptions on the island of Stromboli. I cannot believe I'm here. Ever since Zio Mario took me and Agata to see the movie *Stromboli* starring Ingrid Bergman, I have had a desire to come here. Though the movie came out in 1950, before I was born, there was a theater in Messina that played old movies in addition to new ones. I was ten when I saw it. Carlo was shocked to hear that it was the only movie I had ever seen in a theater. My father thought it was a waste of time to sit watching movies while work could be done around the house. But Zio Mario had managed to convince Papá to let me go. Agata and I could talk of nothing else for months afterward when we were together.

Finally, we reach Sciara del Fuoco, where there is a large group of spectators. Carlo and I watch the flow of the embers erupting from the volcano in silence. The stream of lava that flows down the hillside makes for a dramatic view against the night sky.

Though we've been watching the spectacle for half an hour, I cannot get enough of it. It isn't until we've been there for about an hour that I finally agree to leave. We begin to make our descent down the hill when suddenly we hear, "Carlo! Carlo!"

A man who looks to be about Carlo's age with blond hair and piercing green eyes hurries over to us, waving frantically.

"Franco! What a surprise!"

Franco shakes Carlo's hand and looks at me questioningly.

"This is Sarina." Carlo turns to me. "Franco worked at the hotel a few years ago until he got married and moved to Messina."

Franco extends his hand. *"Piacere, Sarina."*

"Grazie. Piacere."

"Where is your wife?" Carlo stretches his head to see if Franco's wife is anywhere in sight.

"Ah! It has been some time since we've seen each other. I had a son two months ago. She's at home tending to him. I came here with my childhood friend Vito."

Another young man who has been standing a couple of feet behind us comes forward tentatively and waves. Carlo and I smile and wave back.

"Carlo, I was in Taormina last week and ran into your father. He told me about your grandmother taking a turn for the worse. I'm so sorry."

Carlo's face pales, but he recovers quickly.

"Thank you, Franco. As you know her health hasn't been good for quite some time."

"Si, si. I remember. I will keep you and your family in my prayers. I'm sorry I haven't come around more to visit, but since I got married my wife has been keeping me busy."

Carlo nods his head. "Did my father say anything else when you ran into him?"

Of course Carlo is wondering if Franco knows that he left the Villa Carlotta.

"No. Naturally, I asked about you, and he told me you were

doing well and were busy with the construction of the new hotel in Enna. And then we spoke about your grandmother. That was all."

Franco doesn't seem to find it odd that Carlo has asked him about his conversation with his father. I'm not surprised that Signore Conti kept from Franco the news that Carlo had left. Signore Conti's pride won't allow for it, and he has probably told people who inquire about Carlo that he is in Enna, just as he told Franco.

"Well, it was good to see you, Franco. Please give my best to your wife. If you will excuse us, we need to get going."

"Buonanotte!" Franco and Vito wish us a good night and then return to watch the volcanic eruptions.

Carlo and I make our way down in silence. I don't want to intrude on his thoughts and wait patiently for when he is ready to talk.

While on the ferry back to Lipari, Carlo finally says, "Sarina, I must go immediately to see Nonna Lucia."

"I know."

"I just hope I make it in time. From the little Franco said, it doesn't sound good." Carlo looks at his watch. "I can still catch the last ferry tonight from Lipari to Milazzo."

"I'm coming with you." I take his hand in mine and squeeze it hard.

"You don't have to, Sarina."

"I want to be there for you. I'm not afraid of your father, Carlo."

"Grazie, Sarina." He sighs. "It's about time I face the music with him. As you know, I never did call him even though we've been gone for about a month now, and I haven't had a chance to write to him like I said I would. But no more hiding. I will also tell him I plan on making you my wife soon."

My heart thumps hard against my chest. Though I told Carlo I'm not afraid of his father, I am terrified of what he will say when he hears we plan on getting married. I don't reveal my worries to Carlo. He has enough on his mind at the moment with his grandmother.

We rush back home and pack a few clothes before catching the ferry to Milazzo. I pray to God that we're not too late and Carlo

gets to see Nonna Lucia before she passes away. I watch Lipari getting smaller and smaller in the distance as we get closer to Milazzo.
I remember how much I was looking forward to my new life with
Carlo when we were on the ferry coming to the Aeolian Islands.
Now instead I am filled with dread. How will Signore Conti receive
us? I cannot believe a month has already gone by. Who would have
thought we'd be returning to Taormina so soon? Again, the irony
doesn't escape me that the city I thought I could never leave is now
the one place I want to be far away from.

❧ 19 ❧

Ritorno a Taormina

RETURN TO TAORMINA

September 21–October 1, 1969

We arrive at the Villa Carlotta close to midnight. As we enter the lobby and pass the bar, a woman's soft singing reaches my ears. I stop and strain my neck to get a glimpse. Her black hair is swept up in a severe bun, and her eyes are closed as she belts out a slow, somber song that is quite lovely. She wears a simple, long, eggplant-colored gown with no embellishments, but the color contrasts quite strikingly with her raven hair and the gold chandelier earrings that dangle from her earlobes. Finishing her song, she opens her eyes and bows to the small crowd gathered in the bar. Her eyes then rest on mine. Even from the distance where I stand, I can see she is much older than me—in her forties or fifties. She slightly bows her head to me and smiles. I merely bow my head before walking away, quickening my pace to catch up to Carlo, who hasn't even noticed that I'm not directly behind him. He's making his way to the staircase that leads to the second floor and his grandmother's bedroom.

Though I'm not surprised that Signore Conti replaced me with another singer, it still hurts. The woman's voice was serene and mesmerizing. I can't deny she's talented. My hurt stems mainly from jealousy, for I wish I was the one still singing at the Villa Carlotta. Carlo said he would talk to his friend at the hotel where he works in Lipari to see if they would let me sing at their restaurant—even for free. But that will have to wait now for when we return.

As we near Nonna Lucia's room, the door opens. I hear whispers, and then Signore Conti steps out. Carlo and I both stop in our tracks.

"Papá. I came as soon as I heard. Is she . . . is she still . . ." Carlo's voice chokes up.

"She has not passed yet, but I fear it will be any day now. I will call the priest in the morning so he can administer last rites."

Signore Conti says this all without looking at Carlo. He stares at the floor, and even in the corridor's dim lighting, I can see his lips are pressed tightly and his eyebrows are knit furiously together.

"If I had known where you were, I would've sent word to you. How did you hear about Nonna Lucia?"

Signore Conti finally glances at Carlo. Thankfully, his gaze hasn't traveled over to me yet, though I know he is very much aware of my presence.

"I ran into Franco."

Signore Conti nods his head before saying, "You can go in and see her, but she's in and out." He then turns to me. "Sarina, do you mind if Carlo visits with his grandmother alone for now? You must be tired. I'll have one of the maids prepare a room for you."

Carlo looks at me as if he's torn over leaving me alone with his father.

"Go be with her. I'll be fine."

"I'll come find you when I'm done visiting with her."

Carlo quietly steps into his grandmother's room. He closes the door behind him.

Terrified of what Signore Conti will say to me now that we are alone, I follow him down to the lobby. He asks the clerk to find a room for me. It takes the clerk just a couple of minutes to find a vacant room. He tries handing my room key to me, but Signore Conti snatches it before I can.

"Allow me the pleasure of escorting you to your room, Sarina."

"Grazie, signore," is all I can muster.

Once we reach my room, Signore Conti unlocks the door and finally hands me the key.

"I must say, Sarina, you are looking well. I see my son has been taking good care of you."

My face reddens.

"*Signore*, I know you must be upset with both Carlo and me. He was going to call you when he was ready."

Signore Conti finally smiles. He waves his hand as if to dismiss what I've just said.

"He is a man now and does not need to call me when he's coming home late—or in this case, not at all. Don't trouble yourself, Sarina. I will talk to my son when the time is right. All that's important now is that he is here by his grandmother's side."

"*Va bene, signore.*"

"I will let you get to bed."

Signore Conti turns to leave, and I take a step into my room before I hear him call me.

"Oh, Sarina. Did you hear Teresa, my new singer, when you came in tonight? Isn't she wonderful? Of course, she's not as young or as beautiful as you are, but I learned the hard way that the young workers never last. Anyway, since you are here, maybe you can read a few of the guests' tarot cards? Unlike you, Teresa isn't a gypsy."

And there it is. Right as I'm thinking he's being kind to me for Carlo's sake, he manages to catch me off guard, as he no doubt intended, leaving me with his parting shot. My blood boils, and before I can change my mind, I calmly say, "Carlo doesn't want me reading fortunes anymore, especially since I will become his wife soon."

Signore Conti flinches, but he holds his composure and says, "It's about time he started a family. You know, Sarina, if you're not too tired, perhaps you should go visit Nonna Lucia. Carlo looked devastated. I'm sure your sitting with him at her bedside will help him. *Buonanotte.*"

Signore Conti walks briskly away, leaving me completely baffled. He goes from insulting me to telling me his son could use my support right now. I close the door behind me and realize my body is shaking from my confrontation. I want to go to sleep, but Signore Conti is right; Carlo looked horrible. He must be beside himself, knowing his grandmother will die soon. I wash my face and change into a more comfortable dress before going up to Nonna Lucia's room.

As I approach Nonna Lucia's room, I notice the door is now open. I walk slowly, deciding to peer discreetly before entering in case Carlo is having a private moment with his grandmother. He is sitting on his Nonna's bed, holding her hand. She's asleep. I'm about to step in when suddenly a woman's figure comes into view. She bends over Nonna Lucia and wipes her brow with a wet towel. She is gorgeous! Long wavy blond hair hangs down to her waist. A snug skirt shows off her curvy derrière, and the slit in the back reveals shapely calves as she reaches over Nonna Lucia. She then turns toward Carlo and whispers something. Her shirt reveals a very generous bosom.

Carlo smiles at whatever she says. I step back before they can notice me and am about to walk away when for the second time tonight, a boldness I have never felt before overtakes me. I take a deep breath and knock softly on the door.

"Mi scusi."

Carlo looks up, surprise registering on his face.

"Sarina. I thought you would've been in bed by now. What are you still doing up?"

"Your father thought it would be good after all if I kept you company."

No sooner do I get these words out than I realize that Signore Conti wanted me to see this beautiful siren with Carlo. Anger fills every inch of my body, but for now I must let it go.

"Sarina, this is Gemma Maio. She's a family friend and has been helping my father care for my grandmother since she took a turn for the worse."

"Piacere." I nod toward Gemma and do my best to give her a warm smile.

"Piacere." Gemma nods back, but doesn't meet my gaze. Instead she looks at Carlo and says, "I will leave you two alone. I am in the room next door. Just let me know when you're ready to go to sleep, and I'll take over sitting with Nonna."

"Gemma, thank you, but you've already done so much. You should go home now that I'm here. And Sarina can help me as well."

"You forget, Carlo, that your family is my family. Nonna is as much my grandmother as she is yours. I want to be here for her in her last days, and for you, too."

Gemma pats Carlo's shoulder before leaving. Again, she doesn't glance my way as she walks by. It's as if I've vanished into thin air. Once I hear her step into her room, I close the door to Nonna's room.

Sitting by Carlo's side, I take his hand in mine.

"Has she woken up at all since you've been here?"

"No. I can't leave her, Sarina, until she sees me. I'm going to sleep up here tonight."

"I understand."

"Thank you."

I want to ask Carlo how long he's known Gemma and if there was ever anything between them. The signals she was sending out were loud and clear that she has feelings for Carlo and was threatened by me. But I know now is not the time to trouble Carlo. He needs a strong, confident woman by his side. Not an insecure young girl. I sit with him a little longer before wishing him a good night and making my way back to my room. But once I'm in bed, I cannot relax. I have felt nothing but tension and awkwardness since we returned. And now on top of having to deal with Signore Conti, there is this woman.

I shake my head, disgusted with myself. I'm being silly. Carlo loves me. I have never been surer of anything in my life.

Then why can't I stop thinking about the gorgeous blonde whose room is right next to the one where Carlo will be spending the night?

The following morning, a small group surrounds Nonna Lucia's bed as the local priest administers last rites. Carlo is much the way I left him last night, sitting beside Nonna and holding her hand. He looks at her desperately, as if he is willing her to wake up and see that he has finally come back home. But I fear she will not do so before she dies.

Signore Conti stands next to Carlo. His face looks very grave. Gaetano and Grazia are also there. Not surprisingly, Nonna Lucia was a favorite with several of the employees at the Villa Carlotta. Grazia keeps dabbing her eyes with a handkerchief. A few of Carlo's cousins are also present as well as a couple of neighbors. Of course, Gemma is there. Her head is bowed solemnly, and her hands are crossed in prayer. I can see her lips moving silently.

I should be praying for Nonna Lucia's soul as well instead of glowering at Gemma. But every time I try to redirect my thoughts, they just return to Gemma.

After the priest finishes performing the last rites, everyone leaves except for Carlo, Signore Conti, Gemma, and me. Gemma starts telling funny anecdotes about Nonna from when she and Carlo were children. So they've known each other that long, I note to myself. Carlo laughs. Signore Conti joins in with favorite memories he has of Nonna. I feel very awkward, as if I'm intruding on their private moment. They don't even seem to notice I'm standing there. I leave the room and go outside, taking a walk through the hotel's gardens.

I see clusters of lavender and chamomile growing in abundance. Looking over my shoulder, I walk over and pull a bunch of the herbs so I can make my healing salve. Hiding the herbs in my bra, I smile, feeling a small sense of satisfaction that I am taking something from Signore Conti.

"*Buongiorno.*"

I start at the sound of the voice. Turning around, I relax when I see it's only Teresa, the singer.

"*Buongiorno.*"

"I'm sorry. I didn't mean to sneak up on you."

"That's all right."

"Your secret is safe with me. I've been guilty of not only taking some of the chamomile to make my tea, but also a few of the flowers. They're my weakness." Teresa smiles.

"I love flowers, too."

"I saw you watching me last night during my performance. You should come by tonight."

"I'll try, but I might not be able to get away."

"Nonna Lucia. I know. Where are my manners? My name is Teresa. And you must be Sarina, my predecessor." Teresa holds her hand out, and I shake it.

"I only sang here for a short time."

"Yes, but you left quite an impression. All of the hotel employees told me about you and your singing. I'd love to hear you sing some time. Maybe if you stop by tonight, you can perform a song or two."

"I don't think that would be appropriate, but thank you."

"You're afraid of Signore Conti, aren't you?" Teresa's left eyebrow arches, and a look of scorn crosses her face. Has she already formed a low opinion of Signore Conti?

"I no longer work for him. I don't think he would take too kindly to my singing."

"What can he do? Fire you?" Teresa laughs.

"It's a bit more complicated."

"His son. I know all about it."

"Who has been telling you so much about me?"

"I'm sorry. But you know how it is. People gossip. Don't be upset. Grazia told me how much all the hotel employees loved you. Everyone guessed that Carlo left to be with you. I'm sure it is no surprise to you that the employees detest Signore Conti. But everyone has spoken highly of his son and how well he treated them while he was here."

I nod my head. "I noticed when I was working here that Signore Conti didn't treat his employees well. For the most part, I managed to escape his temper because I brought in a large crowd due to my singing, and I also offered tarot card readings. So I made a lot of money for him. The only thing he did that made me feel slightly uncomfortable was to change my wardrobe and ask that I wear a Sicilian folk costume. I didn't mind that much. It was a beautiful outfit. But Carlo became livid and felt that his father was pulling my strings and trying to put me in my place, since we know Signore Conti suspected we were romantically involved."

"And Carlo was right. There is nothing wrong with wearing the clothes of our ancestors, especially since I have heard you also sing beautiful folk songs. But Signore Conti was trying to show you that you were nothing more than a peasant and needed to be grateful that he was employing you. He wanted you to feel lower and perhaps make you question being with Carlo."

Teresa's words sting, though I know they are true, especially in light of my confrontation with Signore Conti last night. He wasted no time before reminding me I was beneath his son by saying I was a gypsy.

"You love Carlo very much. I see how pained you are over this talk of his father."

My eyes fill with tears. I fight them back.

Teresa walks over and places her hand around my shoulders.

"You must be strong, no matter what happens. Don't let that wicked man get to you. And don't abandon your singing."

"How long have you been singing?"

"Just for the past ten years since my husband died. Well, at least singing in public. I've sung since I was a little girl."

"So have I. When I got the job singing at the Villa Carlotta, I couldn't believe it. I miss it so much."

"Where are you living now?" Teresa asks me.

"Lipari."

"Surely, they must need singers in Lipari with all the restaurants and wealthy tourists who want entertainment?"

"I have had a hard time finding work as a singer there. I'm beginning to think they're just interested in hiring male performers. When Carlo and I return to Lipari, he will ask his boss if I can sing for free. It would be a way to continue singing until I can find someone who will employ me again."

"That is good. But remember why you first began to sing. Remember the troubles that led you to find solace in your singing. Something tells me you have not been singing at all recently, even when you are just alone taking a bath or going about your daily routine."

"Are you a clairvoyant?" I laugh.

"I have been down a very similar road to yours, Sarina. I, too, came from a very humble background. I also ran away from home, but I was a few years older than you. When I married and had children, I sang to them. Then when my husband died unexpectedly,

I sang on the street. A nightclub owner saw me and offered me work."

I'm still amazed at how much Grazia told Teresa about my life. I should be mad at Grazia for gossiping about me behind my back, but part of me is glad Teresa knows what I've been through and to hear we have so much in common.

"Thank you for your kind words."

"*Non è niente.* It's nothing. Now if you want to grab anything else from the garden, I suggest you do it now while I keep an eye out for the ogre."

"You're too much. I think I have everything I need for now."

We head back indoors, and I agree to have an espresso with Teresa at the bar. After all, no one is looking for me—not even Carlo.

A week has passed since Carlo and I returned to Taormina. It has been grueling to say the least. I don't know how much longer I can tolerate Signore Conti's glares and comments toward me, or watching Gemma spend so much time with Carlo as they tend to Nonna Lucia. Much to everyone's surprise, Nonna Lucia is still hanging on.

Finally, this evening Carlo has agreed to let his father sit with Nonna Lucia. I know he has been fearful to leave his grandmother's side lest she pass away, but getting little sleep and nursing her round the clock is beginning to take its toll on him.

Carlo has dinner with me in the Villa Carlotta's restaurant. He doesn't say much. I make some small talk and tell him how I met Teresa. He merely nods politely.

When we are done eating, I manage to convince him to take a walk with me on the beach. We hold hands as we stroll along the shoreline, watching the sun sink lower and lower. I can feel Carlo finally relaxing.

"I'm sorry, Sarina. I know I've been neglecting you since we've arrived."

"Shhh! No need to apologize. Your grandmother needs you now."

Carlo brings my hand to his lips and kisses it.

"I promise I will make it up to you once we are back in Lipari."

My spirits surge upon hearing this. I don't know why I had begun fearing he would not want to return to Lipari. Being around Signore Conti has just made me insecure.

I swallow hard and wait a moment before I ask him what I've been dying to ask since our first night here.

"Carlo, I know you said Gemma was a family friend, and I gather you've known each other since you were children. But how exactly did your family become friends with her?"

Carlo's eyes get a serious look. He shrugs his shoulders.

"Signore Maio, Gemma's father, is good friends with my father. He owns several wineries throughout Sicily and is quite wealthy. He supplies our hotel with his wine. That is how my father met him and how they struck up their friendship. Since Gemma and I were both only children, we loved visiting each other's houses and playing together. We were close like brother and sister, and we became even closer after her mother died. Gemma was only twelve. Since I had grown up without a mother, I could somewhat empathize with her, although I always felt it was harder for her since she had gotten to know her mother and felt the loss even more. I, at least, had Nonna Lucia, who had become a surrogate mother for me. Gemma's grandmothers had both died when she was a baby. Her maternal grandfather died when Gemma was six years old. So their family is now just made up of Gemma, her father, and her paternal grandfather, who lives with them."

"She mentioned the other night that Nonna Lucia was as much her grandmother as yours."

"*Si.* Nonna would sew dresses for her and do other things that her mother would have done for her if she had been alive. They became extremely close, and Gemma called her Nonna, too. That is why Gemma thinks of Nonna Lucia as her own grandmother."

"Gemma has been through a lot."

"She has. Sarina, I don't want to keep any secrets from you. My relationship with Gemma became a romantic one about a year and a half ago. But I ended it a few months before I met you."

"She still has feelings for you, Carlo."

"You're mistaking her affection for me as a good friend. I made it clear to her when I ended our relationship that we would always be in each other's lives as friends, but nothing more."

I shake my head. "I don't know, Carlo. My intuition is telling me she is still in love with you. And I see the way she looks at you. I know because it's the same way I look at you, and I'm madly in love with you."

Carlo stops walking. "Sarina, I have no desire to be with Gemma. I was never *in* love with her. It was a mistake. I should have respected our long friendship and not crossed the line by getting romantically involved with her. I think I mistook our friendship for something more. And now I know it was a mistake. The love I have with you is so much stronger than what I had with Gemma. You have to believe me."

"I do. I'm sorry. It's just you have such a long history with Gemma. That's powerful."

"Not as powerful as what I have with you."

Carlo strokes my face with his hands before pulling me toward him. He hugs me tightly, and we stand on the beach for what feels like forever. I wish it were just him and me alone here, just as it often was when we explored the Aeolian Islands. But for now, I let myself be comforted in his warm embrace, the cool breeze kicking up from the ocean, and his assurances that I am the only woman he loves.

Nonna Lucia died earlier this morning. Unable to sleep, I woke up very early, just as the sun was beginning to rise. I was sitting in the bar area, writing in my diary, when Grazia came over to tell me. Carlo had spent the night, sitting up with Nonna Lucia. I found out later that she had woken up a few minutes before she died. At least she saw Carlo one last time.

Rushing up to Nonna Lucia's room, I hear crying. Slowly I walk over, not sure if I should be here just yet. I want to give Carlo and his father privacy. But I also want to be there if Carlo needs me. I place my hands on the wall next to Nonna Lucia's door and peek. My heart drops to my stomach as I see Carlo sitting on Nonna's bed, crying hysterically. But he is not alone. Gemma sits beside him as she consoles Carlo, who has all but collapsed in her arms. Gemma is stroking Carlo's hair and telling him it will be all right.

My head is telling me I should interrupt them, but my limbs remain paralyzed even as my blood simmers because this woman is caressing my lover. I want to scream at her, but no, this is not the time or place. I should burst in and push her out of the way and take Carlo into my arms, but I don't.

Someone taps my shoulder lightly. Reluctantly, I pull my gaze away. Signore Conti.

"Please, Sarina, come with me," Signore Conti whispers, and before I can respond, he leads me away by my arm. I let him. I don't care.

My chest feels like it's been stabbed with knives. The image of the Three of Swords tarot card comes to mind. Frantic thoughts race through my mind. Reason is warring with my insecure feelings over what I saw. Reason is telling me it was natural for Gemma to be consoling Carlo after he lost his grandmother. It means nothing. But my insecurity tells me perhaps Carlo still has feelings for Gemma.

I don't realize that Signore Conti has led me outside until the sound of birds' chirping startles me from my thoughts.

"Sarina, despite what you think, I do like you. That is why I am going to be honest with you."

Naturally, I don't believe him for a moment. But I remain silent, waiting for him to continue.

"Sarina, it's no use. This thing that you and Carlo have will not work out. You are from entirely different worlds. But more important, Carlo and Gemma have loved each other since they were children. They are soul mates."

I curl my hands into fists. What does he know about soul mates? And I can't believe he is having this conversation with me now, just minutes after his mother died. Shouldn't he be up in Nonna Lucia's room, consoling his son?

"Carlo and Gemma used to tell me when they were children that they would get married when they grew up. In fact, they were seeing each other not too long ago."

"I know. Carlo told me. We don't keep secrets from each other." The anger is quite apparent in my tone.

Signore Conti smirks at my last line. "So you think. Men are never fully open with their women."

Ignoring his obvious intention to rile me, I say, "Carlo assured me that while he cares about Gemma and respects her, he thinks of her as merely a good friend. Nothing more. I believe him."

"Sarina, do you ever wonder why Carlo fell for you, especially since you come from such opposite backgrounds? I mean, after all, what could my son have in common with you? He was just dazzled by your beauty. I should have known you would be trouble when I saw that red hair on you. But I am straying from my point. Carlo was taken with your looks and your singing. He was probably even charmed by your fortune-telling. How could he not be when all the locals and tourists who visited the beach talked about your beauty and the *special* readings you gave them?"

Of course, I don't miss the emphasis Signore Conti places on "special," and I know what he is implying. I want to defend myself, but then my pride takes hold. I do not need to explain myself or my virtue to him.

"There is something intriguing about a gypsy, I give you that. But no man from Carlo's fine background wants a gypsy for a wife."

"I am not a gypsy. There are no gypsies in my family. I just read the tarot when I first came here to support myself until I could find other work."

"Gypsies might not be in your family, but you became one when you decided to leave your father's household, live with a ring of gypsies on the beach, and swindle people out of their money by professing to know their future."

"You didn't have a problem with my reading the tarot when it made you money."

Signore Conti glowers at me, but I keep my gaze firmly fixed on his.

"I am not going to argue with you. If it makes you feel better to think you are not a gypsy, fine. Keep deluding yourself. Everyone else knows the truth about you. I'm sure you thought, once I employed you as a singer here, that set you on a higher pedestal. It didn't. I will never give Carlo my blessing to marry you. And if he does marry you against my wishes, I will not waste a second before disowning and disinheriting him. In fact, even if he runs off with you again, I will cut him off from his inheritance. And you can trust I am a man of my word, Sarina."

"So you would disown your only child? You have no remorse about that?"

I know the answer, but I'm so disgusted by his behavior that I can't refrain from asking the obvious.

"He is not my child if he disobeys me and takes up with the likes of you. I don't know what he was thinking, running off to Lipari to manage another man's hotel when he owns his own hotel."

"You knew where we were the entire time?"

"Of course I knew. You forget how influential I am, not just in Taormina. I also know he was traipsing around the islands with you and acting as if you were already his wife."

I blush, giving away that Carlo and I have been intimate, just as Signore Conti suspects.

"Sarina, you are a smart girl. You can't deny that you and Carlo come from different worlds. Carlo needs a woman like Gemma by his side. She is accustomed to hosting parties for her father's business and socializing with wealthy people. She is also her father's right hand in his business. Gemma could help Carlo with the running of the hotel, especially some day when I am gone. With you as his wife, Carlo would never again be taken seriously as a businessman. You know how quickly gossip spreads. It would become common knowledge in no time that you read tarots and were a singer. Carlo would become a laughingstock. Sarina, do the right thing. If you love Carlo, let him go. How would you feel knowing that you were the cause of the rift between Carlo and his father? How would you feel knowing he lost his rightful inheritance because of you?"

I want to lash out at Signore Conti, telling him it would be no one else's fault but his own if he disinherits Carlo. But I can't because a part of me knows that much of what Signore Conti says is the truth. I've always known Carlo and I are from different worlds. Perhaps that is why I've had some anxiety about us getting married soon. I always knew that Signore Conti wouldn't approve of us seeing each other. But Carlo foolishly thought he could convince his father that we were meant to be together and that in time his father would accept our union. I wanted to believe Carlo, but I always knew the reality, probably because I've had a lifetime of dealing with harsh truths. Carlo, who is accustomed to a life filled with wealth and opportunity, could afford to be optimistic. He's never had to deal with hardship as I have. He could afford to dream and believe that a rich boy could marry a poor fisherman's daughter. I see now how stupid I've been to actually believe I could have the life I'd always imagined. These past few months have been nothing more than an illusion—a cruel illusion to show me what life is like for other people, but not for someone like me.

Without meeting Signore Conti's eyes, I say in a low voice, "You've won. I will leave, but not until Nonna Lucia's funeral. I want to pay my respects."

"That won't be necessary. The funeral will be just for family and close friends like Gemma and her father."

His words sting me. How can I leave before the funeral? How will I explain it to Carlo?

"I want you to leave immediately. I will have one of the workers drive you to wherever you want to go."

"I can't just leave without saying good-bye to Carlo."

"Either you leave now or I call my lawyer to remove Carlo from my will."

I nod my head, blinking away tears. Perhaps it is for the best that I don't see Carlo before I leave. How would I explain to him that I have had a change of heart? He would probably suspect, too, that his father had a hand in it. I think Carlo would be able to see in my eyes that I still love him and am lying if I say I no longer want to be with him. And I don't think I could take seeing the pain in his face when I tell him I'm leaving.

"You will have fifteen minutes to pack up your belongings. If you should see Carlo in that time, you are to act like everything is fine."

"But what if he asks me why I have my bag of clothes?"

"Lie. After all, isn't that what gypsies are good at?"

With that, Signore Conti storms off.

I walk quickly to my room and throw the few clothes I brought into my bag. Tears are spilling down my face. I keep telling myself this is for the best. This is better for Carlo. He will have a better life without me. Gemma is the wife he needs, just as Signore Conti said. But all I can think of is that I will never see him again.

In front of the hotel's entrance, a car is waiting for me. A man I've never seen at the hotel asks me if I'm Sarina and tells me he'll be driving me. He takes my bag and places it in the trunk before getting behind the steering wheel.

"Where would you like to go, *signorina?*"

I was too distraught to think where I should go. And I'm still in shock.

"Just take me to the village."

I'll figure out what to do once I get there. Hopefully, my head will be clearer by then.

As we pull away from the Villa Carlotta, I whisper softly, "Good-bye, Carlo."

Moments later, we arrive in the village. I decide to go see Angela and ask the driver to leave me in front of her shop. Before I get out, the driver hands me an envelope.

"From Signore Conti."

I break open the envelope's seal and glance inside. Money. Frowning, I hand the envelope back to the driver, but he holds up his hand, refusing to take it.

"Signore Conti told me to tell you it's your last earnings from when you were employed at the Villa Carlotta."

"I still don't want it. Please, return it to him."

The driver places his hand over mine and says, "*Signorina*, don't be foolish. Take it even if it is from the devil. Besides, I'm sure you will need it."

I pause for a moment. The driver is looking at me with sympathy in his eyes. How much does he know about what happened between Signore Conti and me?

"*Va bene.* Thank you for driving me here. *Buongiorno.*"

"*Arrivederci, signorina. Buona fortuna.*"

After wishing me good luck, the driver waves and drives off.

There is a line of people inside Angela's bread shop. I glance at my watch. It is eight in the morning. No doubt the locals are getting their rolls before leaving for work, and tourists who are getting an early start on their sightseeing are grabbing a quick breakfast. I wait until the shop is empty.

It takes Angela a few moments to notice me. She's bent down behind the display shelves, replenishing them with more rolls and breakfast pastries. When she stands up, she jumps.

"Ah! Sarina! You scared me! Why didn't you say anything? It's so good to see you."

Angela quickly hurries over to the other side of the counter and gives me a hug. That is all I need to break down. I collapse against her, sobbing into her chest and dropping my bag of clothes to the ground.

"*Figlia mia!* My poor girl! What has happened?" Angela pats my back while hugging me tightly to her. I try to say something, but can't. I am shaking so hard.

"Come behind the counter. I will close the shop for a break. This way we will not be interrupted."

I quickly shake my head. "Please, don't do that. Don't lose money on my account." Upon uttering those last words, I can't help remembering Signore Conti's words, "How would you feel knowing he lost his rightful inheritance because of you?" And I begin crying hysterically again.

Angela takes me by the hand and leads me to a little room adjacent to the kitchen. She plops me down into a chair in front of a small café-style table.

"I will be right back."

Placing my forehead in my hands, I try to force myself to stop crying. The tears still slide down my face, but I've managed to stop sobbing out loud. After Angela puts the "on break" sign on her door and closes up, she returns, placing an espresso on the table in front of me.

"Drink this. It'll help. I added a little something special in there to calm your nerves."

I take a sip of espresso and can taste the sambuca liqueur Angela has added. It's quite strong, but I don't complain.

"*Grazie,* Angela. I'm sorry. I must've scared you."

"It takes more than a pretty young woman crying to scare me, Sarina!" Angela gives a little laugh. She places her hand over mine and looks at me with concern.

"If you don't want to tell me what has upset you so much, I understand. But if you want to ease your burden a bit, I'm here for you."

"Thank you, Angela. I'm embarrassed for barging in on you like this in the middle of a busy morning. I didn't think I would fall apart like that."

"It happens to all of us. Don't be embarrassed."

Taking a deep sigh, I tell her everything that has happened in my life since I last saw her. I finish by telling her about Signore Conti's threats and how I left Carlo without even saying good-bye.

"How could I do that, Angela? And right after he has lost his grandmother? He's going to think I am some heartless woman and that I never loved him. How could I hurt him so much?"

"You did what you did because you do love him. You don't want to ruin his relationship with his father as well as cause him to lose his inheritance. I can see how tormented you are over this. But listen carefully to me. If Carlo were anyone other than Silvano Conti's son, I would've told you that you needed to give him the chance to decide whether he was willing to forego his inheritance and even have his father disown him instead of you making the decision for him. But you can rest assured that Silvano Conti is a man of his word. He would not only have made good on his promise to disown and disinherit his son, but he also would have made your life hellish. I could even see him causing problems for his son down the road if Carlo managed to secure the funds to open his own hotel as you said he was hoping to do. Silvano Conti is a proud man and is known for his competitiveness—even with his son. All that man cares about is money and looking good to his business cronies, who are just as crooked as he is."

Angela pauses, looks around as if she's checking to see that we are alone when we both know we are. Angela's husband, for some reason, is not at work today. She then leans over to me and whispers, "I never told you this because you can't be too careful, and I assumed you would probably hear of it on your own while you were working at the Villa Carlotta. But something tells me you do not know. It is common knowledge that Signore Conti has ties to the Mafia."

As soon as Angela utters this, she again looks around nervously. In Sicily, many people can get quite paranoid where the Mafia is concerned, fearing their phones are bugged and that spies are lurking behind the seemingly friendly faces of neighbors, shopkeepers, even family members. One can never be too careful.

"How do you think he is funding that new hotel he's building in Enna?"

"But the Villa Carlotta does well. He's had it for so many years."

"It does well, but not well enough to pay for the lavish hotel he's building. It's supposed to be even grander and bigger than the Villa Carlotta. He has connections everywhere. Even if you and Carlo moved to Lipari, he would have spies reporting back to him."

I then remember how Signore Conti told me he knew all along that Carlo and I were traveling through the Aeolian Islands. I also remember how he boasted of his influence.

"Although you feel like your heart is being ripped out of you, Sarina, you did the right thing. I know it is difficult for you to fully believe that now, but in time, you will see. After all you have been through, you deserve happiness and some peace in your life. You already had a tyrant with your father. You don't need another one. Though Signore Conti wouldn't have beaten you as your father did, his controlling ways would have been just as bad. You were so happy when you got the job to sing at the Villa Carlotta that I didn't want to dampen your spirits. But I was worried all along about your working for the likes of him. It's known that he treats his employees poorly. I was relieved when you didn't complain to me about any mistreatment you were receiving from him."

"It's true. He didn't treat his employees well. But other than insisting I wear a Sicilian folk costume while I performed, he treated me fine. I think that's because I was bringing in a huge audience with my singing and my tarot card readings. I made him money. I'm sure if I had stopped doing so, he would've begun to treat me like the others. He said terrible things to me today. So I believe all that you're telling me about him."

"You can stay with me as long as you like. My husband will understand."

"Thank you, Angela, but I will only stay for the night. I just need to rest before deciding where I'll go."

"But where will you go? Surely not back to your father's?"

"No. I can't go back there." At the thought of my family, I begin crying again. "Carlo asked the police to give my father a warning about beating my mother and my siblings. And he checked in with the police from time to time to make sure my family was okay. Now that I am no longer with him, I will not know how they are."

Angela pulls me into her arms.

"Someday, you will be in their lives again. I'm certain of that."

"I hope so."

"Right now, Sarina, you must worry about yourself. Please, reconsider staying with me."

I shake my head. "I cannot take advantage of your kindness. Besides, this is too close to Carlo. Though I love Taormina, I can't stay here. I would run into him, and he would know I was lying about my reasons for leaving. I love him too much to hide my true feelings. The sooner Carlo forgets about me, the better for him."

"Do you need money? I can give you some."

"No. I have enough to keep me going for a little while. I'm sure I'll be able to secure work, even if it's just reading people's fortunes until I can get something steadier."

"Will you return then to Lipari?"

I think for a moment before answering. "That would be the first place Carlo would look for me. Too many memories are there. No, I need to start fresh, somewhere I've never been with Carlo."

I think about all the Aeolian Islands we visited. Maybe I should head west and stay on the island of Sicily instead of going back to the Aeolian Islands. But I still hold hope that I can secure work that will allow me to provide more for my mother and siblings. That someday I can rescue them from my father. I cannot bear the thought of going too far from them.

I then remember that Carlo and I didn't visit all of the seven Aeolian Islands. We never visited Alicudi or Salina. From what Carlo told me, Alicudi is even more remote than Filicudi. I'd never be able to find work there, and since hardly any tourists visit the island, I wouldn't even be able to give tarot readings. I would have a better chance in Salina.

After spending the night in Angela's apartment above her bread shop and promising her that I will write so she'll know I am okay, I take a bus to Milazzo, where I catch the ferry to Salina. For a third time, I am being forced to make a new home in a place I've never been. I wonder when my wandering will finally stop. Perhaps Signore Conti was right after all about me. I am nothing more than a gypsy.

20

Salina

November 1—November 15, 1969

Today is All Saints' Day. I pray that it is a lucky day for me and that I will make some money. Standing at the marina in Santa Marina Salina, I am singing even though it is raining lightly. My straw hat is on the ground with a few liras I've placed inside to make it look like others have given me money. It is a cool day, and my shawl is doing little to chase away the shivers running down my arms. Although summer was not that long ago, it feels far away. I try not to think of those days. So far, my plan of coming to Salina in hopes of not being reminded of Carlo has failed. For every time I look at the sea, I'm reminded of the boat rides we took to the private coves of the islands. Whenever I walk by the few hotels here, I'm reminded of singing at the Villa Carlotta, then going out for the entire night with Carlo. The worst is when he comes to me in my dreams, often angry. Sometimes I dream that I am in his arms again, making love to him.

I have been in Salina for a month now, and the money Signore Conti gave me is rapidly diminishing. I am renting a tiny room from a widow. She is a greedy, miserable witch who would not include any meals with my rent. So I must make my food last as long as possible. My meals usually only consist of bread, fruit, and any little fish I can catch with my shawl. Lately, I've begun feeling dizzy from the lack of nourishment I am getting.

I'm suddenly drawn out of my thoughts and stop my singing when I feel my purse, which is slung around my body, drop to my legs. A sharp pain slices through my leg. When I look down, I see two gypsy boys. One is holding the knife he used to cut through my bag's strap and my leg, and the other takes my purse before they both run away.

"Stop! Someone stop them!"

My cries go unheeded even though several witnesses have seen what has happened. I chase the boys, but they are too fast for me. Bending over, I place my hands on my knees, trying to catch my breath. The cut on my leg is still bleeding. I rip off a piece of my skirt's hem and tie it tightly around my cut.

Standing back up, I wipe the sweat from my forehead with the back of my hand. I cannot believe my purse was stolen. That was all of my money. There wasn't much left, but it would've been enough to pay rent for the next two weeks. What am I going to do now?

Since we are well into autumn and the tourist season has long passed, I have not been able to give many tarot readings. I used some of the money from my last earnings at the Villa Carlotta to buy another deck of tarot cards since I gave my old set to Carlotta. I've had to be careful with the few readings I have given to the locals, conducting them out of sight of the other gypsies who hang around the marina. These gypsies are not kind and generous like Maria's family. They are hostile to newcomers who could take any of their business away. I tried to befriend some of the women when I first got here, but they shouted curses at me and told me to return to where I had come from.

I suddenly remember that, in my haste to chase the gypsy boys who stole my purse, I left my hat with my meager liras by the port. Running and praying that my hat hasn't been stolen as well, I breathe a sigh of relief when I see it's right where I left it on the ground. As I pick up my hat, tears spring to my eyes. I fight them back, refusing to cry any more than I have since I left Carlo. I need to be stronger. Taking a deep breath, I notice people are coming out of church. Maybe they'll feel more generous since it's a holy day today.

I approach an elderly man who's well dressed and is leaning on a very expensive-looking walking cane.

"*Mi scusi, signore.* Can you please spare a lira? My bag was stolen, and I have little money left. I will pray for you and your family."

The man glowers at me and merely says, "You should be more careful," and doesn't give me a second glance as he hobbles away with his cane.

A group of young men, probably about my age, walks by me. One whistles and stares at me from head to toe while the other dares to lift the hem of my skirt, revealing my thighs. I quickly pull my skirt out of his grasp. The third man comes close to me and whispers in my ear, "*Quanto, zingara? Eh?*" "How much, gypsy?"

I run away. I can hear them laughing. Rounding the corner, I take my time walking around the church, giving the vulgar young men enough time to have gone. Once I'm assured they're nowhere in sight, I wait at the foot of the church steps and resume my begging.

A beautiful woman who is on the arm of a young man walks by me. The woman is smiling shyly at whatever her beau has just whispered into her ear. I can remember when that was me, not too long ago.

"Excuse me. I'm sorry to trouble you, but can you spare a lira? My bag was stolen."

The couple stops. The man looks slightly irritated, but the woman holds her hand to her mouth, astonished that I was robbed. She turns to her companion, giving him a pleading look. He pauses for a moment and then takes out a few liras and hands them to me.

"*Grazie. Grazie molto.* May God bless you."

The woman smiles before the man leads her quickly away as if I have some contagious disease.

Today isn't the first time I've begged since I arrived in Salina. But at least now I have the more sympathetic excuse that my purse was stolen. Of course, many beggars lie to elicit more sympathy. But I refuse to do that.

I continue asking for money until the church has emptied, managing to scrounge up a few more liras. I count my money and sigh. It still is not enough for a full week's rent. I suppose I should get it over with and go explain to the widow that I won't be able to pay my rent.

When I reach the dilapidated one-story house, I see the widow is outside, hanging laundry. She is barely five feet and must stand on her toes to place the clothespins on her laundry. A black head-scarf always covers her hair. I now see why. The wind kicks up the flaps of her scarf behind her head, and I can see only a few wisps of gray hair clinging to her bare scalp.

"Signora Bruni," I say in a very low voice, forgetting that she is quite deaf.

She doesn't even sense my presence since she continues hanging her laundry. I tap her arm.

"*Ai! Brutto diavolo!* Ugly devil!" She presses her palms to her chest, but when she sees it's just me, she says, "Ah! It's you! Why did you not just call me? You gave me quite a fright."

I hold my tongue and dare not say I did call her.

"*Mi dispiace, signora.* I'm sorry. May I talk to you for a moment?"

"*Sì.* But hurry. I have a lot to do."

She turns her back toward me as she continues hanging her laundry. I don't understand why she has so much laundry since she lives alone. But then I notice she's washed all of the drapery and linens. I remember seeing the drapery and linens hanging from the clothesline a few days ago as well.

"My purse was stolen at the marina. Most of my money was in it. I'm afraid I don't have all of my rent for next week. Would it be all right if I paid you as soon as I have all of the money?"

"No," Signora Bruni says in a sharp, clipped tone. Again, she doesn't give me her attention as she begins smoothing out the wrinkles from the wet bed sheets.

"I promise I will pay you as soon as I have enough money. Please! I have nowhere to go!"

I step in the widow's line of vision, forcing her to look at me, but she still keeps her gaze averted.

"That is not my concern. I have my problems, too." She tosses her head as she says this.

Her indifference enrages me. Without thinking, I wave my index finger in her face, forcing her to finally look at me.

"*Strega!* You are a miserable witch! You cannot even show some compassion to a poor, starving girl who has no other place to go. I hope when you are shriveling in your old age no one shows you any compassion as you rot away."

For the first time in the weeks I've known her, Signora Bruni finally shows emotion. She blanches at my words. I turn away from her and walk quickly toward the house to pack what few belongings I have.

She follows me into the house and watches me as I throw my clothes into my bag. No doubt she is worried I will steal from her.

As I leave, I give her an icy stare, but she remains silent. I'm sure I have frightened her with my curse. I feel a small sense of satisfaction, for I know how superstitious old Sicilian women are. She will not rest for days, maybe even weeks, wondering if my curse will come true.

Walking back toward the marina, I decide to go to the beach. I think about my confrontation with the widow. I regret that I'd only been paying her rent per week instead of for the entire month. If I had paid for the month, I would have a roof over my head right now. But I also would have starved since I barely would've had enough money left over for food.

The rain has finally stopped, but the sun hasn't come back out. The beach looks quite ugly when the sun is gone. My spirits have continued to sink deeper since I've come to Salina. Perhaps if I had found work at one of the few hotels or restaurants here, that would have kept me from pitying myself so much and from thinking about Carlo. I'm also scared. I don't know how I will provide for myself in the coming days with the little money I can scrape from singing and fortune-telling. And some weeks, I don't earn any money.

My desperation has even caused me to entertain the idea of returning home. What does it matter if my father kills me? I'll die here eventually from starvation if I don't find regular work. Shaking my head, I realize how silly I'm being. Perhaps I should just leave Salina. Go to a city, maybe even Messina. Though my father goes to Messina from time to time, it is quite a large city. I might not ever run into him. And even if I do, I will put up a fight if he tries to take me with him. A small smile slips my lips as I think about the scene.

Not a day goes by that I don't wonder what Carlo is doing. Then I run through the same questions in my head: How did he react when he heard I had left? Is he looking for me? Has he finally accepted it wasn't meant to be between us? Is Gemma still comforting him? Does he hate me?

I keep walking along the shoreline, oblivious to the chill. It isn't until I reach a hotel on the beach that I realize how far I've strayed from the marina.

Walking away from the shoreline, I walk toward the hotel that sits atop the bluff that overlooks the beach. I want to see if there is a shed or supply room to the side of the hotel that is unlocked and where I can possibly sleep for the night. But there are workers everywhere, preparing for what looks to be a wedding. Straining my neck, I can make out the bride and groom behind the window of the hotel's ballroom. The bride looks so happy. I can't seem to escape happy couples.

I leave but am too tired to walk all the way back to the marina. Sitting on the sand, I take out my tarot cards and spread them in a fan before me, hoping one of the hotel's guests might stroll by and ask for a reading. I don't see any gypsies here, so I should be all right out in the open.

An hour later, someone's voice awakens me, but I cannot understand what is being said to me other than "*ciao.*"

"*Ciao.* Are you all right? Do you hear me?"

"*Ciao.*" I greet the man who's speaking in another language, which I believe is English. A tourist. Perhaps he wants a reading. I smile feebly, then point from my cards back to the man, hoping he'll understand I'm asking if he wants a reading.

"Oh! I'm sorry. You don't know any English. Let me switch to Italian. *Ti senti bene?*"

"*Grazie.* I feel fine. So you do know Italian. Would you like for me to read your fortune? I am very good at predicting what your future will be." My desperate circumstances have led me to become more assertive and confident in my promises to potential clients. I remember, when I worked with Maria and her family, how reluctant I was to mislead anyone. Now near-starvation has forced me to lower my morals.

"No. Thank you. I saw you sleeping here, and you looked very pale. I just wanted to make sure you were okay."

I cannot hide my disappointment, but I force myself to be polite. "Thank you, *signore*. I am fine." I begin collecting the tarot cards I've laid out. It's getting late, and I should walk by a few of the restaurants that have alfresco seating to see if I can steal any food the guests have left behind before the waiters clear the tables. The man remains rooted in place, staring at me. As I finish picking up my cards, I notice his foot is bleeding.

"Do you realize your foot is bleeding, *signore?*"

He looks down. "Oh! You're right. I must've cut it on one of the pebbles on the beach. Would you look at that? It's bleeding a lot."

I pull out of my bag a small jar of my homemade ointment.

"This will help it heal, but first let's quickly rinse your foot to clear some of the blood." I stand up, taking him by the hand, much to the man's astonishment, and lead him to the edge of the water.

"The salt in the ocean will sting you a bit, but we have no choice unless you want to hobble over to the hotel and create a sight with the wedding that's going on." I smile.

"Oh no! That's okay. They would probably laugh and call me 'the stupid American'!" He returns my smile.

Laughing, I say, "That is true. They would call you that!"

I instruct him to quickly dip his foot in the water. After he does so, I'm about to tear off another strip of fabric from my skirt's hem, but when he sees what I'm about to do, he shouts, "No, don't ruin your skirt." First he takes off the linen button-down shirt he is wearing over a plain white cotton T-shirt. Then he takes the T-shirt off and uses it to stop the bleeding from his wound.

"Now you've ruined your shirt. On the other hand, my skirt was already ruined." I point to my leg that still has the strip I tore from my skirt earlier to stop the bleeding from the cut the gypsy boys gave me.

"What happened to you?" The man looks genuinely concerned.

"Nothing. It's a minor cut."

I take over pressing on his wound with his shirt. After a couple of minutes, I check to see if his foot is still bleeding, which it's not. I apply some of my healing ointment on his cut with one of the clean corners from his shirt. Tearing off a strip of the shirt that hasn't been soiled with blood, I tie it firmly over his cut.

"That should be fine until you get back home and can apply a more proper dressing."

"*Grazie molto. Mi chiamo Paulie.*"

"Poli?"

"Paw-lie. Paw."

"Puhli?"

He scratches his head as if he's trying to remember something. *"Paolo! Come l'apostolo."*

I nod my head. "Ah! Paolo! *Si.* Like the apostle." I laugh. "Why don't you just go by Paolo then?"

"That's not how they say it in America. It's Paul in America. But everyone calls me by my nickname Paulie. But if it's too hard for you to say, you can call me Paolo."

"Where in America are you from?"

"New York."

"Very big city."

"It is."

"You're here on vacation?"

"Yes, I'm here on vacation with my parents. I was actually born in Calabria. My parents and I immigrated to America when I was six years old. That's why my Italian is not so good. I didn't keep up with it, and my parents were more concerned with my learning how to speak English."

"It's enough for you to get by, and I can understand you."

"That's kind of you to say. May I ask your name?"

"Sarina."

"Nice to meet you."

I nod my head. "I should get going."

"Wait. I'd like to thank you properly for taking care of my cut. Would you like to have an espresso with me?"

My stomach grumbles lightly at the thought of espresso. Of course, I need something more substantial. I feel a bit uncomfortable having espresso with this man I just met, but he was right when he suspected I wasn't feeling well.

"You don't have to do that. *Buona sera.*" I turn and begin walking away, but Paolo calls me.

"Sarina. Perhaps you could tell me more about your cards. Maybe I'll buy a reading after we have some espresso. I promise I don't bite." Paolo holds his hands up.

Though I barely know him, I sense he has never hurt a fly. And who knows? Maybe he will let me read his cards, and I can make some extra money.

"*Va bene.* All right."

Paolo and I are seated at a café. Not wanting to be rude, I only order espresso, but Paolo insists I order a panino, too, saying I can't let him eat alone.

"You look better now that you have some food in you."

As I suspected, this was Paolo's plan all along, to get me to eat.

"Thank you, Paolo, but you didn't have to feed me. I work and can provide for myself."

"I see that. But like I said I just wanted to show my appreciation, and I didn't want to eat alone."

"You said you were here with your parents. Where are they?"

"They're visiting relatives who moved from Calabria to Sicily a few years ago. There's only so much I can take of the relatives. They talk so fast, and I can't always keep up with the Italian and what they're saying. You're not going to believe this but our surname is Parlatone."

"Parlatone. That means big talker." I can't help but laugh.

"I know." Paolo whistles. "And boy, can they talk forever!"

Ironically, from that moment on, Paolo doesn't stop talking for a good half hour. He talks about everything under the sun, from the amazing fresh produce of Sicily to wondering how his life would have been different if his parents had never gone to America and so on. I let him talk, only too grateful that he isn't asking me questions about myself.

When Paolo pays the check, he offers to walk me home. My face reddens as I try to think of something to say. And for some reason, I decide not to lie to him. I don't have the energy for coming up with an elaborate lie tonight, and there's something kind about his eyes that compels me to be honest.

"I'm afraid that as of today, my home will be on the beach until I can find another room to rent. My purse was stolen earlier today, and my landlady would not let me stay until I have the money to pay her rent. But I'll be fine. This isn't the first time the beach has been my home."

"Oh. I'm so sorry to hear that, Sarina." Paolo looks away as if he's embarrassed for me. His hands are in the pockets of his Bermuda shorts. He starts jangling loudly the coins in his pockets and shuffles his feet from side to side.

"Thank you again for the espresso and panino. Have a good night." I turn around quickly and begin traipsing through the sand.

"But you haven't given me my tarot reading yet! I was talking so much that I forgot to ask you to explain more of it to me," Paolo shouts to me.

Once again, Paolo has managed to stop me in my tracks. Before turning back around, I ponder whether I should give him a reading. I know I need the money, but I also don't want to give Paolo the wrong idea. It's obvious he is trying to help me without causing me to lose my pride.

I turn around. "I'll tell you what. If you are still interested in a reading tomorrow, come by where you found me earlier today on the beach, and I'll give you a reading then. It's late, and I'm sure you must be tired, too. I really must get going now. It was nice to meet you, Paolo. *Buonanotte.*"

"Sounds like a plan. Oh! What time will you be there?"

"I'll be there all morning."

"I'll see you then, Sarina. *Buonanotte.*"

As I walk away, I wonder if Paolo will come by tomorrow after he's had some time to think. It won't matter if he doesn't keep his word since he is a tourist. He can disappear, and I'll never see him again. I'll just remain for him the Sicilian gypsy who took care of his cut and kept him company while he was feeling lonely.

Two weeks have passed since I met Paolo. He has been coming to the beach every day for a reading. But after the first week, I refused to give him any other readings. I could tell he had taken pity on me and was merely getting the readings so he could give me money. The other gypsies on Salina would probably think I am a fool for turning away Paolo's money. But I know it's the right thing to do.

I am standing at the shoreline watching the sun begin her descent. My stomach rumbles, but I ignore it. Though I have money, thanks to Paolo, I am being careful and saving as much as I can since I don't know when I'll have a week in which I won't earn any. All I ate today was a blood orange, a roll, and a small piece of cheese. My ribs are beginning to protrude from my chest and my cheekbones are much more pronounced now. Carlo would probably not recognize me if he saw me.

Shaking my head, I stare at the sea. Her waters are calm this evening even though we are in mid-November. I wrap my shawl tighter around me, but it's doing little to keep me warm against the light winds that have been blowing today. How much longer can I continue sleeping out on the beach, especially since winter will soon be here? While the winters do not get that cold in Sicily, by the water it can be quite uncomfortable at night. I need to get away from the beach, from the Aeolian Islands. It all reminds me too much of Carlo. But where will I go? Perhaps I could find employment at a hotel in Messina. I don't care if I'm not hired as a singer, for I've abandoned those dreams.

I was a foolish girl, thinking I could support myself as a singer and have Carlo, the son of a wealthy hotel owner. I was a fool for letting Carlo convince me I was no different from the rich tourists on the islands we visited. Now, the ache of all I have lost in the past few months can be quite unbearable at times. If I had never sung at the Villa Carlotta, met Carlo, and traveled to beautiful places, I would be stronger now. Now, in addition to my family, I ache for

Carlo. But it was my choice leaving him. I loved Carlo too much to watch his father destroy him. No. I had to let him go. I just pray someday he can forgive me and possibly understand why I left without saying good-bye.

Tears wet my face as they do every night that I stand here, staring at the sea. It's the only time of the day I let myself lose control. It hurts too much to constantly keep it in.

"Sarina?"

I look up.

"Paolo. What are you doing here? Shouldn't you be with your parents having supper?"

"We ate early tonight. I was bored and decided to take a walk on the beach. I was kind of hoping I'd run into you. Are you all right?"

Nodding my head, I wipe my eyes.

"You miss your family, don't you?"

I told Paolo about my family and how I ran away from home. I even told him about my being a singer at the Villa Carlotta. But I haven't told him about Carlo.

"Yes, I miss them every day and always will. But they're not the reason I was crying now."

"I see." Paolo looks pensively at the sun, which is just barely visible before it completely sinks behind the horizon. "Sarina, I hope you have come to think of me as a friend in the short time since we met. If you ever need someone to listen, I'm here."

"*Grazie,* but Paolo, aren't you going home soon?" I can't help but laugh. Paolo's face colors, and I regret being so callous. "I'm sorry. I just—"

"No, you're right. It sounds absurd to confide your deepest troubles to someone who you will most likely never see again. I understand. You don't need to apologize."

Paolo sits down on the sand. He begins tossing pebbles into the water. I sit down next to him and join him in throwing pebbles. Soon, it becomes a game over who can throw the pebbles farther out. Before I know it, we are laughing and my worries from a moment ago have been forgotten.

"What am I going to do when you leave Salina, Paolo? I've had fun talking to you and giving you daily readings." I smile playfully at him.

"Well, you put a stop to the daily readings. You could've been rich."

"I suppose." I laugh. "So when do you return to New York?"

"Day after tomorrow." Paolo looks as if he wants to say something else, but he doesn't. His eyes darken, and his expression becomes serious. He rustles the pebbles on the ground next to him. I decide to remain silent and wait to see if he is ready to tell me what is on his mind. But he remains quiet.

"You know, Paolo, it goes both ways—what you said before. You can talk to me, too."

Paolo looks at me, surprised. "Thank you. That's very kind of you."

The silence deepens. I try to think of something to say, but nothing comes to mind. Sometimes it's better to just let the silence be. Closing my eyes, I begin humming softly a song I wrote and sang at the Villa Carlotta about the spell summer casts on lovers. I'm about to cry again as I think that I, too, fell prey to the season's enchantment and let myself fall in love with someone who could never truly be mine.

When I open my eyes, Paolo is staring at me, and I realize I had gone from humming to singing the words of the song softly. Blushing, I say, "I'm sorry. Sometimes I get lost in my head, especially when I am remembering a song."

"It was beautiful. But you weren't just remembering the song. You were somewhere else."

I shrug my shoulders. "Another time, another place."

"Sarina, I wasn't just hoping to run into you tonight. I came here to talk to you about something. You can't go on living like this. I think you know that. You shouldn't be living on the beach, all alone like a wild dog."

Pain flits across my face, hearing Paolo use such a harsh comparison.

"I'm sorry. But it's true. You're a lovely young woman. I understand why you ran away from home, and that was no life for you, either. Sarina, I want to help you."

"Paolo, you are too kind. You have already helped me so much by buying readings from me and taking me to eat a few times. You owe me nothing. But thank you. I appreciate your wanting to help me."

"Sarina, this might sound absolutely crazy, but I've grown to care about you in the two short weeks since we met." Paolo pauses. He swallows hard. "If I don't just say this now, I might never do it and will always wonder, so here it goes. Marry me, Sarina, and come with me to America. My family has money. I have money. You would never have to worry again about when you can eat or where you will live. I know you keep saying you like to be independent and make your own money. That's fine. You can find a job in New York once you're settled if that's what you want. I can make you happy, Sarina. In time, I know we could have a good life together."

I'm too stunned to respond, but I'm also moved. Part of me had wondered these past couple of weeks if Paolo was beginning to develop feelings for me. I knew I should have avoided him and not led him on. But I had been so lonely ever since I arrived in Salina. When I talked to Paolo, for those moments, I let myself stop worrying about my fate or aching for Carlo. But I cannot marry him. And leave Sicily? I would most likely never see my family again.

"You don't have to give me an answer now. Like I said before, I'm leaving in a couple of days. I know that's not a lot of time to ponder changing your life."

"Paolo. I'm sorry, but it is a tremendous change. I would be giving up my home, the chance of ever seeing my family again, for a world I know nothing of."

"We'd come back and visit your family. Your father could do nothing to you once we are wed. This would be your chance to have contact with them again. You could write to them and telephone. Sarina, I know you don't have feelings for me now, but maybe in time. I wouldn't rush you, and I'd treat you like a queen." Paolo glances nervously away from my gaze. I can tell he thinks I am a virgin. Would he feel the same way about me if he knew I gave myself to another man—a man I still long for?

Placing my hands on Paolo's, I say, "I do care about you, Paolo. But I don't want you sacrificing yourself for me. Don't worry about me. I will be fine. I always am."

Paolo grips my hands. He looks into my eyes, but doesn't say anything. I see the pain in his eyes. Once again, I've managed to hurt someone.

If only I could leave Sicily and all of my memories of Carlo behind. Start fresh somewhere else. I'm tired. Tired of mourning the people I can no longer be with . . . tired of being hungry . . . tired of looking for work . . . tired of begging for money . . . tired of asking people if they want their fortunes read . . . tired of the stares some people give me . . . tired of the curses from the other gypsies . . . tired of the men who think I'm also a prostitute . . . I'm just so very tired.

And in that moment, I hear a voice—a voice that sounds so far away, as if I've stepped outside my body and am looking down from the sky above—and I tell Paolo, "All right. Take me with you."

❧ 21 ❧

La Terra Senza Lacrime

A LAND OF NO TEARS

November 25, 1969

The Mediterranean winds that blow in from the Sahara, known as *lo scirocco,* have been blowing since yesterday. An oppressive, humid heat often accompanies these winds. The heavy air matches my spirits. For today, Paolo and I will set sail for America. I feel conflicted and scared—unsure of what to expect when we arrive in this new strange land that will become my home.

Instead of leaving for America in just a couple of days as Paolo was originally supposed to do, he extended his departure for another week and a half. We decided to marry before leaving and needed the extra time to make preparations. Somehow Paolo was able to find a priest who was willing to marry us so soon. Of course the priest had asked if I was pregnant and perhaps that was the reason for the hasty wedding. But Paolo explained that we were leaving for America and he didn't want us to be sharing a room on the ship without being properly wed. The priest was happy to hear that and gave us his blessing to get married in church. The wedding was two days ago in Messina. Angela and her husband were kind enough to close their shop for the day and be our witnesses. Paolo had wanted his parents to do the honors, but the moment they heard of his plans to marry me they returned to America, saying they wanted nothing to do with this sham marriage. Of course they didn't approve. Paolo had been honest with them and told them how I had run away from home and had been forced to make a living reading tarot cards. They told Paolo he would regret marrying me and asked how could he trust that I wouldn't steal his money since I was a gypsy and used to swindling people. His insistence that I was a good person fell on deaf ears. They believed I had cast some sort of spell on him that was clouding his judgment. When he tried to tell them that I was also a talented singer and had sung in the reputable Villa Carlotta hotel in Taormina, they said a woman performing in a nightclub was no better than a gypsy. Naturally, their opinions stung, but I had become accustomed to people looking down at me. I did try, however, to give Paolo a chance to back out of the wedding when I heard how his parents felt, in case they had influenced him. But he assured me he hadn't changed his mind.

After I had accepted Paolo's proposal on the beach, he insisted on getting a room for me in the same hotel where he was staying. But I was terrified of meeting his parents. Even before I knew what they thought of me, I suspected they would not approve. I begged him to just let me continue living on the beach until we were married. But instead, he booked a room for me in a different hotel so I would be spared being so close to his parents. I know I will have to meet them when we are in America. But at least then I will look more presentable than I had looked while staying on the beach. Then again, they might not ever want to meet me.

Paolo took me to a dress shop to buy a dress for our wedding. I chose the simplest dress I could find, not wanting to spend a lot of Paolo's money. I also felt silly choosing an elaborate gown since it would just be me, Paolo, Angela, and her husband at the church.

As we stood at the altar, listening to the priest's words, I stole glances at Paolo. He is a good man, and I already care about him. Perhaps in time, I can fall in love with him. I want to please him since he is doing so much for me.

On our wedding night, Paolo sensed my anxiety and told me we could wait until we were in America to consummate our marriage.

I was relieved, but I also felt guilty. I just was not ready yet to be intimate with another man. How could I be when just a couple of months ago I had been with Carlo? After we had returned to the Villa Carlotta, Carlo and I had not shared a room. We had both known Signore Conti would not allow it since we weren't married. It didn't matter, of course, that we had been living together on the Aeolian Islands. Besides, I would not have felt comfortable, even if Carlo had suggested we stay in the same room.

Now here we are standing at the port in Messina. I feel very small in comparison to the massive ship that will take us to America. Although Paolo had flown to Sicily for his vacation, he wanted to sail back home. He thought it would be a nice honeymoon for us.

"Wait 'til you see the size of the ship, Sarina! And the inside is supposed to be very luxurious."

I try to act as if I am as excited as he is. But all I can think about is leaving my family behind. I keep looking to see if they've come to see me off. Paolo went to my family's house yesterday to let them know that we'd been married, and that I would be leaving for America. I didn't go with him out of fear that somehow my father would stop me from leaving with Paolo. Paolo told me he would not let that happen, but he is so gentle and so much smaller in stature than my father. I was not convinced that Paolo stood a chance against him. I begged Paolo to hide behind the tree that stands outside the house and wait until my father was out. While Paolo was gone, I was sick with worry. When he returned, he told me he had seen my father leaving the house just as he was approaching. So Paolo waited until my father was gone. Paolo told me for a moment he was tempted to approach my father and tell him that I was his wife now, and that my father could do nothing about it or ever harm me again. But on second thought, Paolo feared that if he did this, he would not have a chance to talk to my mother.

Paolo told me that my mother, Carlotta, and Enzo had been happy to hear that I was well. But they had looked crestfallen when they heard I would be moving to America. My mother had given Paolo her blessings and had asked him to take care of me. When he had asked her if she would be able to come to the port to see me off, she had said she would try but did not know if she could get away without my father's noticing.

I know the chances of my mother's coming are slim. Still, I would feel a bit better about this trip if I could see her one last time.

"It's almost time for us to board the ship, Sarina." Paolo glances at his watch. He seems nervous, as if he's afraid I won't be able to go through with this.

"Please. Let's just wait until we absolutely have to board."

Paolo nods his head. "All right."

I am wearing a black-and-white checkered suit—another gift from Paolo. In fact, he insisted on taking me shopping so I could buy clothes for the trip. And he said he would outfit me with a new wardrobe once we were in New York. When I put on the suit this morning, I no longer saw the naïve, desperate girl who had run away from home almost six months ago. I was now a woman.

Lo scirocco is still fiercely blowing, whipping up my hair, which I had cut into a chin-length bob for the wedding. I tuck the unruly strands behind my ears, and shade my eyes from the sun as I look into the distance for any sign of my family.

The ship's horn sounds, resembling the deep, mournful tone of a death knell. I look frantically at Paolo, not wanting to give up hope that my family will come. Paolo's eyes fill with sadness.

"I'm sorry, Sarina. It'll be time soon to board the ship."

"Please, Paolo. Let's wait until we absolutely can't wait any longer. It's not like we're far. We're only steps away from the boarding ramp."

Paolo glances again at his watch and then at the ship.

"All right. I can't say no to you." He gives me a sheepish smile, and I reward him with a kiss on his cheek. He looks surprised but pleased.

Ten minutes later, the ship's second horn blasts. My heart sinks. *Stupida!* I chide myself. Haven't I learned well these past few months that it's useless having dreams or hopes? Closing my eyes, I accept that I won't see Mama or the children again—or at least for a long time. I think about how Paolo told me we could visit. But it seems a distant reality.

"Let's go, Paolo. They're not coming. No use for us to wait until the final ship's horn."

Paolo places his arm around my shoulders as we begin making our way toward the ship's ramp. I lean into him for support. This last disappointment is too much of a blow for me. We're about halfway up the ramp when I hear the voices of children screaming.

"Sarina! Sarina!"

I turn around and see Carlotta and Enzo jumping and down, waving their hands to get my attention. I don't see my mother, but then I see her doing her best to catch up to the children.

Running off the ramp, I bump into several other passengers who are boarding the ship.

I bend down as Carlotta and Enzo rush into my arms. Tears are blinding my vision. I pull away and stand up and all but collapse into my mother's waiting open arms.

"Mama! Mi sei mancato così tanto."

"I've missed you so much, too, my daughter. And now we'll be losing you again."

"We'll visit," Paolo says.

I turn around. The somber expression he had earlier has returned.

My mother nods her head. Her lips are pursed tightly together. I've seen her do this before, usually after my father has given her a beating, when she is doing her best not to cry in front of my siblings and me.

"And I'll write to you, Mama. Is there any way you can get to the mail before Papá does?"

"They're delivering the mail later in the morning now, while he is still working. I have been checking it every day to see if there were any letters from you since we hadn't heard anything in a couple of months."

"I'm sorry I haven't been able to send you any money."

My mother holds up her hand. "Paolo explained to us that you had been having a hard time lately." She is about to say something else, but then glances at Paolo. "Paolo, I'm sorry, but can I have a moment alone with my daughter?"

"Of course. But we will have to board the ship soon. I've asked one of the crewmembers to allow us a few minutes to say good-bye."

"It'll just be a minute."

Paolo takes Carlotta and Enzo aside. I can't believe how much taller they both have gotten since I last saw them. I then realize I missed both of their birthdays. Enzo is now seven, and Carlotta is five. Paolo takes his wallet out and hands each of them a few liras. Once again, his kindness and generosity move me.

"Sarina. What happened to that other young man you told me about in your letters? The one who rescued you after Papá found you?"

I shake my head. "It's too long to explain now."

"He broke your heart, didn't he?"

"No, Mama. I broke his. Please promise me if he ever comes to see you that you won't tell him I've married. I don't want him thinking that was the reason I left him."

"But Sarina, do you love Paolo? Or are you doing this to get off the streets?"

"Paolo is a wonderful man. I care very much about him. I will have a good life with him. Don't worry about me, Mama."

"My child. You've grown up so much these past few months. I wish I could tell you to come home with me. But we both know that's not possible. Not as long as your father is still breathing."

"Sarina," Paolo calls to me.

I look over to where he is standing and see one of the ship's crew imploring him to get on the ship.

Carlotta and Enzo come over to me.

"Write to us, Sarina, and we'll write to you. Tell us all about America. When I grow up, I'll come find you." Enzo smiles.

I bend down and kiss him. "You are going to be such a strong man when you grow up. Take care of Mama, Carlotta, and Pietro." I frown and look at my mother. "Where is Pietro?"

"I left him with Agata at Giuseppe's house."

"Giuseppe?"

"Zio Mario caught them together at the end of the summer. They were just kissing behind the boulders on the beach. But Zio Mario did not care. Needless to say, Giuseppe proposed to Agata after Zio Mario caught them. They got married in September. Agata now lives next door to us with Giuseppe and his parents."

I can't help but smile thinking about Agata and Giuseppe hiding behind the boulders, the same boulders where my father had chased me, thinking I was there to meet my lover.

"Is she happy?"

"She seems to be. They're trying to start a family."

"Tell her I miss her and wish nothing but the best for her."

"I will. She has told me how much she's missed you, too, since you left home."

Carlotta cries as she walks over and hugs me.

"Don't cry, my beautiful little sister. Remember, when you see the stars at night, look for the brightest one and think about me. And I will also look for the brightest star I can see in the skies in America as I think about you. When you get sad, sing the song we always used to sing."

"'Stella Mia.' I still remember the words."

"Good." I kiss her on the forehead.

Carlotta pulls away. *"Sarai sempre con me.* You will always be with me." She curls her small hand into a fist and taps her chest. I'm amazed by the maturity of her action.

Before I fall to pieces, I mimic her gesture and say, *"Vi sarà anche sempre con me."*

I then turn to my mother. We embrace one last time. She whispers, "Don't worry anymore about us. Your husband is your family now."

"Ti voglio bene, Mama."

"I love you, too, Sarina. Be happy." She kisses me.

"Mama, if you say the word, I will leave with you and the children. I don't care about Papá."

Mama takes my face in her hands. Tears are now in her eyes, too. "I would never forgive myself if something happened to you. And even if nothing were to happen, I can't let you return to that kind of life. There's nothing for you back home but constant abuse at your father's hands. When Carlotta and Enzo are old enough, I will encourage them to find a way to leave, too. The same for Pietro. Go, my sweet daughter." Mama gives me one last hug before pulling away sharply. She gestures with her hand for me to go to Paolo.

I take a tentative step toward my husband and stop. Mama's words come back to me: "Your husband is your family now." Taking a deep breath, I wave to Mama, Carlotta, and Enzo before turning my back to them. I link my arm in Paolo's as we head over to the ship's ramp. Though the crewmember is motioning for us to hurry, I walk slowly. Paolo tries in vain to lead me along more quickly. With each step, my heart grows heavier. Halfway up the ramp, I pause and look at my family. Mama, Enzo, and Carlotta have their arms wrapped around each other's backs, as if they're trying to give one another emotional support. I bite my lower lip, still tempted to run off the ship. But then I see the boarding ramp being hoisted up. My stomach feels queasy as I realize this is it. I really am leaving. I look out at my family once more. They wave to me. Mama's large onyx eyes seem darker than usual.

We go up to the top deck, which is swarming with crowds of people.

"*America! America!*" Many of the men laugh and shout, pumping their fists in the air. Their wives smile and laugh along with them. But many of the other women, especially the younger ones, look as sad as me. Their eyes hold vacant, glassy stares, and their complexions are as white as the linens that their mothers and grandmothers have painstakingly embroidered for their trousseaus.

"Sarina, don't cry anymore." Paolo pulls me close to him and strokes my hair, whispering into my ear, "*America é la terra senza lacrime.* America is a land of no tears."

"*La terra senza lacrime,*" I silently whisper to myself.

As the ship glides away from the docks, I finally am able to squeeze past the throngs of people leaning over the edge. I spot my family.

"Carlotta! Enzo!" I scream, but my voice gets drowned in the din of the other passengers calling to their families.

Tears roll down my cheeks as I watch my family become smaller and smaller until they are mere specks in the distance. I then fix my gaze on the mountains. I remember from my geography lessons that mountains do not exist in every part of the world. Yet in that moment I never would have dreamed that these mountains, which had surrounded me all my life, would disappear as quickly as the years I had spent in my homeland. *Surely, there will be mountains where I am going,* I tell myself. It is, after all, as Paolo has said, "a land of no tears."

PART THREE

Astoria, New York, and Messina, Sicily

July–September 2013

22

Revelations

I turn over the remaining pages in my mother's diary, but they are all blank. While I feel like I know more about her, especially from her life before she met my father, I can't help but feel disappointed since I had hoped there would be clues in the diary as to why she left me. Sighing, I rub my temples, feeling a headache coming on.

Notes from Kyle's bagpipe reach my ears. I get up from the bed where I'd been reading and walk over to the window. The melancholy tones match my spirits, but there's also something soothing about the music.

"Shut that racket! You're going to get the whole neighborhood up in arms!" Daddy's voice booms. Soon, he enters my line of vision, holding a bag of groceries with two loaves of Italian bread sticking out.

Kyle stops playing, and I see him laugh as Daddy scolds him about the bagpipes.

Shaking my head, I go back to the bed and lie down. I pray that Kyle finds a job soon so we can move back home. While it's been nice living with Daddy again, it's also been tense due to the back-and-forth ribbing between him and Kyle. I'm sure Kyle is close to losing his temper with Daddy, but he hasn't out of respect toward

Daddy and me. He's a saint—another reason why I love him so much.

Thinking about my love for Kyle makes me think about Carlo. So my mother had a great love before my father. Did she ever come to love Daddy as much as she had Carlo? Something tells me no, and I can't help feeling sad for Daddy. Did he know about Carlo? For his sake, I hope not. Though I wish the diary entries about Carlo and my mother had been about her and Daddy, I can't deny that my mother and Carlo's love was special. I wonder what ever happened to Carlo? And what about my grandmother and Sarina's younger siblings?

Reading my mother's diary these past two weeks has just left me with more questions—and a deeper ache than ever. All these years, I've been deceiving myself, trying to convince myself that I was fine without my mother and that I had little curiosity about her. Of course, there were moments when I was a child and I cried for not having a mother, especially when I would go over my friends' houses and see their mothers doting over them. Aunt Donna was the closest thing I had to a mother, and though she did her best to fill my mother's shoes while she stayed with Daddy and me, it wasn't the same.

While I read my mother's diary, at times it almost felt as if she were sitting at the foot of my bed, reading to me. Wiping away the tears falling down my face, I close my eyes. I should take a nap. I feel so drained. The past couple of weeks have been hard as I learned more about my mother. The emotions that ran through me have left me spent. And I know I must confront Daddy about the diary, for now something tells me he knows more than he's ever let on.

I manage to fall asleep but am awakened only fifteen minutes later.

"Click on the blue *e!* Click on the blue *e!* How hard is it to re-member that?"

Kyle's exasperated voice reaches my ears, followed by Daddy's.

"Have some patience, for crying out loud!"

Kyle must be showing Daddy for the ten millionth time how to get on the Internet. Our bedroom is right next to the office Daddy uses. With us staying here for the summer, Daddy decided it would be a good time for him to finally become savvier with the computer. He's been driving Kyle and me nuts, to say the least.

"Okay. I remember this part. I type in the Internet address in this white bar at the top."

"That's right."

There's silence for a moment, and I think that Daddy has finally remembered how to access a Web site, but then I hear, "How many *w*'s do I need to type again?"

"You've been really out of it lately, Paulie. I know you're not suffering from dementia yet."

"Funny. And I have not been out of it. I just need some time to get used to using this machine."

"It's not a machine. It's a computer." Kyle groans loudly.

"Whatever. You know what I mean."

"I know what your problem is. You've been thinking too much about Penelope Anastasos."

"What? That's crazy. And lower your voice. I don't need you putting ideas into Julia's head."

Penelope? Why would Daddy be thinking too much about the Greek café owner who bought the late Signora Tesca's house, dubbed the Mussolini Mansion by the neighbors on Daddy's block? Penelope opened Olympus Café on Ditmars Boulevard back in April. The café is just a block away from Antoniella's Bakery. Antoniella, or The Hunchback as Daddy's neighbors have secretly nicknamed her, is a force to be reckoned with. According to Daddy, she feels threatened by Penelope, whose café has been a hit since it opened. While the Olympus Café serves Greek desserts and sandwiches unlike Antoniella's Bakery, which serves mainly Italian desserts and pastries, Antoniella still has been fretting, fearing she's losing business. But whenever I walk by Antoniella's, it's still as packed as ever with customers. Daddy mentioned the other day that when Antoniella found out a few of her loyal customers were also patronizing Penelope's café, she stopped talking to them. If she keeps acting that way, she will begin losing business. And she refuses to be cordial to Penelope, who has made several attempts to befriend her.

The only logical explanation I can think of for Kyle's comment to Daddy about Penelope is that Daddy has probably gotten in the middle of the feud between the two women. Daddy must be trying to find a way to either get them to quash their quarreling or to convince both women he's on their side. If only he could finally stop meddling in other people's affairs. Kyle mentioned to me that the neighbors call Daddy "The Mayor" behind his back, which infuriated me even though I know it's true that he has a tendency to poke his nose where it doesn't belong. I'll have to ask Kyle later what exactly he meant by his comment about Penelope, but right now I just want some peace and quiet. Getting out of bed, I head over to the office.

"Can the two of you lower your voices? I was trying to take a nap, and you woke me."

"Tell your husband. Danny Boy gets so worked up over nothing."

" 'Danny Boy' is an Irish song. I'm Scottish, remember?" Kyle sounds very irritated.

"I swear this is the last time I ask Danny Boy to show me how to use the computer."

"Do you really swear, Paulie?"

"I don't like your tone. I've been patient because I know you're stressed with looking for another job, but—"

"You've been patient? What about Julia and me?"

"Stop it! Both of you! I've had enough of your going back and forth with your constant jokes and bickering! This was a mistake! We should have never come here!"

My yelling shuts both Kyle and Daddy up. But they continue staring at me, shock registered all over their faces. It's rare that I lose my temper, and even when I'm upset, I hardly ever resort to yelling.

"I'm sorry, sweetie. Are you feeling all right? You look a bit pale," Kyle says as he comes over to me and picks up my hand, placing a kiss on the back of it.

Daddy looks up from the computer monitor. "She's right, Kyle. We have been acting ridiculous. I'm sorry, Julia. We should have realized this would upset you."

I pull my hand out of Kyle's grip and rub my head.

"Do you have a headache?"

"I do. Can you get me a couple of Advil?"

"Sure. I'll be right back." Kyle disappears down the hall.

I rub the back of my neck, which, along with my head, is also feeling very tight.

"Julia, sweetie, is everything all right? You have been so quiet and withdrawn ever since you and Kyle came to stay here. I know it's stressful being displaced, but is anything else wrong?"

I look at Daddy. Worry is etched all over his face. I suppose I should just get it over with and tell him about Sarina's diary now.

"Remember that family tree assignment I told you about?"

"Sure."

"Since I'm planning on participating in the assignment as well, I went down to the basement to find that binder you had shown me when I was a kid. You know, the one that has our family's ancestry recorded in it?"

"Oh yeah! Wow! That was a long time ago. I'd almost forgotten I had it. Then again, I haven't looked at the stuff in the basement in quite some time."

"I figured. Anyway, I found a trunk. It looked like . . ." My voice trails off as I ponder what to call Sarina; when I talk about her to others, I just say "my mother." Suddenly, I'm reminded of the day before she left, as I pointed to the grapevine and pleaded, "Mama! Up! Up!" right before she lifted me in her arms. Throughout my life, whenever I've thought about my mother, I've often replayed in my mind this memory, and every time I remember it, a jolt of pain flashes through me. I knit my brows.

"It looked like what, Julia?"

"A few of my mother's belongings were in there."

"Oh." Daddy's face goes pale.

"I found her diary."

"Oh," Daddy repeats.

"Sorry it took me so long. I couldn't find the Advil. Your father doesn't keep it in the medicine cabinet like most normal people do." Kyle hands me two Advils and a glass of water.

Daddy doesn't respond to Kyle's crack. Kyle looks from Daddy to me.

"What did I miss? You two look like you saw a dead person."

"Well, I guess you could say that," I say nonchalantly after swallowing my Advil. I place the cold glass of water against my throbbing head.

"So is one of you going to tell me what's going on?"

"A few weeks ago I found my mother's diary along with a few of her other possessions in a trunk. I've been reading the diary and learning all about her."

"So that's what you've been reading the past few weeks? From the book's cover, I thought it was some primer on teaching."

"Yeah, well, I covered the diary with the teaching primer's jacket."

"Obviously. But why the big secret, Julia? Couldn't you have told us you found the diary when you did? It's natural you'd want to read it and learn more about your mother."

I shrug my shoulders. "I know it sounds crazy, but I wasn't ready yet to let you and Daddy know I'd found it. I guess I wanted to be left alone while I read it."

Daddy still hasn't said much since Kyle returned with my Advil. He looks as if he's deep in thought.

"Are you all right, Daddy?" I ask.

"I'm fine. Just thinking. It must've been hard reading your mother's diary."

"It was. But I have to admit it was kind of nice to know more about her finally. She had quite a fascinating life before she met you. Why didn't you ever tell me, Daddy, that she also loved to sing?"

"So that's where you get it from," Kyle interjects.

"The subject of your mother has always been a touchy one for me. I guess you could say I was tiptoeing around you, not knowing what to say and not wanting to hurt you by bringing her up. You also never really asked to know more about her, other than why she left us. And you haven't even asked that question since you were in grade school."

Something about Daddy's excuse really irks me. "So are you saying it's my fault that you chose not to tell me more about her?"

"No, no, no! That's not what I'm saying. It's just you seemed to be adjusting well without having your mother in your life. I didn't want to rock the boat is all."

"You didn't want to rock the boat?" I can't hide the derision in my voice. The Advil still hasn't kicked in, and my head is pounding now.

"Julia, please. Calm down. I wasn't trying to intentionally hide anything about her from you. Just ask. I'll tell you whatever you want to know."

Kyle comes over to me and rubs the back of my neck, something he always does when I have a headache, but instead of making me feel better right now, it's just annoying me. I pull away.

"What did you know about my mother's past other than that she ran away from home, was a singer, and read tarot cards?" I really want to ask him if he knew about Carlo, but I can't bring myself to hurt him if he doesn't know.

"Wow! Your mom sounds interesting!" Kyle says. I shoot him a look that says to be quiet.

"That's about it. I know she had a rough childhood, caring for her younger brothers and sister and dealing with her father's rages and abuse. That's all."

"So you didn't know about this diary?"

"No. I didn't even realize there was still stuff of hers in the basement. I thought Aunt Donna had cleared it all away when . . ." Daddy pauses before continuing. "When we knew she wasn't ever coming back."

"So you knew for certain she wasn't coming back?"

"Not at first, but after a few years." Daddy's eyes look pained, and I regret my earlier anger toward him, but that quickly changes when he says, "Since you're ready to know everything, Julia, I want to come clean with you. Your mother and I were still communicating with each other for a few years after she left."

"What? I always got the impression that she walked out and that was it. You never heard from her again." My pulse begins racing as I wonder what else he hasn't told me.

"Now hold on, Julia. I never actually told you that."

"No, you just never told me anything, and you thought because I hadn't asked I didn't need to know."

"Julia, I don't expect you to fully understand. I'm sorry. You're right. I should have told you, especially when you got older. But I was dealing with what had happened and being a single parent the best I could. It's hard as it is being a single parent, but then being a single father to a daughter whose mother has left, you can't imagine how difficult that was. I consulted with Aunt Donna and even my parents, but they also felt it was best I just focus on the present and not hurt you by bringing up your mother."

"Of course your parents didn't want you bringing up my mother. They hated her."

"No, that's not true. They didn't approve of my marrying her, but they didn't hate her."

I don't believe for a second that my grandparents cared about my mother, but I decide to let it go.

"So you were saying that you were in touch with her after she left. What happened?"

"Let me start at the beginning, although you might know about some of this already if it's in her diary."

"The diary only covered the time shortly before she ran away from home until when she left for America with you."

"Okay. So you must know from reading her diary how hard it was for her to leave her mother and siblings again?"

I nod my head. "Yes, she wrote about her family a lot, especially her guilt over running away and abandoning her family and then her sadness over leaving them when she left for America." Suddenly, I realize that my mother's walking away from the people she loved had become a habit for her. First, she left her family when she ran away from home, then she left Carlo, and then she left Daddy and me.

"As you can imagine, it was very difficult for her, adjusting to life in a foreign country and one in which she didn't speak the language. I taught her a little English when I had the time, and she picked some up from watching soap operas on TV. But it wasn't just the language and cultural barrier that made life here so hard. Naturally, she missed her mother and siblings. But living in a large city like New York was something new for her. She really loved Sicily, and she was so accustomed to always being in contact with nature, whether that was the beach or the countryside. She told me she couldn't believe how much time Americans, or at least

New Yorkers, spent indoors. That was very unusual for her since from the time she was little she was always outdoors. The winters here were especially tough on her. She hated the cold and even the snow, which she saw for the first time in her life when she came to New York. When I met your mother, she was living on the beach and was having a hard time making ends meet."

"I read that in the diary."

"I know that was part of the reason why she agreed to marry me and come here. I loved her very much, and I have no doubt she loved me in her own way, but I often questioned if my love and providing a stable life for her were enough." Daddy's eyes look so far away and sad when he says this. And I know what he gave her wasn't enough. How could it have been when she had been in love with Carlo and probably was still in love with him even after she married Daddy?

"Anyway, I bent over backwards trying to make her happy. I showered gifts on her, took her to the famous sights in Manhattan. She did seem to enjoy many of the places we went to, but I always sensed a deeper sadness and even a restlessness in her. At first whenever I asked her what was the matter she would assure me she was fine. But eventually she did admit to me she missed her home very much.

"About six months after we were married, I began telling her I wanted to start a family. She seemed a bit reluctant, but I didn't question her, and then when she got pregnant with you three months later, I was so thrilled. She was also very happy and wasted no time before starting to knit clothes for you."

"She knit clothes for me?"

"She did. They should be in the basement along with your other things from childhood. I made sure Aunt Donna saved them for when you would have your own kids.

"Well, her sadness over missing home and her family seemed to turn the corner while she was pregnant with you. She truly was looking forward to becoming a mother, and I saw a glow in her I had never seen before. But not long after you were born, her depression returned, and at times it was so bad that she wouldn't get out of bed. We didn't know about this then, but looking back now, I realize she must've had postpartum depression. I was watching Oprah a few years ago, and she did a show on it."

I notice Kyle roll his eyes.

"Sarina sensed something was the matter with her and would tell me she was disgusted with herself for not snapping out of it, especially now that she had such a beautiful baby. The only time she seemed at peace was when she was holding you and singing to you. She loved singing this song called 'Stella Mia' over and over to you."

"I remember the song."

"You do?"

I nod my head. "It's one of the few things I remember about her. I read in her diary that she had made up the song herself and used to sing it to her little sister, Carlotta."

"That's right. Sarina mentioned to me that Carlotta loved that song. She used to call you her *stella mia*. 'You are my star, my beautiful shining little star,' she would say."

Tear spring to my eyes as I remember how she wrote in her diary that Carlo had called her his *stella mia*. I let the tears flow freely down my face. Hearing all of this stuff about my mother hurts so much. Perhaps my father was right in shielding me all those years? Kyle comes over and places his arm around my shoulders. This time, I don't pull away, but instead lean into him.

"So she would have these mood swings. One moment, she was content, and the next she was saying she had made a mistake coming to America. Then she started talking crazy." Daddy looks likes he's about to continue, but instead stops.

"Don't hold back now. I need to hear it all, even the bad stuff."

Daddy's eyes meet mine. He nods his head and then looks down before he continues.

"As I was saying, she started talking crazy. She said that maybe she wasn't cut out to be a mother and that it wasn't fair to you since she couldn't shake her depression. She said a child needs to see her parent happy and confident. Then one day, she caught you playing with her favorite bracelet. It had a fish trinket dangling from it. She—" Daddy stops talking once again, and I notice his gaze is fixed on my wrist. Glancing down, I see what he's staring at—my bracelet. My hand covers my mouth.

"This was *her* bracelet?"

Daddy nods his head.

Of course. I had read about the bracelet in Sarina's diary. Carlo had given her the bracelet as a gift after they made love for the first time when they were in Filicudi. How could I not have made the connection that my bracelet was the same one? I look at my bracelet, and a shiver runs through me now that I realize it belonged to her.

"But I remember when you gave it to me, right after I graduated from kindergarten." I stare at my bracelet. Of course, it was too big for me to wear when Daddy gave it to me when I was five. He had doubled it around my wrist and secured it with a safety pin.

"She had told me she wanted you to have it. She felt horrible that she had lost her temper that time when she found you with it. She hit you on the arm. When Sarina realized what she'd done, she started screaming that she was no better than her father. I told her she was overreacting, and there was no way she could ever be like her father. But she wouldn't hear it."

"Is that the only time she hit me?"

"That I know of. But it's not like I ever came home and found you with bruises or any other marks. She did yell at you a few times, especially when she was in one of her darker moods. But I also saw how she adored you. I still to this day don't believe that she would've become her father."

I'm kind of amazed that my mother had the foresight to see that she could possibly continue her father's cycle of abuse and become the abuser. Then again, from her diary, I could tell she was a very smart, intelligent woman. I glance down at my bracelet again. I'm not surprised she'd gotten upset when she found me playing with it since I know how much this bracelet meant to her. But then she decided to give it up and let me have it. That alone shows me she did love me.

"Are you feeling all right, Julia? Maybe we should stop talking about this—at least for tonight," Kyle asks me. His face looks somber.

"I'm fine. I want to hear it all. Please, Daddy, go on."

"About six months before Sarina left, she stopped receiving letters from her mother. Sarina thought that her father had probably intercepted them and put a stop to her mother's writing to her. She tried writing to her mother, but nothing—until finally her cousin Agata wrote to her. Agata explained that Sarina's father had died earlier that year of a heart attack. Sarina's father had few savings, and they had already run through all of the money. They were struggling to survive. Agata was helping them as much as she could, but she and her husband were also having financial problems. She asked Sarina if she could send them any money. Agata also mentioned that she was worried about Sarina's mother. She had lost a lot of weight and hadn't been feeling well, but they didn't have the money to go to the doctor.

"Naturally, Sarina told me she wanted to go to Sicily. I hate to say this, but I didn't want her to go, and I told her that."

"How could you not want her to go, especially if her mother was sick?"

"I know it was horrible of me to tell her that, but I think I knew deep down that if she returned to Sicily, she might never come back. I told her we could send her family as much money as they needed since my family was well-off. But your mother had a lot of pride, especially where money was involved. You remind me of her that way." Daddy looks at me and smiles.

"She did accept some money from me to give to her family, but she said she couldn't expect me to continually support her family. I told her I didn't mind, but she wouldn't hear of it. She said she would go to Sicily—just for a little while—and find some work so she could help them out until they were back on their feet. I told her that was crazy since they needed regular income and her mother didn't work. But Sarina said that her mother could take in seamstress work and do other jobs, once she was feeling better. We got into an argument. I told her that you were too young for her to take an extended trip. She said that Aunt Donna and my parents could help while she was gone. And again, she said it would just be for a little while. In the end, I gave up. But even if I had insisted that she not go, I'm sure she would've left in the middle of the night. When she got something in her head, there was no stopping her.

"She was only supposed to be gone for a month. But then shortly after she arrived in Sicily, she learned her mother had stomach cancer. Naturally, she couldn't leave then, and I wouldn't have expected her to. So the one month she was supposed to be there turned into several as she cared for her mother and siblings. After six months, her mother died. I waited several weeks after she buried her mother to ask her when she was returning home. I didn't want to upset her and knew she had a lot on her plate with her mother's funeral and all. But she wouldn't bring it up. So I did. I told her she could bring her siblings to come live with us in America. But she told me she was afraid they wouldn't adjust to life here. After all, it had been so hard on her, and she hadn't been as young as they were. I got upset and told her to just admit to me that she was the one who didn't want to come back, and that it had nothing to do with how well her siblings would adapt to America. She tried to deny it, but I broke her down, and finally she admitted that she couldn't come back. She told me she was afraid that if she returned she would take her own life—that's how bad her depression was. I had known she had been depressed, but I had had no idea it was that severe. Then she brought up again that she was afraid she would hit you, and that if she did, that's all it would take to cause her to end her life. I tried telling her that I would get her help and take her to the best doctors. But again, in her stubbornness she refused to listen to reason. She said if she killed herself, then you would have that scar for the rest of your life. I went into a rage. I asked her how she thought you would feel growing up without a mother, with a mother who abandoned her. Sarina said I could send you to Sicily for the summers when you got older. I told her I wouldn't do that to you and that you deserved a full-time mother, not a summer mother. I then accused her of making up this excuse about committing suicide so that she wouldn't be painting herself as the bad guy. That upset her. She began crying hysterically. I can still hear her sobs in my head. I'd never heard her cry like that before. Guilt immediately washed over me, but I was torn between feeling sorry for her and wanting to kill her for what she was doing to us, especially to you." Daddy's voice chokes up.

"Let me get you a glass of water." Kyle begins walking away, but Daddy stops him.

"Better make that a shot of whiskey. I need it."

Kyle nods his head and leaves.

"I don't think I've ever been as mad as I was that day—or as sad. Even though I was angry with her, I still tried to convince her to come back for your sake. I told her it would be different since now she would have her siblings with her as well, and we could all be one big happy family. Nothing I said got through. After two years of trying to persuade her to come back, I finally gave up. Sarina begged me to still send her updates on you and photos. I did. Eventually, she became vague whenever I asked how she was and what her life was like there. I couldn't understand why she had suddenly clammed up. All she told me was that she was working and was supporting her siblings.

"Anyway, Sarina and I communicated by letter for several years after she left, but then one day she told me to send the letters to a post office box because they had moved somewhere rural where mail wasn't delivered to homes. I didn't buy it. I got tired of her games and stopped writing. She still wrote from time to time, but I haven't received a letter from her since shortly after you got married. I actually broke and sent her a photo of your wedding. That's how she knew you'd gotten married."

Kyle returns with two shot glasses of whiskey. "Figured I should make it a double."

"For once, Kyle, you figured right." Daddy takes the shot glasses and downs them one right after the other.

My blood is absolutely boiling. Part of me is stunned and refuses to believe what I just heard. My father was actually having regular communication with the woman who left me—and as recently as my wedding, which was just five years ago! And all this stuff he never told me about.

"Julia, you look like you could use one of these. Just say the word, and I'll go get you a shot," Kyle says.

"How could you?" I ignore Kyle and turn my attention on Daddy, who looks at me with wide-open, innocent eyes.

"I know this all must be very upsetting, Julia."

" 'Upsetting' is a huge understatement. You failed to ever tell me why my mother left, even when I asked you as a child. You never told me she left because her mother was ill and her family was struggling to survive!" My voice rises sharply.

"Does it matter, Julia? In the end, she chose not to return. It's as bad as if she left without a valid reason."

"Yes, you have a point. She never returned, but I always thought she just up and left because she didn't want me."

"Julia, like I said before, I was dealing with this situation the best I knew how. I was so afraid about how you would turn out without a mother. I know it's hard for you to understand now, but please try to put yourself in my shoes."

"Put myself in your shoes? Why don't you put yourself in *my* shoes? I used to cry in bed at night, wondering why my mother left. I used to pray to God to send her back someday. You're right. After those few times I asked you why she left, I never did again because I sensed it was too hard for you. Somehow, I began telling myself it didn't matter that she wasn't around, and I've been letting myself believe that lie, up until when I found her diary. I've always ached for her deep down, but I pushed the feeling away. How could you have thought that keeping all these secrets from me was beneficial to me? You *are* the Mayor of the Block!"

"Huh? The Mayor of the Block?" Daddy turns to Kyle, all baffled. Kyle gives me a pleading look.

"You have to know everyone's business in this neighborhood, but then you keep your own daughter in the dark about her mother all these years. And the kicker? To find out you were still in touch with her, and as recently as my wedding. Don't you think I feel betrayed?"

"Julia, I wasn't trying to betray you or deceive you. Your mother and I both decided it would be better for you to go on as you were with your life."

"But you said she wanted me to visit her for the summers, and you decided against it! You actually thought it was better that I have no mother than one for the summers? What is the matter with you?" I'm absolutely screaming at the top of my lungs now.

Kyle walks over to me and whispers, "Let's get out of here. You need to take a break from all of this."

But I remain standing where I am, shooting Daddy my most evil stare. Daddy just bows his head, shaking it, but doesn't dare say anything more.

"For crying out loud! What is going on here? I could hear shouting halfway down the block." Aunt Donna comes running up the stairs and into the office.

"When are you going to stop letting yourself into the house? You no longer live here!" I lash out at Aunt Donna, whose eyes quickly fill with pain, but she doesn't say anything.

"You knew, didn't you?"

"Knew what, Julia?"

"You knew that Daddy was keeping in touch with my mother all those years."

Aunt Donna glances at Daddy, surprise in her eyes.

"She found her mother's diary. I decided it was time to tell her everything."

"It was time! I'm forty-two years old! When were you going to tell me? At sixty? Why don't you just say the truth, Daddy? You were never going to tell me."

"Julia, we did what we thought was best. Paulie felt horrible not giving Sarina updates on you. That's why he still wrote to her and sent her your photographs."

"He felt horrible witholding updates from her, but he didn't feel horrible keeping me from visiting her in the summers? I love how you both can justify your bad behavior."

"Julia, baby! I just brought your father a case of Frangelico. Let me fix you a drink, and we can all relax a bit and talk about all of this calmly. What do you say?"

I hadn't even noticed Uncle Dom was standing in the corridor outside Daddy's office. No doubt he heard me chewing his wife out. Uncle Dom owns Russo's Liquors and has three stores in Astoria. Daddy hasn't had to pay for a bottle of sambuca since Aunt Donna met Uncle Dom.

"Thanks, Uncle Dom, but I'll pass. Not everything can be solved with alcohol."

Uncle Dom looks like he wants to say something, but he must notice from the look in my eyes that it's wise he just back off.

"How about you, Kyle? Scotch?"

"Just because I'm half Scottish, Dom, doesn't mean I drink Scotch." Kyle sounds extremely annoyed—no doubt from seeing me so upset. I wouldn't be surprised if he soon explodes.

"Boy, you guys are wound tight! Didn't I tell you, Donna, that Julia and Kyle's moving in with Paulie was a bad idea? Three is *always* a crowd." Uncle Dom makes his way downstairs, probably to fix himself a drink.

"Julia, I'm so sorry. All I can ask is that you forgive me. I'm human. I made a mistake. Your mother, too. I know her leaving you was deplorable, and I'm not trying to excuse that, but she was young and in so much pain. If only you could have seen how depressed she was." Daddy is wringing his hands and pacing back and forth.

Aunt Donna turns to me. "It's true, Julia. There were days she didn't get out of bed. I would have to stay and take care of you, especially during the day while your father was at work. Sarina wasn't an evil woman, but she wasn't equipped to be a mother—at least at that point in her life. When I heard about her childhood and how she ran away from that monster of a father, and then how she lived alone on the beach, making a living as a gypsy, I was amazed that poor girl had survived it all. It's no wonder she almost had a nervous breakdown."

"She wasn't a gypsy," I mutter.

"What?" Aunt Donna is looking at me as if I've lost all my marbles.

"She wasn't a gypsy—not in the true sense of the word. I read her diary. She just read tarot cards until she could get other work. Not that there is anything wrong with being a gypsy, although Grandma and Grandpa thought otherwise."

"Oh, Julia!" Aunt Donna places her arm around my shoulders. "Grandma and Grandpa were just worried about their golden child—Paulie—as always."

"What is that crack supposed to mean?" Daddy glares at Aunt Donna.

"We're speaking the truth here, aren't we? It's no secret you were Ma and Daddy's favorite. That's all I'm saying."

Daddy lets it go. He's probably too spent from my yelling at him to battle it out with Aunt Donna.

"Look, Julia. You'll know how hard it is to be a parent when you have a child someday. I hope that you can not only forgive me, but your mother as well. It's not good to let this bitterness fester inside of you."

I really wish Daddy would just keep his mouth shut. He's only making things worse.

"I can't believe you want me to forgive the woman who left me! Okay. Fine. She was severely depressed, but she stayed away all these years. You can't tell me she never got over her depression. I was three years old! Three years old! I needed my mother."

"Yes, you did, Julia. But unfortunately, she wasn't able to be a mother. She was practically a child, seventeen years old to be exact, when we married. And she was only eighteen when she had you. Granted, it was a different time then than it is now. People got married younger, but still. And she had left her family behind in another country. She was also in a desperate situation, as your aunt pointed out. When I met her, she was barely eating, living day to day on just a few liras."

Kyle finally chimes in. "I don't know what it is about the Italian culture that makes people think it's best to keep the truth from their loved ones, especially when it's something negative. It's like you think we're going to fall apart and can't handle it. I've seen it with my own Italian relatives. They keep the truth from someone if they're sick or even dying! How dysfunctional is that? And then you have the nerve to knock the Scottish, Paulie!"

"Stay out of family business, Kyle. I'm warning you." Paulie narrows his gaze at Kyle.

"I am family, Paulie, remember?"

"You know, I haven't liked your attitude toward me in a while."
Daddy walks over to Kyle.

"My attitude? Look what you've done to your daughter!" Kyle
is pointing at me with his index finger.

"Enough! I can't take this anymore!"

I run down the stairs and out of the house, ignoring my family's
cries. Walking briskly, I don't relax until I've reached my destination—Astoria Park. When I was a teenager, I always loved to come
here, especially when I wanted to be alone and think. I would either stroll along the ramp, watching the tugboats go across the East
River, or sit on one of the park benches, waiting for the sun to set
and the lights to come on in the skyscrapers on the Manhattan side
of the river.

I walk all the way to the last bench along the ramp, letting my
heart slow down, before I take a seat. Tears slowly slide down my face.
I don't even bother wiping them. For a while, I just let my mind
empty of all thoughts—something I've learned to do in my regular
yoga practice.

Taking a deep breath, I regret exploding at everyone back home.
Of course, it was to be expected under the circumstances, but I've
always prided myself on my composure. I was angry. I'm still angry.
I shouldn't regret letting Daddy know that. It's just I remember the
pain in his eyes as he talked about Sarina and the hurt she left in her
wake . . . the pain in his eyes when I lashed out at him.

I still can't believe he never told me he had been in touch with
my mother for all those years. I can't deny I'm a bit disappointed in
Daddy. He was never the bad guy in my eyes. After all, he's the parent who stuck around. I guess I had placed him on a pedestal, and
he could do no wrong. While I realize he's human, there's still a
part of me that wants him to always do the right thing by me and
not make any mistakes. Of course, part of me understands that it
must've been very hard for him to suddenly find himself a single
parent of a little girl, and he had wanted to protect me. But I'm
having a hard time getting past the fact that he never had the conversation with me even as an adult. Then again, I'm to blame also. I
stopped asking about my mother a long time ago. I'm sure if I had
asked once I reached adulthood, he would've told me everything.

Naturally, I can't stay mad at him forever. I love him too much for that. But if I can forgive him, can I ever forgive my mother?

I'm shaken from my thoughts when a woman sits at the opposite end of my bench. We make eye contact, and I smile. She looks familiar, but I'm not sure where I've seen her before.

Returning my gaze to the East River, I once again try to let my mind empty of everything. But I'm having a harder time doing so now. My thoughts drift to my mother's diary and what my father told me earlier. I can't help but wonder what happened to Sarina once she returned to Sicily, and why the secrecy? Why didn't she tell Daddy what she'd been up to?

I sigh deeply. Well, at least now I can understand more her motives for leaving and not returning. I don't blame her for going to Sicily to help her family. And I know it wasn't her fault she had postpartum depression. But why couldn't she ever come visit me? Did her depression get the better of her? Or did she simply lose interest in a child she hadn't seen in so long? I wince, feeling the pain of that possibility.

Perhaps I wasn't so wrong all these years to focus on the family I do have and to live my life. While I was in denial about this hole I've tried to bury deeper and deeper in my heart, there's a certain comfort in not digging up ugly truths and pretending everything is fine. But the times I did let myself think about my mother, the curiosity ate away at me. And now that I've opened up Pandora's box by finding her diary and hearing my father's revelations, the curiosity is absolutely driving me insane.

"Excuse me? I'm sorry to intrude on your thoughts, but I thought I'd introduce myself. I've seen you a couple of times on my street. My name is Penelope Anastasos."

"Oh. You're the woman who bought Signora Tesca's house? I'm Julia Parlatone."

"I see word gets around fast in the neighborhood. Yes, I bought the late Signora Tesca's home. Parlatone. You must be Paulie's daughter."

"You know my father?" Although I know that Daddy is aware of who Penelope is in terms of owning the Olympus Café and buying Signora Tesca's house, I didn't realize they had actually met.

"Yes. He comes into my café a lot. I own the Olympus Café on Ditmars. Your father and I have actually struck up a friendship." Penelope smiles.

I then remember what Kyle said to Daddy earlier—that he was thinking too much about Penelope. She is an attractive woman, probably in her late fifties or maybe even early sixties. Her hair is cut in a layered, angled bob and is jet-black with a few subtle cherry-red highlights. Her eyebrows are lush and perfectly arched. She uses just enough makeup to highlight her best features. She's wearing white cropped pants with a dazzling yellow silk top. Large Jackie O–style sunglasses sit on top of her head. Amazingly, she seems to have positioned the sunglasses perfectly so that not a single strand of hair is out of place.

"That's nice." I don't know what else to say, especially since now I'm wondering if Daddy has a crush on this woman. I then anticipate his heart's being broken again and cringe at the thought.

"I'm sorry if I'm being forward, but I couldn't help noticing that you seem to have a lot on your mind. I know we've just met, but I've always been told I'm a great listener and, more important, that I'm good at keeping a secret."

There's something gentle about Penelope's demeanor and a kindness in her eyes that immediately puts me at ease. For a moment, I'm tempted to tell this stranger everything. But we'd be here all night, and I'm sure she has better things to do than listen to my drama.

"Thank you, Penelope. That's very kind of you. But I'll be fine."

"All right. If you are sure you're okay, I should probably head back and check on some things at the café. But you can find me at my café if you ever want to have a frappé and talk. It'll be on the house. And you'll give me an excuse to take a break. It was nice meeting you." Penelope shakes my hand.

"Nice to meet you, too. And I love frappés, so I'll have to take you up on your offer." I smile.

"Good! I look forward to seeing you again." Penelope waves and walks toward a parked BMW. I guess Daddy was right that her business is booming.

She waves one last time before she pulls away from the curb.

"Julia!"

Kyle approaches me, breathing heavily.

"How did you know I was here?"

"It's no secret you love to come here when you're feeling stressed. Besides, even if I didn't find you here, I could use the serenity of the park to de-stress myself."

Kyle sits down next to me on the bench, still trying to catch his breath.

"Did you run all the way here?"

"Yeah. I figured the exercise would lower my blood pressure."

"I'm sorry, Kyle. I should have had that conversation with Daddy in private. I didn't mean to drag you into the middle of it."

"In private? The way you lost it and were screaming, I would've shown up anyway to see what was going on. And you don't have anything to be sorry for. I'm sorry about all the stuff your father told you about your mother. He and I had more words after you left."

"Don't be mad at him, Kyle."

"Oh, so it's okay for you to be mad at him, but not me? You're my wife, Julia. I don't like seeing you upset."

"Well, thank you for being my staunch protector, but Daddy wasn't completely in the wrong. I understand he was doing the best he could under difficult circumstances after my mom left. It's my fault, too."

"What? Am I hearing you correctly? How is it your fault? None of this crazy mess is your fault."

I shake my head. "It is to some degree. I should've asked him about my mother again when I got older. Of course he wasn't going to drop all this stuff on me when I used to ask him as a kid. But he would've probably told me if I had gone to him once I got older and could handle the truth—although the way I reacted today, I'm not so sure I handled it at all."

Kyle puts his arm around my shoulder and bends his head so that he's peering into my face. "Hey! Go easy on yourself. Look. It's no one's fault. Not your father's or yours. I can't believe I'm saying it's not your father's fault, but I know he loves you very much, and he did a great job with you. You're an amazing woman.

Though I still think he should have had this conversation with you a long time ago. But there's no use beating that point to death now. So let's move forward."

"That's just it, Kyle. How do I move forward after learning what I did? If anything, I have even more questions now." I release a deep breath. "I wish I could go back to forgetting about her—or doing my best to—as I have been trying to do my whole life, but I can't."

"So finding her diary and hearing what your father said hasn't given you any closure?"

"No. I want to confront her and hear from her why she never returned. I want to know what's been going on in her life since she returned to Sicily, especially since she was so secretive about it with Daddy. This is going to sound crazy, Kyle, but I want to go to Sicily and find her."

"It's not crazy. I want to come with you."

I place my hand on Kyle's. "Thank you, but we both know you need to stay here and try to land a job."

"Are you sure? That can wait."

"I'm positive. Besides, I think I need to do this by myself. Also, I'm afraid if you don't find a job soon and we continue living with Daddy, you and he will come to blows."

"Don't worry about us. I'll apologize to Paulie for losing my temper with him when we get back home. And I promise I'll make more of an effort not to get so easily riled by his comments and jokes. I know he's just having fun with me. Lord knows he's bored."

"Have I ever told you, Kyle MacLean, how wonderful you are?"

"Yes, but I never tire of hearing it." Kyle presses his forehead against mine and places a kiss on the tip of my nose.

"I'm going to ask Daddy if he can lend me the money for the trip to Sicily."

"Really? What about your rule about never borrowing money from anyone, especially your father?"

"In light of everything that's happened, I think we can both agree he owes me, and I'm just borrowing it. I'll repay it once you've landed a job and we're back on our feet."

"All right. But I want to do something to help. I'm going to hire a private eye to find your mother. If we can get an address for her before you land in Sicily, that would be better—or else you'll be searching for a needle in a haystack."

"That sounds pricey."

"We can swing it, but if you want to ask Paulie to lend you money for that, you can." Kyle smirks.

"If you'd rather I do, I'll—"

Kyle holds up his hand. "I was just kidding. We can afford it, and like I said, I want to do my part to help you."

"Thank you." I lean into Kyle and kiss him.

Kyle breaks the kiss and stands up. "Let's head back. We have a lot to do before your trip. And your father was worried sick about you, so if we don't return soon, I'm afraid he'll have all of Astoria searching for you."

"I'm sure." I laugh.

We walk out of the park, our arms wrapped around each other's backs, and I can't help thinking how lucky I am to have Kyle. My spirits have lifted considerably. Though I'm nervous, I'm also excited about going to Sicily, especially after seeing it through Sarina's eyes in her diary. Finally, after all these years, I'll be reunited with her.

❧ 23 ❧

En Route to Sicily

I'm standing on the top deck of the ferry that transports passengers from Reggio Calabria—or Calabria, as most people call it, situated at the toe of Italy's boot—to Messina, Sicily. It's a picture-perfect day. The sun shimmers on the crystalline blue waters of the Strait of Messina. And the mountains complete the beautiful landscape before me. The closer I get to Sicily, the more my stomach flutters. But it's not from the ferry's motions. My stomach has been acting up since I took the plane from Rome to Calabria. While I was nervous the past couple of weeks as I got ready for my trip, I was too busy to dwell on it. When I told Daddy that I wanted to go to Sicily, he understood but he also expressed concern. He's afraid I still might not find the closure I'm seeking, and he worries that there might be more pain waiting for me in Sicily once I confront my mother. Though he's never believed in lending money, he didn't blink an eye when I asked if I could borrow the funds to cover my airfare and hotel. In fact, he insisted I consider it a gift even though I tried to protest. He told me it was the least he could do after waiting so long to tell me more about my mother.

The private investigator that Kyle hired was able to locate my mother within a few days, which was a relief to me since I wanted to be able to go to Sicily while school is still out for the summer. It's the second week in July, which gives me enough time to make this trip and then return home and get settled before going back to work. I decided to purchase a one-way ticket. This way if things don't go well, I can leave at a moment's notice.

In addition to entering my mother's address into my smartphone, I've also written it down on several pieces of paper and placed them in different places—my wallet, purse, luggage. I guess you can say I'm paranoid. It only dawns on me now that my actions are crazy, since if I were to lose Sarina's address, I could just contact the PI and get the address from him again. I shake my head. Ever since I found my mother's diary, I haven't been acting like myself.

After Kyle told me the PI had found Sarina and had an address, I kept asking the PI to confirm it was really her. I think his finding my mother so quickly also made it hard for me to believe he had located the right Sarina Amato Parlatone. I received another shock when Kyle told me that the reason the PI was able to find Sarina so quickly is that she's a famous Sicilian folk singer. I didn't believe it at first, but then I remembered the songbook I had found in the trunk and how Sarina had sung at the Villa Carlotta. But part of me still doesn't want to believe it until I hear it from her. Of course the thought that she possibly chose her career over me has entered my mind. I began to get angry all over again, but Kyle told me not to jump to conclusions until I hear what Sarina has to say.

In addition to Sarina's address, the PI also gave Kyle a phone number. I thought long and hard about whether I, or my father, should call her first and let her know I was going to see her. I decided not to. I want to make sure what she tells me is the truth and not some rehearsed version of it.

"Messina!"

The announcement that we've arrived at our port of call snaps me out of my thoughts. My palms feel sweaty as I grab my luggage and make my way down to the main level of the ferry. It's just a matter of time now until I see my mother again.

❦ 24 ❧

Reunion

My taxi arrives at a large but modest house that sits about a hundred feet away from the beach. There are no other neighboring houses for miles. An enormous wooden fence wraps around the property. I pay the taxi driver and slowly make my way to the front entrance. My heart is beating so loudly that it's competing with the sound of the waves crashing against the shore. The surf is quite strong today. I look out at the beach, but it's quiet. No swimmers are in sight. It's early evening, so I guess it would be a bit late to go swimming. But I know how much Italians love taking their *passeggiate,* so I'd imagine I would at least see people walking along the beach. Then I notice the private property signs.

I think about what the PI said about Sarina's being a famous Sicilian folk singer. If it weren't for the fence and the fact that her house sits on a private beach with no houses nearby, I would begin to doubt his claims that my mother is famous. I was expecting a much more lavish house. When I reach the door, I see there is a surveillance camera perched near the roof of the house and angled right where I'm standing. An intercom is also present—all likely signs that someone famous does live here and is safeguarding his or her privacy. Then again, many people have cameras and intercoms now, and they're not all famous.

Ringing the bell, I wait. But no one's voice comes through the intercom. I wait longer until I press the bell again. Great. I didn't anticipate that no one would be home. Now I'm stranded here on a remote beach, and my cell phone isn't activated for international use. Turning around, I begin walking away when I hear the door open. I freeze.

"*Ciao! Chi è, per favore?*"

Could this be my mother?

I turn around. The woman who greets me is very tall and has graying brown hair. Nothing about her looks anything like the photos of my mother from when she was young or even the more current photo Kyle's PI had sent him. But even that photo was taken about ten years ago. A person can change a lot in a decade.

"*Buona giornata. Sto cercando la Signora Sarina Amato Parlatone.*" I offer a shy smile to show the woman she has no reason to mistrust me. She still looks at me with a frown.

"Parlatone?"

"*Sì.*"

"Wait a moment, please." She turns to leave, but then turns back around. "I'm sorry, but what is your name?"

I'm taken aback that she knows English and that she knows I speak English.

"How did you know I speak English?"

"Your suitcase has tags for JFK. That's in New York."

I glance down at my luggage. "Oh. Yes, that's correct."

"Your name, please?"

"I'm sorry. My name is—"

"*Julia? Non può essere.* It can't be."

A woman is standing in the doorway. She's staring at me, her eyes are wide open, and her hand covers her mouth. While she looks familiar, again it's not quite my mother's image. Also, her hair is a rich chocolate brown, and she looks too young to be my mother, who would now be sixty-one. This woman looks like she's in her late forties, maybe early fifties. But how does she know my name?

"Yes. My name is Julia."

The woman rushes over to me and takes me in her arms. I just stand there. This has to be my mother, but it doesn't feel right. I always imagined that if we were reunited someday I would instinctively know it was her, even if her looks had changed dramatically.

After hugging me, she kisses me on both cheeks and takes my face in both of her hands.

"It's a miracle. God has answered my prayers."

I scrutinize her face and see she has the same upturned, bow-shaped lips that my mother and I have. She is also petite like my mother, but looks even shorter at 4'11". Still, this is not the face of the mother whom I remember holding me up to the grapevine or the face in the other fleeting images I have kept in my memory. But it must be her. The woman must see my look of confusion.

"I'm sorry. It's just I am shocked. I am Carlotta—your mother's—"

"Sister. Of course." Now it all makes sense. "You know of me?"

"Why, naturally. You are my niece. I recognized you from your wedding photo that Sarina has in her bedroom."

"She keeps my photo in her bedroom?" I don't know why this comes as a surprise to me since my father told me he sent her my wedding photo. But hearing that my mother keeps my photo displayed in her room brings to the surface a bunch of emotions. I swallow hard.

"*Sì.* And photos of you from when you were a baby and little girl. It's quite a shrine." Carlotta smiles. She looks like she is about to cry, but manages to hold her tears off.

"Is she home?"

"Yes. But before we step inside, I have to ask you. Did your mother write to your father? Is that why you're here? I've begged her to write or call. But of course, she has so much pride and would never admit to me if she had."

I shake my head. "No. My father has not communicated with her since a few years ago. She did not know I was coming."

Carlotta frowns. "I see. Then how did you know where we live if she did not contact you?"

"My husband hired a private investigator. I guess I should have called and let her know I was coming, but I preferred not to."

Carlotta's face looks pensive, then she says, "It doesn't matter. What is important is that you are here."

She takes me by the arm and leads me inside. I almost forget my luggage, but the woman who answered the door takes it. She is now staring at me, curiosity written all over her expression. Of course she listened to the whole exchange between Carlotta and me and now knows I am Sarina's long-lost daughter.

"Where are my manners? I'm sorry, Julia. This is Adriana, one of our maids."

One of their maids. So it is true that my mother is rich and famous. I bow my head slightly toward Adriana. She bows her head back and mumbles, *"Piacere."*

The interior of the house has a wide-open design with views of the beach. While the house is quite spacious and comfortable, it is not as lavish or over the top as I would expect the home of a celebrity to be. My eyes scan all around, searching for my mother, but she is nowhere in sight.

"Sit down, Julia. You must be thirsty. Let me get you a drink. I just made some fresh *limonata*. How do you Americans call it?"

"Lemonade. Thank you. That would be nice."

"By the way, Julia, your Italian is quite good. Your mother will be so pleased to see you learned it. I take it your father taught you?"

"No. He hardly speaks it anymore. I took it in school."

"I'll be right back. I'll go find Sarina. She won't believe that you are here." Before Carlotta goes to get my mother she comes over and kisses me on the forehead. She then strokes my hair as if to prove to herself that I'm not a ghost and am really sitting in front of her.

I take out of my purse a tissue and wipe the sweat from my face. My shirt is completely wet and sticking to me. Though I had heard how hot Sicily gets in July, I'm still not prepared. There are just ceiling fans in the house. One of the doors that opens up onto the beach is halfway ajar, allowing the ocean breeze to blow through, but it's a warm wind that offers little relief. Why don't they have the air-conditioning turned on? Lord knows my mother can afford it.

Standing up, I walk around the space, which looks like a casual living room, almost like a family room. There's a photo of a woman dressed in a Sicilian folk costume. I peer closer and see it's Sarina. She doesn't look much different from the photos I have of her, so the picture must've been taken not long after she returned to Sicily.

The folk costume looks different from the one I found in the trunk. She looks back at the camera with a sad smile. Her eyes are also devoid of happiness.

I'm startled by the sound of a door creaking open.

"Meow!" A gray cat runs toward me, its tail high up in the air. It looks like it came out of one of the doors of a china cabinet that sits in the adjacent room, which must be the dining room.

I bend down and pet the cat, who is now rubbing up against my legs. I'm startled by a ball of orange fur that's plopped underneath the coffee table. Another cat. This one is sleeping.

"Ah! You've met Bruno." Carlotta comes back with my *limonata*. A black cat is following her and meowing. How many cats do they have?

"*Grazie.*" I down most of the lemonade. I see Carlotta is staring at me. Our eyes meet, and she realizes she's gawking and smiles before glancing away.

"Do you also live here?" I ask.

"I do."

I'm not surprised. From what I read in Sarina's diary, she absolutely adored Carlotta.

"There are so many cats."

"Sarina can't bear to see any strays. We start feeding them when we see them on the beach, and before we know it, they're a part of our family. We have six."

I then remember Tina, the family's beloved pet that Sarina and Enzo were forced to abandon. No wonder she takes all the strays in.

Placing my glass of lemonade down on the coffee table, I cross my arms in front of my chest and pace around the room, going over to the doors that lead to the beach. I stare at the ocean, and for a few moments I'm able to still my thoughts. I don't hear footsteps behind me until I feel a hand on my shoulder.

Turning around, I am face-to-face with my mother. She looks much older than the mother I remember from my childhood photos. Her beautiful auburn hair, which I've inherited, has darkened considerably, and gray hairs are quickly overtaking it. Her hair is pulled up into an elaborate, braided bun. Large gold hoop earrings dangle from her earlobes, which look quite stretched. She wears a loose, copper-orange tunic and a long skirt with an intricate pattern that resembles mosaic tiles. Three rings adorn the fingers of each of her hands and gold bangle bracelets circle her wrists. She looks like a well-dressed gypsy. Except for the lines beneath her eyes and on her forehead, she has few wrinkles. But her face holds a worn, tired expression, which makes her appear much older than sixty-one. But I guess that's no surprise when I remember the difficult childhood she had and her severe depression. Still. I would have thought becoming a famous singer and having a more comfortable life financially would have helped her to maintain more of her youthfulness. She obviously isn't vain since she has chosen not to dye her hair. She wears no makeup. Though she has aged considerably, there is still a regal beauty about her. It's the way she holds herself, though there is a slight stoop to her back. She looks shorter than I remember her. But again, I was just a child when I last saw her. When I was a toddler, she seemed to tower above me. Now, her arms look painfully thin as do her legs, and there is a fragileness to her.

She pulls her hand away from my shoulder as if she's been burned and holds it in the air, unsure if she wants to touch me again. But thinking better of it, she slowly lowers her hand. Tears trickle down her face.

I remain frozen in place. I've imagined this moment countless times from when I was a little girl right up until I rode here in the taxi. When I was a child, I imagined running into her arms, screaming "Mama!" as I wrapped my arms around her neck and never let go. But in the past couple of weeks, when I knew I would be making this trip, I imagined a very different scenario. I pictured us standing here, just as we are now, not knowing what to do or say. I thought I would cry, but I'm not even close to tears. Numbness is all I feel.

"*Mia figlia.*" My mother whispers "my daughter."

Hearing those words uttered from her lips hurts so much, but I refuse to let her see my pain.

"I'm sorry I didn't let you know I was coming." I walk past her and go sit down on the couch, keeping my eyes averted from her gaze.

"No need for you to apologize. I'm just shocked. Do you mind if I sit with you?"

"Of course not. It's your home."

I hadn't even noticed Carlotta was no longer in the room until she reappears with a glass of white wine for Sarina.

"I'll be upstairs if you need me." Carlotta places her hand on Sarina's shoulder and gives it a light squeeze before walking away.

An awkward silence follows. I take my glass of lemonade from the coffee table and slowly sip what's left of it. I sneak a sideways glance at my mother. She's still staring at me. Just like Carlotta, she must be wondering if I'm real.

Of course I'm dying to get right to it and ask her why she left me. I'm dying to know what she's been up to since she left America. But now that I see the years have not been too kind to her, I'm afraid of giving her a heart attack, especially since I know I won't be able to contain my anger.

"I have a few of your things that I wanted to return to you." I get up and walk over to my luggage, which Adriana left in the foyer. After wheeling it into the living room, I unzip my suitcase and take out her Sicilian folk costume, the notebook with her songs, and the pack of tarot cards. I hand them to her.

"I found these in Daddy's basement. I thought you might like to have them back." I place them on her lap. She begins examining them, and her lips turn upward into a small smile.

"Thank you, Julia, but I had told your father whatever I left behind was yours. I remember leaving mostly winter clothes since I'd have little use for them here."

I nod my head. "I found them. I also found this." I take her diary from my suitcase and hold it out to her.

She stares at the diary for a moment before taking it. Opening the cover, she flips through the pages and then pauses to read a few of the entries. Closing her eyes for a moment, she releases a deep breath and says, "I thought I would never see this again."

"But you must've realized you left it behind?"

"I could've sworn I packed it. I never would have left my diary behind out of fear that your father would find it. He's a good man. I didn't want to hurt him, and then later . . ." She pauses before continuing. "Then later when I didn't come home . . . Well, I suppose at that point it wouldn't have mattered if he found it. For I had already broken his heart by not going back home."

"So he never knew about Carlo? I was too afraid to ask him for the same reason. I didn't want to hurt him any more than he's been hurt already."

My mother shakes her head. "He didn't know. So you read the diary then."

"I'm sorry. But I couldn't resist. I wanted to know more about you."

"I'm glad you read it. Please, don't be sorry." My mother says this in English, surprising me. She sees my surprise and says, "As you must know, your father was teaching me, but I learned little while I was in New York. A few years after I returned to Sicily, I took lessons."

"But why? You didn't really need to know English here."

"I wanted to be able to speak to you in English someday."

I'm stunned.

"You were planning on coming back?"

"I was."

"So why didn't you?" I can't hide the irritation from my voice. I try to restrain myself, but I can't, and the anger I've kept inside me for almost four decades is unleashed.

"How could you have left your three-year-old daughter behind? Do you have any idea how hard it's been for me growing up without a mother? I had to watch my friends' mothers attend their graduations, bake cookies for them, go shopping with them for their prom dresses and wedding dresses, while I wondered why my own mother couldn't be there for me. I used to cry myself to sleep at times, going over and over in my mind that last day I saw you when you played with me in our yard. I used to fantasize that you would come home and never leave. I drove Daddy nuts when I was a little girl, crying and asking him when you would come home. And then when I got a little older, I asked him why you had never returned. Your absence from my life has made me question whether I can ever be a good mother if I decide to have children. How can I be when I don't know what it's like to have a mother's love? And what about Daddy? Do you know how lonely he's been since you left? He's never allowed himself to fall in love with anyone else, and I don't know why, but he never wanted to get a divorce from you. I guess it didn't matter once you fell off the Earth—and then when you refused to tell Daddy where you were or what you'd been up to? But it all makes sense now. You didn't want us to know about your other life as a rich, famous singer."

"You know about that?" Sarina's face pales.

"My husband hired a private investigator to find you. He told us. I didn't believe it, but now that I'm here and I see this house on a private beach and your servants, I know it's true. Of course you didn't want Daddy to know. For how could a rich, successful woman still abandon her child and not even go to see her? You had the money. And even if you didn't, Daddy had money. He would've sent it to you to come home or to come visit me. But the truth is you were worried if your fans found out you had a child whom you had abandoned, that would've ruined your career. You were selfish and didn't want to be tied down to a husband or a child. Who knows? Maybe you never returned because you met up with Carlo again and wanted to be with your old lover. For all I know, you could have faked that letter from your cousin."

Sarina's eyes fill with tears. She blinks them back.

"You have every right to be angry with me and hate me. I wouldn't expect anything less," Sarina whispers, her voice choking up.

Seeing her in pain hurts me, but I try to quell the feeling. I can't let her break me.

"But you're wrong in thinking that I faked my cousin Agata's letter just so I could return here and find Carlo. And you're wrong in thinking that I was ashamed of you and feared my fans would find out I had abandoned my child. They knew about it."

"What?" I ask incredulously.

"In my songs, I talked about leaving you. So they knew."

"But they probably thought you were talking about someone else or a fictitious person."

"I was asked about it in interviews, especially since a few of my songs were about my pain over leaving you. I didn't lie. I told the truth. It cost me fans, and my record that was out at the time had the worst sales, but I didn't care. I refused to deny you existed and to pretend to the world I was something I was not. It was a small punishment for me to pay for leaving you.

"Julia, I'd like to tell you everything that happened when I returned to Sicily. But if you'd rather not hear it, I understand. I'm not telling you this to defend myself, but I believe the time for secrets is over. I think you can agree."

"There have been too many secrets. It's time I hear the truth from your lips."

She begins recounting what transpired after she left me. I can't help but wonder if her story will merely create a deeper rift between us.

～ 25 ～

Sarina's Other Life . . .

"When I returned to Sicily, it was bittersweet. I knew I wouldn't see you for some time, and then I found out my mother had stomach cancer. I tried to remain optimistic for the children's sake, but I knew her days were numbered and vowed to make whatever time Mama had be as comfortable as possible. While I was happy to be reunited with Mama and my siblings, those first few weeks were extremely difficult. They had all lost so much weight and were basically starving, relying on whatever food my cousin Agata could give them. Thankfully due to your father's kindness, I had money to buy food and Mama's medicine once I arrived in Sicily. But I knew the money would not last long, and I had too much pride to ask Paolo to send more."

"Paolo?" I ask.

"That's what I called your father. Paulie was too hard for me to say when I first met him, and then even when I did learn how to pronounce it correctly, he preferred I keep calling him Paolo."

Of course, I forgot that I had read in Sarina's diary that she had a difficult time saying "Paulie." It's hard for me to picture my father as anything other than Daddy or Paulie. Even when I see his real name, Paul, on mail he receives, it's odd for me.

"So I did what I knew how to do. I set up shop in my mother's home and began reading tarot cards. It was slow though. Wives were afraid their husbands would find out they were spending money to have their fortunes read. Of course, many of the ones who came did so behind their husbands' backs. But it was barely enough to feed a household of five. I went into Barcellona to try to find work at one of the shops or restaurants. I was able to get work as a dishwasher in a restaurant. Agata looked after the children while I worked at night. By day, I took care of my mother and ran the household. Enzo and Carlotta helped as much as they could. Like me when I was their age, they were forced to grow up beyond their years. But they didn't seem to mind. They were so happy I was with them again, and they kept asking me to regale them with stories about America and the tall buildings I had seen in New York. They were curious about you and asked me why I hadn't brought you with me."

My lips purse tightly at hearing this. I meet Sarina's gaze, but she lowers her eyes.

"I showed them photographs of you, which they loved. Anyway, when I learned of my mother's illness, naturally there was no way I could return to New York within a matter of weeks as I had initially planned on doing. Paolo understood of course."

"I know. He told me. He also told me you refused to return to America with your siblings after your mother died."

Sarina folds her hands in her lap and looks down at them. "That is true. Did he tell you why I was afraid of returning?"

"He said you were afraid you were going to kill yourself."

"I was, Julia. You have to believe me."

"But you might've been happier in New York the second time around with your siblings there. You would have had them and me to occupy you."

"It wouldn't have mattered, Julia. Lord knows I was busy taking care of a newborn, and that still didn't block out the dark thoughts that ran through my mind. I hit you once. Did your father tell you about that?"

"He did, but you just lost your temper. All parents lose their temper. It's not like you kept hitting me."

"No, but I found myself with my hand raised in the air more than once. Somehow I realized what I was about to do and stopped myself. But the time I completely lost control and hit you, I just reacted. I didn't even stop to think about what I was doing. It was in an instant. That horrified me—how I could go into a rage in mere seconds and without any warning. I was terrified I was becoming my father. You read my diary and of the abuse I suffered at his hands. I could never forgive myself for doing that to you. I was twenty-two when I left you. While I was no longer the teenager your father had married, I was still quite young. I didn't have the foresight to completely grasp the consequences my leaving would have on you. Had I known then the extreme pain I would cause you, as well as the guilt I have had to carry, I might have acted differently. I might have returned to New York. I really thought you would be better off without me. But there is more to my story.

"The money I was making washing dishes at the restaurant still wasn't quite enough. And as I said earlier, I wasn't making much reading tarot cards out of my mother's home. I worked up the courage to ask the owner one evening if he would let me sing one or two nights a week. I convinced him that by having entertainment he would get more patrons dining at his restaurant. He agreed to let me sing two nights a week, and he paid me for those nights. He also let me keep whatever tips the patrons gave me. After a month, his restaurant was beyond full on the nights I would sing. He asked me to sing from the middle of the week through the weekend, when the restaurant was at its busiest. I took a chance and told him I would only perform on those extra nights if I could stop washing dishes and if he doubled my earnings as a singer. He agreed. After about three months, I again worked up the courage to ask him for a raise. I knew how well the restaurant was doing, and it was largely because of my singing. He tried to talk me out of a raise, and can you believe I threatened to walk out on him?" Sarina laughs. "I was no longer the naïve teenage girl who worked for the likes of Signore Conti. I was becoming more confident in my talents as a singer, and I wanted to provide for my family as best I could. Finally, I was able to buy Mama the china set I had promised her. And I bought new clothes for the children. I even bought Carlotta a new doll, and I bought two cats for Enzo. I also began sending money to your father. It was for you of course."

"You did? He never told me."

"That's because he returned it. I knew he didn't need the money, but it was my small way of trying to provide for you, just like I was doing for my mother and siblings. Since he wouldn't accept my money, I sent packages with little toys and clothes. Many of the clothes I knit myself in the middle of the night. I had begun having insomnia after I returned to Sicily. I think I did not want to go to sleep because my dreams were always filled with you. So I knitted when I couldn't sleep, which was most nights. I was relieved you lived in a place that had very cold winters and could use the warm clothes I was knitting for you."

"My father did tell me you had knit clothes for me, but he only mentioned the ones you made while you were pregnant with me."

"He might have forgotten. Ask him when you talk to him."

"He told me he saved the clothes you had knit when you were expecting me. I'll look for them when I go back home."

Sarina smiles. "I know it didn't compare to having me with you, but knitting those clothes made me feel in a small way like I was still caring for you."

"You said you also sent toys. What were they?"

"I bought for you the same doll I had bought for Carlotta. She had beautiful long red hair and was dressed in a Sicilian folk costume. I imagined your own hair would look the same when you got older and let your hair grow."

"Bella! That's what I named that doll. I remember her! Daddy gave me that doll, but he told me it was from him."

My mother's face looks pained at hearing that my father lied to me about the doll. I begin getting angry at my father again for all the secrets and even the lies.

"He shouldn't have done that. He should have told me the doll and the other gifts were from you."

Sarina leans over and places her hand over mine. I'm startled for a moment by the contact. Her hand is warm, and it manages to calm me. Part of me wants to pull away. But I don't.

"Don't be mad at him. He did what he thought was right by you."

I shake my head. "It's funny. When I confronted him after I read your diary, he told me not to be mad at you. I would think he would still be mad at you for leaving us. I would think he'd want me to be angry with you."

"Your father was a saint. But he was angry at me and let me have it on the phone when I told him I wasn't coming back—at least not anytime soon. I don't blame him for being angry. He had every right to be."

"So did you have some idea when you thought you might be able to return?"

"No, not really. I kept waiting for when I was ready."

"I guess you were never ready. Here I am forty-two years old, and you're in your sixties. I assume it's safe to say you weren't ever going to come back."

"Let me finish my story, Julia. One night while I was singing at the restaurant, a man was watching me very closely. He was sitting at a table in the front. After I was done performing, he came over and introduced himself to me. He was the owner of a record company. He was on vacation in Sicily and had asked for a restaurant recommendation from one of the local people. He had also heard about the singer whom everyone was flocking to see at the restaurant. His curiosity had been piqued. He told me I was one of the best singers he had ever heard. I was stunned. He wanted to make me famous and offered me a recording contract. I didn't know what to do. I felt overwhelmed. Never in a million years had I imagined myself having an opportunity like this. I sang for myself and to help support my family and me. I never dreamed it would go beyond that. He told me to think about it for a couple of days, and he would return to the restaurant then to get my answer. He also told me that I would never have to worry about money again.

"I went home that night to tell Mama." Sarina's voice lowers as she turns her head, letting her gaze wander toward the view of the beach. Her eyes look far away.

"She was so happy for me when I told her. I said, 'Mama, if I do this, you will never have to worry about money again. I will take care of you and the children. I will buy a villa by the beach. You'll never have to live again in this shack of a house that Papá built. You can leave your horrible memories of him behind in this house.'

"Mama stroked my cheek. She was so weak at that point. Her illness had caused her to lose a lot of weight. She looked very small in her bed, and her nightgown swam around her frail body. She said, 'Sarina, you make me so proud. You always have. Go. Sing for this man. Let the world hear your beautiful voice. Make me and your daughter proud.'

"When the record company owner came to see me, I told him I would do it. I signed the papers that night. The next day, Mama died." Sarina's voice chokes up.

Tears come to my own eyes.

"I think she was ready to die then because she knew after hearing my news I would be all right. She knew I would be able to take care of my siblings, and they would never have to worry about where their next meal came from.

"So I buried my mother, and then I threw myself into writing song after song. My record came out six months later. The radio stations all over Sicily played it. It wasn't long before everyone knew who I was. I quit my job at the restaurant and began touring, but I would only perform in northeastern Sicily. The children came with me, and the record company even hired a woman to look after them and tutor them while I was working. I was adamant that they resume their studies since I was never able to.

"Singing my heart out to hundreds of people was a strange but wonderful experience. I became another person when I was on stage. Most of my songs were about the struggles I'd had—my father beating me and my mother, finding love and losing it, living day to day trying to get enough money to eat, leaving my beloved island of Sicily for the shores of America, giving birth, leaving you. I sang about all of it, and I felt the pain of everything that had happened to me all over again.

"Enzo, Carlotta, and Pietro loved coming to watch me sing. As I said, I made sure they got the best education. But everything I did for them, I know was also my way of trying to make up for not being able to do the same things for you. The years went by, and every year I resolved I would find the courage to return to you. But then a deep depression would set in. I was terrified of becoming that shell of a person I had been in America. And then the thoughts of ending it all would surface. It was like a demon that would not completely loosen his grip on me. And when he appeared, he reminded me he was only too eager to let me drown in that bottomless pit. You see, Julia, though I was happy to be in Sicily and reunited with my family, there were still times I thought about ending my life. I hated myself for not returning to you and for not being able to be a real mother to you. I think what kept me from carrying the act out was my singing and the hope that someday I would find the courage to come see you."

Sarina pauses before continuing.

"I bought this villa within a year of my record's coming out. My brothers moved out when they reached their twenties and got married. We're still close, and they come visit me every other weekend. They have children. Enzo has two boys, and Pietro has two girls and a boy. Carlotta also got married, but the only child she had—a girl—died while she was still an infant. Carlotta tried to have other children, but none came. Though she and her husband were very happy, Carlotta still couldn't bear to be far from me, so they bought a house about half a mile from here. Her husband died suddenly of a heart attack five years ago, and she came to stay with me shortly afterward." Sarina begins coughing. She tries to resume speaking, but the coughing starts up again.

"Do you want me to get you some water?"

She nods her head.

I take her empty wineglass and walk over to the kitchen, which is just off the dining area. I see a bottle of water sitting on the counter and then remember learning during one of my Italian lessons in school that Europeans often like their drinks at room temperature and rarely use ice. Rinsing out her wineglass, I pour water. Sarina's coughing has subsided, but now I hear her clearing her throat. Maybe I should give her a break. No doubt my showing up unexpectedly gave her the shock of her life. Guilt washes over me that I didn't call to let her know I was coming. I could've even called after I landed at the airport. Here I am accusing her of being selfish when all I cared about was confronting her and getting my answers—though what I've heard so far hasn't convinced me yet that her leaving was justified. I also can't help wondering if she's being sincere in telling me she always thought about me and planned on coming to see me someday. However, the knowledge that she sent me gifts while I was growing up is a small comfort. At least I was on her mind. Up until now, I always figured I hadn't been. Sighing deeply, I head back to the living room.

I hand the glass of water to her.

"Grazie." Sarina takes a long gulp, then holds the glass to her head. I remember the water wasn't that cold and ask, "Would you like me to get you a cold, wet towel?"

She holds her hand up. "I'm fine. Thank you. Sometimes when it's this hot, my throat gets so dry. I'm sorry."

"May I ask why you don't have the air-conditioning turned on?"

"I only turn it on at night. I prefer the fresh air, coming in from the ocean. The ceiling fans are enough for me. But where are my manners? I should have Adriana turn it on for you." Sarina begins to get up, but I place my hand on her arm, stopping her. She glances down at my hand. I immediately remove it.

"That's all right. I'm fine. I was just thinking if you weren't feeling well, you should have the air conditioner on. If you're tired, we can talk later."

"No. I want to finish telling you everything. I'm almost done."

"Take your time."

Sarina smiles. I wait for her to continue, but she keeps looking at me. My face reddens, and I look away.

"I'm sorry. I know I'm staring. It's just that I still can't believe you're here and how beautiful you are. I mean I could tell you'd grown into a beautiful woman when I saw your wedding photo, but seeing you in person . . . It's just . . ." Sarina doesn't finish her sentence. She looks overcome with emotion, but she quickly regains her composure.

"Where was I?" Sarina scratches her head as she tries to remember where she left off in her story.

I can't resist asking, "What about Carlo? Did you ever see him again?"

A spark appears in her eyes.

"Not long after I returned to Sicily, I went to see my friend Angela who owned a—"

"Bread shop in Taormina. Yes, you wrote about her in the diary."

"*Si.* She was a dear friend to me. She passed away just last year. Well, I went to see Angela in Taormina to let her know I was back. I didn't ask about Carlo, but she knew I was wondering if she'd heard anything about him. Naturally, when I went to Taormina, I looked for him on every street corner. I suppose if I had strolled by the Villa Carlotta and hidden behind a tree, I might've caught a glimpse of him in the hotel or on the grounds. But I wouldn't have dared. Angela told me he did end up marrying Gemma, just as his father had wanted, about a year and a half after I left for America. Even though a few years had passed since I'd last seen him, hearing that he was married to another woman still hurt me so much. But I didn't blame him. I was the one after all who had left him without an explanation and without saying good-bye.

"Instead of managing the Villa Carlotta, he and Gemma had moved to Enna right after the wedding. Once the hotel his father was building there was completed, Carlo managed it. The locals said he left because he couldn't stand to be around Signore Conti, and he knew if he stayed his father would try to control his life. But Angela thought Carlo also left because be couldn't bear to be in Taormina with his memories of me. I didn't know about that. I was certain he hated me for leaving him the way I did." Sarina looks at me. I know she is wondering if I hated her all the years she was gone and if I still hate her now. She takes a sip of water and resumes her story.

"So the years went by, and I continued to make records and tour Sicily. But our paths never crossed, even when I performed in Enna. I knew Carlo had to have heard about my fame, but I wasn't surprised that he didn't try to find me or come to any of my concerts. Though I had accepted he was no longer mine when I made the choice to walk out of his life, a small part of me always hoped to see him again. I would have been happy to even catch just one glimpse of him.

"Five years ago I retired from singing. I began to think more about you—not that I had ever stopped. But I guess you can say I was more aware of how much time had slipped by and how I'd wasted so many years being apart from you. While I knew that at this late stage in your life, you didn't need me anymore to care for you, I wanted to try and finally forge a relationship with my daughter. I was terrified. I didn't know how you would receive me. I kept changing my mind about whether or not to go to America. Carlotta convinced me to make the difficult journey. I was going to book my airline tickets right after I called your father to let him know I was coming. As I was working up the nerve to get myself ready for whatever reaction Paolo might have on the phone, my doorbell rang. I ignored it since one of the maids always answers the door.

"I dialed your father's number, but got a busy signal and hung up. I waited and was about to dial again when the maid interrupted me. I looked up and almost fainted when I saw Carlo standing behind her. Though he was now in his early sixties, sixty-one to be precise, I immediately recognized him. His tender eyes were still the eyes of the kind, young man I had fallen in love with, and he still possessed that magnificent head of wavy hair. But it had all gone gray now.

"We went to sit down on my terrace that faced the ocean. I wanted to make sure that none of my maids eavesdropped on our conversation. My heart wouldn't stop racing, and I could barely look Carlo in the eyes though I felt his gaze on me throughout.

"I waited patiently for him to begin speaking. While I had so many questions, I was afraid that he would finally unleash all of his anger on me. I was shaking so hard that I don't think I would've been able to talk in that moment without betraying my anxiety.

"He told me that he had married Gemma. I told him I already knew. He looked surprised, but didn't ask me how I'd found out. He then said that Gemma had died two years earlier in a car accident. He had been tempted to try and find me a few months after Gemma had died, but then he had decided it would be best to let bygones be bygones. But he couldn't stop thinking about me. In fact, he told me he had never stopped thinking about me from the time I left him.

"I can't tell you, Julia, how my heart sang when I heard him say that, but I was still waiting for him to get angry with me as I knew he would. He told me he knew his father had a hand in my leaving, but he was still hurt and mad that I let his father come between us. He had been busy with his grandmother's funeral and all that needed to be taken care of in the wake of her death. But two weeks later, he had tried to find me. He took a guess and went to see if I had returned to Lipari, but no one had seen a woman who fit my description. Carlo then went to my parents' house, thinking I had returned home. He waited until he saw my father leave for work, and then he approached my mother while she was hanging the laundry. My mother told him that though she had heard from me and I was fine, I hadn't shared with her where I was out of fear that my father would intercept my letters and try to find me again.

"I then told him how I couldn't bear to return to Lipari without him and instead went to Salina, where I met Paolo and then married him and moved to America. I explained to him that my mother had known about my marriage and that I had gone to America, but that I had made her promise not to tell Carlo if he ever asked her about me. He asked me why I didn't want him to know. I told him I couldn't bear to hurt him any more than I had, and I knew he would be pained to know I had married another man. I also told him about you, Julia. I told him everything—how I left you to care for my ailing mother and provide for my siblings. I even told him how I had never gone back for you. I thought he would judge me and hate me for leaving my child. But all he said was how sorry he was that I had been through so much since we last saw each other.

"Carlo then said that shortly after I left him, he remembered the tarot card reading I had given him, and he realized the cards had accurately predicted our fate—that we would be torn apart and a strong, authoritative figure, whom he now realized was his father, would be an obstacle. I couldn't help laughing when Carlo told me this, for I had stopped reading tarot cards a long time ago and had given up believing in them. I had also stopped believing in fate, for I made every choice in my life—good and bad. I have no one to blame but myself for my mistakes.

"Carlo told me I was always so hard on myself, and he could see that hadn't changed over the years. He then told me that when he couldn't find me in Lipari or Taormina, he became very distraught and went into a deep depression. Gemma visited him a lot after his grandmother died. Finally about a year and a half after I had left, he realized I wasn't coming back, and he decided to marry Gemma. They'd known each other since they were children, and he knew she was a good woman. But he swore they never shared the same passion we had shared. He had thought of her more as a loyal companion.

"In addition to the hotel he oversaw in Enna, he ended up opening another hotel after his father died. The hotel was in Lipari and was called Sirena.

" 'Sirena'?" I asked him.

"He said, *'Si, ho chiamato dopo di te.'*

"I was so moved that he had named the hotel for me. I couldn't stop the tears that were rolling down my cheeks. Carlo had wanted to call the hotel Sarina, my actual name, but he couldn't do that to Gemma. She never suspected the hotel's name was a variation of Sarina, especially since the Straits of Messina are known for the *sirene*, or sirens, that were made famous by Homer's *Odyssey*.

"After hearing he had named his hotel for me, I didn't hold back any longer. I told Carlo that many of my songs were about our love. He told me he knew, for when he learned of my fame, he had secretly bought and listened to all of my records. When Gemma was out, he would listen to them. He had even attended two of my concerts when I was in Enna, and once he had driven all the way to Agrigento just to see me perform. I asked him why he hadn't come to talk to me after my concerts. He said his duty had been to his wife, and he couldn't break his vow to her. He shouldn't have even been going to my concerts. I told him he could have just said hello to me as an old friend. Nothing more had to happen between us. But Carlo told me he knew if he had come that close to me, he would have taken me in his arms and kissed me. And he would've never returned to Gemma.

"He then said he needed to see me one last time before . . . His voice trailed off, and his face went absolutely ashen. I became alarmed and asked him if he was ill."

Sarina closes her eyes and shakes her head.

"Would you like me to get you some more water?" I ask her.

She shakes her head. "I'm sorry. Just remembering what he told me and how I felt when I heard it is still painful for me." Sarina opens her eyes, blinking back tears.

Swallowing hard, she clears her throat and says, "Carlo told me he had been diagnosed six months earlier with Alzheimer's disease. He wanted to see me one last time before he lost all memory of me, and he wanted to tell me he had never stopped loving me.

"At first, I didn't believe it. I thought his doctor had made a mistake. Carlo was only sixty-one when he came to see me. He still seemed too young to have Alzheimer's. When I expressed that I thought he had been misdiagnosed, he told me he had early-onset Alzheimer's. Apparently, four percent of the population gets Alzheimer's under the age of sixty-five, and even some people in their thirties and forties can get it. I was stunned.

"We were both quiet for a moment, but then I stood up and went over to the bench Carlo was seated on. I sat next to him and placed my head on his chest as I wrapped my arms around his waist. I hugged him and told him I, too, had never stopped loving him. I apologized for hurting him and leaving him the way I did. I told him I had been a fool to listen to his father and let him convince me to leave. And I expressed how much I had hated myself for leaving without saying good-bye or giving Carlo an explanation. He said he realized I did that because I was afraid his father would disinherit him. But he wouldn't have cared if that had happened. He would have been able to find work and provide for himself and me, just the way he had when we were living in Lipari. I told him I had been very insecure and had believed his father that Gemma would make a better wife.

"Carlo lifted my chin so that our eyes met, and he said, 'Sarina, you should have known that no other woman could ever make me as happy as you did.'

"I cried so hard then. I cried for my foolish mistake . . . for all the years we'd lost . . . for what we could have had. He held me and waited patiently until I was all cried out. He then told me he didn't expect anything from me now. He would go back to Lipari, where he'd been living since Gemma died. All he truly wanted was to see me one last time and let me know he'd always cared about me even though he had married another woman."

Sarina stops talking when we're interrupted by what sounds like a heavy club hitting the floor. Carlotta holds the arm of an elderly man who is walking with a cane. They don't pay us any notice as they make their way to the doors that lead to the beach. At first I think he is Carlotta's husband. But this man seems too old to be her husband, and then I remember Sarina said Carlotta's husband died a few years ago. My eyes then open wide as realization hits me. I look at Sarina.

"*Sì.* He is my Carlo."

I do the math in my head. Sarina had said Carlo was sixty-one when he came to see her, and that was five years ago. So he is sixty-six now. But this man looks as if he's already in his early seventies. His movements are very slow and deliberate, and by the way Carlotta was assisting him, I gather that his Alzheimer's has progressed quite a bit.

"When Carlo told me that day that he just wanted to see me one last time, and he would not bother me again, I told him I wasn't letting him go a second time. I wanted to spend the rest of my days with him—no matter how long that might be. Carlo told me he couldn't let me make that sacrifice, and he said my life would become very difficult, taking care of someone with Alzheimer's, especially when it advanced. But I told him he must not make the same mistake I had made. He must not walk away from true love like I had. So not long after, he came to stay with me. He had no one, Julia. Gemma had not been able to have children. He had been planning on going to a nursing home since he knew the time would come that he could not care for himself anymore. I refused to let that happen to him.

"His Alzheimer's has progressed quite rapidly in the past six months. It's been very difficult watching the man you love disappear. He hasn't lost all of his memories, but I know the day will come when he doesn't recognize me anymore. I try to stimulate his memory as much as possible by reminding him of the days when we first fell in love and of the time we spent together in Taormina and the Aeolian Islands. I tell him these stories over and over." Sarina's gaze turns toward the beach. I look over and see she's watching Carlo, who's now sitting in a folding chair on the beach. Carlotta is positioning a beach umbrella over him. I look away. It is all so sad.

"Carlotta has been an angel, helping me care for him. I don't know what I would have done without her help these past few years."

"Yes, you are very lucky to have her."

"So that is my story, Julia. Now you know everything that has happened since I left you."

"I'm sorry about Carlo, Sarina."

Sarina flinches when she hears me call her by her first name. But she can't expect me to start calling her mother as if nothing has ever happened.

"Thank you, Julia. Has any of what I said helped you?" Sarina's eyes look hopeful. I know she really wants to ask me if I've forgiven her. But I don't know if I have, and even if I have, I'm not ready to tell her just yet.

"I want to be honest with you, especially since you and my father kept so much from me all these years. I'm sorry if what I'm going to say will hurt, but I must be honest."

"Please, tell me the truth, Julia."

"I do feel bad about what you have been through and how things turned out with Carlo. But I can't help feeling hurt that you chose him over me. You were going to come see me, but then when Carlo arrived on your doorstep, you changed your mind. You chose your old lover over your own child."

"I was still planning on coming to see you, Julia. But then the next day, coincidentally, I received a letter from your father, telling me you had gotten married. That was the letter that contained your wedding photo. I saw how happy you were, and I couldn't help thinking that I was about to disrupt your peace and happiness by showing up after all these years. I realized my coming to see you was purely selfish because I wanted your forgiveness. But since I had chosen to stay away from you for all that time, I couldn't just now reappear and wreak havoc for you. If I truly cared about you and your well-being, I would accept that I could not be part of your life anymore. Carlotta was angry with me and tried to change my mind, but I wouldn't.

"I don't expect you to forgive me, Julia. Of course, I would be lying if I said I didn't want your forgiveness. I desperately do, but I know I have caused you so much pain. All I can hope for is that perhaps someday you might understand. When you get to be my age, Julia, you reflect over and over about your past and how you could have done things differently. You have clarity that you didn't have when you were younger. I realized just a few days ago that I have always run away when things got difficult. I ran away from my father; I ran away from Carlo; I ran from you and Paolo. So when Carlo reappeared in my life, I was through with running.

"I will never forgive myself for leaving you, Julia, but you have to believe I did plan on returning someday. I know that is little consolation. But you have to believe I always loved you. I can see all the hurt I have caused you, Julia. Seeing how much pain you are in, I now know I made a mistake in thinking you were better off without me all those years. And I realize I should have listened to Carlotta and come to see you five years ago. But I can't take back what I have done."

"Did you ever love my father?"

Sarina looks surprised that I've asked her this question.

"I did."

"But it was a different kind of love than what you share with Carlo." I say this as a statement rather than a question for I know the answer.

Sarina nods her head.

"Carlo was my first love, and what is it they say? 'You never forget your first love'? Well, that was true for me. I never forgot about him even when I was certain I would never see him again after I went to America. You read my diary, Julia. So you know how it was between Carlo and me. But I cared about your father. As I said earlier, he was a saint, and his kind heart endeared him to me. I wanted him to be happy, especially once I knew I wasn't returning. I even told him in a letter a few years after I left that he could file for divorce. Naturally, I wouldn't contest it, but for some reason he refused." Sarina's face looks sad before she says, "I suppose it's because he always held hope I would return."

"I think that is the reason why Daddy didn't file for divorce. And he never dated. I asked Aunt Donna when I was in my teens if there was anyone when I was a child. But she said there hadn't been."

"I've hurt so many people who didn't deserve to be hurt—Carlo, your father, you." Sarina's eyes fill with tears, but she manages to keep them at bay.

"I have one last question. Why didn't you ever tell Daddy that you had become famous?"

"I was ashamed, for I knew there would be no excuse for me not to return to you, now that I had the means and my family was fine. But I see how foolish that was of me. Like you said, Julia, even if I hadn't had the money, your father would have gladly paid for my ticket to return home."

I don't say anything, and neither does Sarina. We sit in silence for a few minutes, both of us lost in our thoughts.

"So, Julia, what are your plans now? You're welcome to stay here if you like. I don't know how long you were planning on being in Sicily."

Glancing down at my watch, I'm surprised to see how much time has passed since I arrived. "Thank you. I think I will stay just for the night since it's getting late, and I've had a long day. I have a hotel booked in Messina, so I'll head back there tomorrow. May I use the phone to let the hotel know I won't be arriving tonight?"

"Of course. There's one in the bedroom where you'll be sleeping. That's fine if you just want to stay for the night. No pressure."

"Thank you. As for how long I'll be in Sicily, I don't know. I purchased a one-way ticket. I didn't want to be tied to a concrete date just in case . . ." I let my voice trail off as I realize what I'm about to say.

"Just in case you wanted to return home as soon as possible." Sarina smiles, but I can tell it's forced.

"I'm sorry. I had no idea how things would turn out."

Sarina holds up her hand. "It's all right, Julia. I understand.

Well, I'll go get Adriana to set up your room. Excuse me." Sarina gets up and crosses her arms across her chest as she walks slowly away.

"I might be mad at you, but I don't hate you."

Sarina stops, but doesn't turn around immediately. When she does, there's a spark in her eyes. She merely nods her head before turning back around and walking away.

Rubbing my temples, I feel a headache coming on. I can't help wondering if this is a mistake. Maybe I should go back to my hotel? But I'm too exhausted—both from my long trip and the emotional drain of meeting Sarina and hearing everything she had to say.

Is this all really happening? I still can't believe I'm here in Sicily and in my mother's house. And my mother is a Sicilian star. How bizarre is that?

"Julia, your room is ready. Please follow me." Adriana beckons me toward her with a wave.

My head is absolutely exploding now. No more pondering—at least for tonight. Hopefully, my dreams won't be filled with the anxiety I've been experiencing since I got on the plane to come here. And with that last thought, I follow Adriana to my room, having no idea what will be in store for me tomorrow—or how I'll feel.

26

A Daughter's Heartache

The sound of voices wakes me from a deep slumber. For a moment, I'm disoriented and not sure where I am. Sitting up in bed, I see the view from my bedroom window, and the sight of the beach reminds me I'm in Sicily—in my mother's home.

Getting out of bed, I hear the voices, louder now. They sound like they're coming from the room next to mine. I then hear singing. It's my mother's voice. Curious, I step out of my room and see there's only one room adjacent to mine. I walk quietly over to it. The door is slightly ajar. Peeking through the crack, I can make out Sarina sitting in a wooden chair that's placed alongside a bed. I stretch my neck a bit more and see she is holding a man's hands—Carlo's. Sarina is still in her nightgown, and her hair hangs down her back in a long braid. She's no longer singing. Carlo talks to her, but his voice is too low for me to hear. I shouldn't be eavesdropping, but I can't resist seeing them together. It's almost as if I feel I have a right to listen to their conversation since I read about their love in Sarina's diary. It's as if I'm reading the final chapters of their story.

"Remember when we dove into the waters off Panarea, Carlo? We had the cove to ourselves as we swam and floated on the water, staring at the sky, feeling the sun warming our skin. Remember?"

"I remember, Gemma. You weren't swimming. You hated the water."

My heart drops as I hear Carlo call her Gemma.

"No, Carlo. Gemma was not there. It was me, Sarina. I loved to swim."

"Ah! Sarina. My Sarina."

"Si! Your Sarina."

My mother sounds relieved that he has remembered her. I feel guilty now for listening in on their private conversation and am about to walk away when I hear Carlo say, "I called you *stella mia* when we were in Panarea."

Stopping in my tracks, I remember how Daddy said Sarina called me her *stella mia.* I then remember the scene from her diary when they were in Panarea, and Carlo called her that for the first time.

"Yes, Carlo. That's what you called me that day. I said, 'It's so beautiful here.' And you said, 'Not as beautiful as you, *stella mia.*'"

"That's right. What a gorgeous day that was."

"Remember, Carlo, I told you about my daughter?"

I wait to hear Carlo's response, but nothing comes. He must not remember Sarina's telling him about me.

"That's all right. She's here! I will introduce you later."

"We had a daughter? I thought you couldn't have children."

I close my eyes, feeling for Sarina. Again, Carlo has confused her with Gemma.

"That was Gemma, Carlo. I lived in America and had a husband and a daughter."

"No. That's not right. You were mine. You were always mine." Carlo sounds hurt and angry.

I can't bear to listen anymore. I return to my room.

It must be torture for Sarina seeing Carlo deteriorate. Seeing him forgetting her and confusing her with his late wife. If that happened to Kyle, I think I would go mad.

There's a soft knock on my door. I answer it and see Carlotta is holding a tray containing a cup of espresso and a plate with a slice of frittata as well as a couple of cactus pears.

"*Ciao,* Julia. Did you sleep well? I brought you something to eat."

"*Grazie,* Carlotta. You didn't need to do that. I could've eaten in the kitchen."

"It's my pleasure. Besides, you can't leave Sicily until you have my *Frittata con Patate e Cipolle.* And please, call me Zia. I am, after all, your aunt."

"All right." For some reason, I don't feel strange calling Carlotta Zia even though I only met her yesterday.

Zia Carlotta steps into my room and places my tray on the dresser.

"Do you mind if I keep you company while you eat?" she asks me.

"No. You ate already?" I take the tray over to the bed and get in, propping up my pillows so that I'm seated and can eat my breakfast. Zia Carlotta remains standing, leaning against the dresser.

"*Sì.* I wake up very early."

I take a bite from the *Frittata con Patate e Cipolle,* or Omelet with Potatoes and Onions. My father also makes these at home, but I must say Carlotta's wins hands-down.

"This is so good!"

Carlotta smiles, obviously pleased by my enthusiasm for her cooking. "Do you have cactus pears in America?"

I nod my head. "We do, but they're hard to find even when they're in season." I take a bite from one of the cactus pears, which Carlotta has already peeled and cut for me. "Wow! The cactus pears I've had in New York don't taste this sweet."

"That is the fruit of Sicily. You must've noticed all the cactus pear plants on the way here?"

"I did."

I take a sip of espresso. Again, I feel Zia Carlotta's eyes on me. Glancing up, I see she looks nervous.

"Have you decided if you will stay here?"

"I was planning on going to my hotel in Messina today."

"I meant if you would stay in Sicily for a while longer? Sarina told me last night you bought only a one-way ticket."

"I did. I thought about staying a week, but I don't know now."

Carlotta comes over to my bed and sits on the edge.

"Julia, forgive me if I'm being forward, but please stay. You are a teacher, no?"

I nod my head, knowing where this is going.

"It is only July. I understand the schools in America don't resume for the new year until September. Why not stay until the end of August? Sarina would be so happy."

"Oh, I don't know. I was thinking maybe just a week. You have to realize, Zia, this is a lot for me to handle. I'm still processing it all, and I don't even know yet how I feel toward my mother."

Zia Carlotta takes my hand in hers.

"Julia, your mother hurt you, very much. I do not deny that. She had the world on her shoulders from when she was a child, caring for me and my brothers, and trying to ward off our father's temper. The way he beat her . . ." Zia Carlotta closes her eyes tightly as if she's trying to shut out the painful memories. "It was horrible. There were times I thought he would surely kill her. We all did. That's why we never blamed her when she ran away. And she married your father so young. She was forced to become an adult when she was still practically a child. But I know. There is no excuse for her not returning to you and staying away for so long. But please don't let her mistakes keep you separated now. Not when you've come this far. Get to know her. I believe it was fate that led you to find her diary and brought you here. Just as I believe it was fate that reunited her and Carlo. Julia, you will regret it if you leave now. You will always wonder if the two of you could have gotten past this. Maybe you won't. But shouldn't you at least give it a chance and see what happens? Please, don't be mad at me. I just care about you and my sister. *Ti voglio bene.*" Zia Carlotta strokes my cheek.

I'm touched by her telling me she loves me. And I'm torn. Throughout the night, I dreamt of nothing else but my mother. I woke up several times and kept asking myself if I should return home. But I don't want to feel pressured in the moment to make a decision.

I take Zia Carlotta's hand in mine. "I'm not mad. Thank you for caring so much. I just need some time to think. I'll let you know what I've decided after I eat and take a shower."

"*Va bene.* I will let you get dressed. Let me know if you need anything." Zia Carlotta kisses my cheek before leaving my room.

Sarina's singing reaches my ears again. The sound is soothing, but it also creates a deep sadness within me. It's the same sadness I've felt since I was a child and thought of my mother. Zia Carlotta is right. If I leave now, I will always wonder what could have happened between Sarina and me if I had stayed. This is my opportunity to finally get to know the mother who has been a stranger to me for so long. I can't lie to myself anymore. There is still the little girl inside of me who aches to have her mother's love.

⁓ 27 ⁓

The Dream

The past month and a half has been surreal as my mother and I have struggled to get to know each other. It is now the last week in August and my last week here in Sicily. I will be returning to work soon and cannot prolong my trip any longer, not to mention Kyle has been so patient about my being away so long.

The morning after I first arrived, I decided I would stay for another week. Then I extended my stay for an additional week, until I finally just gave in to my mother's and Carlotta's pleas to remain until the end of August. Now that my time here is almost over, I feel torn and anxious. I haven't let my mind wander to what it will be like once I go back home and won't have my mother with me anymore—although I know it's now different, for I can pick up the phone and talk to her and come visit her whenever I like. Still. I wish she could come back to New York with me.

The first week we tiptoed around each other, afraid of saying the wrong thing—well, at least my mother was afraid of saying the wrong thing. I still hadn't decided if I had forgiven her for staying out of my life for so long, yet I couldn't deny the strong pull to want to get to know her more. And to want to know what it would feel like to have her in my life again even if just for a few weeks.

I finally started to relax during my second week. Every day, Sarina would do something for me. One morning, I woke up to find my laundry had been washed and was folded neatly and placed on the chair next to the dresser in my bedroom. Another morning, she made for me *granita di caffè*, coffee granita. She even made her own *panna,* or whipped cream, to top it off. I didn't think anything of it, even though I have loved coffee *granitas* since I was a teenager. Daddy used to take me to a bakery in Williamsburg, Brooklyn, that sold *granite*. But then the next evening when Sarina presented me with another favorite of mine, Arancini di Riso, or Sicilian Rice Balls, I suspected something was up.

"How did you know that I love *granita di caffè* and Arancini di Riso?" I asked her.

She gave me a sly smile and said, "A mother knows these things about her daughter."

I almost cried when she said that, but I merely mumbled, *"Grazie,"* and quickly began eating before I lost all control. There could be only one explanation. She must have phoned Daddy and asked him what my favorite dishes were. I was moved that she would go to this trouble, but it also made me incredibly happy.

Now, here we are seated in the outdoor terrace behind her house. A sprawling grapevine encircles the entire terrace. Pots of jasmine, bougainvillea, red crimson lilies, and hibiscus are everywhere. There is even a large orange tree as well as a fig tree. My back faces my mother as she braids my hair. I almost feel silly having her braid my hair as if I were a young schoolgirl, but whenever she's asked if she can do my hair, I haven't refused. Sometimes I've imagined that I am still a little girl, and my mother is styling my hair before sending me off to school.

Carlo hobbles out onto the terrace. Sarina begins to stand to help him, but he holds up his free hand, motioning to her that he can manage. Leaning heavily on his cane, he makes his way over to a folding chair and carefully eases himself into it.

"How are you today, Julia?"

My eyes meet my mother's. We were waiting expectantly to see if he would mistake me for Sarina as he's done a few times during my stay here. Sarina told me my being here has helped his memory, especially since I resemble the younger her. She said he's remembered more of their time together in Taormina and the Aeolian Islands. But I can't help feeling guilty when he does mistake me for my mother.

"I'm well, Carlo. Thank you. How are you?"

"Tired. But fine otherwise." Carlo's eyes focus on Sarina braiding my hair. His gaze remains fixed that way until Sarina is done styling my hair. He often goes into a bit of a trance.

"Carlo, let's go for a walk on the beach." Sarina stands up. "Please join us, Julia."

"That's all right. I'll let you enjoy each other's company."

"Please, Julia. I'd like to take a walk with both of you."

I've found it has become harder and harder for me to say no to her. Even in her old age, there is something enchanting about her and vulnerable. When she asks me to do something that I know would make her happy, I see the teenage girl who ran away from her abusive father and who had to fend for herself. And the more she tells me about herself and her days as a folk singer, the more I find myself drawn to her.

"All right."

Sarina hooks one arm through mine and the other through Carlo's arm. We walk very slowly for Carlo's sake. None of us says a word. I listen to the sound of the ocean's waves crashing against the shore. The voices of children chasing a dog reach my ears, but soon the only sounds are those of the ocean and the seagulls. I let myself steal a sideways glance at my mother and Carlo. Their gazes are fixed on the water. My mother's face looks serene and content. A small smile dances on her lips. Carlo's eyes appear again as if he is somewhere else, remembering another time, another place—or perhaps struggling to remember an event. Still, there is something tranquil about his expression as well.

Never would I have imagined this scenario, especially when I was reading Sarina's diary. Never would I have thought I would be walking on a beach in Sicily with my mother and her first lover—the only man she ever truly loved. Suddenly, I realize why she insisted I walk with her. Yet my heart refuses to believe what I suspect, even though I desperately wish it to be true. Could it be that she wanted to walk with the two people she loves the most?

As if reading my thoughts, my mother turns to me and looks into my eyes, smiling the most beautiful smile I've ever seen. And in that moment, I decide to let down the last wall.

"Ti voglio bene, Mama," I say.

Sarina stops walking. She lets go of Carlo's arm and takes my face in her hands. She is overcome with emotion as tears race down her face. She kisses my cheek and hugs me in a tight embrace. We stand like that for a long time. I don't want to let go. I cry, silently at first, but then I sob louder. The pain I have felt since I was a little girl comes rushing out. I don't try to push it back as I've always done.

When we finally pull away from each other, I see Carlo is staring at us and smiling.

Mama leans over to me and whispers, "I love you, too, my dear daughter."

We resume our walk, but this time the three of us have our arms wrapped around each other's backs.

After dinner, Mama has convinced me to play her piano. Zia Carlotta, Carlo, and a few of the maids listen. I'm surprised she even has a piano since she doesn't play, but she told me she had always hoped to learn, but the opportunity never arose.

"Julia, perhaps now that you know us and are more comfortable, you can sing? I have been dying to hear your voice," Zia Carlotta says.

Mama turns to me, her eyes glowing. *"Si!* Please, don't be shy."

"All right. I suppose it's only fair since I have heard you sing." I smile as I say this to my mother.

I pause a moment, thinking of the few Italian songs I know. Clearing my throat, I begin to sing the song that my father and I danced to at my wedding—Vittorio Merlo's "Piccolo Fiore," "Little Flower." I dare not look at my mother while singing the song. The real reason that I haven't sung before now is that I feel like I could never measure up to her talent. I know she is by far the better singer of the two of us.

I'm so absorbed in my thoughts that I don't notice Mama come over and sit beside me on the piano bench. She places her arm around my shoulders and begins singing along with me. There is something in her face that I've only seen in my father's when he listens to me sing. She is proud of me. We continue singing together through the end of the song. Our small audience applauds us and begs for an encore. We sing a few more songs before everyone decides to go to bed. But Mama and I remain, discussing our favorite songs.

"Julia, I would love to give you a tarot card reading. If you're not too tired, let's go to my bedroom, and I'll get my cards."

"I thought you didn't believe in them anymore?"

"I don't, but it's still fun. There's no harm in it, is there?"

"I guess not."

We head over to Mama's bedroom. Though Mama does share a room with Carlo, there are some nights when he isn't feeling well, and she sleeps in her own room so that he'll be more comfortable alone in bed.

An hour later, and after an in-depth tarot card reading that covered my past, present, and future, Mama predicts I will have a transformative experience. Secretly, I can't help wondering if she's mixed up her cards and if that prediction is really supposed to be about my present and not my future, especially since meeting my mother has definitely been a transformative experience. But I don't question her.

I yawn and see it's almost one in the morning. Mama looks especially tired, and I regret keeping her up so late.

"Mama, I'm going to bed now. Good night."

"Julia." Mama pauses.

"What is it?"

"This is going to sound silly, but . . . but I was wondering if maybe you would want to sleep here tonight. We can talk until one of us falls asleep first." She utters a light, nervous laugh.

I see what she is doing. What she has been doing these past six weeks that I've been here. She is trying to make up for the lost time—for not being there to tuck me in as a little girl . . . for not being able to watch me fall asleep.

"I love slumber parties! Why not?" I hop under the covers, making her laugh.

We talk for another couple of hours. Though I'm tired, part of me doesn't want to go to sleep. I want to prolong this night forever, just listening to Mama tell me stories about her and Carlo that weren't in the diary or stories from her days singing on the road. She also tells me stories about when I was a baby and a toddler. After Mama is done going down memory lane, she asks me to tell her more about Kyle and how we fell in love. I then remember something.

"I'll be right back."

I go to my room and take out of my purse the bracelet with the fish charm that Carlo had given to my mother that night they were in Filicudi.

Returning to Mama's room, I see her eyelids are beginning to close. But she hears me and opens them, forcing a smile. She looks so tired.

"I'm sorry. Why don't you go back to sleep. We'll talk more tomorrow, and I should let you have your bed to yourself. You'll be more comfortable."

"No, Julia. Please. This bed is huge. There's room." She motions to me with her hand.

"Are you sure?"

"Sì."

I get back under the covers.

"I can't believe I've forgotten to give this to you." I hold out the bracelet.

My mother gasps, placing her hand over her mouth. She takes the bracelet from my hand and examines it. Her eyes get this far-away look; no doubt she is remembering that night in Filicudi, when she and Carlo made love for the first time and he gave her the bracelet.

"I told your father you could have this."

"He did give it to me, but I always thought it was a gift from him. He gave it to me when I graduated from kindergarten. After I read your diary and realized it was the bracelet that Carlo had given you, I didn't feel right keeping it."

"You loved this bracelet when you were a toddler." My mother's face grows somber. "That was when I hit you. I found you playing with the bracelet, and before I knew what I was doing, I hit your arm, causing you to drop the bracelet."

"I know. Daddy told me."

"I'm so sorry, Julia."

"It's understandable. There was such enormous sentimental value attached to this bracelet."

"No. There's no excuse. I shouldn't have lost my temper with you."

"I've worn the bracelet since Daddy gave it to me. He had to wrap the bracelet twice around my tiny wrist until I got older. It's almost as if I sensed it was your bracelet. I was so fond of it."

My mother takes my arm and places the bracelet around my wrist, fastening its clasp.

"It's yours. Please, keep it. Carlo has given me so many gifts since we reunited."

"But this was extra special."

"And that's why I want you to have it. Please, don't argue with me. It would make me very happy to know you have it."

I nod my head. "Thank you."

We talk some more before I feel myself drifting off to sleep. And soon, I hear my mother's voice in the distance, singing the lullaby she always sang to me as a toddler: *"Stella mia, stell-ahhh mia, tu sei la piu bella stella. My star, my star, you are the most beautiful star."*

I am dreaming of the beach where my mother grew up with her family. Staring up at the many stars in the night sky as I bravely walk alone with my lantern to the boulders on the beach. Though I see myself in the dream, I also see my mother, and it is as if I am one with her, living her life and experiencing her feelings. Soon, the beach transforms into a lush countryside. I am now holding hands with my cousin Agata as we skip and sing before getting to work, harvesting the crops from our fathers' land. Once again, the landscape changes, and I am transported to beautiful Taormina with scenes of Mount Etna looming in the distance. Tambourines and flutes reach my ears as I dance the *tarantella* with Maria and her family of gypsies on the beaches of Taormina. Then I am staring into Carlo's eyes as he watches me singing in the bar of the Villa Carlotta. A beautiful stallion appears, and my heart races against

Carlo's back as we ride the horse on the beach in Isola Bella. My body feels weightless as he and I hold hands while we float in the waters of Panarea. Then I am standing with Carlo on the island of Filicudi as a heavy rain soaks our clothes, and later we watch the moon rise across the waters of the beach. I am telling Carlo I love him in our candlelit room that we rented in Filicudi. Then I am staring into my mother's sad eyes as I say good-bye to her and my younger siblings before leaving for America. Pain shoots through me, followed by elation when I stare at the baby girl I've just given birth to. Suddenly, Sarina's face disappears, and I only see myself climbing up the grapevine in my father's backyard in Astoria. Though I'm scared the grapevine's thin branches won't support my weight, I continue climbing higher as my father cheers me on. Then I hear Mama's voice also encouraging me to keep climbing. I look over my shoulder and see that Mama is now also climbing the grapevine. Soon, she passes me and keeps climbing higher and farther away from me. I try to catch up to her, but she's climbing too fast.

I'm awakened by the sound of something banging loudly. I sit up in bed, and my clothes are nearly drenched in sweat. The window shutters are open and are swinging violently back and forth against the walls. I can hear the wind whipping up outside, which I find strange since it's the end of August. It shouldn't be this windy in Sicily now. I get up to close the shutters, but stop in my tracks as one last howl of wind screeches through. The shutters bang back into place against the windows. It's then eerily quiet. I stare out the window, and though it's cloudy, I see the sun is beginning to break through.

Glancing at my wristwatch, I see it's almost eight o'clock. I'm surprised Mama is still sleeping. She's usually up at six, getting breakfast ready for me. I walk over to her and nudge her shoulder gently to wake her up.

"Mama," I call her repeatedly, but she doesn't wake up. I then notice her complexion looks awfully pale. I touch her cheek and am stunned to feel how cold it is. A thought enters my mind. I try to push it away, but it won't let me. I feel for her pulse. Nothing.

"No. No. Not now. Mama, please. I need you. Please. Not now after we've been apart for so long. I still need you, Mama. Please."

My legs buckle beneath me as I fall onto my knees. Placing my head on my mother's chest, I cry uncontrollably. I don't know how long I remain there until Zia Carlotta walks in and pulls me off my mother.

28

Losing Paradise

I am sitting at the airport in Calabria, waiting to board my plane to Rome. It has been a week since my mother died. I extended my stay and let work know I would not be able to return at the start of the school season.

Mama's funeral was beautiful. We kept it small. Besides me, Zia Carlotta, and Carlo, the only other people in attendance were the priest and Mama's brothers, Enzo and Pietro. Zia Carlotta asked me if I wanted to sing at the service. I sang "Ave Maria," one of my mother's favorite hymns.

I am leaving on the day after the funeral even though Zia Carlotta wanted me to stay longer. Kyle has been worried sick about me and wanted to fly to Sicily to be by my side. But I told him I would be fine. He finally found a job, and I didn't want him to risk losing it by taking off so soon. Kyle told me he didn't care. But I assured him I would be okay and would be home in a matter of days anyway.

Before I left, Zia Carlotta made me promise to stay in touch with her. Even Enzo and Pietro extended an invitation for Kyle and me to visit them next summer. I promised them all I would stay in touch and come back to visit when I could.

Poor Zia Carlotta. After the initial shock of my mother's dying so suddenly, I asked Zia if Mama had been sick. She admitted to me that Mama had been diagnosed with breast cancer two years ago. It had been in remission, but had come back earlier this year. It was too aggressive to treat. I then remembered how much older than her age Mama had appeared to me when I first arrived in Sicily. I also remembered the regular coughing she did, which I had just attributed to old age. And her body had looked so frail. But other than that, I wouldn't have known she was dying. I unleashed my anger on Zia, furious that she had not told me when I first arrived about Mama's illness. She told me she came close to telling me the morning after I had arrived when she brought me breakfast in bed. But Sarina had made Carlotta promise not to tell me. She couldn't go against the wishes of a dying woman. That was why she had implored me to stay longer in Sicily. Zia Carlotta knew I would never again have the chance to see my mother.

I would have hoped that after being reunited with me and seeing how much I had been hurt by her secrets as well as my father's, Mama would've learned her lesson and chosen to confide in me about her cancer. Zia Carlotta said Mama didn't want me to feel any sense of obligation toward her. She wanted me to stay in Sicily because I truly wanted to finally get to know her and not because she was dying.

Zia said that Mama had asked her to take care of Carlo if she should die before him. I was stunned that Zia Carlotta would sacrifice so much of herself and her own life to take care of the man her sister had loved, but as she explained to me, Mama had given up her life in New York and her daughter to help Carlotta and her mother and her siblings when they needed her. Zia Carlotta was honored to be able to repay her sister. Enzo and Pietro would now help with Carlo as well.

Carlo didn't stop crying at the funeral. We all thought he would confuse me with Mama and refuse to believe she was really gone. But amazingly, he knew she had finally left him forever.

I glance down at an envelope with my name written on it. It's a letter from my mother that she had written about a week before she died. Zia Carlotta found it among her belongings and gave it to me the day before the funeral. Mama had told her about the letter and instructed her to send it to me after Mama died. Apparently, she thought she had at least another six months before the cancer would finally get her. I haven't been able to bring myself to read the letter. Taking a deep breath, I break the envelope's seal and pull out the letter.

> *Dearest Julia,*
>
> *I'm sorry I have left you again. But this time, I truly had no control over it. I am just so grateful to God that I was able to see you again.*
>
> *One of the happiest moments in my life was when I held you for the first time after you were born. Yes, I was incredibly terrified of being a mother and turning into my father, but I was also so proud of you. And then when I saw what a kind, beautiful woman you have become, I was even more proud.*
>
> *Over the years when I thought about you, I would often close my eyes and remember back to when I held you in my arms and lulled you to sleep by singing "Stella Mia." You cannot know how happy I was when you told me you actually remembered my singing that song to you. I had always imagined you had little or no memory of me since you were so young when you last saw me.*
>
> *And then when you told me about how you still care for the grapevine I had planted in the yard of your father's home, I knew you had never stopped loving me, even if you were hurt and angry that I had left you. When I would stare at my grapevine here in Sicily, I would hope that you were looking at the grapevine in Astoria and that you were thinking about me, too.*
>
> *I will never forgive myself for not returning to you. I will never forgive myself for hurting you the way I did.*
>
> *I was a coward, afraid of taking on the responsibilities that motherhood entailed. I see now I used as*

*an excuse that I feared I'd become my father and
would abuse you. I could not let go of my home in
Sicily and my family who remained here, but I didn't
give America enough of a chance. I didn't give you
and your father a chance.*

*I suppose you are wondering why I didn't reach out
to you when I learned I was dying. Just as when I had
reconsidered coming to see you after your wedding, I
didn't want to suddenly waltz into your life and then
disappear from it again so soon once I died. That
would not have been fair to you either. It truly was a
miracle that you found my diary when you did and
decided to come here. Though I was so overjoyed at
seeing you, I also felt immensely sad. For I knew our
time together would be short, and then I would be
hurting you all over again after my passing. I almost
wished you had remained mad at me and left. That
way you would have been spared this additional pain.
But I am glad you stayed. These past few weeks have
been a dream come true and the happiest in my life.
They've also been extremely difficult for me because I
see now what I could have had if only I had faced my
demons and dealt with my depression. I threw away
all those years we could have spent together. I've also
come to realize that I was wrong in thinking I was
losing paradise when I left Sicily for America. For the
true paradise I lost was you, my beautiful daughter.*

*Please don't be mad at me or Carlotta for not
telling you I was dying. Someday we will see each
other again. Until then, think of me whenever you
sing or look at the grapevine.*

Ti voglio bene.
Tua Mama

I take out a tissue and wipe the tears that have fallen down my
face.

"Flight 380 from Calabria to Rome is now boarding at Gate 11."

I put my mother's letter in my purse and make my way to the airline attendants collecting boarding passes.

Half an hour later, my plane is in the air. I have the window seat and am staring at the serene panorama below. How could my mother have left such a beautiful place behind? Seeing how stunning her homeland is makes me finally have some understanding as to how difficult it must have been for her to leave all of this behind and adjust to life in America, no less New York City. She went from an island paradise to a densely populated metropolis with views that are almost always marred by scores of skyscrapers.

If only my mother had been able to convince my father to move to Sicily, things could have been so different. But then I suppose Daddy would've been the one to be unhappy? I guess I'll never know how that could have played out. I just wish Mama had been able to get the help she needed with her postpartum depression. All I know for certain is that I'm through with wishing things had been different in my life. It's time I look to the future.

I continue staring at the magnificent view when my mother's words come back to me: *"The true paradise I lost was you."*

EPILOGUE

Sarina's Grapevine

Astoria, New York, August 2016

As I stand in the backyard of my father's home, looking at the grapevine, I can't believe three years have passed since I went to Sicily and was reunited with my mother. I think of all that has happened since then.

When I returned to work, I had forgotten about the family tree project I had assigned to my students before the summer break. I couldn't believe I'd forgotten about it since if it weren't for that assignment, I would've probably never found my mother's diary. Of course, my students reminded me on my first day back to school, and they were actually excited to share their family trees. When my class was all done relaying their essays about their ancestors, they told me it was my turn. I had nothing prepared since I had forgotten about the assignment. So I skipped to telling them about one of my ancestors. I told them about my mother, but I decided to tell the students she was my grandmother instead. I didn't feel comfortable revealing the fact that my mother had left me, and I was concerned they would have asked me why she lived in Sicily, while I grew up in New York. So I told them about how Mama's father had mistreated her and how brave she had been to run away from home when she was just seventeen years old. I told them how she read people's fortunes. The students seemed to especially love that. I relayed her love of singing and how she sang at the Villa Carlotta, where she met her first love Carlo. And of course I told them about Sarina and Carlo's storybook romance while they went from one Aeolian Island to the next. My class was impressed to learn she had become a famous folk singer in Sicily, but what they really loved was hearing how she had been reunited with Carlo after so many years. I ended my story there. It was still too painful for me to talk about her dying or even to tell them about Carlo's Alzheimer's and how he was slowly, but surely, forgetting Sarina.

When it was time to vote on which student had the best essay, I was surprised that my class had unanimously voted mine the winner. But I reminded them the rules of our contest and that as the teacher, I could not win. So we took another vote and chose a different winner.

Believe it or not, Daddy got remarried about a year after I returned from Sicily, and to none other than Penelope Anastasos! I guess it wasn't that much of a shock to me that he had fallen for her. I eventually added two and two together after I overheard Kyle teasing Daddy about thinking of her too much and also after I met Penelope at Astoria Park, and she told me that Daddy had been visiting her at the café regularly. While Daddy was dating Penelope, he had a strong feeling he would ask her to marry him if things continued to go well between them. He was planning on finally getting a divorce from my mother. But then he received the news that Mama had passed away. Daddy actually cried when I told him over the phone. Though I knew he was no longer in love with her, he never really stopped caring about her.

I also learned after returning from Sicily that Antoniella had found out that Daddy was a regular customer at Penelope's café. Naturally, Antoniella blew up at Daddy and stopped talking to him. And whenever Antoniella crossed paths with Penelope on the street, she gave her the dirtiest looks. But Penelope smoothed things over when she asked Antoniella to make her wedding cake. Nothing makes Antoniella happier than making money—even if it's from an enemy. But I think Antoniella also appreciated that

Penelope was respecting her talents as a baker by asking Antoniella to make her wedding cake. The two women soon became friends, and Antoniella finally stopped fretting that she was losing business to Penelope's café.

After all these years of having Daddy to myself, it felt strange to see him remarry. But the feeling quickly vanished when I remembered there were times that I had worried about his being alone and never having loved another woman besides my mother. Now he would have the love he deserved to have—and should have had—a long time ago. My thoughts drift to my mother and Carlo. I think about how they were apart for all those years and how Mama and I were also separated for so long. All that wasted time only to be reunited and then to lose her again so quickly. Life is too short to spend it alone or apart from the people we love. I hope that Daddy and Penelope have more years together than Carlo or I had with my mother.

A month after I returned from Sicily, Kyle and I moved back into our house since he had found another job and we were back on our feet financially. I was saddened to see that the grapevine in my father's yard had inexplicably died while I was gone. Kyle assured me that both he and my father had been regularly tending to it, but no matter what they did, it just seemed to get weaker. The following year, the grapevine didn't grow back. I couldn't help but see the irony in it, since the grapevine had always been a reminder of my mother and now it had died just like she had.

"Mama!"

I'm startled out of my thoughts by my two-year-old daughter, Sarina, who runs to me. I pick her up and raise her high into the air, just like my mother had done with me all those years ago. She squeals and giggles. I then lower her and hold her against me. Sarina's head nestles against my chest. The sun brings out the auburn highlights in her light brown hair. Like my mother, she has an olive complexion. But she has Kyle's large blue eyes.

I had found out I was pregnant a month and a half after Kyle and I returned to our house. We were both stunned since we had been trying to have a baby for so long to no avail. I had begun to think it simply wasn't meant to be. It wasn't until I was pregnant that I remembered the tarot card reading my mother had given me the night she died, and how she had predicted that I would have a transformative experience in the future. That experience was Sarina's birth. It has changed me so much and given me new understanding, especially where my mother is concerned. For ever since Sarina was born, I have been filled with some anxiety, worried for my child and worried that I will not be a good mother. To think I had stood in this yard three years ago, fearing I would be a terrible mother if I ever had children because of how my own mother had left me. Once I had this epiphany, I understood the fear that had gripped Mama so tightly when she had hit me and thought she would become the abuser her father had been. My mother's fears of being a bad mother no longer seemed so unjustified. And then I remembered how young she had been. She was seventeen years old when she married my father and eighteen when she gave birth to me. Though she was in her early twenties when she chose not to return to me, she still possessed the spirit and fears of that lost teenage girl who had run away from home, dreaming of a better life.

While my healing began when I was in Sicily, reconnecting with my mother, I am still healing. Sometimes I still get sad for that little girl who had to grow up without the love of her mother. I have finally forgiven Mama. I only wish I had told her that before she died. But I was still trying to fully come to terms with her abandoning me and figuring out where she belonged in my life then. The time for regrets is over though. I made a promise to myself on the plane when I left Sicily that I would let go of the past and focus on the future. Having Sarina has definitely helped ease the ache of Mama's loss.

Kyle was a bit surprised when I told him I wanted to name our baby Sarina. But then I told him about Mama's prediction when she read my tarot cards and how I couldn't help feeling she had a hand in the miracle of our conceiving Sarina. It's also my small way of showing my mother, wherever she is now, that I have forgiven her.

My thoughts return to the grapevine. Ever since that first year when it didn't grow back, I have tried to plant offshoots from the grapevine in one of my father's neighbor's yards to see if those would take hold. Finally this past spring, a grapevine is growing once again in Daddy's garden. It is now August. The grapevine has grown, but it still has a few years to go until it becomes once again as lush and beautiful as the previous one was. But I have faith it will get there.

I talk softly to my daughter as I take her hand and let her touch one of the grapevine's leaves. "When you are older, Sarina, I will teach you how to garden and care for the grapevine. Then you can grow one in the yard of your home. This way you, too, can continue the tradition that Nonna Sarina started with this first grapevine. And I promise I will tell you all about your namesake—your Nonna Sarina—and what a fascinating life she led."

Sarina begins to cry. I rock her as I softly sing, *"Stella mia, stell-ahhh mia, tu sei la piu bella stella. . . . My star, my star, you are the most beautiful star."*

Author's Notes

In Chapter 14 ("Furia dell' Etna") I mention that Mount Etna was erupting. I exercised creative license here since Mount Etna did not have any eruptions in 1969.

In Chapter 17 ("Panarea and Filicudi") I mention that there is no electricity in Filicudi. This was true in 1969, when the story took place. However, electricity did come to the island in 1986.

RECIPES FOR *STELLA MIA*

Tetu (Clove-Scented Chocolate Cookies)

1 cup blanched whole almonds
4 cups unbleached all-purpose flour
8 tablespoons (1 stick) unsalted butter, softened
2 ounces unsweetened chocolate
1 cup milk
1½ cups sugar
1 teaspoon ground cloves
2 teaspoons baking soda
½ teaspoon salt
1 teaspoon vanilla
1 egg, beaten lightly to blend

GLAZE

2 cups sugar
1½ cups water
12 ounces unsweetened chocolate, roughly chopped
2 cups powdered sugar, sifted

Preheat the oven to 375 degrees.

Spread the almonds on a baking sheet and toast in the oven for 15 to 20 minutes, or until well browned. Let cool. Grind the almonds to a coarse powder in a food processor or in a coffee grinder in small batches. Transfer to a large bowl, stir in the flour, and set aside.

In a medium saucepan over low heat, melt the butter, chocolate, and milk, whisking until the butter is melted. Whisk in the sugar, remove from the heat, and let cool to lukewarm.

Whisk the cloves, baking soda, salt, vanilla, and egg into the butter mixture. With a wooden spoon, stir the liquid ingredients into the flour-almond mixture just until combined. Chill the dough, covered, for 1 hour, or until easy to handle.

Preheat the oven again to 375 degrees.

Grease two baking sheets.

Pinch off a tablespoonful of the dough at a time, roll between the palms of your hands into a smooth ball, and arrange balls 2 inches apart on the greased baking sheets.

Bake the cookies for 15 minutes, or until puffy but still slightly soft in the center. Allow the cookies to cool for 10 minutes before removing them from the pan.

Meanwhile, make the glaze: In a medium saucepan, bring the sugar and water to a boil, whisking constantly. Boil for 3 minutes, then remove from the heat and whisk in the chocolate until melted. Whisk in the powdered sugar until smooth.

While the cookies are still warm, immerse them, a few at a time, in the warm glaze, then place them on a cooling rack over a baking sheet to catch the drips. It's important that both the cookies and the glaze be warm so that some of the glaze soaks into the cookies. Cool on the rack.

Makes about 3 dozen.

Granita di Caffè (Coffee Granita)

¾ cup finely ground Italian espresso
4 cups water
2 tablespoons sugar, or to taste
Whipped cream (optional)

In an espresso maker or drip coffeepot, make coffee according
to the manufacturer's directions, using the espresso and water. Add
the sugar if desired, and stir until dissolved. Let cool slightly, then
cover and chill until cold.

Pour the coffee into a chilled 12- by 9- by 2-inch metal pan or
8-inch square glass baking dish. Freeze for 30 minutes, or until ice
crystals begin to form around the edges.

Stir the ice crystals into the center of the mixture. Return the
pan to the freezer and continue freezing, stirring every 30 minutes,
until all of the liquid is frozen, about 2 to 2½ hours.

Serve in large goblets, with whipped cream if desired.

Makes 1½ quarts.

Arancini di Riso (Sicilian Rice Balls)

2 cups Italian Arborio or American Carolina rice
1 cup meat sauce
1 cup grated Pecorino Romano cheese
1 (10-ounce) package frozen peas, thawed
2 eggs
1 pound ricotta
1 cup flour
2 cups dried bread crumbs
3 cups canola or vegetable oil for deep-frying

Boil the rice until tender and drain. When the rice is still hot, but cool enough to handle, add the sauce, Pecorino Romano cheese, peas, and eggs. Mix well and let cool. Take a handful of rice mixture, make a depression in the middle, and fill with 1 table-spoon of ricotta. Cover the ricotta with more rice, and shape into a ball. As you shape the *arancini,* place them on a tray.

When you have finished making all of the *arancini,* make a paste out of the flour plus 1 cup of water, and using your hands coat each one with the flour paste. When all have been coated, roll each one in bread crumbs. Refrigerate for at least 1 hour or overnight.

When ready to serve the *arancini*, deep-fry them in the oil until golden, drain on paper towels, and serve hot or at room temperature.

Makes about 16.

Pasta alla Norma (Pasta with Eggplant)

2 eggplants
Kosher salt
½ to 1 cup canola or vegetable oil
1 pound uncooked spaghetti or macaroni
2 cups marinara sauce
8 ounces ricotta salata, shredded, or Greek feta cheese,
   crumbled

Cut the eggplants lengthwise into ½-inch slices. Layer them in a colander, sprinkling salt in between the layers. Top the stack of slices with a weight and let them drain off the dark bitter juices for at least 30 minutes. When ready to fry them, rinse off the salt, dry on paper towels, and fry in the hot oil.

Cook the pasta according to the package directions. Drain, place in a bowl, and add the sauce and the cheese, reserving some of each for the topping. Arrange the fried eggplant all around the serving platter, allowing the slices to hang over the edge. Spoon the pasta into the serving platter, fold the eggplant slices over the pasta, top with the reserved sauce, and serve hot or at room temperature.

Serves 6 to 8.

Frittata con Patate e Cipolle
(Omelet with Potatoes and Onions)

6 tablespoons extra-virgin olive oil
2 potatoes, peeled and cubed
2 onions, sliced
6 eggs
Salt and black pepper to taste

Heat 2 tablespoons of the olive oil in a medium frying pan, and fry the cubed potatoes until they are golden brown. Place in a bowl, and set aside. Add another 2 tablespoons of olive oil to the same pan, and cook the onions until browned and fragrant. Add to the potatoes. Heat the last 2 tablespoons of olive oil in the frying pan.

Meanwhile, in another bowl, beat the eggs with the salt and pepper; stir in the potatoes and the onions. Pour the mixture in the heated pan, and, running a fork along the bottom of the frittata, pierce it, allowing the egg to run to the bottom. When the top is just dry, turn the frittata onto a plate, and slip it back into the frying pan to cook the other side.

Serves 4.

The recipe for *Tetu* was adapted from *Sweet Sicily: The Story of an Island and Her Pastries*, by Victoria Granof (HarperCollins). The recipe for *granita di caffè* was adapted from *La Dolce Vita*, by Michele Scicolone (William Morrow and Company). All the other recipes were adapted from *Sicilian Feasts*, by Giovanna Bellia La Marca (Hippocrene Books). For more recipes, special reading group features, and blog posts, please visit RosannaChiofalo.com.

Please turn the page for a very special
Q&A with the author!

What was your inspiration for *Stella Mia*?

I often have more than one inspiration for writing my novels. For *Stella Mia*, I knew I wanted to set most of the book in Sicily. I also wanted to capture some of the mysticism that pervades Sicily. I thought it would be interesting to have a character who sang Sicilian folk songs and who also read people's fortunes. So that was one inspiration. My other inspiration was my father's grapevine. I had told my editor about the grapevine my father had planted when he and my mother bought my childhood home in Astoria, Queens, New York. In my family, we were all very proud of the grapevine my father had planted in our small concrete backyard. Some people thought the grapevine would never grow, but it did, and it made our tiny city backyard look so beautiful. The year that my father had cancer, the grapevine inexplicably didn't grow as lush as it had the previous years. And after my father died, the grapevine all but died as well. Of course, my family and I couldn't help seeing the irony, especially since my father had planted the grapevine and loved it so much. About fifteen or so years later, sometime after my mother had sold the house, I was visiting our old next-door neighbor and was talking to her in her yard, which faced the yard of my childhood home. I was surprised to see that my father's grapevine was growing again. My mother had tried to replant the grapevine with an offshoot of a grapevine she had received from a friend. But we never got to see if the grapevine would take hold and grow to be the lush vine my father's had been, since my mother had sold the house. Needless to say, I was very moved when I saw the grapevine had grown back and was on its way to looking as beautiful as the one my father had planted. In high school, I had written a college application essay that centered on my father's grapevine, and I always knew that someday I wanted to work it into a novel. When my editor heard the story of my father's grapevine, he, too, felt I should try and work it into my next novel.

Does the song "Stella Mia" hold any personal connection for you?

I made up the words for the song "Stella Mia," but I got the idea for Sarina's singing the song to Julia when she was a baby because a few years ago I learned that my father used to sing to me a lot when I was a baby as he was rocking me to sleep. My father died when I was sixteen, and I had never heard before that he sang to me when I was a baby. My brother told me my father was always singing, and later I did remember him singing a song or two, but I had no idea he sang to me as well when I was a baby. So when I knew I wanted to write about a woman whose mother had left her, the idea came to me that Julia's mother, Sarina, sang her the same song, "Stella Mia," over and over. And the song is one of the few things Julia has to remember her mother by. Songs and music can be very powerful since we often attach a memory, milestone, or other significant life event to them. Every time we hear the song, inevitably the memories associated with that song come to mind. For Julia, the song "Stella Mia" still connects her to the mother who left her. For Sarina, the song at first reminds her of her little sister, Carlotta, whom she used to sing the song to. But later, when Carlo calls Sarina his *"stella mia,"* the song and phrase then remind her of the love she shared with Carlo. In *Stella Mia,* I do mention a song that is tied to a milestone in my life. The song that Julia mentions she and her father danced to at her wedding, Vittorio Merlo's "Piccolo Fiore," was the same song I danced to at my wedding with my older brother Anthony.

This book is different from your previous two novels in that most of it is set in Italy and only a small portion is set in Astoria, New York. Why did you choose to make Italy the main setting in *Stella Mia*?

I learned from many of my readers that the scenes that took place in Italy in both *Bella Fortuna* and *Carissima* really resonated with them. And as an author, I especially enjoyed writing those scenes that were set in Italy, so I decided to make the main setting for *Stella Mia* Italy and just set a small portion of the book in Astoria, New York. I like to challenge myself as a writer and shake things up a bit from book to book.

Domestic abuse figures prominently in Sarina's story. Why did you decide to touch on this subject?

I was fortunate enough to have parents who didn't hit me as a form of punishment when I was a child; however, I knew other kids who were repeatedly physically abused. I also remember the mother of an ex-boyfriend of mine recounting the horrible physical abuse she had suffered as a child at her father's hands. With my friends whose parents had abused them, I saw the effect the abuse had on their lives as they got older. It eroded their self-esteem, and many times caused them to treat others poorly, whether it was through verbal or physical abuse. In Sarina's case, I believe her father's vicious abuse of her ultimately played a role in why she chose not to return to Julia. She never trusted fully that she could be a good mother and avoid becoming the monster her father was. Likewise, she was never fully confident in Carlo's love for her and was easily made insecure when Gemma came into the picture. It was almost as if she didn't believe she deserved to have someone love her the way Carlo did because her father had never loved her.

In *Stella Mia*, you made us understand the character of Paulie Parlatone better as well as made him more likeable than when he appeared in your previous two novels. What were your motives for doing so?

Though Paulie could be quite an annoying character with his nosiness and crude habits, as we saw in *Bella Fortuna* and *Carissima*, he was also an unforgettable character for those same traits that made him so irksome. I've always believed there is more than meets the eye with most people. We often forget that people have histories and that the events that have happened in their lives make them who they are today. I wanted readers to understand better why Paulie is the way he is, particularly where his need to know everyone's business is concerned. In *Stella Mia,* when we see that he has been lonely since Sarina left him and Julia, we can understand why he might try to distract himself from his problems and loneliness by focusing instead on his neighbors' affairs. I also thought it would be fun for readers to encounter him again in *Stella Mia,* and to learn more about him, especially from the perspective of someone who loves him—his daughter, Julia.

In all of your novels, you depict different relationships and their dynamics. In *Bella Fortuna*, we saw the dynamics between Valentina and her mother and sisters. In *Carissima*, we saw the dynamics of sisters, both when they're close and when they're estranged. And in *Stella Mia*, we have the dynamics between a daughter and her mother who abandoned her. Why are familial bonds a strong recurring theme in your writing?

I think some of the most fascinating relationships are familial ones. I'm close to my family, and I do enjoy writing about families and their interactions with one another, whether they are good or bad. Families are quite complex, and the way we act with some of our family members might not necessarily be the same way we would behave in some of our other relationships. I love the multifaceted complexity of the bonds that hold family members together and when something happens that tests those bonds or breaks them.

Have you ever had a tarot card reading, and do you believe they can give one a glimpse into what the future holds in store for them?

When I was a teenager, my friends and I used to get regular tarot card readings from a fortune-teller. My brother had bought a deck of tarot cards, and my sister and I used to practice giving each other readings. I haven't had a reading since my twenties when a coworker and friend gave me one. Though I was very intrigued by tarot cards when I was younger, I don't believe in them now. I also didn't like how for a while you carried in your mind the reading you received and were waiting to see if what transpired in your life matched the reading. I don't believe we are intended to know the roadmap in our future, and we shouldn't be living our lives trying to figure out what is in store for us. But I still do love the mysticism and allure that tarot cards hold, even though I've given up on using them to tell me my future or to help throw some light on whatever obstacles I might be facing currently in my life.

Can you give readers a tarot card reading for the future and let us know what subject you might be writing about in your next book?

I haven't completely formulated the idea for my fourth book, but I do know it will be completely set in Italy, and pastries will figure prominently in the novel. Sorry to be mysterious, but that's all I can predict for the future right now!

STELLA MIA

Rosanna Chiofalo

About This Guide

The suggested questions are included to enhance
your group's reading of Rosanna Chiofalo's
Stella Mia.

DISCUSSION QUESTIONS

1. After Sarina runs away from home, she is torn with guilt over having left her mother and siblings behind. Do you believe she made the right decision in leaving her mother and younger siblings behind?

2. Sarina goes from living an abused, hard life in her father's house, to living an idyllic life in the coastal resort town of Taormina and on the magical Aeolian Islands, and her dream of singing becomes a reality. How do you think her life would have been different if she had remained at home and continued to be abused by her father?

3. Sometimes Sarina feels that Carlo is being idealistic when it comes to their romance since they are from opposite worlds; he is rich and has had a privileged life, whereas Sarina has only known poverty and hardship. Discuss the pros and cons of being romantically involved with someone who's from a different social class.

4. In *Stella Mia,* the author goes against the long-held stereotype of gypsies as thieves and swindlers by depicting Maria and her family of gypsies as honest and hardworking, yet the author also shows how people immediately mistrusted them. Do you feel gypsies have been judged unfairly over time?

5. Sarina is intimidated by Carlo's father, Signore Conti, especially when she realizes he knows she has been seeing Carlo. Does Signore Conti intimidate Sarina so much because subconsciously he reminds her of her own stern father? Did she give in too easily to Signore Conti's demands that she leave Carlo?

6. Paulie tells Sarina that America is a "land of no tears." What do you think he meant by this? Do you feel that many immigrants believed this before immigrating to America? For Sarina, America instead proves to be a land full of tears. Discuss what could have become of Sarina if she hadn't married Paulie and moved to America.

7. Why do you think Julia gave up on asking her father more about her mother, especially when she reached adulthood? Do you feel she was too harsh toward her father when she confronted him about Sarina's diary?

8. How has Paulie failed Julia? How has he done right by her? How has Sarina failed Julia? Has Sarina done right by Julia by staying out of her life for so long?

9. Are Sarina's motives for not returning to Julia valid? Do you think she deserves Julia's forgiveness?

10. Toward the end of *Stella Mia,* Julia has a dream in which she is experiencing a few of the major moments in Sarina's life. It is as if she has become Sarina until the end of the dream, when it is then just Julia watching her mother climb higher, and away from her, on the grapevine. What do you think the author was trying to achieve with this dream sequence?